J. W. KITSON

PEOPLE FROM THE LAKE

Copyright © 2022 J.W. Kitson

ISBN: 978-1-7333001-2-4

Any references to historical events, real people, or real places are used fictitiously. Names, characters, and places are products of the author's imagination.

Front cover image by Josh Menning
Book design by Lara Helmling

Printed in the United States of America

First printing edition 2022

Kitson Books, LLC
www.jwkitson.com

ENDORSEMENTS

"I had the pleasure and privilege of working on the film *Beasts of Our Fathers* with J. W. Kitson, and now I am thrilled to go on another journey while reading his new novel, *People from the Lake*, a truly twisted journey of a family tormented by dark souls still yearning for life." **Lorenzo Beronilla, an American film, television, and voice actor; notable for the comedy *Furlough* (TBA) starring Melissa Leo, and *Super Dark Times* (slated as one of the top 50 American Films in 2017)**

"Anyone who loves great writing, hard-hitting stories, and compelling characters needs to put J.W. Kitson's books on their 'must read' list. If *People from the Lake* is as great as *Song of the Tree Frogs*, it will be a winner." **Maria Olsen, Actress in *Percy Jackson & The Olympians: The Lightning Thief*; *Paranormal Activity 3*; *Starry Eyes*.**

"A great combination of action, horror, and romance. This deftly told, spine-tingling story appeals to adults and teens alike. I was on the edge of my seat wondering what this likable family would be forced to deal with next." **Brooke T. Harman, English and Creative Writing Instructor**

"J.W. Kitson is an amazing storyteller; a wordsmith who paints vivid images with rich, compelling, characters that will take you on an emotional and thought-provoking journey. Given his storytelling prowess and writing talent, it's no surprise that he is also an accomplished film producer, having worked on the inspiring documentary *Gateway to Hope: Overcoming Heroin*, and the upcoming thriller *Beast of Our Fathers*. His latest story delivers on everything a reader would expect from an accomplished writer." **Jason Klingensmith, Award Winning Screenwriter, Director, and Actor in such works as "Open Casket," "One More Run: The Powerhouse Indians of Yesteryear," "Relative Justice," "Rivals," *Unwavering*, "Grassman," and more.**

"As an actor used to reading screenplays and manuscripts from various authors, I can easily distinguish between a good author and a great one. J.W. Kitson is an exceptional writer. His first novel, *Song of the Tree Frogs* is maintaining a 5-Star rating after dozens of reviews. This writer delivers on his work, and I've been waiting for the release of *People from the Lake*. Having worked with this author on various films and projects, this bone-chilling thriller is just another reflection of a gifted author." **Georin Aquilla, Actor from "Empire,"** *For My Man, Love the Coopers*, **and Superbowl commercials.**

This story is dedicated to these special people:

To the "Three Blessings" in our lives:
Madison, Matthew, and Nathan

I also dedicate this book to my wife, Connie,
our dear friend, Kathy (Mathias) Jordan,
and my "Momma Ruth"
Thank you all for your encouragement

I also dedicate this book to our beloved Tabbie ("Tabs")
for the countless times we tried to scare
each other over the years.
We miss you!

Table of Contents

CHAPTER 1

Seth was motionless, lying face down in the mud at the water's edge.

"Seth!" Aeron fell beside his brother. He turned Seth over and hoisted him onto his weakened, trembling legs. "Oh God, come on, Seth! Wake up! *They're coming!"* Aeron peered out into the fierce squall—desperate for any living soul who might rescue them. "Seth, we gotta go—*I mean it!"*

The storm raged as Aeron violently shook Seth, trying to stir life back into his unconscious brother. As the roaring winds muffled Aeron's frenzied cries, wind-driven torrents of rain pelted Seth's limp body. Blood poured from his mouth and nose, leaving a crimson flow running down Aeron's forearm like the splintered veins of lightning raging overhead.

"Oh God, this can't be happening *again!"* Aeron tightened his embrace around his brother and cried out, "Come on, Seth . . . *please!"* Aeron attempted several times to lift his brother out of the lake, but his wounded leg, and the slippery mud, caused him to fall hard onto the saturated ground.

"Dad, I found him!" Aeron's cries were devoured by the violent, howling winds. *"Daaaad!"* His heart was thrashing about in his chest, as his lungs begged for precious air. *"I need you!"*

As Aeron gazed into the blackness, lightning blazed across the sky, revealing nearly a dozen decaying corpses standing waist deep in the turbulent lake. The menacing creatures were determined to abduct the brothers from the realm of the living.

"*God . . . help us!*" Aeron wailed. He forcefully shook Seth again. "Come on, Seth! *Pleeease!*"

As another flash of lightning dashed across the sky, Aeron saw the rotting, outstretched arms of the deadly creatures even closer than before.

Spasms seized control of Aeron's muscles as he struggled again to stand and lift his brother from the edge of the water. He collapsed once more. "*Noooo! Leave us alone!*" he pleaded.

Drowning in weakness and despair, Aeron finally lowered his chin and rested it on the top of Seth's soaked, wet hair. Seeing no escape, but to punch into the darkness, Aeron frantically rocked back and forth with Seth held firmly in one of his arms. "*Please wake up, Seth!*" Aeron cried out. "*They're gonna kill us!*"

In desperation, Aeron attempted one last spine-tingling shriek. "*Someone help us!*"

Streaks of lightning shot across the sky, affirming Aeron's worst fears: the hands of the creatures . . . only inches away.

Days earlier, and many miles away, Josh Wallace sprang from his bed, as if being yanked out of it by some unknown force. Sweat rolled down his flushed cheeks and dripped onto his bare chest. The salty perspiration eventually made its way to the floor as his racing heart pounded a sadistic rhythm. His legs weakened, finally causing him to collapse onto his bed.

He sat there surrounded by pulsating flashes of light in his eyes, leaving him unable to make sense of the darkness smothering him. He tried to swallow, but his parched mouth was a desert. Each spasm in his gut caused his fists to press even harder into his stomach.

He shivered as the agonizing nightmare that awakened him haunted his thoughts.

The lake! Why were those boys in the lake? Who was trying to take them away?

He leaned forward and rested his elbows on both knees. His hands became a pillow for his throbbing head.

The terror finally subsided, and he was able to inhale more of the cool air circulating throughout his room from the fan spinning above his bed. When he sat up, he licked his dry lips, which had an overwhelming salty taste. Attempting to wipe away some of the moisture, it felt warm, not like the coolness of the sweat that had been rolling down his face. He rushed to the bathroom. "Please, God, not again!" he whispered, as he turned on the light.

The reflection in the mirror revealed another nightmarish discovery: blood flowing from both nostrils. Josh grabbed a towel and wet it down in the sink. When he held it to his nose, he observed the redness in his eyes. He dropped the towel and turned on the faucet. After splashing water on his face, he lifted the corner of the towel and wiped off the beads of water that clung to his reddened skin.

His nostrils were a river of blood, so he held the towel to his nose again before returning to his room, longing for the comfort of his bed. As soon as his back hit the dampness of the mattress and sheets, he stood and grabbed his pillow. He threw it on the floor and sat beside it with his back against the mattress. Looking upward, he whispered: "God, why is this happening again?" His head drooped, and he rolled onto his side on the hard floor and rested his head on his pillow.

CHAPTER 2

"Mom, where am I supposed to put all of my stuff?" Aeron complained. "All of Seth's junk is in my way. I don't even have room for my guitars."

A frown spread across Teresa's face as she eased her shoulder against the doorframe. "You and Seth will somehow have to work it all out without an attorney present. It's not like I don't have my own stuff to put away, including the twins' belongings." She sighed. "As you can see, there's nothing easy about moving into a new house."

As she turned to leave, Seth bumped into her as he entered his room with another box. "Oops! sorry, Mom, I didn't mean to run into you." He dropped the box on his bed.

"Another one! Are you serious?" Aeron barked.

Exasperated with the disorder, Teresa grumbled, "You two try to get things sorted out without killing each other. I certainly don't think my law firm would appreciate having to prosecute a murder case that took place in my own home." Before leaving, she said, "Oh, and I need you two to help bring in some more furniture from the garage in a little bit."

"Sure, Mom," Seth replied. "After all, I am the *good son* around here." His smirk ignited a bomb in Aeron's chest.

"You are such a—" Aeron paused after seeing his mother's glaring eyes.

"Aeron Tyler Douglas, don't you dare! You remember what happened the last time you used that word! I caught Kieran saying it the other day." His mother's look of disdain subdued Aeron's conscience. "You need to get your attitude in check, and I mean it!"

"Yes, Mother Teresa, I'll do my best," Aeron replied. "May I call him 'Richard Cranium' instead?"

"You're impossible, Aeron! I can't believe I haven't needed a defense attorney to defend me in court for the murder of my own son." She stepped back into the hallway. "Oh, and if you *don't* want to find yourself grounded *again*, I would suggest you watch what flies out of your mouth from now on."

"I know, Mom, because you'll put me in solitary confinement again."

"Exactly!"

After Teresa walked away, Seth turned to Aeron. "I have to admit that "Richard Cranium' was a good one, but it almost got you grounded."

Returning to his unpacking, Aeron murmured, "Who cares."

Seth shook his head. "You know, I can't believe we have to share a room again."

"Yeah," Aeron snapped, "I still have to listen to you snore all night."

"Real funny. I just don't understand what I ever did to Mom and Dad to deserve such a life sentence with someone like you." Seth chuckled at his own joke. "At least you let me have the bed closest to the window where I can see some of the lake."

"What's the big deal about that stupid lake?" Aeron bellowed. "That's all you've talked about for weeks. It's like you're obsessed with it or something!"

"Man, who peed in your cereal this morning? I just think it's cool that we have a lake. Is that such a crime?"

"Whatever," Aeron replied, while rubbing his temples.

"Why are you so moody lately?" Seth asked. "You've been nasty almost every time we've come out here to bring stuff from the townhouse."

"Maybe I'm tired of listening to you," Aeron retorted. His phone dinged again. Aeron looked at it and tossed his phone onto his bed.

"Who keeps bugging you?" Seth inquired.

"Whitney's been busting my rear end all day with her texts."

"Well, at least I'm not obsessed with keeping a control freak for a girlfriend."

"*What a funny guy!*" Aeron replied. He leaned over and rested his elbows on his dresser and massaged his temples.

"What's wrong, man?" Seth asked.

"I can't get rid of this bad headache, and my ears are ringing again. It's probably all this country air out here screwing up my head." He stood straight up and looked around the room. "Let's just get this done."

As the boys sorted through their belongings, Seth looked up and stopped rummaging through the box he'd placed on his bed. Aeron made his way over to his closet, wondering how to organize the heaps of clothing he'd thrown into a pile near the closet door. Seth walked over to the window and looked toward the lake. The embankment up to the lake was quite steep, and no matter how hard he looked, Seth could only see a few patches of shimmering light radiating from the lake's surface.

"Come here, Aeron!"

As he joined Seth at the window, they observed someone at the top of the embankment. The antique manufacturing of the glass caused some warping of the image, but they were able to see a woman in a long black dress, which was flowing like a pennant in the breeze. She appeared to be floating leisurely in the direction of the barn on the other side of the lake.

"Who is that?" Seth inquired.

The woman stopped. She saw the boys glaring at her from the bedroom window, so she gestured with her arm for them to come to her. The boys looked at each other before darting for the stairs.

"Where are you two going?" Teresa yelled, as she stepped out of her room.

"Go to my room, Mom," Seth yelled, "and look toward the lake. There's a strange lady up there." Seth rejoined his brother at the bottom of the stairs, and they darted out the front door.

"It's probably our new neighbor," Teresa yelled.

After arriving at the location where they'd first seen the lady, they were panting like dogs that had been running for hours. Beads of sweat dripped from their foreheads. "This is too weird! There's no way she could've outrun us," Aeron said. "Where did she go?"

Both boys glanced around the lake for the stranger. "Aeron, look!" Seth grabbed his brother's shoulder and spun him around. "Is that her standing in the doorway of the barn?"

Sweat dripped into one of Aeron's eyes, and he wiped it away before it stung too much. "Yeah, I see her now!" he said. With hearts pounding, they rushed toward the barn.

From their bedroom window, their mother saw them point and take off running. She wanted to investigate as well, but she didn't want to leave the twins, Darcy and Kieran, alone in the house.

"She's still standing there! Let's try and stop her!" Seth insisted.

"Where in the world is she going?" Aeron squawked. The stranger took a few more steps backward and disappeared into the shadows.

Once the boys arrived at the entrance, Aeron bent over and placed his hands on his knees. "Do you see her?" he huffed, desperate for air that seemed to be smothered by the humid August afternoon.

Seth leaned against a large wooden beam. He could feel the splinters piercing the back of his head. Also panting from the sprint, he put his hand up to his forehead and wiped away more sweat. "No," he wheezed, "I can't see her!"

"Surely she couldn't have gone up into the loft," Aeron said. The boys shivered from the welcomed breeze wafting through the barn, momentarily chilling their clammy skin.

"Aeron, I—"

"What?"

"I think I wanna go back to the house."

"Stop being such a—"

A sudden thump echoed from the loft, startling both boys.

"Okay, man," Seth gasped. "What was that?"

"I bet it's that neighbor of ours," Aeron whispered. "We have to see why she's snooping around. I'm not having some weird old woman spying on me all the time."

They each climbed two different ladders, leading into the two lofts, which were separated by the center of the barn with its high, vaulted ceiling.

They reached the top at the same time. They looked around, but only the remnants of hay and ropes were seen. They looked over at each other and shrugged their shoulders.

"Toss me that rope," Aeron requested. Seth pushed it over, and Aeron caught it. It was attached to the center beam. He tugged on it several times before swinging above the main floor and into the same loft as Seth.

"This is too weird, man. She must have gone downstairs instead," Seth suggested. "Let's check down there."

Reaching for the top of the ladder, Aeron looked down and exclaimed, "What the—" Aeron complained, as he lifted his palms toward Seth. "Where'd this black stuff come from?" He wiped his hands on his shorts.

"You realize that Mom's gonna make you wash that out."

"Don't worry about it," Aeron said. "Let's check out the basement."

After they returned to the main floor of the barn and descended the stairs leading into the basement, Aeron teased, "Hey, maybe she's down there waiting to slaughter us."

Seth hit his brother on the arm. "That's not funny, you jerk!"

Once they reached the bottom of the steps leading into the basement, Aeron suddenly forced his forearm against Seth's chest. "Wait! Look over there!" Aeron whispered.

In the far corner, a shadow swayed from side to side. Aeron's skin erupted with goose bumps. He signaled to Seth to step behind him. The shadow continued to wobble back and forth as the boys slowly approached the corner where the mysterious silhouette appeared to have made its lair.

Sweat rolled down their backs and chests like raindrops cascading down the steep pitch of a roof, and their hearts raced at a vicious pace. Aeron wanted to whisper something to his brother, but his arid throat was like sandpaper scratching away his words.

As they made their final approach, Aeron signaled for Seth to be quiet by placing his finger on this own lips. There was a thick canvas cover hanging from several iron hooks screwed into the wooden support beam above them. Aeron stretched forth his quaking hand and quickly pulled the old, stained cloth aside.

A cloud of dust soon revealed several huge bales of straw, which fell over and tackled Aeron like a football player. He fell backwards, stumbling into Seth. As their shrieks echoed around them, they both plunged to the cement floor, which was still partially covered with remnants of straw. Aeron yelled, as he wrestled to remove one of the huge bales, which was pricking his legs like the quills of a porcupine. Seth's head struck one of the wooden planks behind him.

After sitting up, Seth reached for the back of his head. "Aeron! I think—" he suddenly stopped talking when he saw one of his hands smeared with blood.

"Oh my God! You're bleeding, man!" Aeron roared. "Are you okay?"

"No, I'm not okay!" Seth complained. "Get me to the house before I bleed to death!"

Aeron removed his shirt and pressed it to the back of Seth's head. As the boys ascended the stairs, another woman in a flowing, white gown appeared from behind one of the stalls.

After reaching the main floor of the barn, they failed to notice the woman in the long black dress standing near an open window at the back of the barn. The decrepit ghoul grinned as the boys rushed toward the barn's entrance. Moments later, they stumbled down the embankment toward the house.

"Mom!" Aeron hollered, as the boys hurried through the kitchen door. "Get in here!"

"Oh my God!" Teresa shrieked, as she rushed into the kitchen and saw her wounded son. "What in the world happened?" Seeing Aeron's shirt soaked with blood, she yelled, "Get him upstairs to the bathroom!"

As Seth sat on the edge of the bathtub, Aeron retrieved some towels from the linen closet. "Somebody better tell me what happened!" Teresa insisted, while continuing to press the shirt against her son's head.

"We were in the barn looking for that person we told you about, and a bale of straw fell on me. I fell backwards onto Seth, and he hit his head."

"How bad is it, Mom?" Seth asked.

"I think you might need some stitches."

Teresa wet the towel Aeron handed her, and she gently wiped the blood from his hair.

"Ouch! That really hurts, Mom!"

"I'm sorry, honey, but I want to make sure we get it cleaned out so I can see how bad it is."

A shadow crept across the bathroom floor as Teresa and Aeron fussed over Seth. Just outside the doorway, the woman in black stared at the newcomers trespassing onto her domain. She disappeared when the twins emerged from their bedroom.

When they arrived at the bathroom door, Teresa ordered the twins to hurry and get ready because they needed to go to the emergency room.

"What happened, Mommy?" Darcy asked.

"Just run and get ready, baby. We must go right now!" Teresa insisted.

Kieran was mesmerized by the sight of his brother's blood, but his attention was suddenly drawn to the intruder drifting down the hallway toward his older sister's room. The menacing woman looked back once and smiled at Kieran before disappearing into a bedroom. He rubbed his eyes while peering once more toward Delaney's room where the clandestine stranger had vanished.

"Mommy, what happened to Seth?" Darcy asked.

"Seth hit his head and has a cut, baby. Now, be a big girl and take

Kieran down to your room and get your shoes on!"

Darcy grabbed her brother's hand, and the two fled toward their room. "Come on, Kieran," she pleaded, "we have to help Seth get to the hospital!" His attention was still focused on the entrance to Delaney's bedroom.

"Aeron, you need to put on another shirt," his mother demanded. "Grab another one for Seth."

As Aeron dashed to his room, he heard Delaney's bedroom door slam behind him, causing him to jerk with fright. Seeing nothing, he shook his head before entering his room. After retrieving shirts, he turned to leave and noticed the woman in a white gown standing on the embankment beside the lake. "What the heck's up with the people around here?" he whispered.

"Aeron, where are you?" Teresa hollered.

"I'm coming!" he shouted, while backing away from the window.

After returning to the bathroom, Aeron helped Seth to his feet before rushing toward the stairs. Darcy and Kieran followed closely behind their brothers. Once they reached the landing on the stairway, Kieran stopped and looked up. The lady he'd seen earlier, smiled down at him. After blowing a kiss to Kieran, she waved and moved back in the direction of Delaney's room.

"Hurry, Kieran," Darcy insisted, while standing at the bottom of the stairs.

"Aeron, when we get in the car, call and tell your dad and Delaney to meet us at the hospital," Teresa ordered.

Aeron secured Darcy and Kieran in the back of their Suburban before helping Seth into the middle seat. Aeron sat beside Seth and held what was becoming another bloodstained washcloth against the back of his brother's head. "God, Mom, this is making me sick!" Aeron complained.

"Just call your dad and sister!"

As they pulled out of the driveway, Kieran tapped Aeron on the shoulder and asked, "Did the old lady in black help you get Seth to the house?"

Aeron immediately looked at Seth, and they both yelled, "Old lady in black?"

CHAPTER 3

"Dad, I swear there was this weird old lady up by the lake. Me and Aeron followed her into the barn and that's when I got hurt," Seth insisted.

Adrian placed his hand on Seth's knee and flashed a look at Aeron, who was standing at the foot of the gurney Seth was sitting on. "Young man, how many times have I told you that wrestling around was going to get someone hurt someday?"

"Dad, I didn't do anything except fall back onto him when the bale of straw fell on me. I mean it!" Aeron argued.

"Yeah, Dad, it was all an accident. And there really is an old lady walking around our property," Seth insisted. "Even Kieran said he saw an old lady in black!"

Teresa put her hand on Adrian's shoulder while placing her hand on Seth's back. "Adrian, as your sons' attorney," she chuckled, "I know the boys can be rough with each other, but they really were chasing after someone near the lake. I saw them point and take off running toward the barn."

"I don't know, you guys, it just sounds too far-fetched that some old woman in a long black dress would be wandering around the lake before mysteriously disappearing into the barn." He winked at Teresa. "But if *your attorney* says so, then we'll have to go with your side of the story."

"Maybe it was our new neighbor, Mrs. Murphy," Teresa suggested. "She could have been out for a stroll or something. If it wasn't her, maybe she can tell us who it might have been."

"Yeah, maybe you're right, honey. I can go and meet her when we get home from the hospital," Adrian said.

A nurse appeared from behind the curtain. He walked over to Seth with a syringe in his hand. "I have to numb the area around the wound before we do the stitches," he said. Seth's eyes bulged in their sockets. "This will sting a little, but you won't feel it during the procedure."

"Well, isn't this gonna be fun," Seth protested.

"It won't take too long," the nurse assured him, "but we need to get that gash closed up."

Seth grasped Adrian's hand and squeezed as the needle penetrated his scalp. Aeron held his stomach and turned away. A tear glided down Seth's cheek as Adrian grimaced. "Dang, boy! I'm losing circulation in my hand."

"Sorry, Dad." Seth groaned, and his teeth clenched shut for a moment. "Dang, this really hurts!"

"I know. Trust me!" Adrian jeered. "I've had my share of stitches over the years." Adrian grimaced from his son's grip. "Hey, Aeron, you should be holding your brother's hand instead of me."

Aeron turned and scowled as he saw the nurse still working on Seth. As he patted his father's shoulder, he replied, "You know, Dad, you seemed to be doing a great job. I'd hate to interfere."

Adrian chuckled. "Yeah, some special son you are."

"Yep, I am," Aeron said. "It's about time someone finally recognizes how special I am."

As the nurse removed the needle, Seth's shoulders dropped. "Okay, that wasn't fun at all," Seth complained.

"I'll be back shortly," the nurse said. "Let's give that time to numb the area." He exited the room.

"Honey," Teresa said, "I'll help you clear off your bed when we get home."

"Thanks," Seth replied. "I doubt my *roommate* will help me out."

"Wait a minute," Aeron protested, "I was the one who helped you get your first stitches. My work is done for the day."

Seth looked at his parents and rolled his eyes. "And he thinks I'm the one with the head injury!"

Adrian laughed.

"Okay," the nurse said, as he returned. "We have a wound to stitch."

"My brother said he'd volunteer to take my place," Seth teased.

"Yeah, right," Aeron replied. "I think it's time for me to go for a walk."

CHAPTER 4

That evening, Adrian's rational mind dominated his thoughts, which seemed to be swept up in a hurricane—swirling wildly in his head. He wondered who could have been snooping around their lake and barn earlier that day.

As he meandered up the manicured walkway to Mrs. Murphy's home, the pungent odor of flowers and herbs captured his senses, causing his eyes to fill with water.

He hesitated before finally tapping on the door.

As he began wiping away his tears, a gray-haired woman appeared. "May I help you?"

"Yes," Adrian said, "Please forgive my intrusion this late in the afternoon, but I wanted to introduce myself. I'm Adrian Douglas. My family and I just moved in across the road."

"Oh, yes," Mrs. Murphy replied, "that wonderful realtor of yours told me I was going to have a new family over there." The screen door squeaked open. "Please come in, Mr. Douglas."

"Thank you, ma'am."

As he entered, Adrian was mesmerized by the colonial-style decor of her kitchen. His attention focused on the fireplace mantle, which was decorated with antique kitchen utensils, pewter dinnerware, and various red, white, and blue Fiestaware pitchers. "Wow, your kitchen is amazing, ma'am."

"Oh, it's just some old stuff I've collected over the years. Most of it was handed down from family members who've passed years ago." She extended her hand and shook Adrian's. "It's a pleasure to finally meet you, Mr. Douglas."

"Same here, ma'am. I'm sorry I couldn't have come over sooner, but things have been very hectic over at my place."

"Yes, I know that moving can be such a chaotic time," she said.

Seizing the opportunity, he declared, "Well, one of my sons got hurt in the barn this afternoon and that sort of delayed us from getting more things done today."

"Oh, my goodness," she gasped. "Is he okay?"

"Well, he ended up with some stitches in his head, but we are certain he'll live." Adrian's tone was somewhat sarcastic, and yet, he'd hoped she would be able to provide some rationale for the boys' story about the strange woman.

"I'm so sorry to hear that," she responded. "I certainly would have helped out had I been here today."

Adrian's head jerked backward. "Pardon me, ma'am, but I sort of assumed that you knew about the accident."

"Well, I'm not sure how," she replied, "because I was visiting my sister over on Stewart Road all day. I just got back about an hour ago."

"Oh," Adrian said, intrigued by her response. "Well, my boys said they saw you today up near the lake right before you walked into the barn."

She tilted her head. "Mr. Douglas, I've been at my sister's since early this morning. We've been canning tomatoes all day. Are you sure they said it was me they saw?"

"Well," Adrian continued, "they said they saw a lady in a long black dress by the lake, and then she went into the barn. They assumed it was you, but . . . well, apparently, they were wrong."

Mrs. Murphy's eyes widened as she lifted a hand to her mouth and casually slid it down to her chest. She laughed. "I sure wish I could be two places at once, but I can't. It had to have been someone else. Besides, I don't *ever* go near that barn."

"Would you know who my boys might have seen?"

"I can't say that I do, but occasionally, we do have neighbors up the road who walk down this way." Sensing Adrian's bewilderment, Mrs. Murphy responded, "Wait here, honey." She stepped over to the counter and returned with a sealed jar of tomato juice. "You look like you need some proof as to my whereabouts today."

Adrian's face reddened, and he cleared his throat. "I'm so sorry, Mrs. Murphy, but I didn't mean to imply that it was definitely you at the lake and barn. My boys swore they saw a lady in a long black dress walking near there today, and since we're the only two homes down this far, we all assumed it was you." Mrs. Murphy began to fidget with the strings on her apron. "Please accept my apology, ma'am. I didn't mean to question your whereabouts."

"Oh, honey, you don't need to apologize," she replied. "That makes perfect sense that you folks would assume it was me. Our properties do adjoin."

"Now I'm really confused," Adrian said. "I can't begin to imagine who it might have been."

"Well, as I said," Mrs. Murphy repeated, "maybe it was one of the neighbors up the road."

"Well, I guess so," Adrian agreed, still embarrassed by his tone and assumptions.

Sensing his discomfort, Mrs. Murphy asked, "So, tell me about your family, Mr. Douglas." She motioned for him to follow her into the living room; however, she noticed a shadow retreating up the side wall of the staircase, which was followed by a creaking noise scurrying across the ceiling of the living room. In a sudden, nervous crescendo, she asked, "Can I get you a nice glass of iced tea?"

"No thank you, ma'am. And please call me Adrian."

She smiled. "I will call you Adrian, but only if you call me Virginia."

They grinned as Adrian sat in one of the overstuffed chairs. "You have a remarkable home," he said. "I hope we can get our house in order soon. This is so impressive, especially the antique furniture. All we have right now are a bunch of boxes that we keep tripping over. I certainly need to get my wife over here soon."

"Please tell me about her. Does she work outside the home?" Mrs. Murphy asked.

"Well, yes and no. Teresa is an attorney, and she often spends a lot of time at home during the summer months. When the kids go back to school, she spends more time at the office. I'm an engineer, and co-owner in a computer company over in the Youngstown area. I try to spend a lot of time at home during the summer months as well, but I often must travel out of town."

"So, Adrian, how did you end up in my little part of the world?"

"Well, a couple years ago we sold our other home, but at the same time, my company was hit hard due to a downturn in the market, and we had some unexpected costs related to an expansion project my company was doing. We ended up living in a townhouse longer than we'd planned. It was tight for a family of seven."

"Seven! How did you manage that, Mr. Doug—Adrian?"

"Well, my oldest kids helped us out a lot with cooking, cleaning, and babysitting, so that made it easier for my wife and me to both work at the office a little more than we'd anticipated. We saved as much as we could to buy a bigger house with more property. I know it sounds a bit cliché, but we're so glad we finally found the house of our dreams."

"I'm certainly glad you did," Mrs. Murphy said. "So, you two must have very hectic lives."

"Yes, Teresa and I have five precious darlings," he jested. "Delaney is our oldest. Then we had Aeron, Seth, and the twins, Darcy and Kieran."

"*Twins!*" Mrs. Murphy lunged forward in her chair and clutched her chest. Her reaction forced Adrian's eyebrows to launch upward. "Well," Mrs. Murphy, stammered, "that's very interesting, Adrian." Her lips trembled.

"You know . . ." she stated, before smiling, ". . . having twins and all is . . . quite special." Mrs. Murphy eased back in her chair. Taking a deep breath, and clearing her throat, she asked, "So, what are their ages?"

"Well, Delaney just turned 18 years old, and she's going to be a senior at the high school this year." Finally relaxing again, he explained, "I must confess that I have felt very guilty for moving her right before her last year of high school, but she seems okay with it. I think it has something to do with some drama she wanted to get away from with her last boyfriend, who happens to be my business partner's son." Adrian blushed, wishing he'd omitted that part of the story.

"Awww, what a darling she must be," Mrs. Murphy said.

"Aeron just turned 17 in July, and Seth is almost 16. They both keep us hopping with sports and all."

"I bet they are as handsome as their father."

Adrian chuckled. "You are being too kind, Virginia." He rested his hands on the arms of the chair. "Then, we have the twins, who just turned 6-years-old this past May."

"I'm sure they all make you and your wife so proud."

"Yes, and quite busy, too."

Adrian looked around the room once more. He saw several old photos above the fireplace and in between each large window. "So, who are those people in the photos, if you don't mind me asking?" he inquired. "I've always been intrigued by older photographs. Everyone always appears so somber." He shifted slightly in his chair.

"Well, that one over the mantle is my father sitting on my grandfather's lap. I have that same chair in that photo right over there in the corner." She pointed to it with pride. "My grandfather—his name was George—used to own all the property on both sides of this portion of Murray Road. In fact, he pretty much built your home and the barn. The lake was added several years later because it used to be—" She ceased talking and cleared her throat. "I mean, it used to be filled with a lot of grass and such." She crossed her legs and shifted sideways in her chair.

"You know, the real estate agent told us that you knew a lot about the area. Did your grandfather farm all this land back then?"

"Yes, he was a farmer, but he also raised a lot of livestock for the locals. He slaughtered pigs and sold the meat to almost the entire town of Inverness."

"That's something I've been meaning to ask someone," Adrian interrupted. "I assume that Inverness has to have some connection to Scotland, but how did it get its name here?"

"Well, some Scottish families did settle just up the road, and they apparently brought a lot of their stories with them. Some of them didn't make it here alive, but many did survive the trips and settled there. Inverness is the name they chose for the town." Mrs. Murphy cleared her throat while shifting in her chair again. "You know," she continued, "I've always heard about this Irish family, with the last name Ward, lived in a log cabin on the property before my grandfather acquired it; however, I don't know where they went after they left here. I think some of them were buried in the old cemetery before it was moved up on the hill behind your house."

"Old cemetery? Where was that?"

"It's a long story, and I'll have to share it with you some other time," Mrs. Murphy said.

The huge ornamental clock chimed.

"Oh, I don't want to take up any more of your time. You've had a long day, so I better get home," Adrian said.

"Oh, you're not bothering me one bit. I love sharing the history of this little corner of the world. I must say, though, it has had a very interesting history."

"Why do you say that?" Adrian asked. "And, I hope you don't mind me asking, but why do you stay away from the barn?"

"Well, Adrian, there were some terrible things that happened in that barn, and I just can't bring myself to go near it."

A door unexpectedly slammed shut in the upstairs. A shrill scream raced from Mrs. Murphy's mouth, as Adrian lunged forward, looking toward the ceiling.

Mrs. Murphy clutched her cross neckless and squeezed her eyes shut. She mumbled a few brief words, but Adrian was unable to make sense of them. After releasing her cherished heirloom around her neck, she laughed and said, "Oh, it's just the wind. I need to get that silly window fixed upstairs in the hallway. It lets in too much air sometimes."

The tingling sensation of thousands of tiny ants crawled all over Adrian's flesh. "What did you mean by saying 'terrible things,' Virginia?"

Clearing her throat once more, she replied, "Oh, it's just that I don't like going to the barn because it . . . well . . . let's just say it always smelled like death. It's just a creepy old place to me. I can still see the pigs hanging upside down by their hind legs as they were slaughtered. I just don't like being near that place."

Adrian's breathing eased, as his mind stopped spinning ominous tales of horror.

Sensing Mrs. Murphy was growing weary of his interrogation, Adrian changed the subject. "Who are the two people in that picture over there?" He pointed to a single picture on the wall above an antique table.

"That is my grandfather and his first wife. Her name was Matilda, my grandmother."

"Oh, did his first wife pass, and he ended up remarrying?"

"Yes," Mrs. Murphy replied, "his second wife was sort of crazy, so my family doesn't really talk about her." She chuckled—her face beaming a crimson shade. "I'm sorry, Adrian. I shouldn't be telling you such nonsense about my crazy step-grandmother, especially after just meeting you."

Adrian smiled. "You're only answering my questions." He paused briefly. "I would like to hear the rest of your story about your family sometime. But, if you don't mind, how did he meet his second wife?"

"My grandfather met Harriet in the town of Inverness. There was a tragedy on one of the ships that Harriet came over on, and that was around the same time my grandfather lost my grandmother. Maybe my grandfather and Harriet were grieving and somehow found companionship in suffering."

"What kind of tragedy happened on the one ship?" Adrian asked.

Hesitating at first, she finally responded, "Well, almost all the passengers on that ship had been massacred. Only two people survived."

Adrian's eyebrows leaped on his forehead. "Massacred? By whom?"

"No one knows for sure, but the two survivors said it was another ship that attacked theirs, and the thieves killed almost everyone before robbing them."

"Pirates?"

Mrs. Murphy shrugged her shoulders. "As I said, that was their story, so maybe it was pirates."

"Whatever happened to the two survivors?" Adrian's mind sought answers.

"One of them stayed in the town for a while, and the other happened to marry my grandfather." Mrs. Murphy scooted forward in her chair, waiting for a reaction from Adrian. She wasn't disappointed.

"So, you're telling me that Harriet was one of the survivors?" Mrs. Murphy nodded. "What happened to the other woman?"

"Her name was Dolores, and she was Harriet's sister."

"That is unbelievable!" Adrian commented.

"It is all in the past," Mrs. Murphy said. "Anyway, most of my relatives are buried up there on the hill." She pointed toward the direction of Adrian's new home.

"Madeline, the real estate agent, told me about a cemetery on the property, but I didn't really think much about it until you mentioned it. It kind of seems strange having a cemetery adjoining my property now that I really think about it." After smiling, Adrian said, "I'm not one for all that paranormal crap. My oldest boys, on the other hand, are interested in all sorts of ghost stories, but I'm certainly not."

"I'd like to say I feel the same way, but you know that strange, unexplained things can certainly happen." Mrs. Murphy grabbed her necklace again.

Adrian looked at his watch and stood. "I better get home and check on Seth. He's the son who was injured in the barn today."

"Seth. Now that's a nice name. I have a relative by that same name, and I think it means *anointed one*." She smiled. "Oh, well, I hope he feels better soon." She stood and shook hands. "You know, Adrian, most of those people on the hill have been buried there for decades, so unless you really do believe in ghosts, I would have to say that the lady your boys saw today must have been one of our *living* neighbors up the road." They laughed. "Please give my best to your family. I can't wait to meet them soon."

After watching Adrian make it safely to his own property, Mrs. Murphy walked over from the window and picked up another photo from the stand in the corner. It was the wedding picture of her grandfather and Harriet, his second wife. She could never seem to rationalize why she kept the photo on display, but she somehow justified its existence as some sort of appeasement: a personal sacrifice to what she thought was a vengeful goddess. She gazed down at it intently and then pointed her finger and warned, "Now, don't you dare run these ones off, Harriet. Mr. Douglas seems like a nice man." After she straighten it on the table, she pointed at the image again and demanded, "You also better leave his children alone, especially those twins! They're not yours, Harriet!" Suddenly, Mrs. Murphy clutched her chest after the lights flickered and another door slammed shut upstairs.

The battle over souls had begun once again, and the Douglas family was about to experience a war they were not prepared to fight.

CHAPTER 5

That night, Adrian sat up in bed, as if jolted by a static shock. The eerie sound of squealing pigs awakened him out of a deep sleep. As Adrian rested for a moment, rubbing his eyes, he wondered what could have caused the dreaded sound.

Not wanting to disturb Teresa, Adrian slipped out of bed and stepped quietly into the bathroom. After walking to the sink and splashing water on his sweaty face, an apparition peered into the bathroom through the small opening in the door. It gazed at Adrian as he dried his hands and face.

The apparition drifted past the bathroom door and was absorbed into the darkness of the shadows in the bedroom. The menacing creature stepped farther back into the darkness when Adrian turned off the bathroom light and returned to his bed. Teresa stirred and pressed her body against his once he pulled the sheet over his waist. After wrapping his arm around her, Adrian gently kissed her forehead before closing his eyes.

The decomposing corpse remained in the corner until Adrian was sleeping soundly. It finally moved across the room and stood next to Teresa. It meticulously examined her. Aroused, it stooped next to her and inhaled, savoring the remnants of a perfumed aroma emanating from her skin.

The prowler stood and meandered toward the oldest boys' bedroom, stopping briefly to examine a table full of family photos that Teresa insisted on displaying earlier that day, hoping to give her children a sense of home. A faint, hazy reflection appeared in the glass of one of Delaney's senior photos. An agonizing, moaning sound pierced the silence, and echoed down the hallway. The apparition soon completed its journey to Aeron and Seth's bedroom.

Seth was on his stomach with both hands tucked under his pillow. As he slept, his sheet slid gently down his bare back and legs and drifted like a feather to the floor at the bottom of his bed. Seth twitched from the sensation. He turned his head as the intruder knelt to the floor beside his bed.

As Seth inhaled the cool, night air streaming in from the open window, the face of the creature was only inches away from him. It sniffed up the cheek of the unsuspecting teen as he rested on his bed, innocently dreaming. Decades of worm-ridden, festering rot clothed the decaying flesh of the intruder's exposed skin. Its one remaining eyeball dangled from its crushed eye socket. The creature sniffed the back of Seth's head and soon discovered where the once gaping lesion had now been stitched closed. The creature stood and stared, envious of Seth's young, warm body.

The apparition anxiously approached Aeron and lowered onto its knees beside his bed. It placed its ear close to Aeron's chest. The muffled sound of the teen's tranquil heartbeat stirred a memory of its own vibrant life radiating from its soul. Its nostrils flared, and the wrinkles of the creature's neck were momentarily smoothed when it lifted its head into the air, savoring the faint odors of cologne clinging to Aeron's flesh. Resembling the cunningness of a predator sizing up its prey, the apparition admired Aeron's features from only inches away from the teen's own face. It moved its head slightly to the right before easing to the left. Aeron suddenly rolled onto his side, causing the creature to stand and retreat toward the door.

Delaney's room was its next destination.

The trespasser entered and stopped at the foot of her bed. Delighting itself in the scent of Delaney's room, the creature's chest was set ablaze with intense desire. Delaney was lying on her back with her sheet at her waist. The apparition moved to the right side of her bed and positioned itself between her and the attic door on the far side of her room.

Slowly collapsing forward like a falling tree, the creature's feet lifted from the floor. Moments later, it was hovering above Delaney, only a foot from her peaceful body. After lowering just inches from her, the creature stretched forth its arms and placed one hand on each side of Delaney's head. Its bony, grimy fingers brushed the hair away from her face. The creature's head moved closer to Delaney's neck and sniffed. Delaney stirred, causing the creature to quickly ascend. The intruder returned to an upright position on the floor and retreated for the hallway, stopping only once to gaze back at Delaney.

Satisfied with the close contact it had with several of the living residents of the house, the creature descended the stairs and passed through the front door. It ascended the embankment and soon slipped peacefully into the lake, disappearing below the surface of the water.

CHAPTER 6

The alarm buzzed at 6:30 A.M. After Adrian sat up in bed, he kicked the sheet from his legs and spun around, placing his feet on the cool floor. He looked over at Teresa before slipping on a pair of jeans and walking down the hallway to Aeron and Seth's bedroom. He peeked in and noticed Seth was uncovered. The slight breeze blew the curtains aside, sending a damp chill throughout the room. Adrian walked over and retrieved the bed sheet from the floor and eased it over Seth. He leaned over and examined the stitches before smiling and turning toward Aeron.

He walked over to Aeron's bed and reached for the covers, assuming they'd been kicked off sometime during the night. Aeron's eyes opened. "Oh, I'm sorry," Adrian whispered, "I didn't mean to awaken you." He smiled at Aeron. "Did you sleep well?"

"Yeah, but I don't think Seth did. He seemed restless last night."

"Well, maybe his head was hurting or something," Adrian replied. He felt dampness under his toes, but he ignored it while he reached down and pulled the sheet up to the middle of Aeron's chest. Still whispering, he said, "I'll be home in a few hours. My meeting shouldn't take too long. And I'll really need your help then," Adrian said.

"Okay," Aeron replied, as he turned onto his side.

Adrian patted Aeron's arm. "Hey, please make sure you two help your mom out this morning." Aeron nodded.

Adrian moved Aeron's bangs from his forehead before whispering, "I'll see you soon."

Adrian entered Delaney's room and walked over to her bed. She was curled up with the sheet, which was pulled up to her chin. Admiring the peaceful slumber of his eldest daughter, Adrian gently kissed the top of her head. Suddenly, he noticed something green laying on the sheet. It was slimy to the touch. There was only a trace amount, but enough for him to wonder how it got there. He grabbed a tissue from the box on the stand beside her bed and wiped it away.

As he started to leave, he lifted his foot and noticed another damp spot on the floor. Not knowing for sure what to think, he left to check on Darcy and Kieran. He was relieved to see that they appeared undisturbed, and thankfully, he didn't notice any damp spots on their floor. He kissed them and retreated to his room to get dressed for his meeting.

Seth awakened and looked out the window at the lake. He rubbed his eyes and glanced over at Aeron, who was lying on his stomach. Seth quietly stood and jumped from several feet away. "Incoming!" he hollered, as he landed on top of his unsuspecting brother. Seth laughed as Aeron thrashed about, trying to get untangled from his sheet.

"What's wrong with you, you idiot?" he protested. Aeron slammed his pillow into Seth's face as he bellowed, "You're such a dumb—"

"What's going on?" Teresa inquired, as she walked into their room with some folded clothes in her arms. "I was just coming in here to awaken both of you. You guys need to get dressed and start helping out around here," Teresa demanded. "Your dad's friend, Brian, and the other contractors are coming soon. There's lots of renovations to do around here."

After Teresa left, Seth hit Aeron on the arm and said, "Hey, I wanna go over to the lake just to see it in the morning. Wanna come?"

"I guess, but Mom will shoot us if we don't help out," Aeron insisted.

"It's just for a few minutes. I'll ask Delaney, too," Seth said.

"I gotta take a leak and get some clothes on, so I'll meet you in the sunroom," Aeron replied.

Fifteen minutes later, the three siblings walked across Murray Road and up the embankment to the lake. The grass was manicured like the landscaping on a golf course. Delaney looked at her brothers and said, "You know something, this is pretty cool!"

"You two sound alike. Are you sure you guys aren't sharing the same brain?" Aeron teased. Delaney slapped his arm.

"I can't wait to go for a swim," Seth said. They walked to the pavilion and sat on one of the picnic tables for a moment. "I think we need to have a party with some of our friends," Seth suggested.

Aeron laughed and replied, "Yeah, like you actually have any!" Aeron grinned. "I'll ask all of mine, so you don't feel lonely."

"You are so conceited, Aeron Douglas!" Delaney rolled her eyes. "You know," she chuckled, "you'll never get a girl to love you as much as you love yourself." The fist bump between Delaney and Seth was like a slap to Aeron's face.

"I wanna see the dock," Seth said, as he stood. The dock extended about fifteen feet out into the lake. The three of them meandered out to the ladder, which was attached at the far end. Delaney sat down, removed her sandals, and soaked her feet in the water.

"That's where that old lady disappeared, Delaney," Seth said, as he pointed toward the barn. "It was so weird." Goose bumps rose on his skin.

As they sat, speculating about the strange visitor in their yard from the day before, a hand approached slowly under the water toward Delaney's submerged feet. As the hand was inches from grasping one of Delaney's ankles, the siblings stood and walked to the shore and made their way over to the far end of the lake. Cattails stood like fence posts, surrounded by green scum. It was too swampy for them to pass through, so they walked back in the direction of the pavilion.

"Okay, Seth, this is kinda cool up here," Aeron concurred. "Maybe you aren't so psycho about it after all."

"I told you," Seth answered confidently. "Let's get stuff done at the house so we can come back and swim."

"Not so fast, Aquaman!" Delaney jeered. "Remember, you have stitches, and you can't get dirty lake water in the wound."

Disappointment possessed his body. "That sucks! I forgot."

"Let's get back over home. Mom needed our help, so we better get there before she sends out a search party," Aeron said.

"Yeah, we need to get back over home," Delaney agreed.

As Delaney, Aeron, and Seth descended the embankment, small circular waves rippled outward across the lake's surface. Bubbles raced upward, but they quickly disappeared, much like the fading voices of the three siblings making their way back home.

CHAPTER 7

After the contractors left, Kieran begged Adrian to take him to the lake. Darcy, stomped her foot and insisted on going with them.

A few minutes later, Teresa walked out of her room with a tissue in her hand. "Honey, what is this?" she asked, but Adrian had already left for the lake with the twins. Still curious about the mysterious substance she held in her hand, she yelled for Aeron, who was exiting the bathroom.

"What's up, Mom?"

"I'm not sure what this is, but look here," she said.

In the tissue was a green, slimy substance. "That kinda looks like the green scum we saw at the lake earlier today," Aeron said.

"I didn't think about that, but you know, the floor was also wet on my side of the bed this morning, and that's where I found this green stuff." She shrugged her shoulders. "It's probably something we brought in with one of the boxes from the garage."

"Maybe," Aeron said, as he walked toward his room. "This moving is really kicking my butt. I *really* need to take a quick nap. Hope that's okay." Aeron grimaced and rubbed his forehead.

"Is your head hurting again?"

Aeron sighed. "Yeah, and my ears are ringing, too, and it's starting to really bother me."

Teresa hugged him. "I'm so sorry, honey. Maybe a combination of the heat and all the heavy lifting has gotten to you."

"Who knows," Aeron replied. "Anyway, I just need to rest for a little while."

Teresa smiled and brushed his bangs out of his eyes. "How about we go for a walk up the road later? I miss our little talks."

"Sure," Aeron replied with a grin. "You know, it's not easy talking with your mom when she's an attorney."

"What do you mean?"

"I rarely win an argument with you," he said with a forced smile. He rubbed his forehead again.

Teresa winked and tapped his shoulder. "Yeah, like how you've been trying to negotiate with me over getting to use the car more often."

Aeron smiled, as he lifted his eyebrow. "Any chance I might borrow it later today? After all, I've been a good little boy, helping you move things and all."

"Well," Teresa smiled, "I'll think about it." Teresa hugged Aeron again. "How about you get your nap, and we'll discuss it later. You really look like you're hurting. I'll bring you some medicine if you'd like."

"No, I'll be okay."

"If you say so," Teresa replied. "I'll call up for you later."

Aeron removed his shirt and collapsed onto the soft mattress before adjusting his pillow. Within minutes, his eyelids were weighted down with fatigue, and he soon drifted off to sleep.

The door to his closet opened. Standing in the shadow was a man in an old pair of bib overalls. His clothing was moth-eaten, and the hems of his pants were tattered. The creature's gray hair was matted to his forehead, and his ashen skin was tattooed with purplish veins, splintering off like lightning racing across an evening sky. Water seeped from his swollen face as he stood and watched Aeron resting peacefully on his bed.

An hour later, Adrian tapped on the door and entered. He didn't notice the closet door easing shut at the same time. Adrian sat on Aeron's bed and gazed at his son for several moments. He wanted to awaken Aeron, but his son's peaceful countenance caused Adrian to pause.

Over the years, as Adrian tucked his children into their beds, he would sometimes rub their backs until they fell asleep, especially if they'd had a rough day. There were also many times when he would stand in the doorway and watch them sleep for several minutes.

As Adrian sat in silence, listening to the breaths of his son, he'd realized that Aeron was becoming the young man he'd hoped to have in his life. He admired Aeron's charisma, which was every bit as attractive as his model-like appearance. His engaging eyes often drew a host of admirers, and his dark, ash brown hair dangled just above his brow, when it wasn't slicked back. The pinnacle of his provocative smile was his dimples. Aeron was his first son, and he remembered the countless times he'd held him as a newborn and hummed many hymns he'd sung on Sundays in church. But now, he knew his son's independence only symbolized a small part of the man he was becoming each day, and his son's relationship with Whitney, although disappointing to him and Teresa, was evidence of an even deeper journey into adulthood.

The feeling of sorrow was a flock of vultures hovering above Adrian's world, for he knew it wasn't long before his oldest son and daughter would be leaving for a life of their own. His children were everything to him, and those moments of peace and quiet were some of his greatest treasures—a kind of legacy he knew he'd cherish forever in the secret recesses of his heart.

Knowing Aeron had company waiting for him, Adrian reached forth his hand and tenderly placed it on the top of his son's shoulder. Aeron's eyes opened. "Oh, sorry, Dad," he whispered. "How long have I been out?"

"About an hour. I'm glad you got to rest, though" Adrian said. "I hope you're feeling better. Your mom said you're still having that problem with a headache, and she said something about your ears ringing."

Aeron reached up and rubbed his eyes. "Yeah, it's better, but I've been feeling really tired ever since we moved out here. All I wanna do is sleep."

"Maybe we should get you checked out. We'll keep an eye on it for a few more days. Maybe it's all the unpacking. It might be all the dust, too." He stood and extended his hand. "Seriously, though, if the problem persists, we'll get it checked out." Adrian helped Aeron out of bed. "By the way, you have a guest downstairs."

"Who is it?"

"Why don't you come down and find out," Adrian teased.

"I hope it's Jake. I haven't seen him in a while."

"Just come down and see for yourself."

"I'll be down in a minute. I have to go to the bathroom first," Aeron said.

"Okay, I'll meet you in the kitchen."

Aeron picked up his shirt from the floor and held it to his nose. He dropped it and walked over to his dresser and pulled out a clean shirt. On his way to the bathroom, the woman in the black dress walked out of the twins' room and stopped. She watched Aeron walk down the hallway. When he closed the bathroom door, the woman disappeared into Delaney's room, destined for the attic.

After relieving himself, Aeron gazed at his fatigued expression in the mirror before reaching for his toothbrush. When he bent over to brush his teeth, a bloody corpse appeared in the reflection of the mirror. The entity had a noose around its neck as it stood in the doorway. It was dressed in a flannel shirt and jeans, which were threadbare in the knees. The frayed cuffs of his shirt were stained with the same sticky, black substance Aeron discovered on his hands from the rope in the barn. The disfigured creature grinned as he watched Aeron. When Aeron stood upright, wiped off his mouth, and finally slipped on his shirt, the stranger had already disappeared.

Aeron ran his fingers through his hair, trying to regain some style to it. He picked up a stick of deodorant and applied it before checking his chin and jawline for whiskers.

"Aeron!" Adrian called up from the bottom of the stairs. "Are you coming down?”

“On my way.” Aeron darted from the bathroom and down the stairs.

CHAPTER 8

Aeron's heart plummeted into his stomach when he entered the kitchen and saw Whitney seated at the table. "Hi, Aeron," she said, as she quickly stood and pushed in her chair.

"Hey," he murmured, while staring at the annoyed expressions on his parents' faces. "Sorry that I haven't been in touch, but I've been busy helping out around here."

"Yes, Whitney, we have kept him quite busy," Teresa said.

Whitney ignored her and embraced Aeron, but she felt as though she'd embraced her enemy. Although annoyed at first, Aeron's stomach tingled when he felt her chest brushing against his. "Let's go to the sunroom," he suggested.

Adrian and Teresa glanced at each other. Teresa rolled her eyes as Adrian's cheeks puffed outward, forcing air from his tightening lips as he shook his head.

Aeron attempted to sit in one of the chairs, but Whitney pulled him over to the loveseat. Although desiring to have him close, her wrath was still building in her gut. She didn't want to immediately announce her displeasure with his lack of responses to her texts and voicemails. "I've missed you, baby," she said, while rubbing his leg.

"I've been so busy getting stuff unpacked and moved around here that I haven't had much time to contact anybody. My parents haven't given me much time to myself."

She looked toward the kitchen before saying, "Let's go for a walk." She grabbed his hand and pulled him up. "You can show me the rest of the house later."

Her strategy was quite simple: keep Aeron Douglas at all costs, and she knew exactly what to do to ensure that. She had grown accustomed to having him exclusively to herself. He was, after all, her strongest desire—an addiction of sorts.

"Okay," he replied. "How about I show you our lake again? The house is still kinda messy anyway."

"Yeah, I'd like that," she responded, as her heart danced inside her throbbing chest. "I really liked the antique kitchen, though."

"Yeah, my mom does, too," he replied.

As they walked around the lake, Aeron shared the story about the old woman he and Seth followed into the barn. Whitney seemed intrigued at first, but she had more important things on her mind.

"I remember when you and I drove out here a couple weeks ago," Whitney reminded him.

"Yeah, that was an interesting visit."

"I'll never look at that picnic table the same anymore," she said, with a provocative smile draped across her face. "I just hope that old woman who lives over in that house didn't see what we were doing." Whitney laughed before rubbing her hand across his chest.

"Yeah, I was thinking about it when Delaney and Seth came up here earlier with me. We were pretty crazy that night."

"Aeron," she interjected, "I've really been worried about you."

"I'm fine. I've just been so busy, and it's hard getting used to a new house, so I haven't been sleeping too well, either."

She grasped his hand and smiled. "I can always come over some night and tuck you into your bed." Aeron grinned. Whitney reached up and brushed her hand through his hair. "Do you remember that night my parents were out of town, and you came over without your parents knowing about it?"

His crimson face beamed in the late afternoon sunlight. "Yeah."

Whitney stopped and gently caressed his chest. "Me, too." She lifted her eyebrows. "I'd like to relive a little bit of that night." She grabbed his hand and pulled him toward the barn. "Come on. I've been wanted to see the inside."

As they approached the towering structure, she grabbed his hand even tighter, prompting him to move faster toward the entrance. Once they entered, Whitney raved about the distinct, euphoric atmosphere, and she whispered into his ear seductive suggestions about being alone with him again. Aeron grinned. His initial inhibitions from the kitchen were quickly melting away.

She rubbed his arm as they walked toward the back of the barn.

"What's up there?" she asked, as she pointed to one of the lofts.

"That's a loft where the farmers stored hay for animals."

"Can you take me up there?" she asked.

"It's an oven up there right now. Are you sure you want to? It only has some old ropes and scattered hay."

"I'm not into sweating. What about those?" she asked, as she pointed toward a gate on one side of the main floor.

"One of the stalls. There's just some old junk in them now. You can check it out if you want."

"Later, because I have something better in mind," Whitney said. She led Aeron over to several bales of hay near one of the stall doors. She sat and patted where she wanted Aeron to join her. His heart pounded against his ribs, as other familiar sensations gained his attention. He sat down, and Whitney leaned over and kissed his neck. "I've really missed you, Aeron," she whispered, once her lips moved up to his ear. Aeron's mind exploded with the possibilities of where their encounter was heading. His annoyance with her intrusive texts quickly dissipated like smoke in a brisk wind, especially when she pressed her lips to his.

Whitney eased onto her back, pulling Aeron with her. "I've *really* missed you, Aeron," she whispered.

"I know!" Aeron pushed himself upward and removed his shirt. After he dropped it onto the floor, he rested again onto her chest.

Unknowingly, a man was hanging by a noose from one of the rafters high above them, but somewhat closer toward the entrance to the barn. The pitiful creature was dressed in black, with a white shirt, which was saturated with blood. Flies swarmed around his body as blood flowed from his swollen eyes, which bulged in their sockets.

Whitney pulled slightly away from Aeron and whispered, "Do you love me, Aeron?"

Aeron opened his eyes, and just as he stumbled over his words, they heard Seth yelling for him. His breaths suddenly became rapid and shallow. "Oh, my God! My brother sounds like he's close."

Aeron pushed himself up and grabbed his shirt. He jumped to his feet and pulled the shirt over his head while struggling to get his arms through the holes.

"I can't believe this," Whitney protested, as she brushed the remnants of hay from her clothing.

"If I don't answer, he'll know something's going on," Aeron said.

Whitney rolled her eyes. "Yeah, something *was* going on until your annoying brother interrupted us!"

A sudden, dull ache in Aeron's head triggered the familiar ringing in his ears. When he turned in the direction of the entrance to the barn, the hanging creature was gone.

Unhindered in her anger, Whitney words were abrasive and bitter. "Look, I don't know why you're trying to be some innocent boy around your family. Everybody knows what we do every time we're together." She brushed hay from her clothing when she stood. "I feel like you only use me for a good time."

"I don't use people!" he snapped.

"Oh, come on Aeron, everybody knows you only keep me around for your own selfish reasons. And besides, everyone knows your rich parents spoil you guys, and they're just worried people might talk bad about them when their precious kids do something they don't approve of." Aeron's eyes narrowed, and his hands clenched into fists. "After all, it's not like you always behave like the wonderful church-going boy your parents think you are. And I know they hate my guts."

"Where is this coming from?" Aeron asked.

The ringing in his ears intensified.

"I'm just tired of you not wanting to spend time with me," Whitney rebuked. She brushed her fingers through her hair, trying to remove the hay. "And what do you think they'd say if they knew you were hanging out with Jake Winters the nights he . . . well, you know." She pinched a couple fingers together and held them to her lips, pretending to blow smoke into the air.

"Why are you doing this?" Aeron rubbed his forehead and shook his head. "There's no reason to make a federal case out of this. It's not my fault we got interrupted!" Aeron pressed his fingers to his ears before shaking his head again. "And you need to leave Jake out of this. I'm not smoking anything with him! I would never do anything like that, and you know it!"

"I just feel like you're more worried about what your parents think of you. You're supposed to worry about me, you know!"

"You've got to be kidding me!" Aeron rubbed his forehead.

"Come on, Aeron, let's get out of here before we end up in another fight," she insisted.

"I'm not the one who started any of this," Aeron argued.

As they walked toward the entrance to the barn, the creature who'd been hanged was dangling above them once more.

"I'm on my way, Seth," Aeron yelled.

CHAPTER 9

Aeron was nearly intoxicated with adrenaline as he and Whitney walked toward the lake while ignoring each other's presence. Aeron saw Seth near the top of the embankment, so he waved and yelled, "I told you I am on my way!" Seth motioned back and started walking toward the house.

As Aeron and Whitney walked up the driveway, she asked, "How does my hair look?" Aeron didn't answer. "You know, you were really enjoying that way too much while we were sitting on the hay," she said, as she grabbed onto his arm. Aeron pulled away. "Oh, come on, Aeron, just give me that boyish grin. You know I can't resist your gorgeous smile."

He refused.

As the tension hovered like a storm cloud over their heads, Whitney inquired, "Aeron, you never did answer me in the barn. I asked if you loved me." His answer was glued to his tongue. Whitney hit his arm. "Oh—my—God! You don't love me, do you?" Her hands were thrust to her sides. "That's why you won't answer my texts. I knew moving out here was just one of your ways of getting away from me."

The woman in the black dress appeared in a bedroom window on the second floor. Joining her was a woman in a long white dress. She glared down at the young couple arguing in the driveway. Whitney quickly became the object of indignation to the woman in white.

"Yeah, right, Whitney. Do you really think I said, 'Hey, Dad, let's move out to the middle of God knows where just so I can get away from my girlfriend'?" He rolled his eyes. "Just relax! I told you I've been super busy, and that's why I haven't called you that much over the last few days." He shook his head and massaged his temples. "And besides, you're the one who doesn't act like you love me! All you do is accuse me of cheating on you, especially when I don't check in with you every stinking minute." He pressed his index fingers into each ear, trying to ease the pain. Disgusted with the interrogation, Aeron yelled, "And besides, everyone knows what you're like when things don't go your way. They all run for cover when you throw one of your temper tantrums and start destroying everything."

Whitney slapped Aeron across the face. "Go to hell, Aeron!" He turned toward her and glared. "Well," she threatened, "how do you think people will feel about you when I tell them how abusive you are to me? And what about the trouble you'll be in with *Mommy and Daddy* when they hear about your little pot and drinking parties with Jake? No decent girl would have anything to do with you after I tell them everything!"

Strangle her Aeron . . . she doesn't deserve you!

Aeron shook his head. "So, Princess, what are you doing with a guy like me if I'm such a horrible person? What's that say about you?" Whitney punched his arm. He sarcastically grinned and said, *"Oh, wow! That really hurt."* The feel of her moist hand against his cheek caused Aeron's head to jerk to one side. As he rubbed the side of his face, his anger burned inside his chest like a raging inferno, and his hands suddenly clenched into fists again.

Aeron saw her mouth moving, but the ringing in his ears smothered her words like a thick blanket of smoke. He suddenly thought about Jake Winters, and how Jake had warned him about her so many times. Whitney's best friend, Mariah, had also pursued Jake as much as Whitney had been chasing after him. Aeron knew he should have listened to his best friend—

"Aeron! Did you hear me?" Whitney yelled. She grabbed his chin and jerked his head toward her face. He pulled away.

"What?" he bellowed.

"See if I ever give you anymore—" She immediately stopped when she saw Seth stepping out onto the side porch.

"Dad really needs you, Aeron," Seth announced.

"I'll be there in a minute!" Not wanting to show the indelible red mark he was certain was spreading across his cheek, Aeron turned slightly away from the direction of his brother. "Just leave me alone and get back into the house!"

"Look, I have to go anyway," Whitney jeered. "You can at least walk me to my car." Once they approached her car, Whitney grabbed Aeron's hand. "I'm sorry, baby, but I don't like being used."

Aeron rolled his eyes. *"I'm—not—using—you!"* He shook his fists. "I don't get you!"

As she opened the door and sat down, she looked up at Aeron with a scowl. "You know, baby, I'm just being a jealous girlfriend. You're probably going to go to that new school and find some piece of trash who'll throw herself all over you."

Like you, he thought.

Aeron sighed. "Whitney, I wouldn't cheat on you. Loyalty is something I've been taught by *those parents* of mine that you don't like."

Whitney forced the keys into the ignition and turned again toward Aeron. "Just remember one thing, Aeron Douglas!" Aeron rolled his eyes. "I have dozens of guys who would be happy for me to—"

"Happy for you to what, Whitney?" Aeron boldly asked.

She smirked. "Trust me, you're not the first guy I've had to break in."

Aeron started to walk away, but suddenly he turned and yelled, "Fine! They can have you 'cause I'm done with you anyway! Besides, I got what I wanted!" He turned and stormed over to the side door.

Whitney peeled out of the driveway.

The woman in black peered out the upstairs window. She watched until the taillights of Whitney's car disappeared in the distance. Her lips widened with happiness, exposing her rotting teeth.

CHAPTER 10

Aeron stormed through the kitchen door and slammed it shut. Adrian climbed down from the stepladder and placed a screwdriver on the table. A sickening feeling came over Aeron as he looked at the screwdriver with an ominous sense of need and desire to do something he knew he'd regret.

Adrian noticed the red mark on the side of his son's face. It wasn't the first time such unexplained marks had appeared on his son. "What's wrong, Aeron?" Adrian asked.

Aeron's rage was about to detonate like a bomb, and his throat burned from the acid erupting from his stomach. "Nothing, Dad," he said with clenched teeth. "I was just showing Whitney the lake and barn."

Seth smirked. "Yeah, right. You were probably showing her a lot more than that."

"Shut up!" Aeron shouted.

Seth laughed as he walked into the dining room. "Yeah, I hope you kept your clothes on this time when you showed her around the barn." Aeron started after him, but his father stepped into the doorway, blocking him.

Seth kept walking toward the living room.

"You two need to knock this off right now!" Adrian demanded. "Aeron, what in the world is wrong? And where did those red marks come from *this time*?"

The muffled sound of a baritone voice suddenly disrupted Aeron's thoughts.

You don't have to answer him! He's not the father you deserve!

A sharp pain jabbed Aeron's ears, causing him to press his fists against the sides of his head. He kicked a chair against the kitchen table and hollered, "I suppose you're gonna yell at me about something too!"

"Whoa! Where's this coming from, young man?"

"I'm not in the mood for a lecture, Dad!"

"What in the world happened over there in the barn that got you into this mood?"

"Just leave me alone!" Aeron slammed his fist against the refrigerator.

"Did you have another fight with Whitney? What happened?"

"Dad, I said I'm not in the mood. Besides, I'm done with her! *You happy now?* You've always hated her!" Adrian walked over and put his hand on his son's shoulder. Aeron shoved it away. "Keep your stinking hands off me!"

"Aeron, what in the world is wrong with you?" Adrian asked. "I've never seen you this mad before, so what really happened between you two?" Aeron started to walk out of the room causing Adrian to yell, "Aeron Tyler Douglas, don't you dare walk away from me like that! I don't deserve that from you. I'm just trying to help."

Aeron squeezed his eyes closed for a moment, trying to ease the feeling of a sword piercing his ears. The voice returns.

He's deceiving you!

Aeron slammed his hand against the refrigerator again. "I said I don't wanna talk about it, Dad!"

"Now, just settle down, Aeron," Adrian warned. "Just tell me what I can do to help you."

Aeron's face grimaced with intense animosity. The ringing in his ears was like fingernails across a chalkboard, and the excruciating throbbing in his forehead pounded like a hammer against his skull.

Adrian's stomach sank from the malevolent expression on his son's face. "Here's how you can help, Dad! How about moving us back to civilization! I *hate* it here! *This is all your fault!*" With clenched fists, Aeron glared at his father—anger possessing his muscles. "*I hate you!*" Aeron attempted to leave the room again, but Adrian stopped him. Aeron pushed his father, causing Adrian to fall into the table, knocking several chairs to the floor. The screwdriver bounced several times off the floor.

Teresa and the twins were on their way down the stairs, but when she heard the yelling, she told Darcy and Kieran to go back to their room. Delaney came from the bathroom in time to intercept the twins after they ran up the stairs, frightened by the commotion coming from the kitchen.

Teresa bolted to the kitchen. Seth ran in to the hallway from the living room just as Teresa reached the bottom of the stairs.

Adrian quickly regained his balance and grabbed Aeron from behind before slamming his son against the refrigerator. Adrian's size was also intimidating. He was well built, tall, and a former linebacker from his college years, but he still struggled to subdue Aeron. With his broad chest pinned against his son's back, Adrian gritted his teeth and demanded, "Don't you *ever* lay a hand on me again, young man! I don't care how ticked off you are at the world!"

Kill him!

"Stop it, Dad!" Aeron yelled. "Leave me alone!"

Teresa ran into the kitchen and saw her husband pinning Aeron. "What in the world is going on in here, Adrian?" She grabbed onto her husband's arm and tried to pull him away from Aeron. Adrian refused to release his enraged son. Seth also tried.

"Let go of me, Dad!" Aeron hollered.

"No! Not until you settle down!" Adrian insisted.

"Dad, you're hurting me! You're gonna break my back!" Aeron pleaded.

Teresa tugged as hard as she could, but Adrian's forearm was pressed firmly against the upper portion of Aeron's back. "Adrian! Stop this! Right now!" Teresa ordered.

"Dad, please, you're gonna hurt him!" Seth pleaded.

Adrian looked at the side of Aeron's face and saw blood running from his son's lip. He immediately released him. After stepping backward, Adrian leaned against a wall, stunned by his own violent reaction. Aeron was panting as he slid sideways, coming to rest against the wall beside the refrigerator. Blood was flowing from Aeron's nose and lip, as well as cascading down the side of the appliance.

Adrian pressed his hand to his forehead in disbelief.

Teresa clasped her hand around Aeron's wrist and said, "Honey, are you okay? You're bleeding! Seth, grab a towel from the counter." She jerked her head toward Adrian. "Somebody better tell me what just happened in here!"

Adrian's breathing intensified. "I . . . I don't know what—" Adrian stormed out the kitchen door.

Teresa took the dish towel and held it against Aeron's nose. Exhausted and grieved by the fierce battle with his father, tears flowed down Aeron's face. The ringing in his ears had barely dissipated, and the pain seemed to be crushing his skull. Aeron buried his face in his hands.

Teresa gently stroked the back of Aeron's head and whispered, "It's okay, honey. Just tell me what's wrong."

"I don't know, Mom!" Aeron cried out. "I swear I really don't know! I haven't felt this way before." He rubbed his temples. "My head feels like it's gonna explode!"

"Well, no wonder, Aeron." She continued to comfort him.

His eyes squinted when he looked at Teresa. "Mom, my head feels like it's being crushed in with a sledgehammer, and my ears feel like they're gonna bleed." He rolled his head around, trying to relieve the pain. "And it's like someone is trying to say things in my head that I don't wanna do."

Teresa's heart sank, but she chose to ignore Aeron's comment while she rubbed the back of his head, hoping to provide some relief. She looked up at Seth and said, "Can you give us some time alone, honey?" Seth nodded. "Oh, and can you go upstairs and let your brother and your sisters know everything is calm now."

"Mom," Aeron mumbled, "I don't understand what happened. I just threatened Dad. That's not like me!" Exasperated, Aeron pressed his hands against his ears and leaned his head against the wall. "I just don't know anymore. Maybe this whole move is really getting to me."

Teresa gently placed her hand on his knee. "Honey, I know this move has been hard on all of us, but everything's going to work out soon." She brushed her fingers through Aeron's hair.

"Mom, I threatened Dad! I've never done that!"

"Just go to him," Teresa whispered. "Your father is the most understanding man I know. He loves you, and you guys will work it out."

"I don't know why I felt so mad all of a sudden."

"Honey, I promise you'll feel better about everything once school starts up and you begin to make some new friends." Aeron's silence tugged at her heart. Teresa caressed the side of his head and retrieved the dish towel from him. "See, you're all better. No bleeding." Teresa turned his head sideways. "Boy, Whitney sure did a number on your face, didn't she?" Aeron's face reddened again. "Aeron, I'm really concerned about you. This relationship is way too serious!"

"It's fine, Mom. I got it under control. It's probably over anyway."

Teresa sighed. "Why don't you go upstairs and let everyone know you're okay."

"Yeah, I guess I better." Teresa helped him to his feet. He staggered slightly, while pressing his fingers into his temples again.

"Are you okay, Aeron?"

"Yeah, I'll be fine."

Seth walked out of Delaney's room after Aeron reached the top of the stairs. They both stopped. "I'm sorry, man. I didn't mean to be such a jerk."

"It's okay, Aeron. I know you can't help what you are."

Aeron shook his head and smiled. "Yeah, I deserved that." Aeron asked if Delaney was in her room.

"Yeah, she's pretty ticked off, though."

"Where are you going?" Aeron asked.

"I told Delaney I would watch the twins, but I needed something from our room."

Finally sensing some relief from his headache, Aeron walked to his sister's room and taped on the door. "Who is it?" Delaney inquired.

"Your demon possessed brother."

"Oh, it's you," she said, as Aeron popped his head through the doorway. "Well," Delaney said, "you are not allowed completely into my room unless you are coming to apologize for *scaring us all to death!*"

Aeron smirked. "Okay, I've come to apologize."

"Okay then, you're permitted in my room," Delaney said, with her own smirk.

Aeron entered and closed the door. "Hey, I'm really sorry. I just don't know why I'm so angry these days."

"Look, Aeron," she said, as she walked over to her vanity and sat down. "We are all struggling to get adjusted to this move. You're not the only one dealing with this."

He sat on her bed and sighed. "I know, but it's just hard."

"Right, it is, but you need to get over it before you really do something bad," she warned.

"Delaney, can I tell you something?"

"What?"

"I really wanted to hurt someone. It was like someone was saying things in my head."

"You were totally psycho, if you ask me," Delaney replied, as she stood and walked over and sat on her bed beside him. "Aeron, you really did scare us."

"I know," he said, "and I'm really sorry. I've been ticked off before, but I really felt like I could have hurt someone. I've not felt that angry in my whole life."

"We all feel that way sometimes, Aeron."

Aeron dropped his chin to his chest. "Yeah, but have you ever thought about smashing someone's brains out by bashing their head off the floor, or stabbing their eyes out with a screwdriver?"

Delaney's eyes grew larger. "Aeron, who were you thinking about when you felt that way?"

When he looked away, Delaney grabbed his chin while lifting his head. She examined his face. "Ouch! Whitney sure left a nice mark this time." She turned his head from side to side. "Okay, Aeron, who were you thinking about hurting? Was it Whitney?"

A tear rolled down his cheek as he quickly stood and walked toward the door. "I can't!"

"You know, Aeron, it sounds like you really were possessed or something. I heard almost everything, and you don't ever say that kind of stuff to Mom or Dad." Aeron was silent. "Was it Whitney or Dad?" Delaney asked. "You were thinking about hurting one of them, weren't you?"

"Don't," he replied. "I shouldn't have said anything to you or Mom." He eased his back against the door. "I looked at Dad, and all I thought about was that he didn't deserve to be my dad. I just wanted to—" Aeron sighed. "Please don't repeat that!"

Confused by his response, Delaney said, "Aeron, if you ever feel that way again, you need to come to me. I mean it!"

"I will."

"Hey," Delaney interjected, "you know you *really* scared Darcy and Kieran."

"Shoot," Aeron replied, "I really screwed up on this one, didn't I?"

"Yeah, you better let them know you're sorry about everything,"

Delaney suggested.

"I better do it now." Aeron opened the door and turned back toward his sister before leaving. "Delaney, I really am sorry for what I did."

"Okay, you've convinced me," she smiled.

"About what?"

"That I should forgive you." Delaney grinned while Aeron smiled back.

As he approached the twins' room, he heard Darcy say, "Yeah, my brother isn't always like that."

"Yeah," Kieran agreed, "you don't have to be afraid of him."

Aeron opened the door and walked in. Darcy and Kieran jerked from fright. "Hey guys. Listen, I'm really sorry for yelling downstairs. I won't do it again," Aeron said.

Kieran ran over to his big brother and hugged him around his waist. Darcy joined them.

"That's good, 'cause Lilly and Cain are afraid of you," Darcy stated.

"Who's Lilly and Cain?" Aeron inquired.

"They're our new friends," Darcy said. "They play games with us."

Aeron smiled. "Oh, okay. Just tell them for me that I'm not always a mean, nasty guy."

Darcy turned toward the open closet door. "Aeron really isn't mean like that. So, it's safe for you guys to come out and play."

Playing along, Aeron looked at the closet door and said, "Yeah, come on out and play with my brother and sister."

Kieran smiled before walking over and closing the closet. He turned toward Aeron and said, "Thanks, Aeron. They said they aren't afraid anymore."

Aeron smiled. "You guys have a good time. I'll see you later."

He left the room.

Aeron paused briefly outside the twins' bedroom door. He listened as his siblings giggled and ran around the room.

CHAPTER 11

Adrian was sitting on the dock with his legs pulled up to his chest. His head was buried in his arms, which were resting on his knees. He didn't see Aeron approach until the noise of his son's footsteps thumped on the wooden planks of the dock. Adrian looked up as Aeron squatted beside him.

"Hey," Aeron whispered.

"Hey," Adrian replied.

Aeron bent over and picked up a small pebble from a crack between two boards and tossed it into the lake. Some of the ripples soon disappeared under the dock. "I'm sorry, Dad. I didn't mean to act like such a lunatic with you in the kitchen."

"I'm sorry, too," Adrian said. "I know this move has been tough on you guys. I just felt it was the right thing to do, Aeron. Besides, I wanted to get you away from some of the crazy city life. I was really getting concerned about—" He stopped and shook his head. "I just thought I was doing the right thing." Adrian's shoulders lowered. "I promise. I'll do everything I can to make it better. You'll see."

Aeron sat next to him. "Dad, you *did* do the right thing. I'm just being a jerk about it. I'm sorry! I'll honestly try to get used to it here."

Adrian reached over and pulled his son closer. "Aeron, I was afraid you were going to hurt someone today. I've never seen you behave like that before."

"I know. It's just that Whitney really set me off, and then I thought you were going to yell at me, too."

Adrian wiped a couple tears from his own face. "Aeron, you know we never work things out in our family through violence." He gently brushed Aeron's bangs from his eyes. "Look, I understand why you're hanging in there with this relationship with Whitney. I'm not dumb, so I just hope some *certain talks* we've had sunk into your brain. Your mother and I have prayed so many times that God would help you make the right choices. It doesn't take a genius to figure out that Whitney is determined to hang on to you at *any* cost. I think today proved to me that the pressure of everything is crashing down on you."

"I don't know, Dad. I was really thinking about breaking up with her until she showed up today. Once we got in the barn, it just kinda . . . I don't know anymore."

"Look, I know this move was, and is hard on you, and it will be for a while, but I know you, and you'll make different friends quickly at the new school. I also put in another call this morning to the football coach about you and Seth joining in the practices with the team. I'm sure he'll call me back soon."

Aeron smiled. "I hope because that will help a lot if I get to play again this season. I'd like to also wrestle again this year."

"Yeah, I hope so as well. I love watching you in sports." He looked down at his watch. "We better get back to the house. I promised your mom I would help with dinner tonight—that's if she's still talking to me."

"I'm sorry about that, too. Mom was really ticked about what happened."

"Yeah, she was, and I don't like being on her bad side, if you know what I mean."

"Yeah, I do. You've always told us not to mess with Mom when she's angry."

Adrian stood and extended his hand to Aeron.

As they walked toward the shoreline, Adrian patted Aeron on the back. "I love you, son."

Aeron stopped and embraced his father. "I love you, too, Dad." He stepped back from his father. "And I'm so sorry for the things I said and did to you in the kitchen. You didn't deserve that, especially coming from me."

Adrian grabbed Aeron's shoulders and they locked eyes. "Aeron, you know that you kids mean the world to your mother and me, but I can't let you have another outburst like that ever again."

"I know." Aeron said. "I promise I won't ever behave like that again." They embraced once more. "I still don't understand why I felt so mad. I agree that everything is just crashing down on me right now. Mom thinks things will get better once school starts."

Adrian smiled. "Yes, I agree with your mom." They continued walking toward the top of the embankment. "Hey," Adrian said, as he wrapped his arm around Aeron's shoulders, "I really meant it when I said I can't wait to see one of my favorite football players on the field again." Aeron smiled.

As they descended the hill, bubbles rose to the surface of the water about ten feet from the end of the dock. Blood spread across the water as several corpses floated to the surface. Their entrails drifted outward from their torsos like the tentacles of an octopus.

The rotting bodies then sank once more into their watery grave once Adrian and Aeron descended the embankment toward the house.

CHAPTER 12

That evening, while Aeron and Seth lamented over the mound of dishes they had to wash after dinner, Seth suggested they venture up to the old cemetery on the hill behind their home. As Aeron dried off some of the dishes, he shivered from the creepy reality of having such a dwelling for the dead about one hundred yards from their back door. With curiosity quickly replacing the morose feelings, Aeron decided to go.

Adrian walked into the kitchen and pulled Aeron aside. They walked into the dining room, where Teresa had started to do some work at the table. "Have a seat. Your mom and I need to talk with you."

"Am I in trouble?" Aeron inquired.

Teresa removed her glasses and placed them on the folder she'd been sorting through. "No, but Aeron, whatever happened earlier today, we are very concerned. But first, how are you feeling? How's your head?"

"It's just a dull ache right now, but I really can't explain why I was so angry today. Whitney has pis—I mean, ticked me off before, but I really couldn't control myself for some reason."

"Is she leaving you alone? Adrian asked. Aeron's head drooped toward the floor.

Teresa glanced at Adrian. "Aeron," Teresa said, "I am just going to say it: We're very concerned about this relationship. You know what her best friend did to Jake Winters."

"Yeah, I know." Jake was scared to death about Mariah being pregnant, and—"

"And you don't think that could be a possibility in your relationship with Whitney?"

"Okay, this is a little uncomfortable," Aeron jeered.

Adrian sat back in his chair. "Yeah, and so is changing diapers at 3:00 a.m."

Aeron sighed. "Guys, I said I was sorry for what I did today."

"Yes, you did," Teresa said, "but we will not tolerate any kind of behavior like that ever again. When something isn't going well, you know you can come and talk with us. We can work through it together."

"I know, Mom, but I think it's over anyway. I told Whitney I was done."

"But she doesn't seem to believe that now, does she?" Teresa interjected.

Aeron looked at his mom's phone on the table. "I guess not."

Adrian reached out and touched Aeron's arm. "We need to know something, Aeron."

"What?"

"What you said to your mother about something in your head telling you to hurt people."

Aeron's heart raced. Like a neon sign flashing on and off, he could see the words "*strangle her . . . kill him!*" He swallowed hard. "I think it was because I was out of control, and maybe I was—" His words clung to the roof of his mouth. Looking at his parents' eye to eye, he couldn't share the truth just yet. "I'm not hearing voices if that's what you mean!" He looked away; the guilt was bearing down on his shoulders like a heavy weight.

"Well, since I finished your chores for you, can we leave now, Aeron?" Seth jeered, as he walked into the dining room.

Relieved, Aeron sprang to his feet. "Yeah, let's go!"

"Wait, Aeron. We aren't through with this conversation," Adrian said. "Sit back down for a minute."

"But me and Seth wanted to go for a walk."

"Seth, give us a few minutes," Teresa said.

"Okay, but if you're going to ground him for a while, could you make sure he can still drive me wherever I need to go?" Seth smirked at Aeron. Teresa pointed toward the kitchen, and Seth quickly retreated into the kitchen.

"Where are you two thinking about going?" Adrian said.

"Up the hill." Aeron finally sat, somewhat annoyed by the delay in his plans.

"Honey, are you sure you weren't like…hearing voices?" Teresa asked with caution.

"Seriously, Mom? You think I'm schizophrenic or something?" Aeron's head slammed against the back of his chair.

"No, Aeron," Adrian reassured, "it's just that—"

Aeron stood and stepped behind his chair. "Look, I told you guys I was really angry, and I've apologized how many times?"

"Calm down, Aeron, this isn't an interrogation," Adrian said.

"No, but Mom knows how to do her job as a prosecutor, and I feel like I'm on trial for something I already know I did wrong!"

Teresa stood and walked over to her son. She embraced him from behind. "Aeron, listen to me. We don't think you're mentally ill. It's just that you told me earlier today that you thought someone was trying to tell you to do things—things you didn't want to do."

Adrian walked over and hugged Aeron as well. "Son, you know we love you, and we don't want anything bad to ever happen to you." Adrian pulled away, but he held on to Aeron's shoulders. "Aeron, truthfully, you scared everyone in the house today, especially your mother and me, and we know you've been under a lot of pressure with the move…and Whitney."

"I know I scared everybody, and I promised you guys I wouldn't do it again, but Dad, I just want to get things back to normal."

"We all do, honey," Teresa agreed. "Maybe when you start football practice, that will make a huge difference in how you're feeling around here."

Seth peered around the corner from the kitchen. "Am I allowed to finally come in?"

Teresa smiled. "Yes, you're allowed."

"So, has Aeron been sentenced to the electric chair yet? I really would like my own room," Seth teased.

Adrian chuckled as he placed his hand on Aeron's back. He remarked: "Dang, boy, you ought to be able to plow right through anybody on the field this season." He squeezed Aeron's shoulder. "Let's just hope the coach can get you two on the team soon. I know it's already late in the summer."

"Aeron won't make it on the team. He would be lucky to make it onto the cheerleading squad," Seth taunted.

"No, I think your scrawny rear end would fit better into their outfits. Football uniforms are for *real* men." Adrian and Teresa laughed.

"Well," Adrian said, "I did what Coach Bryson instructed about calling the new coach as soon as we enrolled you guys at Inverness High. I checked with the principal, and he said it shouldn't be a problem finding a place for you two on the team, especially since we officially moved into the school district."

"Can we call the coach again tomorrow? I would really like to start back," Aeron said.

"Already had it on my agenda, Aeron."

"Hey Dad," Seth interrupted, "me and Aeron want to go see the cemetery. Is that okay?"

"First of all," Adrian corrected, "it's *Aeron and I*, and is that the walk you mentioned earlier, Aeron?"

"Yeah. It's up the hill."

"I know," Adrian said. He raised his eyebrows to Teresa. "Why don't I think this is such a good idea?"

Adrian saw her glare. His heart fluttered, knowing what that look meant. Teresa folded her arms. She glanced at the boys. "Unleashing you two in a cemetery is certainly asking for trouble. Which one of you isn't coming back?" Teresa raised her eyebrows.

"Come on, Mom, we won't do anything stupid," Seth pleaded.

"It's getting late, so make sure you're back before dark," Adrian ordered.

Seth raced for the kitchen door. Aeron rolled his eyes. "He's such a child." As he turned to leave, he looked back and said, "I'll take a shovel with me. When he does something stupid, I'll just bury him up there. That way he won't be such an embarrassment to the family."

Teresa shook her head. "You are so rotten, young man!"

"Go after him before he hurts himself," Adrian said.

Aeron smiled and left the room. The kitchen door closed moments later.

Teresa pulled out a chair and sat. Her nostrils flared. "So, am I going to end up in the cemetery tonight?" Adrian commented, as he sat down. "I know that look of yours."

"What just happened?" Teresa rebuked. "I don't think we accomplished anything, especially when we changed the subject without getting to the bottom of what's truly bothering him."

"Teresa, did you not see his hands?"

"What do you mean?"

"The fists he had! He was on the verge of another outburst. I'm sure of it. That's why I changed the subject."

"No, I didn't see that."

"Earlier today," Adrian continued, "it was like he became possessed or something," He lowered his hands and grasped Teresa's. With his thumb, he gently rubbed the top of her folded hands in a circular motion. He choked back tears before suggesting they should take Aeron to see a counselor. Teresa's chin quivered. "Teresa, the bigger he gets, the harder he'll be to control if this continues. I didn't let him see it, but as I told you earlier before dinner, I was really struggling to pin him against the refrigerator. He's solid, and I don't know what will happen if he picks a fight with one of you guys instead of me." Adrian squeezed Teresa's hands. "You should see what he's capable of lifting in the gym."

"I just hope it was an isolated outburst caused by Whitney, and nothing more," Teresa said. "It's hard to believe one relationship can change him so much. At least it sounds like it's over between them."

Adrian sat back in his chair. "I'm fairly certain I know why he's been so different with *this* girlfriend. Trust me, Teresa, there's a reason why he's been tolerating her like he is."

Teresa cleared her throat. "Yeah, I think you're right. His level of arrogance sometimes makes me think he's been quite active with this one for several months. I hope your talks with him have been working." Teresa rested her forehead in one of her hands. "Aeron's still a bit clueless about where this relationship is taking him, and we didn't raise him to behave like this."

"I know, but . . ." Adrian sighed. "You have no idea what Matt went through with Jake and his girlfriend. There were days he could barely function from the chaos Mariah caused."

"I know some of it. Remember how Ginny called me in tears on many occasions? As Jake's stepmother, she was really struggling to sort it all out without making things worse."

"Let's hope we don't have to go through it." Adrian leaned back, releasing Teresa's hands.

"Adrian, do you really think Aeron needs to see a counselor? I can call Dr. Ferro. She's helped me out with a lot of my clients. I trust her completely."

"If you go to her in confidence, are you sure she'll keep it quiet?"

"Absolutely. She can't share anything like that."

Look, he's excited about football, so let's keep focusing on that. Once he gets into school and meets some people, I have no doubt he'll find some other girl he'll get along with much better."

"That's my prayer," Teresa said.

As Adrian began wringing his hands, he whispered, "I feel so guilty for uprooting my whole family, and I hope it doesn't completely blow up in my face like it did today." He stood and walked over to a window and stared out into the fading sunlight sinking into the horizon.

Teresa walked over to him and wrapped her arms around his waist. Her head gently rested on one of his shoulders. "Honey, it won't. Maybe it was nothing more than him having a bad day after Whitney and him got into an argument or something."

"Maybe. They do argue a lot."

Teresa turned Adrian around. She grasped his hands. "Honey, do you think Aeron really heard something in his head?"

He pulled her closer. "Not really," he said. "Haven't you ever thought something so strongly in anger that it was like something was prompting you to lash out when you weren't thinking clearly?"

Teresa leaned the side of her head onto his chest. "Yeah, I guess you're right. Maybe it was just the way he worded his feelings that made me think something else was going on." She smiled as she looked up at Adrian. "I'm glad he is looking forward to something at the new school. Hopefully that coach will get back to us soon. In fact, I think I'll call him right now."

Teresa leaned over and kissed him. "I think that would be a good idea."

Before releasing her, Adrian remarked, "God, I'll never forgive myself if the decision to move here hurts you and the kids in any way. My job is to protect my family, and I'll die doing just that!"

Teresa stepped back and grasped Adrian's hands. "Honey, you are the best husband and father, and somehow I just know the kids will adjust better once they get into a routine again." Adrian kissed her hands. "As for Whitney, hopefully Aeron will meet someone new, and we can put this whole relationship with her behind us for good," Teresa said. "It's tearing him apart more than he realizes."

"Yeah, I agree. It's obviously had an impact on all of us."

Teresa released his hands and walked to the table. She picked up one of the folders and looked at it before placing it back down on the table.

"Adrian, I don't think I can do anything else today. My paperwork will just have to wait until tomorrow. Let's just relax for a while and see what's going on with the rest of the world."

Adrian placed his arm around her waist as they walked to the living room to watch television. "I'll call the coach in a bit. Let's just relax for a few." His stomach tingled at the soft touch of her hand in the back pocket of his jeans.

Several minutes into the news, Teresa looked over at Adrian. "Honey, I really think that one end table would look great over by that Windsor chair in the corner."

Adrian smiled. "Let me guess, it's the one stacked in the far corner of the garage."

"Do you mind?" Her innocent eyes left Adrian with no recourse but to honor her request. "I'll go check on Delaney and the twins while you go and find it." She stood. "After all, in our vows, we did promise to 'love, honor, and *obey*,' right?"

"I should have known that marrying an attorney would somehow obligate me to follow through with every detail in our *marriage contract*." They kissed before they departed from the living room. In the hallway, Adrian asked: "Are you sure you don't want to tie a rope around one of my ankles before I go into the garage?"

Teresa grinned. "Let me guess: it's in case you get lost in there and I have to drag you out?"

"Exactly!" Adrian smiled. "The garage is a jungle of furniture and boxes, so just make sure my life insurance is paid up. I might not survive."

As Teresa walked up the stairs, she joked, "Don't worry about your life insurance, because when we take a cruise from the money we'll get, we'll sprinkle your ashes somewhere in the ocean near Bermuda."

"Gee, thanks," Adrian murmured as he walked toward the kitchen door. "I love you, too."

CHAPTER 13

The boys finally reached the huge iron gate of the cemetery. "Is it me, or do you find it kinda weird having a cemetery just up the hill from our house?" Aeron asked.

"I think it's cool," Seth replied.

Aeron pushed Seth. "Yeah, but aren't you the wimp who was afraid to look in the barn with me for some old woman?"

Seth smirked. "I just went along to protect you."

Aeron rolled his eyes. "Yeah, sure you did."

As they entered onto the cemetery grounds, they looked at the different headstones. As they walked around, Seth pointed, saying the names on the headstones as he meandered down the center between two rows, moving his head back and forth like he was watching a tennis match. "There's quite a few different names here. There's Clark . . . Murray . . . Boyce . . . Wallace . . . ." Seth paused and sounded out the next name: "Harts . . . horne. I think I said that right. Anyway, here's a Loy, and then a Ketchum, and one stone with the name Ward on it." Seth stopped and read the inscription on the last stone in that row. "Hey, Aeron, this Stewart Ward guy was almost one hundred years old when he died."

"That's weird. I see one over here that was in her teens." Aeron shivered.

After moving to the next row, Seth sounded out one of the names: Aber . . . nathy. That's a different kinda last name." He looked at Aeron. "Did I say that right?"

"Yeah, stupid, that's what it says." Aeron stepped into the next row behind the headstone and said, "There's another Abernathy here, too."

Seth got down on the ground and brushed some dried grass from the letters engraved on the stone with the name George Murphy. "Isn't Murphy the last name of our neighbor lady?"

"Yeah, it is," Aeron said. "Do you see any stones with our road's name on them?"

"Yeah, I saw the name Murray in the first row," Seth replied.

Aeron raised his hand to his chin and scratched. "That one says George Murphy and the one next to his says Matilda Wallace-Murphy. That must have been his wife."

"Yeah," Seth replied, "but on the other side of him it says Harriet Abernathy-Murphy. It says she was a wife and mother." The intrigue of the names stirred a fascination within the boys, causing them to wonder how the people in the cemetery might have been related. "Do you suppose he had two different wives?" Seth inquired.

"It's possible." Aeron swatted a mosquito on his arm. "Hey, Seth, there's a grave here that doesn't have a last name. It just has a small cross with a date and the name Henry on it." Aeron noticed the child's age. "Dang, he was only nine years old."

"Lilith and Cain Murphy," Seth said, as he pointed to another stone. "Hey, Aeron, they were only 6 years old. That's Darcy and Kieran's age, too." The boys glared at each other. "They had to have been twins, because they have the same birthday, and it says they died on the same day! That's way too weird." Seth scratched his chest and swatted at a few gnats buzzing around his head. "I wonder what happened to them."

"Wait a minute!" Aeron interrupted. "Seth, I just remembered something!"

"What?"

"Darcy and Kieran said they were playing with some imaginary friends in their room today. Their names were Lilly and Cain. I'm sure of it!" Aeron ran both hands through his hair. "Okay, that's so freakin' weird. I just thought they made them up, so do you suppose Mom or Dad already brought them up here and they saw those names?" Aeron looked around nervously. "Seth, this is starting to creep me out." Aeron shivered again as a cold breeze raced across his body.

"Yeah, I think I agree with you." Seth slapped a mosquito on the back of his neck.

As they approached the gate, Seth pointed at the ground over one of the graves. It was sunken in nearly three feet. "Why do you suppose it's collapsed in like that?" he asked.

"I don't know," Aeron replied. "Maybe the casket rotted and fell in." He smiled before saying, "Then again, maybe someone tried to dig him up." Aeron's attempt at scaring his brother suddenly caused his arms and legs to tingle. Goosebumps rose on his arms.

As they looked toward the amber horizon, the sun was fading behind a row of trees on the next hill. "We better get back 'cause it's gonna be dark soon, and I definitely don't wanna be in a cemetery after dark, especially with you!" Aeron said.

Unexpectedly, the gate at the entrance to the cemetery banged shut. The clanging of the iron caused both boys to jump. "What was that?" Aeron yelled.

As Seth started to reply, he stepped backward and fell into the sunken grave, almost striking his head on the tombstone. "Aeron!" Seth hollered. Aeron suddenly looked down. "Help me outta here!" As Aeron started to laugh, he reached forth his hand and pulled Seth up beside him. "God, I hope I didn't anger Mr. Norris," Seth chuckled, as he brushed dirt from his clothes. The two stared at each other and swallowed. The ghostly, darkening shadows from the trees, and the sounds of different nightly creatures sent a surge of fear throughout their bodies. "Okay, Aeron, I'm definitely ready to go now."

As they approached the gate, a grunting noise, followed by a high-pitched scream from some animal not far from them, paralyzed their muscles, and they suddenly froze in place. "What in the world was that?" Aeron whispered.

"It sounded like an animal being killed or something."

"Where did it come from?" Aeron asked.

Seth pointed toward the woods on one side of the iron fence surrounding the cemetery. "I think it was a deer and a fox," Seth speculated.

Determined to survive their adventure, their legs regained strength, allowing them to run to the gate. As Aeron attempted to open the gate, a terrifying rustling of leaves and branches in the woods startled them. The scream echoed around them, and their hearts nearly shot through their ribs. The gate was jammed, and as Aeron used more force, it only rattled, creating a louder noise.

Just as the gate popped open, several grunting sounds echoed throughout the cemetery, and weeds moved violently in three different spots in the woods.

Seth tripped over Aeron's foot as he dashed past his brother. After falling face-first into the grass, Aeron grabbed his brother by the shirt and they darted off toward the house, never looking back as they raced down the path leading to their backyard.

By the time the boys made it to the bottom of the hill, the eerie shadows of trees and shrubs gave the path a foreboding sense of danger. Just as they saw the back of the garage in the distance, Seth suddenly disappeared. A huge splash took both boys by surprise. "Aeron!" he yelled.

"Oh my God!" Aeron hollered. He dropped to his knees and reached out to his brother. Seth resurfaced from a circular pool of murky water and was choking as he gasped for air.

"Aeron!" he begged. "Get me . . . outta . . . here!" Aeron managed to grab Seth's shirt. Just as he tugged on him, Seth was swiftly pulled under, but he resurfaced again moments later. Seth screamed for help again. He was struggling to breathe as the tug of something around his legs seemed to pull him under again.

His ankles were entangled in something, and the sensation of being yanked downward sent waves of panic and desperation throughout his body. "Aeron, something keeps—" Once again, Seth's cries for help were cut short when his head plunged beneath the surface of the frigid water. He came up again for air, but he was choking from the flow of water into his nose and throat.

"Give me your hand, Seth!" Aeron shouted.

When Seth submerged again, he felt a tightening in his chest. He knew he had seconds of air left before he was forced to open his mouth and gulp the remaining amount of liquid needed to end his life.

As the seconds waned, Aeron frantically yelled his brother's name. Agonizing seconds passed before Aeron saw bubbles rising to the surface of the water. Aeron plunged his hand into the water, trying to grab onto his brother.

Seth finally surfaced, and Aeron grabbed his brother's arms and pulled him upwards with all his strength. "Come on, man! Lift your legs out!" Aeron pleaded. He tugged once more, and Seth was finally freed from the old well.

Both boys collapsed onto the ground next to each other. Seth continued to choke as Aeron sat up and yelled, "What just happened? Why'd you keep sinking?"

Seth started to cry as his chest heaved. Seconds later, he vomited, causing him to gag even more. Aeron patted his brother on his back. "Are you okay, man?" Seth collapsed onto his hip and nodded his head. As they gasped for much needed air, Aeron asked, "Where did that hole come from?"

Seth managed to talk without choking. "I don't know, but I want Dad!" he cried out. "Aeron, get me to the house!"

Aeron clutched his brother's cold flesh and assisted in helping him stand. "Can you walk?"

"Yeah, but don't let go of me!" Seth pleaded. "And watch out in case there's another one of those holes around here."

They stumbled into the yard beside the garage. "Daaaad!" Aeron yelled.

Adrian ran from the garage and saw Aeron supporting Seth's body by one arm. "Oh my God! What in the world happened to you two?"

"Seth fell in a hole filled with water." Adrian grasped Seth's other arm and helped him to the house. They entered through the kitchen door.

"Teresa! Get in here!" Adrian yelled.

Teresa ran down the stairs and into the kitchen. "What happened?"

"There must be an old well or something out there, and Seth fell into it," Adrian said.

"Oh my God!" Teresa rubbed her hands through Seth's soaked hair and down his arms. "Adrian, we need to get his clothes off. He's freezing!" Seth was covered in goose bumps from the chilled water and cool air being forced into the room from the air conditioning. "Aeron, run and tell Delaney to get down here with some dry towels," Teresa commanded.

Moments later, the woman in black drifted near the top of the stairway and watched Delaney feverishly descending the stairs with her arms full of towels. Adrian helped Seth get his shirt and shorts off. He wrapped him in the dry towels. "My God, Teresa, he's freezing! That water must have been deep to be that cold." Teresa grabbed a towel and quickly dried Seth's hair. Adrian yelled, "Will somebody turn off the air before he freezes to death!" Delaney ran toward the thermostat.

Darcy and Kieran scurried into the kitchen like mice, frightened by the boisterous commotion of their parents and siblings. Teresa looked at the twins and said, "Seth's okay, babies! He just fell into a puddle of water behind the garage." Teresa looked at Aeron. "Tell us exactly what happened to your brother?"

"We were almost to the back of the garage," Aeron said, "and suddenly, Seth was gone! He fell into the water!" Aeron looked at his father. "Dad, I tried my best to get him out, but he kept going under. I almost couldn't pull him out!" Aeron swallowed. "I almost lost him!"

"Yeah, I swear something was pulling on my ankles!" Seth insisted.

"I'm serious! I swear! Aeron's right, I really thought I was gonna drown in there." Teresa and Adrian embraced Seth. "If Aeron wasn't there, I know I would've died! Aeron saved me!"

Teresa looked up and saw Darcy and Kieran still standing near them. "Delaney, please take them into the living room and turn on something for them to watch." She leaned over and embraced Seth. "I know he did, honey!" She looked up at Aeron as a tear rolled down her cheek.

Adrian stood and hugged Aeron. His heart pounded as he held onto Aeron.

Teresa looked upward at the ceiling. "Yes . . . thank God he's okay!"

Adrian's rational mind was at war with the story he'd been told about someone pulling Seth downward in the well. *Impossible!* he thought, until he looked down at Seth's ankles, and there were thin red streaks on both—about the width of fingers.

Later that night, Adrian and Teresa entered the boys' room. Teresa sat on the bed next to Seth. "How are you feeling, honey?" She kissed his forehead. It was warm.

"I'll be okay, Mom . . . seriously."

"Honey, you're a little fevered. We need to check your temperature." Teresa exited the room and returned shortly with a thermometer. As she placed the device under Seth's tongue, Aeron laughed. "What's so funny?" Teresa asked.

"Hey Seth, I hope Mom isn't using the other kind of thermometer."

"Real funny, jerk!" Seth mumbled.

"Honey, keep your mouth closed, and Aeron, you need to behave." She removed the thermometer and remarked, "101.5." She stood. "I'm getting you some meds."

"Mom, I'm good. You really need to go to bed. It's been a long day."

"No, I'll be right back."

Seth leaned his head back with a sigh. "Seth, just let her fuss," Adrian said. "You probably do have something going on between the stitches and the dirty well water you probably swallowed or inhaled."

Teresa returned with two pills and a glass of water and handed them to Seth. She leaned over and kissed him on the forehead before walking over to Aeron and kissing him. A tear rolled down her cheek as she whispered, "Please keep an eye on him tonight." She also knew Aeron was the real reason for their ability to be at peace that night.

Teresa sat on Seth's bed and pulled the covers up to his waist. "Honey, if you need me, please have Aeron come and get me."

"I'll be fine, Mom."

"Okay, but if your fever isn't broken by the morning, we are getting you looked at immediately." Teresa leaned over and kissed him again. "I love you, honey."

"Love you, too," Seth replied. She stood and walked to the door with Adrian.

"We love you guys," Adrian said. "Seriously, don't hesitate to get us."

After turning out the light, Adrian and Teresa left the room.

Aeron wanted to sleep, but visions of his brother struggling in the well haunted his thoughts. Several minutes later, Aeron heard his brother sniffling. It was barely audible, but he knew Seth still needed him. He sat up and turned on the small light next to his bed. "Are you okay, man?" Seth didn't reply.

Aeron stood and walked over to his brother's bed. "Hey, move over." Aeron sat and looked at Seth, whose face was soaked with tears. "Are you thinking about the well?" Seth nodded. "Hey, I know you're upset," Aeron whispered, "but you're safe, and I'm not gonna let anything happen to you. I promise."

Seth lifted his body and propped his pillow up against the headboard. "I know, but I was really scared, man. You don't know what it feels like to almost drown."

"I know. I just can't figure out why you kept going under the surface when I had a tight hold on you. It was so crazy. And besides, how did we not see the well? Don't they usually have walls around them and a bucket overhead?"

"I guess not," Seth replied. "Weeds must have grown over the edges of it, and it was getting darker, so I didn't see it." Aeron turned and rested his back against the headboard as well. "That was the scariest thing I've ever gone through. I really thought you were gonna drown."

"Aeron . . ."

"Yeah?"

"I *know* something was pulling me down," Seth insisted. "You know when we were wrestling a couple weeks ago, and you were dragging me by my ankles through the living room at the townhouse?"

"Yeah."

"That's what it felt like. It was the same kind of grip," Seth explained.

"Are you sure it wasn't something caught on your shoes, like some debris or something?"

"Aeron, I'm telling you, it was like someone's hands were tugging on my legs." Seth leaned over and rested his head on Aeron's shoulder. "I can't believe I almost died today. If you weren't there, I know I would have." Aeron felt the bed trembling. "I was thinking about going up to the cemetery by myself, too. I'm glad I asked you to go with me."

"Well, you didn't die, and you're gonna be fine. I promise!" Aeron rested his head against the headboard. "You know, it was kinda funny when we heard those noises in the woods by the cemetery, and then you tripped over my foot trying to run away. I would've laughed if I wasn't so scared myself."

"Yeah, that was kinda funny, now that I think about it. My face was planted in the grass."

"Well, you better get some rest," Aeron suggested. "I know this sounds stupid, but I'll stay with you if you want, or will you be okay?

"I'll be okay." As Aeron stood, Seth asked, "Can you leave the little light on? I think it might help me sleep better."

"Sure." Aeron crawled into his own bed. "If you need me, just wake me up."

"Thanks, brother. I guess this makes you *my hero*."

"Yeah, yeah, yeah. I guess I wasn't ready to trade you in yet for a room to myself."

"Seriously, Aeron, I love you, man."

"I love you, too."

As Aeron rested for a while in his own bed, he still couldn't get the visions out of his mind from Seth's near-fatal drowning. Tears welled up in his eyes as the full realization of what occurred that day hit him harder than expected.

Life without Seth—simply impossible to imagine!

CHAPTER 14

As the oldest boys slept, the determined, mysterious woman dressed in white stood at the bottom of Seth's bed. She drifted over and knelt beside her desired possession. She examined Seth's features adoringly before lifting her hand toward his head and softly stroking his dark, wavy hair. Moments later, she stood and left the room.

After making her way to the kitchen door, she passed through it and traversed the short distance to the old well behind the garage. As she stood at the edge, small bubbles surfaced, causing the water to ripple. A young boy slowly ascended straight out of the well and drifted toward his mother, whose outstretched hand grasped his wrinkled fingers. She pulled him close to her bosom. Once more, she felt maternal—almost alive in the presence of her beloved son, Henry.

Across the road, the crystal smooth surface of the lake was suddenly disrupted by a dozen circles of small waves spreading outward. The tops of human heads began to emerge. Clumps of algae clung to the creatures' shoulders, arms, and clothing as they rose and stood waist deep in their watery grave. The moonlight radiated down upon their resurrected bodies. A white, glowing mist rolled in from the surrounding fields and hovered just above the surface of the lake, making them appear as though they had no lower extremities. They slowly made their way to the shoreline.

An ambiance of death saturated the darkness. Slowly, they sauntered from the murky water and leisurely formed a line, which stretched across the embankment. With their hands hanging at their sides, they faced the direction of the Douglas home. For several minutes, they waited while bursting with anticipation over the five vibrant children they steadfastly desired to abduct from the world of the living. The lonesome howl of a coyote echoed across the ghostly fields, which was soon joined by the yipping, growling sounds of its fellow predators.

With one foreboding step at a time, the creatures walked down the embankment and crossed Murray Road. They assembled on the front lawn of the Douglas home in a semi-circular configuration—as if assembled for some sacrificial ritual. Innards protruded from their abdominal cavities and draped down the front of their decaying bodies like a veil. The creatures smelled with the stench of a rotting carcass left to die along the side of the road. Their swollen, purplish lips were sealed with the silence of death. Eye sockets, once brilliant with the joy of life, now glowed with a white, glassy film, which glistened from the moonlight overhead. The whole assembly began to moan—smothered with the dreadfulness of unending bereavement. Their long, stringy hair was saturated with the slick texture of lake water. Their youthful looks had long been erased by years of decay.

They stopped and gazed upward toward Darcy and Kieran's room. The poltergeist from the well, along with the maternal apparition who beckoned him, joined the other creatures. There was a mystical fog hovering low above the ground, and the apparitions stirred the mist into spherical currents as they began moving closer to the house. Imprints of bare feet dotted the wet grass throughout the yard.

Three ghouls walked over to the house and entered through the sunroom door, which was closed and locked. They passed through the kitchen door and moved toward the stairway leading up to the bedrooms. Their shadows were cast upon the floors and walls from the beams of moonlight streaming though the large windows. The other corpses remained outside and simply waited for what they expected to be the delivery of the Douglas children into their hands. Like prisoners trapped in solitary confinement, the wretched beings instinctively desired companionship with the living. Unable to fellowship with their own offspring, and having never said goodbye to them, these grieving creatures desired the chance to have children with them once more.

Once the three creatures reached the stairs, they paused and gazed upward into the darkened stairway, illuminated by the faint glow of nightlights from the upstairs hallway. The basement door opened as the three apparitions continued to wait for another ghostly companion to join them. Slowly ascending the cellar stairs, a disfigured creature heaved his putrid body into the kitchen. Delaney's room was his destination.

The four invaders finally assembled at the bottom of the stairs before ascending toward their desired companions: the Douglas children. Stepping forward, they viewed photos of the family, which hung on the wall leading up the entire length of the staircase. The woman in black, Harriet, stopped at one of the twins' pictures and ran her lanky fingers across their images.

The four beings soon lined up in pairs as they rounded the landing and moved toward the remaining few steps into the serene, faint light of the second floor.

Once inside Darcy and Kieran's room, Harriet moved over to Darcy's bed and stood above her as the child slept soundly, unaware of the grieving mother affectionately gazing down at her. A gangly, wrinkled hand eased down onto Darcy's chest.

The heartbeat—she *needed* to feel the heartbeat of the innocent child.

Harriet grabbed the sheet covering Darcy's chest and delicately pulled it up to her chin. The reminiscence of evenings tucking her own twins into bed caused a solitary tear to roll down her pale, gaunt cheeks and hang onto her chin briefly before dropping onto Darcy's forehead.

"Mommy?" Darcy whispered, as her eyes opened slightly.

In a gruff tone, Harriet answered:

It's just Mommy checking on you, darling. Now go back to sleep and dream pleasant thoughts.

Still groggy after the sudden disturbance, Darcy rolled onto her side. The creature pulled the sheet up to Darcy's neck again and kissed the young child's cheek.

Kieran was sleeping on his stomach with an arm hanging over the side of his bed. Harriet reached down and pulled his chilled limb onto the mattress. Kieran moved slightly as he pulled his arm under his chest and continued to sleep. Harriet rubbed his bare shoulders before pulling the bed sheet up to the middle of Kieran's back. She lifted her dress slightly from the floor and knelt and began caressing the back of Kieran's head. Another tear rolled down her cheek and dropped onto the mattress, disappearing into the fabric. Kieran moved slightly again as he turned his head toward the phantom kneeling beside him.

"Daddy?"

No, sweetie, it is your mother. I'm just checking on my baby boy.

As her lips moved even closer to Kieran's ear, the creature murmured tenderly, as if caring for an ailing child with a fever.

Mother loves you. Now rest quietly, for eternity soon awaits your arrival.

While lying on his side, Kieran pulled his legs up, as the sheet was pulled up to his neck by Harriet. She rose and stood between Darcy and Kieran's beds for several minutes before moving over to a rocking chair and sitting. Calmly, she rocked, softly humming "Brahms' Lullaby." As the music resonated from her chest, the closet door opened and revealed Lilly and Cain holding hands. They emerged and stood in the doorway of their domain. They looked over at each other and grinned.

As Harriet rocked, the young apparition from the well entered the room. Henry, her nephew, walked to the foot of Kieran's bed before looking back at Harriet and smiling. He moved over to his aunt and stood beside her chair, placing his pale hand on her shoulder. For several minutes, both watched the children sleeping in the warmth of their beds.

Henry bent down and kissed his aunt's cheek before departing.

Farther down the hallway, Dolores stood at the foot of Seth's bed once again. On the opposite side of the room, Mors, a hawkish bloke, stood over Aeron like a guard protecting a prince. In almost every way possible, Mors wanted possession of Aeron as his son. He had missed the companionship of Wyatt, his own male child who'd died years earlier. Mors never said goodbye to Wyatt, and he longed for a second chance to know such closure. Driven by the need to be close to Aeron, he quietly levitated above the bed, observing the sleeping boy from above like a falcon waiting to swoop down for the kill of an innocent prey.

Dolores floated off the floor and positioned her body parallel to Seth's. His vibrant body reminded her of every attribute she still desired from her very first young lover, Gabriel.

As the boys slept, the apparitions continued to float above them in a euphoric state of ecstasy. The male specter drifted closer to Aeron's face and gently kissed his forehead. Aeron jerked slightly, but he did not awaken. A clear, slimy secretion clung like glue to his forehead.

The female stretched forth her puckered fingertips and pushed Seth's dark hair to one side on his forehead. She descended just inches from his body. Dolores exhaled a mist from her mouth into Seth's nostrils, almost as if she was releasing her spirit. He inhaled, but the sensation did not cause him to stir. She drifted down even closer and barely kissed him on his lips.

Seth reached to his lips and wiped. "Huh?" he whispered.

His eyes squeezed closed before opening slightly. Not observing anything above him, his eye lids strained under the weight of fatigue, and he soon drifted back to sleep.

Both creatures floated back to a position beside each boy's bed. After rejoining each other in the center of the room, Dolores and Mors clasped hands and gazed at their secret desires.

Henry entered the room and stood beside Seth's bed, causing Mors and Dolores to smile. He reached out and touched Seth's shoulder before moving over to Aeron. Henry leaned over and tilted his head from side to side, closely examining Aeron's features. He thought of Wyatt, Mors' dead son. He then joined Mors and his mother in the center of the room.

Alastor, the creature from the basement, slipped into Delaney's room and stood in the center of the floor. For nearly five minutes, his decaying muscles were frozen. His forbearance finally reaped the reward of allowing him access to her. He dragged his wounded, rancid body over to the bottom of her bed. He cocked his head and scrupulously studied her features. A yearning to be alive consumed his entire body, much like the bacterium that now devoured his flesh. He strolled to the side of her bed and sluggishly knelt to the floor. With deliberate, gradual movements, the sheet slid down her body so slowly that she hadn't felt it flowing across the curvature of her chest. He positioned his face near one of her shoulders and inhaled the aroma that saturated her locks of silky hair.

Backing away slowly, he stood and watched her from the center of the room. Henry arrived moments later and moved closer toward Delaney's bed. He touched her hair, rubbing several strands between his fingertips. There was a stirring in his gut, even though he didn't fully understand the sensation. He stepped back and joined Alastor in the center of the room. Henry looked up at Alastor and smiled, his teeth bearing years of decay.

Soon after their invasive surveillance, the four trespassing marauders met in the hallway and descended the stairs together. The four spirits desired the Douglas children more than ever before. As they moved about the downstairs, they growled with malevolent intonations when they viewed all the photos of Adrian and Teresa, especially the ones with their children. Jealousy devoured them like a parasite as they turned each photo of the couple down on every stand. Dolores spoke.

We must wait until the oldest boy rids us of them for good!

Harriet placed her hand on her sister's shoulder and uttered,

Yes, the children will resist us until their parents are gone forever.

Three of the apparitions eventually made their way to the kitchen door and exited. Alastor entered the basement doorway and descended into the darkened abyss, heading back to his lair under the stairs. The three other apparitions rejoined the sinister assembly in the yard, anxiously waiting for the appointed time when they could seize the children their fellow companions.

That night, however, they had to wait—wait for the time when Adrian and Teresa were no longer a threat to them.

Henry returned to the well and descended into his cold, watery crypt. As the mist drifted down the embankment from the lake, like an avalanche of snow, the creatures sauntered back to the shoreline and entered the still waters of their grave. Their heads slipped peacefully below the surface of the water.

CHAPTER 15

The next morning, Teresa walked into Delaney's room and sat on her bed. "I'm sorry to bother you honey, but why in the world are there all these damp spots all over my rugs?"

"Damp spots?"

"Yes, your dad mentioned he stepped in some wet spots the other morning, but we didn't think anything about it, but I've stepped in a lot of them around the house this morning, especially in the hallway."

Delaney sat up and rubbed her eyes before reaching over to her nightstand for a hairband. "What are you talking about, Mom?" she asked, while pulling her hair back into a ponytail.

"There's a trail of damp spots from the kitchen, up the steps, and in the hallway. My feet were soaked by the time I made it downstairs for my coffee."

"It was probably Aeron and Seth," Delaney suggested. "Those two are always into something."

"I don't know, honey. Both boys had a rough day yesterday, so I doubt they would be up to their usual antics. Besides, I peeked in on them, and they were still asleep. I didn't have the heart to wake them up." Teresa rubbed her hand along the side of Delaney's head and pushed a few loose strands of hair behind one of her daughter's ears. "I also discovered that your father's and my photos were all turned down on every stand downstairs. It had to have happened during the night."

Delaney pulled her sheet to the side and stood. "No wet spots here," she said. "Did you check the other rooms?" When Delaney stepped away from her bed, she suddenly felt the few damp spots near her bed, as well as in the center of the room. She quickly lifted her foot and stared at her mother.

"This is the first bedroom I've actually walked into besides my own," Teresa said, "but I'm planning on checking the others." She walked toward the door. "I'm sorry to have awakened you, but I thought you might be able to help. This whole thing just baffles me, especially since there weren't any in my bedroom."

"I'll check, too, but give me a minute to put in my contacts," Delaney said.

After Teresa left the room, Delaney walked over to her vanity and gazed at her reflection in the mirror. She pulled out the chair and sat before removing her hairband and running her fingers through her silky, golden-brown hair. Her fetching, brown eyes sparkled in the morning sunlight pouring through her bedroom window. She was a strikingly beautiful young woman, beaming with pride. Her charisma was an aphrodisiac to the swarm of boys who admired her from her last school. She attracted the admiration of her peers, and like her brothers, her model-like characteristics were a lure to the male companions who did everything to gain her attention.

She looked at the corner of her mirror and saw the remnants of tape left over from a photo of Jake Winters that she'd once attached to the shiny surface. Whether it was out of spite, or self-preservation, Delaney kept a comfortable distance from a lot of guys. Jake Winters, her last boyfriend, had tainted her once confident attitude towards the opposite sex, and the festering wounds from their breakup had built up a resistance to any advances from those she'd perceived as potential disappointments, much like Jake was to her.

After putting in her contacts, curiosity persuaded her to seek answers to the mysteries concerning the damp spots and overturned photos. She walked out the doorway, heading toward her brothers' room.

Aeron was flat on his stomach, so she gently tapped his back and whispered, "Hey, it's me."

Aeron turned his head towards her and replied, "What?"

"You're really scaring Mom with all your stupid pranks," she whispered back.

"What are you talking about?" he asked, as he rolled carefully onto his side while holding onto his sheet.

"Why are you putting water on the rugs and pushing over pictures of Mom and Dad?" she insinuated. "I mean, come on! When are you going to grow up?"

His eyebrows squeezed inward. "Seriously," he whispered, "you're not making any sense."

"Mom came into my room a little bit ago and said a lot of the rugs were damp down the hallway and downstairs leading to the kitchen. She also said that every photo of her and Dad have been pushed over. It's like someone was mad at them."

Aeron pushed himself up to his elbows. "Look, I have no clue what you're talking about."

Delaney sighed as Aeron rolled his eyes at her. "You need to come with me so we can talk to Mom," she demanded. "You need to tell Mom you didn't do all that stuff—that's if you're being honest about everything. And you better tell her the truth because she looked really upset." As Delaney stepped away from the bed, her foot encountered another damp spot on the floor. "This is crazy," she complained, as she raised her foot and looked at the bottom of it.

"Mom," Delaney said, as she walked into the kitchen with her brother, "I don't think Aeron knows what we're talking about."

Before Teresa could respond, Aeron blurted out, "I didn't put water on the floor, or fool around with any pictures last night. I sat in bed with Seth for a little while, and then I went back over to my own. I didn't even leave the room to pee."

Teresa cocked her head slightly, while creases formed on her forehead. "Why were you in bed with your brother, Aeron? Is he okay?"

"Yeah, but he was still a little upset when you left, so I sat with him for a few minutes."

"You should have called for me! I would have sat with him."

"I don't think he wanted you to know he was still upset," Aeron suggested. "He was shaking badly for a while, but then he finally relaxed and fell asleep."

Teresa stood and pushed her chair in. She closed her eyes and lowered her head before an audible sigh escaped from her lips. She cleared her throat and glanced at Aeron. "Are you sure you didn't do the wet spots or anything to the pictures?"

"Yeah, because I actually slept well after everything last night," Aeron innocently responded.

Delaney looked at her mother and said, "Mom, I stepped in a wet spot in Aeron's room, too."

Kieran unexpectedly walked into the kitchen. He was irritated. "Mommy, why is my bedroom floor wet?"

Teresa had been hoping that her youngest children wouldn't have noticed any dampness. Darcy also walked in and said, "Mommy, why did you tuck me in again last night?" Goose bumps erupted all over Teresa's skin.

"What do you mean, honey?" Teresa asked. She glanced at Delaney and Aeron. "You pulled my sheet up and said you loved me," she said. "You already did that after our prayers." Darcy stepped closer to Teresa. "Is your voice better this morning, too?"

Teresa licked her lips and ran her hand down her neck, stopping at her upper chest. She replied nonchalantly, "Oh, Mommy was just making sure you were comfortable." After a few seconds, she asked Darcy, "And why did you ask about Mommy's voice?"

"I thought you had a sore throat. You sounded funny last night," she answered. Delaney's eyes bulged while Teresa's hand rushed to her own gaping mouth.

Teresa lowered her hand and replied, "Yes, Mommy is a lot better this morning. Now, you and Kieran go get dressed. I'll be up in a few minutes to help you make your beds."

"Mommy," Kieran said, "I think my closet door is still broken. I heard it open again last night. Daddy said he'd fix it after we moved in." The twins turned and left for their room.

"Mom, what in the world is going on around here?" Aeron asked. "And where's Dad?"

Teresa's eyes widened—her extremities tingled. "I honestly don't have a clue, and your father had an early appointment this morning with Matt Winters." She gripped the back of one of the chairs. "Guys, I didn't go back into the twins' room during the night, and I don't think your dad did either!"

Teresa grabbed Aeron's arm. "Oh my God!" She quickly dashed for the upstairs. Delaney and Aeron followed.

"Where are you going, Mom?" Delaney yelled.

Trying her best not to alarm Darcy and Kieran, Teresa stopped outside of their bedroom door and waited for Aeron and Delaney to get closer. "What if someone is still in the house?" Teresa whispered.

"Mom, you're really scaring me!" Delaney whispered back.

"What if someone came in last night while we were sleeping?" Teresa said—her instinct refusing to allow her to accept any other explanation.

As they contemplated what to do outside the twins' bedroom, Seth, awakened in his room, rolled over onto his back, and coughed. The weight of a boulder rested on his chest, and he couldn't seem to get the phlegm out of his throat. He struggled to sit up before placing his feet on the floor. He suddenly lifted them when he felt a wet sensation on the bottom of his feet. "What the—"

An intense, sharp pain pummeled his chest like a wrecking ball slamming into a wall. He grimaced while rubbing his chest vigorously, but the soreness only deepened. He coughed into his hand, and when he pulled it away, he noticed a trace amount of blood splattered onto the palm of his hand. He took the back of his hand and wiped it across his nose. It was smeared with blood when he pulled it away. "What is this from?" The walls seemed to close in on him, and the floor appeared to roll like waves. Seth started to slip off his bed. "Aeron, I'm gonna—" The daylight faded into darkness as he collapsed onto the floor like a ragdoll.

Teresa stepped into Darcy and Kieran's room, and Aeron and Delaney followed closely behind. Their hearts were dancing wildly, and the kids jumped from the unexpected interruption. "What's wrong, Mommy?" Darcy asked.

"Delaney—the kids!" Delaney whisked the twins from their room and into the hallway. "Aeron," she whispered, as she pointed to Kieran's baseball bat in the corner. He quickly grabbed the bat and headed toward the closet. Teresa moved over to the door and held the doorknob. She nodded her head several times, giving him the okay to swing at whatever was hiding behind the door.

"*One, two, three*," she whispered, before swinging the door wide open. Aeron yelled as he plunged the bat into the closet like a sword.

Fear struck Kieran, and he ran toward Seth's room. Delaney ordered him to stop, but he pushed the door open and darted into the safety of his brother's room. He stopped and shrieked. "Delaney, Seth's hurt!"

Delaney ran in and dropped to the floor next to her brother. As she rolled Seth over, blood was pouring from his nose. "Mom, get in here right now!" she hollered.

Finding nothing in the closet, Teresa suddenly heard the yelling from down the hallway. "Now what?"

Aeron took off for his room. Upon his arrival, he saw Delaney's hands soaked with blood. "What happened?" he yelled.

"Good God, you guys! What happened to Seth?" Teresa frantically asked.

"I don't know, Mom, but he's out cold!" Delaney cried.

"We have to get him to the hospital!" Aeron insisted.

"Wait!" Teresa said. "I don't want to move him. We don't know what happened. We need an ambulance, right now!"

"I'll call!" Delaney said.

Aeron slid his leg under Seth's back and held him close. "Mom, I don't want him to choke."

"Yes, hold him up to your chest."

"Seth! Come on. Wake up!" With his eyes bulging, and his face contorted from confusion, Aeron looked at Teresa, who was falling to her knees beside them. "He's not waking up, Mom! Please get him to wake up!" Aeron rested his chin on the top of Seth's head. One final time, he pleaded, "Come on, Seth. Talk to me!" He wrapped his arm around Seth's neck and begged, "Mom, do something!"

"Honey, we're calling an ambulance now," Teresa replied. "Don't jostle him about! We don't know what's going on!" She gently lifted Seth's arm and tapped his shoulder. "Seth, please answer us!"

As Delaney spoke with the 911 operator, Teresa stayed beside Seth. After Darcy retrieved her mother's cell phone, Teresa frantically called Adrian. Moments later, one of the executive assistants interrupted the conference Adrian was having with his business partner. "Adrian, your wife is on the phone and needs to talk with you right away."

Adrian sprinted to the room where Seth was lying on a gurney in the emergency department. A nurse was administering medication into an IV. In a cracked voice, Seth spoke softly, forcing everyone to lean in closer to him. "How long was I out?"

Adrian looked at the nurse before whispering, "Seth, you're going to be fine now."

"You've been in and out of consciousness since the ambulance got you here," Aeron explained.

Seth closed his eyes. A tear seeped from the corner of his right eye and rolled down onto the pillow. Aeron reached over and grabbed a tissue from a small box near Seth's bed. He wiped the tear from the side of his brother's face. Aeron looked up at Adrian and lamented, "Dad, what in the world is going on with him? This is really scaring me!"

Adrian moved over to Aeron and put his arm around his shoulders. As he pulled him closer, Aeron reached around, too, and hugged his father tightly. "Everything's going to be fine, Aeron. I promise," Adrian whispered.

Seth reached up and grabbed Aeron's arm. "Hey." Aeron pulled away from his father and glanced down at Seth. "Stop acting like such a sissy," Seth teased. Aeron leaned over and hugged his brother. "Wow! Maybe you do love me after all?" Seth jested.

Aeron stood and smiled, suddenly acting brave. "Not really. I'm just pretending so you feel better." Aeron smiled. "And by the way, you still haven't gotten me a new Ohio State shirt."

"What do you mean?" Seth asked, his voice still weak.

"You ruined my other one when you bled all over it after you got cut in the barn. I pressed it against your head to stop the bleeding, remember?"

"Oh," Seth recalled, "that's right. Maybe I'll just buy you a Michigan State shirt instead."

"Yeah, real funny, *Richard Cranium*," Aeron retorted. Adrian snickered, relieved by the familiar joking between his oldest sons.

Moments later, the doctor came into the room and said there was something cloudy on the chest X-ray, which looked like pneumonia. He wanted to keep Seth overnight for further tests.

"Absolutely!" Adrian said. "We need to find out why my healthy teenage son is suddenly having all these problems. I can't understand any of this," he said.

Teresa was relieved when Seth asked if anyone could stay with him throughout the night. Aeron knew why his brother was too frightened to be alone.

"I can stay," Teresa insisted.

"I can, too, Mom," Aeron said.

"No, I would like you to stay at home for the twins. They must be confused over what's going on." Teresa knew she wanted to stay more than anything.

Adrian caught a glimpse of hope in his wife's tone. "Hey, Teresa, I think it would be best if you stayed here with Seth."

Seth shrugged his shoulders. "That's fine, if you want to, Mom."

Teresa smiled. "Yes, that's not a problem at all."

Maybe he wasn't too old to still need her, she thought.

CHAPTER 16

That night, Aeron battled sleep, along with his covers. Frustrated, he rolled onto his back and folded his hands behind his head. "I can't believe I really miss that annoying little punk," he whispered to himself. As he chuckled, he was startled by several creaking sounds above him. He hoisted himself up onto his elbows and listened.

Silence.

After flopping himself back down onto his back, the noises returned and seemed to travel across the ceiling like mice scurrying across a wooden floor in the darkness.

He hurried from his bed and dashed to Delaney's room. Light emanated from the bottom of her door, so he tapped lightly and opened it. "Delaney, did you hear that?"

"Hear what?"

"I was lying in bed and heard noises upstairs in the attic."

Delaney looked over at her attic door and then back at Aeron. "Did you really, or are you just trying to scare me?"

Aeron excitedly ran over to the attic door and opened it. "I really did hear something!"

"Ummm—no thanks! You are not getting me up there!" Delaney insisted. "Especially at night!"

Aeron stepped into the entryway leading up into the attic. "I'm going up, so you can either go with me or just sit there like some wimp."

"I'd rather be a wimp than a corpse," she said. "You go without me." After Aeron started up the steps, Delaney gazed around the huge room and shivered. "Wait for me, Aeron!"

The dust and stale odor of the attic penetrated their nostrils as they ascended the stairs together. "It really smells up here, Aeron."

"It's kinda like no one's been up here in years," he replied.

The squeaky noises of the steps echoed throughout the stairway, and the temperature warmed considerably with each step. Once at the top, Delaney and Aeron looked around at the cobwebs clinging to the timbers. Delaney sneezed. "I can't believe the amount of dust up here," she complained. The single light bulb cast their shadows on the walls. Their heartbeats accelerated as sweat seeped from nearly every pore of their skin. "I feel like I'm standing on someone's grave—you know—kinda like we shouldn't be up here." Delaney said.

Aeron pointed over to a corner. "What is all that?"

Several old trunks, and a few antique oak trinket boxes, were stacked together in a corner. They walked over and stood in front of the long-forgotten remnants from previous owners. "What do you think is in them?" Aeron asked. "They look really old."

"Why don't you open one and see," Delaney suggested.

Aeron lifted an antique rosewood and maple banded box from one of the two trunks. The latch was rusty and hard to open at first, but with a little force, he separated the two metal connectors and opened the lid slowly. Years of musty remnants overwhelmed their senses. "Man, I hope I don't find a dead mouse at the bottom of the box," Aeron remarked.

There were also several old Gurkha cigar boxes full of photos, which Delaney pulled from the trunk. She began sifting through the pictures. "These must be over a hundred years old. Why would someone leave behind family photos like these?" she asked. "There have surely been several families who've lived in our house since these things were stored up here. Why would anyone just leave them?"

"Maybe they are the family members no one liked," Aeron joked.

Delaney identified a photo that was taken near the lake. She assumed it was a family reunion photo because of the various poses of people, some sitting on blankets in the grass. The women were dressed in ankle-length dresses and long sleeve tailored blouses with ornate lace collars. Some were wearing Panama hats. Their hair was pulled back into buns or worn in short bobs. The little girls had pigtails with large bows, and their dresses were mostly knee length with dark stockings.

Most of the men were dressed in bib overalls, but a few were in dark pants and white shirts. Some of the younger boys were dressed in Buster Brown suits, and one boy, who looked to be around 10 years old, was wearing a Fauntleroy suit, along with a frown on his face.

After blowing some of the dust from several other pictures, she examined the different facial features and discovered that no one seemed to be smiling for their portrait. "What a somber looking bunch of freaks. I bet their reunions were a blast," Delaney sarcastically remarked. She paused. "Aeron, why's this guy standing so far away from the rest of them?" A gentleman dressed in a black suit—although somewhat hazy in the photo— was positioned about ten feet behind some of the children. He was wearing a black bow tie.

"I'm not sure, but he's sort of dressed like a preacher," Aeron replied.

Aeron pulled out a baby rattle and a rag doll from the trunk. He examined them, shook the rattle, and put them back into the trunk.

After sorting through a few more photos, Delaney jeered at the photographs of some children. "Hey Aeron, look at this!" She pointed quickly. "Look at the white smudge in these photos of the kids. It's just like the one we saw in our photo that real estate lady took of us in front of the *sold* sign in the front yard. Dad was so proud that day. Remember?"

Aeron closely examined the photos. "Yeah, the fuzzy image is like the one standing behind Darcy, Kieran, and Seth that day. Remember how Dad was ticked about it? He didn't see it until he made a copy of it from his phone."

Delaney suddenly stopped. "Oh my God! Who in the world takes these kinds of photos?"

"Let me see." Aeron grabbed one of the photos before Delaney handed a couple more to him, which quickly caused a look of disgust to spread across his face. "That's weird. Seriously, who takes photos of their dead kids?"

Delaney interrupted. "Look at this one. This must have been taken right before they were put into their caskets." There was a younger boy and girl propped up in a chair together. They appeared as though they were about 5 years old at the time. The little girl had a lace ribbon in her hair, which almost covered the side of the face of the boy seated beside her. Both were wearing black stockings and high-top black leather shoes. The white dress, with an inlet white lace sewn around the collar, fit loosely around the little girl, except for a lace tie wrapped around her waist. In a similar fashion, the boy's sailor style shirt fit snugly around his wrists; however, it was also baggy in the arms. His knickerbockers were solid black and flailed out near the knees.

Delaney turned the photo for Aeron to see. "They're cute kids, but why would someone photograph them in that way? They looked so sad and a little swollen," Delaney remarked. "I think we're both right about them being dead. Their eyes are just . . . different."

"I can't believe all the junk some people leave behind. Who wouldn't want to keep their own family photos? Mom always fills the walls with ours," Aeron commented.

Delaney jerked her hand back and dropped another photo she was holding. "No way!" she exclaimed. She picked the photo up quickly and pointed to the wall in the picture. "Isn't that Darcy and Kieran's room? Look at the wallpaper between the two windows!"

"No freakin' way!" Aeron exclaimed. "That *was* taken in their room! Mom just commented yesterday about the weird pattern in the wallpaper." He saw Delaney's hands trembling. "This is a little too weird for me." He pushed the photo firmly back into her hand. Goosebumps rose as he shivered from a sudden wave of cold air swirling from the stairway.

As they rummaged through the trunk, Aeron pulled out another box and removed the lid. The box felt as though it could have disintegrated in his hands. There were some stains and worn papers tucked inside. As his fingers fumbled through the contents, he saw a couple documents that looked official. He opened one of them carefully, trying not to tear it.

"This is a death certificate," he said to his sister. His head shook a little, and chills surged up his back. "So, when was the last time you heard the name Lilith?" he jested.

"I've heard the name Lilly before."

"Lilly is the name of one of Darcy's and Kieran's imaginary friends!" Aeron said. He scanned down the certificate and noticed the cause of death. "Delaney!" His eyes squinted. "It says here that this little girl drowned." Delaney and Aeron looked at each other.

"Where do you think it happened?" Delaney asked.

"I'm not sure." Aeron shivered again.

As Delaney and Aeron sorted through the boxes, the man in the black suit, from one of the photos, appeared about ten feet behind them. He stood quietly as the siblings rummaged through the old remnants of the past.

Delaney also removed a couple documents and started reading through them. "Aeron!" she said, as she grabbed his arm. "This one here says Cain Murphy on another death certificate. He also drowned!"

"No way! What are the odds?" Aeron wiped sweat from his forehead.

The apparition walked slowly toward them. His teeth were clenched, and his hands squeezed into fists.

After picking up the death certificate Aeron recently held, Delaney kept looking back and forth at them. "Aeron!" she gasped, "Lilith and Cain Murphy weren't just ordinary siblings." As she pushed the documents in front of her brother, she said excitedly, "They have the same birthday, and they were both six years old when they died *on the same day*! Aeron, they were twins!"

"Delaney! Lilly and Cain are the imaginary friends Darcy and Kieran told me yesterday! There's even some grave markers up in the cemetery with their names on them." As he glared at his sister, blood drained from his face. "Okay, my heart is pounding out of my chest. How about we call it a night!"

Standing behind them, only several feet away, the ghost's hands opened. He was close to seizing the back of Aeron's neck.

"I'm with you," Delaney agreed.

As they stood to leave, a creaking noise came from the opposite end of the attic. Delaney grabbed Aeron's arm and squeezed. "What was that?" she whispered.

"I don't know, but I'm not staying up here to find out," Aeron insisted.

When they turned to leave, there was nothing behind them.

Just as the two started to dash toward the stairs, their father yelled, "Hey, what are you guys doing up there?"

Delaney clutched her chest and screamed, while Aeron hollered and stopped abruptly, grasping the railing at the top of the stairs.

"Dad! You scared us to death!" Aeron yelled.

Delaney was still gasping for air.

Adrian laughed as he walked up the stairs. "Well, well, well, Delaney, it looks like your brother isn't as tough as he thinks."

"Yeah, Dad, it's hard to be tough when you're trying not to have your bladder explode," Aeron jeered.

His father chuckled.

"Seriously," Adrian inquired, "what are you guys doing up here? I thought you two were exhausted and would be asleep by now."

Delaney walked over and hugged her father. "Aeron thought he heard noises up here, so he wanted to investigate. We found some old trunks and started looking through them." She pointed in the direction of the corner where they were located. "There's some really creepy stuff inside of them."

"Like what, honey?"

They walked over to the trunks and started showing him some of the photographs and documents. "Look at these pictures, Dad. These kids look dead, and they were taken inside of Darcy and Kieran's room."

"Really? Let me see them," Adrian insisted. He examined them closely before saying, "You're right, that is creepy." He turned to Delaney and explained, "These are postmortem pictures, honey. People often took them of family members, especially if they didn't have photos of their loved ones prior to their deaths."

"Dad," Aeron interrupted, "the names of the kids in the photo might be Lilith and Cain Murphy. Those are the names Darcy and Kieran told me about when I went in to apologize about our fight we had in the kitchen. They said they'd been playing in their room with kids by the names Lilly and Cain. That must be the same kids, don't you think?"

"Are you sure those were their names?" Adrian asked.

"Yeah," Aeron responded, "I just thought they were imaginary friends or something. How would they have known those names? Did you take them to the cemetery or something because there are grave markers up there with their names on them?"

"Not at all," he replied.

"Dad, these documents say they died from drowning," Delaney stated. "You don't suppose it was in our lake, do you?"

"No, I'm sure it's all just a coincidence. The twins must have heard someone say something about other twins living here. Maybe the real estate agent or someone." The stunned faces of his oldest kids convinced Adrian to suggest they should return to their own rooms for the night.

"Listen," he said, before they walked down the stairs, "please don't say anything to your mother or Seth about this. We've dealt with enough already."

As the three of them descended the stairs, two small children—a boy and a girl—stood behind them at the top of the stairs. They turned their heads toward each other and back toward the bottom of the stairs. Harriet walked up behind them. She placed her arms around their shoulders, reassuring her offspring they would soon have their new, desired siblings with them forever.

The apparitions turned and walked back to the open trunk. Lilly lifted the rag doll to her chest and hugged it tightly. Cain picked up the rattle and shook it. The three of them walked over to the opposite end of the attic and disappeared into the darkness.

Once inside Delaney's room, it didn't take long for Aeron to push a dresser in front of the attic door. "I'm not ever going back up there, unless it's daylight," Aeron said.

Delaney laughed. "I'm never going up there again, and by noon tomorrow, you and Seth are moving into this room instead!"

"Nope! You wanted this room, so it's yours," Aeron replied.

"Some nice brother you are!" Delaney hissed.

"I'm gonna head to the bathroom. I wasn't joking when I said my bladder exploded. I gotta go. I'll see you in the morning."

Aeron returned to his room after a quick trip to relieve himself. He texted Seth about the items found in one of the antique trunks. Goosebumps formed on his skin with each letter he added into his text. Just when he was about to send the message, he remembered what his father had told them in the attic about not mentioning anything, so he deleted the message and placed his phone on the nightstand. He picked up the remote for the television, and after finding something familiar, with some humor, he sat and watched until fatigue finally overwhelmed him.

CHAPTER 17

"Well, the whole thing is confusing to me," Dr. Gates said. "I've tried to make sense of it, but the second X-ray revealed that nothing was wrong. I can't explain why the first X-ray showed something that looked like pneumonia. I still suspect the incident with the well might be the reason behind all of this."

"But there was so much blood," Teresa said.

"I understand, but he hasn't bled since last night. Listen, just take him home, let him rest, and he'll be running around the yard playing football with his brothers before you know it. I'm going to prescribe a steroid, and that should help him out, along with the antibiotic. The well water was likely stagnant and full of God knows what."

Adrian pulled the doctor aside while Teresa fussed over Seth. "Look, Wes, I wish I could understand all that's been happening to Seth, but he's really been through a lot in just the last few days."

"Look," Dr. Gates said, "if you have any questions or concerns, you guys call my cell phone." He placed his hand on Adrian's shoulder. "Heck, Adrian, I'll pick up even if it's you who's calling." They both smiled. "Now, get him out of here and let him rest in his own bed."

After Adrian, Teresa, and Seth walked into the kitchen at home,

Darcy and Kieran ran to Seth and hugged him. Aeron swallowed some milk from the carton, while standing in front of the open refrigerator door. "Dang, I thought I was gonna have the room to myself again tonight."

Seth laughed. "Sorry to ruin your plans."

Aeron put the milk away, walked over, and hugged Seth tightly. "Glad you're okay," Aeron whispered. Seth patted his brother on the back.

"Aeron," Teresa said, "why don't you help your brother to your room, and I'll put together a good lunch for everyone."

"Sure, Mom. Would you like me to carry him up the stairs, too?" Aeron replied.

"If you keep up the sarcasm, young man, I will hold you in contempt and place you under house arrest," Teresa smirked.

"Yes, your Honor," Aeron said. He and Seth smirked and walked into the dining room.

CHAPTER 18

"No, it's my turn to pour the tea!" Darcy argued.

Teresa was taking a basket of laundry to the boys' room when she heard Darcy's plea. She stopped and quietly opened the bedroom door and leaned into the room. "Who are you talking with, honey?"

"Mommy," Darcy cried, "Lilly won't let me pour the tea."

"Lilly?"

Thrusting her hands to her sides, Darcy insisted, "Lilly's my friend. She's always nice, but today she's being mean to me and won't play fair!" Darcy whipped her head around to the closet door and pointed. "Now she won't come out and play with me." Darcy's brown, wavy hair was disheveled, and tears streamed down her soft, suntanned cheeks.

"Is Lilly hiding in your closet?" Teresa inquired.

"Yeah, Mommy. She lives there, but now she won't come out and play with me unless I let her pour the tea for our party. I keep telling her it's my turn today!"

"So, when does Lilly come out of the closet?" Teresa asked—her eyes fixated on the door.

"She only comes out when me and Kieran are alone," she innocently responded. "Lilly says she likes this room and wants to play in here with me for all *in . . . ternity*." Darcy paused for a moment. "Mommy, what does that mean?"

Teresa stared intently at her youngest daughter and swallowed, nearly choking from the strain to her throat. "Do you think Lilly would come out and join us if we have a tea party together?"

"No, 'cause she says she only wants to play with me and Kieran." Teresa's eyes were glued once more on the closet door.

Just then, Aeron walked in and tapped Teresa on the shoulder. Teresa's scream echoed around the room and down the hallway. The basket fell from her hands, scattering clothes over the floor.

Aeron yelled, grasping his chest. "What the he—heck is wrong with you, Mom?"

Teresa turned and pointed her finger in her son's face. "Watch your mouth, young man!"

Aeron threw his hands upward and shrugged his shoulders. "What did I do?"

"I'll be right back, Darcy," Teresa said. She pushed Aeron into the hallway and whispered, "Darcy says she's playing with a little girl in her room named Lilly." Aeron's eyes widened. "Aeron, she's upset and crying over her friend. Kids don't do that with imaginary friends. She even said the little girl wants to play with her for all *eternity*. I'm sure that's what she meant."

"Didn't Dad tell you?"

"Tell me what?"

"Lilly is the little girl that Darcy told me about. And that's the name of the little girl who drowned with her twin brother!"

"Drowned? Twin brother? How do you know this?" Teresa inquired.

"I was in the attic last night with Delaney and Dad, and we found death certificates with the names Lilith and Cain on them."

Teresa gasped. "Aeron, what is going on?"

"Honestly, Mom, I don't know?"

Darcy quietly stepped into the hallway and tugged on Teresa's shirt. Teresa shrieked again. Darcy pulled her arms to her chest. Teresa placed one of her hands on Darcy's shoulders. "Honey, why don't you go downstairs to the kitchen and get Mommy's phone? It's on the table."

"Okay," Darcy replied.

After Darcy was out of view, Teresa grabbed Aeron's wrist. She pulled him over to the closet door in the twins' room. The faint creaking sound was heard from behind the door, but when Teresa opened it, no one was there. Once she closed the door, there was nothing but silence. "I swear I heard something moving in the closet," Teresa insisted. "Did you?"

"I didn't hear anything," Aeron responded.

"Okay, this is really starting to scare me. We'll talk to your father when he gets back over here from the lake. He took Kieran over a little while ago."

"I'm sorry, Mom, I probably shouldn't have said anything about what we found last night in the attic."

"Why not?"

"Dad asked us not to because he said there's been enough craziness going on around here."

"I'll talk with your father when he gets back over here, but whatever you do, don't mention anything to Seth about last night. He's already freaked out as it is." Teresa stepped into the hallway and turned. "By the way, Aeron, what did you want from me?"

"Seth says he's pretty tired and wants to take a nap, so I came to see if you had his sheets and blanket."

"Yes, but they're on the floor. Let me get them."

"I'll get them, Mom."

Minutes later, Teresa and Aeron walked into the boys' bedroom. Seth was sitting on the bed, but he stood when they entered.

"How are you feeling, honey?" Teresa placed the basket on Aeron's bed and felt Seth's forehead. "You still feel a little warm."

"I'm fine. Just tired."

As Teresa, Aeron, and Seth were covering the bed with the fitted sheet, there was a knock at the front door. "Can you see who that is,

Aeron?" Teresa asked. Seth helped Teresa with the sheet before grabbing the bedspread.

As Aeron made his way down the stairs, he saw the shadow of someone standing at the doorway. "Can I help you?" he asked, after arriving at the door.

"You must be the oldest boy. It's Aeron, correct?"

"Yes, ma'am," Aeron replied. "Do I know you?"

"Oh, I'm sorry, you must think I'm so rude," the older lady said. "I'm Mrs. Murphy. I'm your neighbor from across the road.

"Oh, I'm sorry. Please come in," Aeron said. He opened the door, and she walked in holding a container. "My mom's upstairs helping my brother with his bed. He had a bad nosebleed yesterday, and my mom had to wash his sheets."

Mrs. Murphy gasped. "Oh . . . well, I'm sorry to hear that."

Just like Josh Wallace, she thought.

"Aeron," Teresa said, as she rounded the corner on the landing of the stairs, "who is at the door?" Suddenly, she noticed Mrs. Murphy. "Oh, I'm sorry," Teresa apologized, "I didn't see you there at first."

Mrs. Murphy shifted the container into another arm before reaching forth her hand to shake Teresa's. "I'm Mrs. Murphy. I'm your new neighbor."

"Oh, I've been looking forward to meeting you," Teresa replied. "My husband said I really need to get over to see your house, but I've been a little overwhelmed the past few days."

"I didn't come sooner because I wanted to give you time to get settled in," Mrs. Murphy said. "I brought this pie for your dinner this evening. I hope you'll like it."

"I have no doubt we will, Mrs. Murphy. That is too kind of you to do that."

"It is my pleasure." After examining Aeron, Mrs. Murphy said jokingly, "Well, young man, you certainly look like you can manage to carry this container to your kitchen on your own."

He grinned. "Yes, ma'am, I'll take it. Thank you."

Teresa laughed. "As you can tell, shirts seem optional with my son." They both smiled. "And thank you, Mrs. Murphy, for the dessert. I know my family will enjoy it."

Mrs. Murphy watched as Aeron walked through the doorway and into the other room. "Yeah, I can see I better make more than one pie next time. He must eat you out of house and home."

"You have no idea," Teresa chuckled.

"Mom, I need to—" Seth suddenly noticed their guest as well, as he descended the stairs. "Oh, sorry," he said, "I didn't know we still had company."

"Mrs. Murphy, this is Seth. He just came home from the hospital today."

"Yes," Mrs. Murphy replied, "I was told by your brother that you had a bad nosebleed, young man." Seth smiled. Admiring Seth, Mrs. Murphy said, "Wow, Mrs. Douglas, you certainly have very handsome sons."

"Thank you," Teresa replied graciously. She turned to Seth and asked if he would get Delaney and Darcy.

A few minutes later, Teresa was introducing her two daughters.

"My goodness," Mrs. Murphy said, "you must be a model!" Delaney grinned.

"Thank you, ma'am."

Looking down at Darcy, Mrs. Murphy smiled and stated, "You must be a model as well, young lady." Darcy giggled.

"No," Delaney replied, "we like buying clothes, not modeling them."

Mrs. Murphy complimented Teresa on her children once more. "There are days, though, where I don't claim them as mine," Teresa laughed. "I just might send them over to you when they get on my nerves. In fact, you better fix up a spare room for the two boys. They might need to stay a lot."

"They are certainly welcome at my place. I just love children," Mrs. Murphy boasted.

"I do, too, but usually when they're someone else's, and I can send them away to their own homes." They laughed. "I have two more kids as well," Teresa stated. "One is my youngest son, Kieran, and the biggest kid happens to be my husband, whom you've already met."

"Yes, I met your husband. He seems like a wonderful gentleman, I might add. Oh, and he's very handsome, too, if you don't mind me saying so."

Teresa politely smiled and replied, "That all depends on his mood."

"I can see that you folks are going to be wonderful neighbors," Mrs. Murphy said.

"I know we will all get along quite well," Teresa responded, with a hint of relief. As they were chatting in the hallway, Adrian and Kieran walked through the kitchen door. Adrian heard the conversation taking place in the front entryway, so he went to investigate, with Aeron following behind him. "Honey, Mrs. Murphy is here, and she was kind enough to bring us a wonderful pie for dinner."

"Yes, I saw it in the kitchen. Thank you, Virginia, and it's good to see you again," Adrian said, as he extended his hand to greet her. Kieran latched onto his father's leg, as Adrian placed his arm around his son and introduced him. "This is Kieran. He's one of our twins I told you about."

Kieran studied Mrs. Murphy closely. After a few moments, he said, "Cain told me about you. He said you are the lady who watches over the people from the lake."

"Kieran!" Delaney and Aeron yelled at the same time.

Teresa's face beamed a crimson shade. Mrs. Murphy stiffened, as if a cold bucket of ice water had been poured over her. "*Cain?* Do you know someone named Cain, young man?"

Kieran's bottom lip extended outward. "Yeah, he plays with me a lot in my room," Kieran replied, as if embarrassed that he'd mentioned his friend. Seeking protection, Kieran moved even closer to Adrian's side. "Cain stays in our closet."

Teresa laughed nervously. "Darcy, why don't you and Kieran go out and play in the side yard. We would like to speak with Mrs. Murphy." Teresa's stomach gurgled—her knees suddenly weakened. "Go now, kids.

We'll call for you soon."

"Dad!" Aeron said. "Mom doesn't know any details about the stuff in the attic!"

"I know, Aeron. Just give me a minute to think." He rubbed his forehead in disbelief, searching for any explanation his rational mind could conceive.

The piercing sensation of daggers shot through Mrs. Murphy's joints. "Is there some place I might sit down?" she asked. Teresa escorted her to the dining room table while Delaney was sent to retrieve a glass of water.

After taking a few sips, which she almost spilled due to her trembling hand, Mrs. Murphy looked at Adrian as she pressed her hand firmly against her chest, almost as if she was trying to tame her wild, throbbing heart. "I know about the mysterious twins, Adrian, but I didn't mention them the other night when you visited my home. I didn't want to frighten you since you also have twins of your own," Mrs. Murphy explained.

Adrian cleared his throat and gazed at his neighbor, who had just opened an interrogation that Adrian had tried to avoid for several days.

"Umm . . . what twins are you talking about, Mrs. Murphy?" Teresa asked.

"Lilith and Cain. They died before I was born. They were my grandfather's children to his second wife, Harriet."

Teresa's hand lifted off the table and slid to her gaping mouth. As an attorney, she was analytical, but her mind was swirling with thoughts too frightening to comprehend. "Mrs. Murphy, what did you tell my husband the other night that he failed to tell me?" She glared at Adrian, but then focused on Mrs. Murphy, anticipating her response.

Mrs. Murphy explained the family connection to the property, and the details about the family burials in the cemetery on the hill. "That was where they'd placed the bodies after they'd been moved," she said.

"Moved from where?" Teresa inquired.

"Well, there was a ship that carried relatives of the people from

Inverness. Tragically, those people had been killed on the way over here, and they'd buried the people across the road."

"Like up near the lake?" Teresa asked.

Mrs. Murphy took another sip from the cup. "Yes, you could say that."

Aeron blurted out, "Near our lake?"

"Yes, dear, but they honestly did move everyone that had been buried across the road."

"Where was the cemetery before it was on the hill?" Seth questioned.

"Well," although lying to them, "Inverness Lake, which is several miles up the road, was built over a junkyard filled with many wrecked cars from accidents around the area," Mrs. Murphy explained.

Delaney leaned forward in her chair. "Mrs. Murphy, were Cain and Lilly buried in the cemetery that was once there?"

"No, dear. They did drown in the lake, though."

Teresa placed her elbow on the table and leaned her head forward into her hand. "Dear God, Adrian! Twins drowned in a lake right up the road!" Teresa shivered. "Mrs. Murphy, "are you telling me there was a real Lilly and Cain who lived here, and they died at Inverness Lake?"

Mrs. Murphy adjusted herself in her chair, mimicking a defendant on the witness stand. "Yes, those children existed, but that was a long time ago. Their deaths were probably just an accident. Well, at least that's what we were told over the years, but quite frankly, we believe it was a lot more than that."

Teresa's heart fluttered like the wings of a bird in distress. She leaned forward. "Darcy says she plays with a little girl named Lilly who lives in her closet." Teresa wiped her brow with a napkin. "Adrian, this is beginning to really scare me."

Delaney and Aeron were both breathing shallow—their air was being blocked by their constricting throats. Seth sat motionless.

Teresa took a deep breath. "I'm sure this is just a coincidence!"

"Yes, of course, honey," Adrian reassured.

Aeron wiped off a trickle of sweat rolling down from his temple. "We know what they looked like from the photos in the attic."

"What are you saying, Aeron?" Teresa asked.

"I started to mention to you upstairs about the stuff we found in the attic. I can go get the photos if you want."

Mrs. Murphy took another sip from the glass. A dribble of water rolled down her chin. She looked at Teresa and asked, "Honey, do you have something a little stronger than water? I could use it right about now."

"Go get the bottle of wine from the refrigerator. And bring *two* glasses," Teresa said to Delaney.

Aeron went up alone into the attic. As he knelt beside the old trunks, emerging from the shadows, at the far end of the attic, was Mors. He quietly moved closer towards Aeron, who sifted through the papers and photos as hastily as he could. Mors' fingers straightened—his stiffened joints cracked. He was yearning to grasp hold of Aeron, the boy he believed was Wyatt, his long-lost son.

Aeron found the photos and documents he needed and stood. As he turned, he was alone in the attic, but he thought he heard a creaking sound emanating from the far end of the attic. Aeron squinted and stared into the shadows. "Hello?" he whispered. He shook his head and blinked several times. "I'm going crazy," he whispered.

When Aeron started down the stairs, the creaking noise of floorboards resonated gain from behind him. Aeron stopped and looked up. He walked back up a few steps and gazed into the attic. "Hello?" Silence filled the dusty air.

As they waited for Aeron, Teresa gulped the wine from her glass while Mrs. Murphy told her all about her dislike for the barn, and the uncanny behaviors of a mad woman named Harriet. Adrian and Teresa glanced at each other often.

Aeron rushed in with the documents and photographs. As they sorted through them, Mrs. Murphy was able to identify many of the people in the photos. "Yes, this is Cain and Lilly," she said with confidence. She continued to show various photos of them with other ancestors, and she explained the documents related to their deaths.

"Mrs. Murphy," Delaney interrupted, "my dad said that some people took photos of dead family members many years ago. They just look creepy to me."

"I'm sorry to say, but yes, honey, they really did," Mrs. Murphy responded. "Some children didn't live very long in those days, and postmortem photos were used to help the family remember what their child looked like. Today, we don't really need such photos unless they want them for some reason, so that's probably why you haven't heard of the practice before."

Teresa also noticed the wallpaper in one photograph. "Oh my God!" she said. "This was taken in Darcy and Kieran's room. Look at the wall!" She pointed it out to Adrian.

"Mrs. Murphy," Adrian asked, "did the people who lived here before us ever complain about strange things happening to them?"

"Well, I'm not all that sure," she said, while looking away. "Those neighbors didn't talk to me that often. Their son, Josh, used to visit from time to time. Josh was very friendly, and he did tell me about a couple things like—" She was silent as she shifted in her chair. "He said . . . he had some bad dreams and didn't feel well sometimes." Mrs. Murphy took a gulp of wine. "The real estate agent, Madeline, told me different families left some things, but I didn't know exactly what it was they'd left behind. In fact, I suspect that stuff in the attic has been there for many years. Perhaps the homeowners were afraid to dispose of it for some reason."

Teresa looked at Adrian. "Honey, there has to be an explanation to all of this," she insisted.

Adrian rolled his eyes and sighed heavily before leaning back in his chair. "Honey, you're talking about some old pictures and some imaginary friends. Besides, no one has been hurt by any of this."

"Excuse me Dad, but what about me?" Seth interrupted. He tilted his head downward and pointed to the stitches. "What about these?" He looked sternly at his father. "And don't forget I almost drowned in that well. And no one can tell me why I started having bad nosebleeds either! It's not like I haven't spent more time in the hospital than in my new home, for God's sake!"

"Seth Matthew Douglas!" Adrian sat up. "You need to settle yourself down right now! Those were just freak accidents. Anything like that could have happened to any one of us, especially since we aren't that familiar with our new home yet. We all need to settle down!"

Seth slammed his hand on the table and yelled, "Dad, this crazy place scares me, especially after hearing about those twins who died in a lake! We have a lake, too!"

"Seth!" Adrian jumped up and reached for his son's face. Blood was streaming from Seth's nose again. "Someone get me a towel! Hurry!"

Teresa gasped and ran into the kitchen. Mrs. Murphy, Delaney, and Aeron rushed over to Seth, as Adrian cupped his hand under his son's nose.

"Dad, what's going on with me?" Seth cried. He coughed from the taste of his own blood flowing down the back of his throat.

"Seth, it's just a nosebleed, so settle down," Adrian insisted.

Teresa ran back into the room, wrapping an ice pack tightly in a cloth. She held the towel up to Seth's nose as Adrian walked swiftly to the kitchen to wash his hands. Aeron went with his father to help turn on the faucet.

At the sink, Aeron whispered, "Dad, what is going on with Seth? Is there something you're not telling me?"

"Aeron," Adrian whispered back, "he fell into that well, and the doctor said he likely has an infection from the bad water." Adrian washed off his hands while Aeron handed him a towel. "Everything is fine. It's just a nosebleed." Adrian dried his hands. "Let's get back in there and help."

"I think it's letting up a little, Seth," Teresa reassured him. "You don't feel like you're going to pass out, right?"

Seth shook his head, and Teresa leaned over and rested her cheek on the top of his head. "Honey, everything's going to be fine."

"So, what does the doctor think is causing these?" Delaney asked. "I thought you guys said something about the dirty water he fell into."

"Yes," Adrian replied, as he walked closer to Seth, "and he said it probably irritated his sinuses. He gave us an antibiotic because he says the stagnant water from the well—"

Unexpectedly, Teresa yelled: "Oh my God! Adrian! The well! *Did you cover the well?*"

"Oh my God!" Adrian shrieked. "Where did you tell Darcy and Kieran to play?"

"Adrian, we forgot about the well!" Teresa dashed for the door.

CHAPTER 19

Seth attempted to stand and leave the room with everyone else, but the room became a merry-go-round and he fell back onto the chair.

"I'll stay with Seth," Mrs. Murphy said. She grabbed the towel and held it gently to Seth's nose.

After the family bolted through the kitchen door, Mrs. Murphy said, "I'm sure the kids are fine, Seth." She smiled and rubbed the side of his head. "You remind me so much of Josh who lived here."

Panic rolled over the family like a tidal wave. They yelled frantically for Darcy and Kieran after running outside. "Mom," Delaney cried out, "do you see them?" Adrian, Teresa, and Aeron ran toward the well while Delaney was ordered to check the front of the house.

After arriving at the well, there were no signs of any disturbance in the water. Adrian yelled, but there was no indication the kids were ever there. They charged back to the side yard and meet up with Delaney. "I didn't find anyone," Delaney said.

"Neither did we," Adrian replied.

"Adrian!" Teresa cried in horror. "The lake! You know how much they love the lake!" Teresa called out to the kids as she sprinted up the huge embankment to the lake. Her lungs burned as she tried to inhale as much air as possible.

"Darcy!" Adrian yelled, while Teresa hollered for Kieran. "Aeron, you and your sister go check the barn." Adrian and Teresa darted around the lake in opposite directions, looking at the water for any ripples. *Lilly and Cain*, Teresa thought, as she ran along the lake, checking the cattails for any sign of the kids. Moments into their search, they arrived at the far end of the lake. They were separated by the shallow, muddy pool at the far end where the water flowed into the lake from a small hill at the bottom of the fields.

"I didn't see them anywhere," Adrian stammered, as he tried to catch his breath. He looked over at the fields and cried out, "Maybe they're playing in the cornstalks and got lost! Kieran asked to do that when we were over here earlier." Without running back around the lake to meet up with his wife, Adrian sloshed through the thick, slimy mud and rejoined Teresa.

Once entering the barn, Aeron anxiously climbed one of the ladders into the hay loft. He saw nothing. He twisted around and gazed into the other loft, only seeing a few bales of hay. "Delaney," Aeron yelled, as his sister searched in each of the stalls, "I can't find them!"

"They're not in the stalls either," Delaney replied.

"I'll check the downstairs," Aeron said, as he jumped down from several rungs on the ladder. "You keep looking up here," he said.

"Darcy . . . Kieran!" Delaney called out, her voice quavering from the fear overwhelming her mind. "Please answer us!" She found nothing but a few burlap sacks piled in a corner, and some old bales of hay scattered around the floor. She walked back to the large open entrance and scanned the area. She was unaware of the man in the bloodstained apron standing in one of the lofts. He began descending the ladder. His blood-soaked hands stained the wooden timbers as he approached the main floor. The machete he held shimmered in the sunlight pouring through the entrance. Delaney started rubbing her temples as she gazed out toward the lake, worried that something terrible had happened to her youngest siblings.

Less than ten feet behind her, the apparition continued to drag one of his legs through the remnants of hay. He grinned with anticipation as he lifted the machete high above his head.

The pounding of Aeron's footsteps caused Delaney to jump and turn around swiftly. "They're not down there either."

The ghost was gone.

Meanwhile, back at the house, Seth told Mrs. Murphy he wanted to help in the search, but the salty taste of blood was making him nauseated. When they removed the towel from his nose, there was still a small trickle of blood flowing from his nostrils. "You still need to hold that to your nose, honey," Mrs. Murphy instructed.

As they made their way to the kitchen sink to get a glass of water, Seth heard laughter coming from outside. He glanced out the window and saw Darcy and Kieran running back and forth in the lower yard. "There they are!" Seth hollered.

He and Mrs. Murphy rushed out the kitchen door. He ordered Darcy and Kieran to come to him. The twins stopped, waved at someone, and ran up to the yard where they'd joined their brother and neighbor. *"Where have you guys been?"* Seth yelled. "Everybody's out looking for you right now!"

"We were only playing hide-and-seek with our friends," Darcy explained.

"What friends?" Mrs. Murphy asked.

"Lilly and Cain," Kieran replied, as tears welled up in his eyes.

Mrs. Murphy tapped Seth on the shoulder. "Honey, if you can, you should run and find your parents and tell them we have the kids safe and sound." She grabbed the hands of the twins and held on tightly. "You guys better stay with me."

Seth heard Delaney yelling from the area near the barn, so he ran in that direction. His muscles were on fire from the trek up the embankment. When he arrived near the lake, he bent over and gasped for air. Blood dripped from his face and landed on a small patch of emerald clovers below him. He lifted the towel to his face once more. His lightheadedness caused bursts of blackness to pulsate throughout his vision with each heartbeat.

When he heard Delaney yell his name, he looked up and waved. "We found them!" Seth hollered. Aeron and Delaney ran from the barn and met Seth at the top of the embankment.

Teresa and Adrian separated briefly to search a larger area amongst the high stalks of corn. When Teresa stopped to take a breath, she heard rustling behind her. She quickly turned. "Adrian, is that you?" She stepped toward the noise, but the cornstalks behind her frantically swayed back and forth, as if caught in the brisk winds of a storm. "Kids? Adrian? Please answer me!"

All around her, the cornstalks whipped violently, causing Teresa to scream out in terror. She crouched to the ground and cried for Adrian. Just as she pressed her hands to her ears, her husband's hand reached out and grabbed her shoulder. She fell to the ground and screamed again.

"Honey, what's wrong?" Adrian asked.

Teresa stood and embraced Adrian as if he was going to leave her alone to die. "I swear there were people in the rows all around me!" she explained. "I want to get out of here right now!"

As they exited the rows of corn, they finally heard their oldest children calling, so they sprinted from the cornfield and met them near the lake. "Seth found them," Delaney announced.

"Thank God!" Adrian bellowed.

"Honey, is your nose still bleeding?" Teresa asked. She panicked when he removed the towel and blood was still oozing from his nostrils.

"Yeah, but I just ran up this hill, and it probably made it worse," he said. "The twins are safe with Mrs. Murphy."

Aeron turned his back to Seth and said, "Hey, hop on." Seth complied, and the family started walking quickly down the hill toward the house. "Hey, I'll kick your scrawny rear end if you get any blood on my clothes. You still owe me a Buckeyes shirt." Seth laughed at his older brother's hollow threat.

After Teresa darted over to the twins, she shook them. "Didn't I tell you two to play in this yard? Don't you *ever* do that to Mommy again!"

Kieran started to cry, as he pleaded, "We won't, Mommy, but we only wanted to play with our friends."

Teresa hugged them. "Mommy's sorry, but we thought something happened to both of you."

Darcy put her arms around Teresa's shoulders. "Mommy, we're fine. You don't need to be mad. We didn't hear you."

"You know," Mrs. Murphy interjected, "I have to say that having you folks around is definitely going to keep me young." She smiled and patted Seth on the shoulder.

Teresa walked over and hugged her neighbor. "Thank you so much for helping us out. You must think I'm a crazy woman with all this excitement I've put you through today."

"Not at all, dear. I haven't had this much excitement in a long time." Mrs. Murphy smiled and placed her hand on Teresa's shoulder. "It looks like you folks need to get some rest, so I need to make my way back home."

When Mrs. Murphy turned to leave, Adrian said, "Hey Virginia, thanks again for tonight's dessert." She smiled, acknowledged Adrian's gratitude, and continued walking toward her own yard.

Aeron suddenly laughed. "Hey Dad, what happened to your legs?" Everyone looked down and discovered the mud.

"Oh, geez. I forgot about that. I need to jump in the shower," he mumbled.

Later that evening, Teresa wanted to show the photos to the twins, to see if her youngest children could recognize the other twins in the pictures; however, she was fearful they might identify the *friends* supposedly living in their closet. A confirmation of the strange friendship was needed, but Teresa was afraid it might frighten the children to see the postmortem photos. After asking them to describe Lilly and Cain, Teresa's skin crawled when their descriptions of their *playmates* were quite accurate to the photos, including their burial clothes.

In bed that night, Teresa and Adrian gazed into each other's bewildered eyes. They needed answers! They pressed their bodies firmly against the twins sleeping soundly between them. A tear escaped and cascaded down the contour of Teresa's face. She and Adrian soon reached out to each other—their arms forming a garrison of protection over their youngest children.

CHAPTER 20

Early the next morning, Aeron grabbed some clothes and headed to the bathroom for a much-needed shower. Hot water poured over his sluggish body, and before too long, steam clung to the mirror over the sink. As Aeron's senses were finally revived, the cabinet above the sink slowly opened, reflecting a hazy silhouette near the door.

The intruder—full of gaping holes in its torso—glided across the floor toward the shower. Festering secretions oozed from its wounds, consisting of four puncture holes in a row—matching the pattern of the prongs of a pitchfork. Maggots fell to the floor in small clumps as the stranger staggered closer toward Aeron.

Words appeared on the surface of the mirror, written by the finger of an unknown entity.

Kill them!

As Aeron was rinsing off, the dark shadow appeared just outside the frosty plastic curtain. "Hey, Seth," Aeron yelled, "let Dad know I'll be down soon." After no response, he yelled for his brother again. Still no response. After turning off the faucet, he took his hands and brushed them through his hair, removing as much water as possible. He opened the curtain. "What the—" he hollered.

Standing at the shower curtain was Seth.

"What are you yelling about?"

"I wish you'd stop trying to give me a heart attack!" Aeron snapped.

"You're the idiot who called for me."

Aeron reached for his towel and started to dry off. "Did you hear me tell you to let Dad know I'd be down soon?"

"No, I didn't, but I'll let him know if he hasn't left already. He said he had another meeting this morning, but he said he'd be home in time to take us up to the high school. I'm glad the coach finally called."

"Did Dad say exactly when he was taking us to the school to meet the coach?"

"No," Seth replied, "but he said something about mid-morning."

"Good. I'll be out in a few minutes. We better be prepared to stay for the practice. I hope we're allowed."

"Sounds good," Seth responded.

As Seth turned to leave, Aeron yelled, "Close the door, will ya!" After approaching the mirror, Aeron noticed the ominous words on the surface. "What a moron," he snickered, before taking his towel and wiping off the mirror.

Aeron combed his hair before returning to his bedroom.

"Real funny, Seth."

Seth looked up from his phone. "What?"

"*Kill them*? Really?" Aeron mocked.

"Kill who?"

"I'm talkin' about what you wrote on the mirror while I was showering."

Seth lowered his phone. "What?"

"Yeah, right! You're such a liar." After slipping on his shirt, Aeron said, "Hey, I know Coach Bryson said he'd talk to the new coach, too, so I hope that was enough to get us good positions on the team." Aeron headed for the kitchen for breakfast.

"By the way," Seth yelled, "I didn't write anything on the mirror!"

"Whatever," Aeron said, as he sprinted down the stairs.

CHAPTER 21

Seth walked the short distance to Murray Road after telling Aeron he needed to see Mrs. Murphy. The pungent odor of the flowers and herbs made his eyes water, just as they had done to his father.

After knocking, Mrs. Murphy entered the kitchen and greeted him. "To what do I owe this pleasure?" she asked.

"I wanted to come over and apologize for my bad attitude when you were at our house yesterday," Seth timidly said. "My dad wasn't too happy with me."

Mrs. Murphy smiled and opened the door. "You come right in here and see me, young man." Seth stepped into the kitchen. "Please sit down right here," she insisted, pulling out a chair for him.

She walked over and poured a glass of milk from the refrigerator and retrieved some cookies from a container. "I was pretty ignorant by yelling at my dad in front of you," Seth said, "so I told my dad this morning I wanted to come over and apologize."

"Oh honey, you didn't need to. I know you've been all out of sorts with your injury and trying to get adjusted to a new home, so I completely understand." She placed a large plate of cookies in front of him, along with a large glass of milk. "I'm certain your family is overwhelmed with the move, so you don't need to apologize at all." She leaned down and hugged him. Seth wasn't sure how to react, but he embraced her in return. "I hope you don't mind, but I'm a hugger," Mrs. Murphy said.

Seth smiled. "No, ma'am, I don't mind. My parents are like that, too. Even Aeron hugs me."

"How is your head, honey? And what about that nasty nosebleed?"

"It's better today," he said. "Thanks for asking." He glanced down at the cookies. The dark spots of chocolate made his mouth water, so he reached over and took a cookie from the plate after she pushed it closer toward him. After one bite, he looked up. "Are these homemade?" He wiped away a few crumbs that had collected in the corners of his mouth. "Oh, and the pie was really great!"

"That's good, Seth, and yes, they're homemade. I don't buy any of those store brand cookies. She smiled as Seth took another bite. "The milk also comes from the dairy farm up the road."

Seth took a gulp from the glass and quickly raised his eyebrows. "Yeah, there's a huge difference in taste. Me and Aeron—I mean—Aeron and I, drink a gallon every day. My mom complains about it all the time, especially when she needs it for her coffee and there isn't any left. Aeron gets in trouble all the time for drinking out of the carton, but Dad says the milk makes us stronger, so he tells her not to complain."

Mrs. Murphy chuckled.

Seth looked around the kitchen. "My dad said your house is really nice. I see what he means now."

"I can give you a quick tour if you'd like," Mrs. Murphy offered.

"Sure," Seth replied. He lifted the glass of milk to his mouth and finished its contents before leaving the table.

As they toured each room, Seth was surprised by the antiquity of all the furnishings, which was something that never interested him before. Much like his fascination with names on the headstones in the cemetery, and the history behind the people, Seth was intrigued with the old photos on the walls, including the ones placed neatly on every stand throughout each room.

On a table in the upstairs hallway, Seth noticed a photo of a couple dressed in wedding attire. "Who is that in the picture? I saw one in your living room, too."

As Mrs. Murphy reached for the photo, she nearly knocked a kerosine lantern off the edge. Seth grabbed it before it fell to the floor. "Thank you, dear! I thought for sure I was going to have a huge mess all over the rug."

"My dad doesn't like having kerosine in the house. He says it's too dangerous, and he doesn't want Darcy and Kieran to get hurt."

She eased the lantern back into its place and picked up the photo. "Your father is probably right. As clumsy as I am, maybe I shouldn't have kerosine in the house either." She smiled and continued. "Anyway, this is my grandfather and his first wife. Their names were George and Matilda. He built the house you live in. His brother, Jabez, also helped build both of our houses."

"They did a nice job on them," he grinned, but he became hesitant for a moment before asking, "Mrs. Murphy, do you really know if other people who lived in our house experienced some of the creepy things we have seen and heard?"

Mrs. Murphy cleared her throat and adjusted her cross necklace. "Well, I've met several families moving in and out of your home over the years. They said there were strange things that did occur, but they didn't really say much beyond that." She smiled. "I just think your family is so used to the hustle and noises of city life that maybe these things you guys are seeing, and hearing, are just different things from what you're used to. Old houses do make noises. They certainly have their own character."

"You're probably right, but it's so weird about the old lady we keep seeing. I'm totally sure there was someone in a long black dress standing over by the lake the day I got hurt, and I'm starting to kinda believe that my little brother is seeing someone like her in the house. The stuff about that Cain and Lilly is really freaking us out, too."

Mrs. Murphy patted Seth on the shoulder. "So, are you saying you think your house is haunted?"

Seth swallowed and replied, "No . . . well . . . maybe?"

Mrs. Murphy laughed again. "Honey, just give it some time and all of this will work itself out. I think it's all a coincidence."

"I hope you're right, 'cause I do like having a bigger house, even though I have to sleep in the same room as Aeron." Seth grinned and shrugged his shoulders. "I do like having a lake, though. It's great, and for some reason, I keep wanting to go over by it. I think it's a peaceful place, and it gets me away from everyone for a while."

"Yes, it is a nice lake. I'm glad my great-uncle Jabez convinced my grandfather to purchase the land, along with the fields surrounding it."

"Your grandfather didn't own it all at that time?"

"No, a gentleman named Stewart owned it at first, but when he suddenly left the property, my grandfather ended up with the lake as an added addition to the land."

"Why did that Stewart guy leave suddenly?" He and Mrs. Murphy walked toward the stairs and started down to the living room. "Was there a problem?"

"Well, to tell you the truth, I believe it had something to do with a dispute with some Native Americans in the area. I'd heard that Stewart may have killed one, so he left to protect his own life."

Seth's eyes became saucers, making his eyebrows leap upward. "Seriously?"

"Yes, I know it seems odd that something like that happened on the property, but back them, cowboys and Indians wasn't just a game that boys played." Mrs. Murphy's legs felt like fragile porcelain, ready to break after the tour, so she sat in her favorite chair. Seth sat on the sofa.

"Mrs. Murphy, how did everyone get here to Inverness? My dad said that some Scottish people settled the town."

"He's correct, but something mysterious happened on one of the ships as they crossed the ocean."

Seth's curiosity pushed him to ask, "So, what happened?"

Mrs. Murphy's words were clinging to her tongue at first, as she looked over at the photo of her grandfather and Harriet. "Well," she finally said, "the ship was located not far from the Virginia coast. It had been adrift for a couple days they assumed."

Intrigued even more, Seth moved forward on the sofa, his mind filled with inquisitiveness. "Why was it adrift?"

Grabbing her cross necklace, Mrs. Murphy eased forward in her chair as well. "When another ship spotted it, the captain decided to move closer to investigate." Mrs. Murphy's body trembled like a frightened child in the darkness. "They discovered that everyone on board the ship had . . . well, perished quite mysteriously."

"You're kidding me! Everyone?"

"Well, all except two women. They were discovered hiding under thick blankets below deck." Again, Mrs. Murphy clutched her cross necklace.

"So, what happened? Did the woman tell anyone why the passengers were dead?" Seth's face was contorted as if in pain.

"After they put a small crew on board, both ships safely made it into port. Several people were there from Inverness waiting on their relatives." Mrs. Murphy shook her head. "Those poor souls were shocked by the news of their family members."

"So, did the women tell them anything?" Seth leaned in even more toward his neighbor.

"They claimed another ship attacked them, but there was never any proof. The women ended up traveling back to Ohio with the others from Inverness, and those women settled here, and one of those women found a companion, whom she married."

"Wow!" Seth replied. "That guy sure had a lot to deal with over her emotional baggage, I bet."

"Yes, but the man who married her had recently lost his wife, so he had some baggage of his own. Maybe that's what brought them closer together when they first met, and he started courting her."

"Courting?" Seth leaned back.

"What you and I would refer to as dating. It became serious, and they married several months after he met her in the town." Mrs. Murphy pointed over to the photo of her grandfather and Harriet. "That is the couple right there."

"Seth stood. "May I see it?"

"Certainly. It might be a little dusty, though." Mrs. Murphy eased back into her chair.

Seth picked up the photo. Immediately, he pulled it closer to his face and spun around. "Mrs. Murphy! I know this lady!"

Mrs. Murphy seemed to be yanked out of her chair. "You couldn't know her. She died decades ago!"

"It's the lady in the black dress! I'm sure of it!"

Mrs. Murphy swallowed hard, trying to hide her fear. "Seth, there were a lot of women who dressed alike in those days. It's certainly not rational that a woman who's been dead for almost one hundred years would be roaming around the property."

Seth held the photo close again. "Well, I guess you're right, but it sure looks like her. Who is she?"

"Harriet. She was my grandfather's second wife."

Seth chuckled as he placed the photo back onto the stand. "Yeah, it would be impossible for some dead lady to be taking a walk by our lake, but boy does she remind me of that creepy lady Aeron and I saw that one day."

"Come, let's get you another cookie, Seth."

Seth noticed the clock in one of the corners of the room. "Shoot, I didn't realize it was getting this late. Me and my broth—I mean—my brother and I have to go meet the football coach at our new school."

"I understand, honey, so let's get you back home." Mrs. Murphy chuckled at the way Seth was correcting his grammar. "Let me wrap up some cookies for you to take back for you and your siblings."

"Thanks, I really appreciate it. They did have a better taste than the ones from the store."

Mrs. Murphy opened the door after placing the cookies into a bag.

When Seth stepped passed her, he turned and asked, "May I ask one more question?"

"Sure," Mrs. Murphy said.

"What happened to the other woman that was on the ship?"

Mrs. Murphy paused. Her brief smile was marred with disdain for what the other woman did to her relatives years ago. "The other woman was named Dolores…Harriet's younger sister," Mrs. Murphy replied.

"Oh. Well, they must have been tough people to handle such a tragedy." Seth stated. "And, what did they do with the bodies of the dead relatives?"

Mrs. Murphy stepped back, easing the screen door closed. "Well, they brought them back by way of a train. The stench must have been overwhelming."

Seth crinkled his nose. "Yeah, that's kinda gross. So, did they bury them in the cemetery on our hill?"

Mrs. Murphy's guilt plagued her conscience. She didn't want to deceive the young man standing before her, but she knew what the answer had to be: "Well," her breaths returned, "they're likely buried in a couple different cemeteries in the area."

"Oh, well, that makes sense."

"Now, you run along, and I hope you have a wonderful time meeting that new coach. I'm sure you miss being in sports."

"Yeah, we do. Aeron is super excited to be back on a team." Seth smiled and thanked her again for the cookies before turning and sprinting toward his home.

After walking through the living room and peering out the window to watch Seth, a crashing noise startled Mrs. Murphy. As she quickly turned, she looked up toward the ceiling and yelled, "I didn't tell him, Harriet!" As several doors slammed upstairs, Mrs. Murphy slowly walked to the stairs and began to ascend to the second floor. "He's a really nice boy, Harriet, and I've already warned you to leave his family alone!"

When she reached the landing on the stairs, standing and leaning against the banister on the top floor were Harriet and Dolores. The women stood in silence as Mrs. Murphy quickly backed up against the wall. "You've had enough men already in your lives, so damn you two to Hell!"

The sinister siblings stepped back into the shadows and disappeared. Mrs. Murphy slowly ascended the stairs before rushing into her room and slamming the door shut.

CHAPTER 22

The car was filled with anticipation as Adrian and the boys drove to the school to meet the football coach. Aeron's heart pounded against his chest, and his palms were soaked with sweat. He was somewhat apprehensive, because he knew his contentment at their new home depended on whether he was able to play football that semester. For now, it was his purpose, paving the way for a peace of mind he lacked since being uprooted and moved to a strange place he neither cared for, nor understood. He was desperate for any distraction from the move to Inverness.

Once they arrived at the school complex, the players were already on the field practicing. Seth suddenly hit Aeron on the arm. "Hey, man." Seth pointed toward the field. "Cheerleader alert!" He tapped Adrian on the shoulder. "Alright, Dad, I'm starting to like this new school already."

"Don't even think about any of them," Aeron teased, 'cause you'll probably have your scrawny butt flattened by the stampede when they see me."

"You know, Aeron," Adrian mocked, "your sister is right about you."

"Right about what?"

"You'll never find a girl who will love you as much as you're in love with yourself." Adrian grinned.

The sound of whistles and cheering lifted Aeron's spirit. For once, he finally felt at home.

They walked over to the coach and introduced themselves. Coach Mathias shook their hands, and after formal introductions, the coach said, "Yeah, I would say based on what Coach Bryson told me about your boys, Mr. Douglas, we would really like to have them come on board with the Tigers." Aeron's adrenaline surged like an erupting geyser. "I couldn't welcome them officially to the team until you guys moved into our district. I hope that didn't create too much confusion." Coach Mathias looked at Aeron, sizing him up. "Coach Bryson told me about you. Weren't you headed towards a school record for the most rushing yards in a season?"

"Yes sir," Aeron replied. "I was really shooting for it, but then we moved out here."

"Well, we will see how we can keep that streak going for you, young man." Adrian's shoulders finally lowered, and his breathing eased. "Since all the paperwork and physicals are completed already," the coach said, "you boys are welcome to stay and practice with us if that's okay with your father."

"Certainly," Adrian agreed.

The coach blew his whistle and yelled for the team to come to the sidelines. While waiting for the team, Aeron happened to notice one particular girl on the cheerleading squad staring at him. She tapped a fellow cheerleader on the arm and pointed at him. Her smile stretched across her face, and when the team ran over to their coach, the girl stood there alone, not realizing her coach was calling for her as well. One of the other cheerleaders ran back to her and pulled her over to the area where the rest of the squad was waiting.

A few of the players removed their helmets, seemingly curious about the two new guys. "Mr. Douglas, this is the team. Gentlemen, this is Mr. Douglas and his sons, Aeron, and Seth. They're the boys I told you guys about earlier. As you know, they're new to the school this year, and they'll also be staying for practice today." Some of the players acknowledged them, while others just gazed—an almost ominous glare that symbolized a potential threat to their playing time. "Chance, get over here," the coach commanded.

Emerging from the center of the players was a tall, husky player with sandy blonde hair. He held onto the facemask of his helmet as it hung at his side. He was several inches taller than Aeron, and somewhat rugged looking with his cleft chin, barrel-chested torso, and tattoos running down both his arms. He was a formidable, Herculean force that Aeron knew he must contend with around school.

"This is Chance Hilliard. He's the team's captain," Coach Mathias announced.

Adrian, Aeron, and Seth shook his hand. "Nice to meet you," Chance said. He paused and looked more intently at Aeron. "Hey, Coach." Chance looked back at his teammates and grinned. "It's nice to finally have someone on the team who looks like he can get things done on the field." Several groans erupted as the coach chuckled.

"Chance," Coach Mathias said, "why don't ya take the Douglas boys up to the locker room and get some helmets and pads. Besides, boy, you look like you might get mowed down out here by your teammates." After blowing his whistle, the coach ordered the players back onto the field.

Adrian thanked the coach and said, "I appreciate this, sir. My oldest son really needed this."

"No problem, Mr. Douglas. Besides, your oldest boy looks like he's ready to get started right away."

After being told the time they would be done with practice, Adrian said, "I'm sorry to bring this up, but Seth had a little incident not too long ago, and he has some stitches in his head. I'm sure he'll be fine, though. And, he's been having these strange nosebleeds, too, so if one starts, just have him call me. They get bad."

The coach put his hand up to his chin. "That's odd. I had a player last year with the same problem. We'd be in the middle of a game, and boom, I'd have to pull him from the field 'cause his nose would just start bleeding. It was the strangest thing."

"What was the kid's name?" Adrian inquired.

"Ummm . . . Wallace was his last name," the coach answered. "His first name was . . . ah . . . now let me think. He was only here that one season." A few moments later, he said, "Josh, yeah, that was his name. Josh Wallace."

Adrian stood silent; his mind swirling with concern.

"I'll be sure to keep an eye on your boy, Mr. Douglas," Coach Mathias reassured.

On their way to the locker room, Chance asked if Aeron and Seth had toured the school. "Yeah, pretty much," Aeron replied, "when we came here about signing papers and talk about schedules."

"So, I heard you guys moved into that old house down on Murray Road," Chance said. "Isn't that the one with the lake and barn?"

Aeron replied, "Yeah, that's us."

"Wow," Chance jeered, "that's quite a house. I've heard some interesting stories about that place."

"Like, what kinda things?" Seth asked.

Chance paused and raised his eyebrows. "You haven't heard?"

"Well," Aeron responded, "some things, but what do you know about it?"

As they walked to the gymnasium, Chance told them about the slaughtering of animals, but it was the murders that took place on their property that heightened the inquisitiveness of the boys. "Yeah, some crazy old lady killed a bunch of people. She slaughtered them like pigs, I guess. I even heard some of them were still alive when she and some butcher guy sliced them open and watched their guts spill out all over the floor. I heard they dumped their bodies in the lake."

Seth's eyes bulged. "Are you kidding?"

"No, I'm serious. This lady named Harriet and her crazy sister killed people with machetes, pitchforks, and all kinds of stuff."

"How do you know all of this?" Aeron asked.

"Really?" Chance heckled. "Everybody knows about Harriet and her psycho sister. Then Harriet was really messed up after her kids drowned in the lake, even though everybody thinks she went crazy and probably killed her own kids."

"What were the names of the kids that drowned?" Aeron asked.

Chance thought for a moment and finally replied, "Laney, or something like that. Maybe Lilly, and . . . umm . . . dang . . . I can't remember the boy's name."

Seth blurted out, "Cain!"

"Yeah, that's it," Chance confirmed. "So, you've heard some of the stories?"

As Seth started to tell Chance about the two kids supposedly in Darcy and Kieran's closet, Aeron immediately interrupted his brother. "Yeah," as he glared at Seth, "we've heard some things like that. It's just a bunch of stupid ghost stories."

"Well, I don't think it is. I heard some people even saw some lady in a black dress wandering around the cemetery not too long ago. I heard it's the cemetery by your house. That wasn't the original cemetery I'd heard about, though," Chance said. "I heard your lake was filled in over an old cemetery." Chance shook his head at the two stunned faces walking beside him.

"Our lake used to be a cemetery?" Aeron asked.

"Yeah, but they moved it up on that hill behind your house. Who knows if they moved the bodies or not." Chance shrugged his shoulders.

Seth glared at his brother. Aeron shook his head slightly, his eyes narrowed as he glanced at Seth.

"Did you know that Harriet and her sister were the only survivors of a massacre that happened on a ship coming here to America?" Chance asked.

"Yeah, Mrs. Murphy told me—" Seth was interrupted by his annoyed brother who interjected another comment to shut his brother up.

"Yeah, as I said, it's nothing but some stupid ghost stories," Aeron insisted.

"Yeah, but you might want to think twice before you go swimming in your lake. You never know what might grab ya." A veil of disgust fell over Aeron and Seth's faces. "Before Harriet got hanged, people believed they slaughtered about a dozen people in the barn after they strung them up by their ankles with ropes. They probably poisoned them or something. People were used to the smell of death in that barn of yours 'cause of all the pig slaughtering they did there also, so no one really knew, at first, that they were actually killin' people, too."

Aeron looked at Seth, whose face was saturated with dread. "Well, we don't believe in ghost stories," Aeron argued. "Besides, it's been calm around there so far."

Anger ripped at Aeron's chest, and a sudden, dull ringing began to echo in his ears again.

Your father has betrayed you!

"Hey," Chance said, "you can believe what you want, but there is definitely something weird going on down there at your house."

Wanting to change the subject, Aeron asked, "Hey, who's that one cheerleader down there in the middle of the others?"

Chance looked. "You mean the one with the brown hair pulled back?"

"Yeah," Aeron answered.

"Why do you want to know?" Chance's eyes narrowed.

Aeron smirked and said, "I think she wants me."

"Listen, Douglas," Chance threatened, "if you think you're going after her so you can get some—"

"Wait a minute," Aeron interrupted, "are you two dating or something?"

"No," Chance replied. "It's just that Brittany is a really cool girl, and we've been friends forever, so I protect her when I think someone's going after her just so he can get laid."

Aeron's gut erupted with rage. "I just asked her name, and besides, she's the one who was definitely looking at me first." Aeron's chest puffed outward, and he squared up his shoulders.

"Relax, man," Chance ordered. "I just don't want her to get hurt, especially from someone who doesn't even know her."

Standing nervously, Seth stepped forward. "Hey, my brother doesn't use girls. I saw her looking at him, too, so he's just curious, that's all."

"What are you? His bodyguard?" Chance said to Seth. "Both of you need to chill. Brittany's like a sister to me, and I'll defend her no matter what."

Aeron's shoulders sank. "Look, I get it. I'm like that with my sister."

"You have a sister? How old is she?" Chance inquired.

"She'll be a senior this year at this school," Aeron replied.

"Hum…" Chance mumbled. "What's she like?"

"Listen," Aeron stated, "she just had a bad breakup with my best friend, so I don't think she's looking to date anyone anytime soon."

"Okay," Chance said, "I'm not asking her to marry me or anything. I was just curious, too."

"I get it," Aeron said. "I'm just curious about that cheerleader, too. That's all." Chance's shoulders sank. "You'll probably meet her at school when we start next week," Aeron said.

"Listen, Douglas, I promised that I would always watch out for her." Chance turned and walked toward the gymnasium. Aeron and Seth followed.

"It's fine, man," Aeron replied. "It's just that my last girlfriend kinda caused a lot of problems, and I was hoping to meet someone that didn't breathe down my neck every second."

"Brittany's not like that at all," Chance said. "She has a lot of guy friends because she says she hates all the drama some of the girls cause around here."

Seth pushed his phone into Chance's face. "This is Delaney, our sister."

Chance took the phone. His eyes ignited with infatuation. "So, Douglas, when are you inviting me down to your house for dinner?"

"Anytime you want," Aeron answered. "It's kinda boring down there. I could use some good company instead of having to put up with this dork." He smirked at Seth.

"Hey!" Seth said.

Chance laughed. "Yeah, little brothers can be a pain sometimes."

"So can older brothers," Seth rebuked.

"So, when can you come down to the house?" Aeron asked.

"Honestly," Chance replied, "I'm not really allowed down there. My parents are freaked out about the stories about that place."

"Seriously?" Aeron jeered. "It's just a bunch of stories."

"I know," Chance agreed. "Then again, I don't always do what my parents tell me to do."

The three boys made it to the gym and entered the equipment room. After finding some shoulder pads and helmets, they returned to the field and joined the practice with the team.

In the parking lot, Aeron paced in anticipation for his father's arrival. His temper swelled like ocean waves, while his temples pulsated feverishly. *Dad,* he thought, *my dad actually lied to me!*

He betrayed you! Make him pay, Aeron! Make him pay!

CHAPTER 23

Aeron slammed the door shut after getting into the truck, and quickly started massaging his head, which felt like it was being squeezed in the iron jaws of a vise. The ringing in his ears was almost deafening—the feeling of a thousand buzzing insects swarming around inside his head.

Before Adrian could ask about practice, Aeron yelled, "What kinda possessed house did you buy for us, Dad?"

"What?" Adrian asked. "Where in the world is this coming from?"

Aeron looked over at Adrian and shouted, "Did you know that some psychotic lady named Harriet, and her crazy sister, slaughtered people in our barn and then dumped their mutilated bodies in our lake?" Adrian cocked his head. "It's not like making new friends isn't hard enough as it is, Dad. Now, everyone will know we moved into some kind of slaughterhouse!"

"Aeron, knock it off, right now! I mean it!" Adrian threatened.

"I even asked Chance if he wanted to come down to the house sometime, and he said his parents won't allow him 'cause they think the place is haunted!"

Seth leaned up from the backseat and told Aeron to shut his mouth. "You're only getting yourself into trouble, man."

"You can just shut up! I don't care if I get into trouble," Aeron bellowed.

"Aeron, I'm starting to get ticked off, so you need to close your mouth, right now!" Adrian demanded. "It's not like the real estate agent is going to reveal that kind of stuff to a client. I didn't know about any of that before buying the house. Besides, you said you would give the place a chance."

Aeron laughed. "Yeah, Dad, I *was,* but that was before I found out about those two crazy women who killed people. Now, nobody will want to hang out with us. You lied to me!"

"How did I lie to you?" Adrian asked.

"You promised you'd do everything to make it better for us, now we look like a bunch of idiots who were tricked into buying a haunted house!" He leaned forward and pressed his fingertips to his ears, trying to ease the sharp pain and ringing sensation echoing in his head.

Adrian's heart pounded, and his hands gripped the steering wheel like a tourniquet. "Aeron, just calm down, and we'll get this all sorted out. Just let me talk to Mrs. Murphy again and see how much of that stuff that football player told you was true. It could be just a bunch of stupid ghost stories."

Aeron slammed his fist into the door and hollered, "It doesn't matter, Dad! You outta know that people don't care about the truth anymore. They already believe the place is evil. I *hate you* for doing this to us!"

"Aeron, if you don't settle down—"

"You'll what?" Aeron taunted. Adrian glared at his son and warned him not to say another word. "When we get home," Aeron insisted, "you better not lay a hand on me!"

Seth yelled out, "Aeron, *stop it!* What's wrong with you?"

Aeron turned around and grabbed Seth by the shirt and raised his fist. "Don't you *dare* lay a hand on your brother, Aeron! I mean it!" Adrian demanded. "I'm still big enough to take you down, boy!"

Seth was thrust back into his seat as Aeron whipped around in the front seat and threatened, through clenched teeth, "I'd like to see you try it!"

Aeron massaged his temples, while squinting from an intense, sharp pain in his head.

"Listen, Aeron, you also promised me that you'd never again act like you did in the kitchen recently. You just need to stop all of this and let me sort it out!"

"I hate you! You've ruined everything by moving us into the middle of hell. No one will wanna hang out around us."

Adrian's face ignited into an inferno. He sped away when he pulled onto the road toward their home. For several miles he refused to say another word, even though Aeron ranted about their new house. When Seth attempted to speak, the glance of his father's eyes in the rearview mirror silenced him. Adrian's nerves throbbed throughout his body in rhythm with his thumping heartbeats.

Less than one hundred yards from the driveway, Aeron started to laugh—a malevolent chortle of sorts—before he said, "Yeah, I didn't think you had it in you! I knew you'd back down."

Unable to resist, Seth pleaded with his brother. "Aeron," still keeping his distance, "please stop it!" Tears filled his eyes. "Dad, it's not Aeron! I mean it! It's not him doing this!"

At an accelerated speed, Adrian traversed the remaining distance and slowed just enough to make it into the driveway without rolling the vehicle. He thrust the gearshift into park and turned toward Aeron. "Don't you ever—and I mean *ever* threaten—"

Aeron pushed the door open and got out. "Whatever!" he murmured, before slamming the door.

Adrian jumped from the driver's side and ran around to the front of the truck where he forced his hand against Aeron's chest. "Where do you think you're going, young man?"

Two apparitions appeared in the upstairs bedroom window where they could watch the imminent clash between father and son in the driveway.

The voice returned, with an ominous message.

You know what you must do, Aeron!

Aeron squeezed both hands into fists. He felt an overwhelming urge—something erupting from somewhere deep in his gut—to comply with the seemingly implanted thoughts controlling his mind. He grabbed Adrian's arm and swung, striking his father on his cheek. Adrian retaliated by thrusting Aeron against the hood of the truck and pressed his forearm against the back of Aeron's neck.

Seth, now outside the truck, yelled for his mother. He begged Adrian and Aeron to stop fighting, but Aeron screamed with anger, "Dad, you're hurting me!"

"Are you going to stop?" Adrian asked.

"*Yes!* Now get off me!" Aeron pleaded.

Teresa ran from the house and screamed at Adrian. "Let him go! I mean it, Adrian! You're going to hurt him!"

"Stay back, Teresa. He's in a rage again, and I don't know what he'll do!" Adrian ordered. "Now, do you promise to settle down, Aeron?"

"Yes, now get off me!" Aeron demanded. He wanted to tear his ears off because of the raucous ringing that clamored in his head.

As Adrian eased up slightly on the back of his son's neck, Aeron maneuvered away from his father's control and lunged forward with his hands outstretched, aiming for Adrian's throat. "I'm gonna tear your head off!" Aeron threatened.

Teresa suddenly screamed for Aeron to stop. Before he can grasp this father's throat, Adrian struck the side of his son's head, causing Aeron to fall backward against the hood of the truck. He rolled off to one side, collapsing onto the gravel below.

Seth stepped in front of his father and grabbed both arms as Adrian yelled, "Get out of my way, Seth!" Teresa ran over to Aeron and stooped to the ground.

Kill them! Kill them both! Do it now!

As she rolled Aeron over, he forcefully pushed against Teresa's chest. She fell backwards onto the ground. "Don't touch me!" He pressed his hands against his ears. "Make it stop!" he pleaded.

As Aeron staggered to his feet, Seth was shoved aside by his father. Adrian quickly seized Aeron by the throat and forced him backward, slamming him onto the hood of the truck again. "Don't you *dare* lay your hands on your mother!"

Adrian snatched a handful of Aeron's hair and slammed his son's head onto the hood. Seth hurried to his mother and helped her up. Adrian drew his face closer to Aeron's and warned, "I'll break every bone in your body if you *ever* lay a hand on her again!"

Adrian's forearm was now obstructing Aeron's ability to breathe. The sky appeared to blacken, and his family's voices become garbled. Teresa tried to pull Adrian from Aeron, but it was like moving a boulder a hundred times her own weight.

Surprisingly, a shriek from behind them startled everyone. "*Stop it!*" Delaney screamed. The apparitions disappeared from the upstairs window. "Stop it right now or I'm calling the police!"

Never in her lifetime did Teresa think such words would flow from the lips of anyone in her family, especially from one of her own children.

Adrian looked into Aeron's eyes, which started to roll back in their sockets. He was only seconds away from passing out. Adrian quickly released him, and Seth caught his brother, gently easing him onto the driveway. Adrian stepped back, as Teresa rushed to the boys.

Adrian slowly turned his hands and looked down at his palms. His chest heaved as he gasped for air, which seemed to be blocked by his tightening throat. He backed up into the yard with his hands outstretched. Finally, Adrian was able to release words that were wedged in his throat. "It was self-defense!" he pleaded. "I wasn't going to hurt him . . . no . . . I—" He rushed to Aeron and fell to the ground beside him. "Aeron!"

Aeron's head bobbled a few times as he blinked his eyes repeatedly, attempting to regained full consciousness. Adrian placed his hand on the back of Aeron's head to stabilize him. "Dad, what's wrong with me?" Aeron cried out.

"You're okay now, just relax," Adrian replied in a gentle tone. "Everyone back away!"

"I think he's hurt, though" Teresa said.

"I said for everyone to step back, right now! I don't know if he's over this yet."

Aeron sat up and opened his eyes completely. "What happened?"

"Delaney, go get a glass of water and a wet washcloth. Hurry!" Teresa ordered.

Aeron shook his head, as if coming out of a trance. His eyes filled with tears, which soon flowed down his cheeks as he grasped Adrian's arm. "Dad, please tell me what's going on with me!"

Adrian pulled Aeron closer and wrapped his arms around his shoulders. "You're okay now. Just rest for a minute." He waved to Teresa, and she rushed over to them.

She stroked the back of Aeron's head and asked, "Do you think you can get up, sweetheart?"

"Let him rest a minute," Adrian said.

Delaney arrived with the glass of water and a towel. "Here, honey," Teresa said. He took several sips. "Take a few more," Teresa insisted. She started to wipe Aeron's face before draping the cool cloth over the back of his neck. "Aeron, do you think you can walk to the house where it's cooler?"

"Yeah," he whispered.

Adrian and Seth helped pull him up from the ground. Aeron staggered to the house, but he gagged and ran for the small bathroom off the kitchen. Adrian knelt beside his son as he vomited. Stained with the contents of his stomach, Adrian helped remove Aeron's shirt before draping a cool, wet towel over his son's back and shoulders.

"Are you okay, now? Adrian asked.

Teresa arrived and knelt beside Aeron as well. "Honey, what can I get you?"

"Just let me sit here a minute," Aeron replied. "I just need to rest."

Teresa wiped his chest and back with the wet towel. "Do you need to lie down?"

"Yeah," Aeron said. "I wanna go to the sofa."

They managed to make it into the living room where he collapsed onto the sofa. Teresa sat on the floor in front of him and rubbed his arms. "How do you feel, honey?"

Through tears, he complained, "My head feels like it's going to explode again."

Adrian moved around to the back of the sofa and tried to get Teresa's attention. When she looked up at him, he motioned for her to come with him into another room. "Delaney, will you and Seth sit here with him a minute?" Teresa asked.

"Sure, Mom," Delaney said. Even though Aeron seemed calm, Delaney remembered what her brother told her after the last outburst of anger. *Would Aeron really hurt me?* she wondered.

Adrian and Teresa walked into the kitchen. "Should we take him to the hospital?" Adrian asked.

Exasperated, Teresa whispered, "How can we? Do you know what a social worker would do to us?"

"What do you mean?" Adrian inquired.

"Yes, I think there's something wrong, but we can't walk in there with both of your faces red and bruised up. Good God, we'll have Child Protective Services on us faster than you can say 'domestic violence.' It's not like we aren't probably on their radar as it is with Seth."

Adrian placed both hands to his temples and replied, "You're right."

"And how would we explain these rages he's having?" Teresa asked. She clasped her hands together and held them to her lips. She exhaled and removed them. "I'm an attorney for God's sake. How can I walk in there and explain that my son had a moment of temporary insanity where he acted possessed by a demon, and my husband had to hit him like he was performing some kind of exorcism? They'll think we've lost our minds."

Adrian tried to hug his wife, but she forced him away. "Teresa," he pleaded, "please don't push me away. I really had to stop him, so please try and understand."

"Adrian," she interjected, "somebody better explain what is happening to our son, and why you two were in a horrible fist fight! I want a straight answer! I mean it! I'm already feeling guilty for not taking him to the hospital as it is. Please explain what is happening!"

Adrian explained the verbal assault and physical threats in the truck on the way back from their football practice. She was shocked over Aeron's behavior unleashed on both Adrian and Seth. Tears cascaded down both of their cheeks. "All I know is that my son hates and resents me for moving us out here, and now, I don't know what to do!" Adrian sobbed.

Teresa stepped back. "I'll call our doctor and see if he can recommend a good psychiatrist." Teresa rested her head on Adrian's shoulder as she whispered, "I can't believe this is happening to our family. I've prosecuted people for this kind of violence. I feel horrible right now."

As gently as he could, Adrian lifted his hand to the back of Teresa's head and stroked her hair. He ran his other hand down and massaged her back in circular motions. "We'll get through this, honey. I promise."

"I hope you're right," she whispered. Moments later, she looked up and said, "I better get in there and check on Aeron."

"I'll be in soon," Adrian said. "I need to get my keys from the truck."

As Teresa made her way through the dining room and into the stairwell, she noticed someone out of the corner of her eyes. She gazed up the stairs and saw Darcy and Kieran standing on the landing, holding hands. Their stares were hollow, as if completely void of life.

"Are you two okay?" she asked. Neither child responded.

Teresa positioned herself on the first step and asked again. "Please answer Mommy. Are you both okay?"

They said nothing.

After taking a few steps toward them, she demanded an answer.

Darcy and Kieran slowly turned their heads toward each other.

They repositioned them back in Teresa's direction and said together, "Yes, Mommy." They peered up into the second story hallway from the landing and then back at their mother. Teresa's eyes and lips were now contorted with bewilderment. Directly above Teresa stood Lilly and Cain. They were also holding hands with Harriet. The three of them smiled as they peered down at Darcy and Kieran.

"Why are you acting so strange?" Teresa asked, as she took two steps up toward them. "Who are you looking at?" Her hands trembled. As she ascended one more step, Teresa looked upward into the second floor of the house. She saw no one.

Darcy and Kieran released their hands from each other and walked nonchalantly to the second floor. "Kids?" she murmured. They ignored her, so she darted up the stairs and grabbed their shoulders. "Kids!" She whirled the twins around and jostled them about as if waking them from a paralyzing dream. "What's the matter with you two? Why are you acting this way? You're scaring Mommy!"

Darcy blinked her eyes and curled her lips. "Nothing, Mommy, we're fine. Can we go play now?"

Teresa cocked her head. She seemed lost in a sea of uncertainty and dread. "Yes, I suppose that would be okay." She placed her hand under Kieran's chin and raised his head. "Kieran, are you okay?"

He squinted his eyes. "Yes, Mommy, I'm fine. I want to play now." Before the twins walked back into their room, Kieran turned and asked, "Mommy, is Aeron okay?"

"Yes baby," she replied. "How did you know something was wrong?"

"Lilly said he was going to hurt Daddy."

Teresa's hand quickly covered her mouth. After removing it, she responded, "Yes, Aeron is okay, and so is your daddy."

The twins walked to their room and closed the door. Teresa ran back down the stairs and into the living room.

Teresa was whispering to Delaney and Seth when Adrian returned from outside. "Hey boys," Adrian said, "why don't you guys go up and get showers. You've had a lot of football practice in the heat."

Seth stood and extended his hand to his brother. Slowly, Aeron stood and embraced his brother before stepping closer to his parents. "I'm really sorry," he said, as he hugged them.

"Aeron," Adrian replied, "just get showered and we'll talk later." Aeron's eyes started to well up with tears as he nodded his head and pressed on his temples. Seth put his arm around Aeron, and they ascended the stairs to their room. Delaney decided to follow them.

Teresa grabbed Adrian's arm as soon as their oldest kids left the room. After explaining the incident on the stairs with the twins, Teresa and Adrian darted up the stairs to their bedroom to check on them.

Adrian's heart sank as he approached the twins' room.

A nightmarish thought invaded his mind: *What have I done to his family?*

CHAPTER 24

After showering, Aeron walked over to the mirror and began wiping away the condensation. He saw something dark in the hazy reflection, so he turned quickly. To his surprise, no one was there. When he looked back toward the mirror, he saw Seth in the reflection, standing in the doorway.

"Will you stop that! God, every time I think I see something creepy, it ends up being you!" Aeron bellowed.

"Gee, thanks, man" Seth murmured. He walked over to the shower and turned it on. "I hope you saved me some hot water this time."

"Stop whining. I did."

"So, what in the world was wrong with you today?" Seth asked, as he stepped into the shower and pulled the curtain. "You're *really* scaring us, you know."

Aeron gripped the sink and leaned forward. "I honestly don't know. It's like I hear someone telling me to—" Aeron sighed and looked into the mirror, disgusted with the young man he saw glaring back at him in the reflection.

Seth peeked out. "Don't tell me you're hearing voices now."

"No! It's nothing. Forget I said anything."

"You better not try and hurt me when I'm sleeping. I'm serious," Seth warned.

"Relax," Aeron said, "I'm more worried about how you'll hurt yourself when you're in bed alone with your thoughts."

Seth slipped behind the curtain and laughed. "Real funny!" he said. "You're the one with the great imagination."

"I'm gonna finish getting dressed in our room. There's too much steam in here," Aeron complained.

As Aeron walked back into the bedroom, his closet door clicked shut. He picked up his phone and saw several text messages from Whitney. He ignored them and collapsed onto his bed. He massaged his temples, trying to ease the dull ache still plaguing him.

Adrian and Teresa finished checking on the twins. They sensed nothing wrong, even though Teresa was still baffled by their odd behavior earlier. Adrian kissed Teresa and said, "I'm going to go talk to Mrs. Murphy. Maybe she has some answers about the things that football player told the boys today at their school."

Teresa grabbed his arm. "Honey, I think we might upset her if she finds out about the fight between you and Aeron. Please be careful what you say to her."

Adrian kissed her. "I'll be back in time for dinner . . . well, that is if you don't mind starting it without me."

"No, honey, you need to go," she said, "we need answers." She wiped away a tear. "I'm going to check on Aeron."

"Please, if you don't mind. I think his head is still hurting him, so when I get back, we'll see what we need to do," he replied.

A few minutes later, Seth stepped into his bedroom. "Hey, how did you think practice went to—" He saw his brother lying on his side. Thinking he was asleep, Seth walked softly over to his dresser and retrieved a shirt.

"I think it went fine," Aeron said, as he rolled onto his back.

"I thought you were sleeping, Seth replied.

"No, I'm just thinking about today." Aeron sat up.

"Aeron, can I be serious for a minute?" Seth said, as he stepped over and sat beside his brother.

"Yeah," Aeron said.

Seth gazed into Aeron's eyes before quickly looking away. His head drooped toward the floor. "Don't laugh when I say this, but . . ." He turned again to Aeron, only this time, his eyes were filling with tears. In a quavering voice, he said, "You're my best friend, and I love you. I truly mean that, but for the first time ever, I was really scared of you today. I truly thought you were going to kill me or Dad." He lowered his head again and sighed.

Aeron put his arm around Seth and pulled him into his side. "I know I give you a rough time but listen to me . . ." Aeron turned slightly toward Seth. "I promise I would never hurt you—ever—and I'll do everything I can to always be there for you. I would die for you, man. I truly mean that!"

Seth wiped his face with his shirt. "Aeron, I do believe you, and I'd die for you, too. God has given me the best brother I could have ever hoped for in this world."

Tears rushed to the surface of Aeron's eyes. "I won't let you down, man. And I agree that God has given me the best brother, too."

Seth stood, as did Aeron. For the first time in a while, they embraced. "If you need me, I'll be downstairs." Seth smiled and walked out the door while Aeron sat on the bed and rolled onto his back.

Within several minutes, Aeron was asleep.

His closet door opened, revealing Mors standing in the doorway. His rotten teeth were exposed when he smiled at Aeron, whom he intended to take with him in eternity.

CHAPTER 25

Adrian rehearsed several ways to engage Mrs. Murphy in a conversation about the murderous past of their new home. His apprehension, as he approached her door, was akin to the awkwardness of meeting someone's parents before a first date. He simply didn't know what to say.

To his relief, Mrs. Murphy was happy to see him standing at the door. "Oh, Adrian, please come in."

Adrian stepped just inside the doorway. "Hi, Virginia, I'm sorry to bother you, but I just wanted to check and see how you were doing."

"Oh, I'm doing fine, dear. How's your family?" she asked, as she subtly tried to hide the half empty bottle of wine setting on the counter.

The sweet aroma of another pie baking in the oven overwhelmed Adrian's senses. He halfheartedly smiled. "Everyone is fine. Thank you for asking."

The welt on the side of Adrian's face screamed out for attention, which caught the observant eyes of Mrs. Murphy. Trying not to pry for information, she amusingly said, "That's your surprise in the oven for dessert tonight. I was going to take it over soon, but I'll just give it to you instead."

"I have to say, that pie you made for us for our dinner was the best I've ever had," Adrian complimented. "Please don't tell Teresa I said that."

He grinned.

"Why, thank you! I haven't always been able to bake a good pie, though. I had to get used to a gas stove and oven. Many pies didn't survive the baking."

"I did notice the huge tank beside the house. I wondered if it was for oil or natural gas. I'm not the biggest fan of heating oil. It's so expensive." Adrian said.

"Yes, it is, but I haven't blown the house up yet, so I must be doing something right," Mrs. Murphy laughed. She turned and checked the timer on the oven and turned back to Adrian. "You know, that Seth of yours is such a wonderful young man. He actually came over earlier to apologize to me for yesterday. You've raised wonderful children, Adrian. You must be so proud."

"Thank you, ma'am. I guess I kind of needed to hear that today. It's been a rough few days for us." Adrian glanced at the floor. "Look, I'm sorry, but I should have called first before stopping over," he stammered. He looked up and sighed. "I just need to talk to you about something, but you're probably busy, and I shouldn't have bothered you so late in the afternoon."

As he turned to leave, Mrs. Murphy confessed, "I know why you're here." Adrian was surprised at her assertiveness, and he slowly turned back and gazed at her. "You're concerned for the safety of your family." Adrian swallowed hard. "I do understand, you know."

His face was a crimson shade. "I should go," he said.

"No!" she insisted, "I want you to stay and talk with me. How about we take a stroll to the lake and chat for a while," she suggested. "Let me get the pie out of the oven. You can take it with you after we talk."

A few minutes later, they strolled toward the lake. She confessed that she hadn't been entirely forthcoming with him concerning the history of the house, lake, and the barn.

Adrian told her about the conversation the football player had with Aeron and Seth, and to his disappointment, Mrs. Murphy stopped and wiped tears from her eyes. "Yes, a lot of that is true," she affirmed.

"Who was Dolores?" Adrian inquired. "Did she do all those things?"

"As I've mentioned, Dolores was Harriet's much younger sister. Most people believe she and her lover were responsible for the terrible things that happened on the property. That boy was right about them *slaughtering* people while they were still alive. It was so gruesome and evil."

Adrian's scowl revealed his contempt for himself for having chosen such a home for his family, but he needed to know what he was battling. Nausea continued to overwhelm Adrian as he thought about the horrible murders that had taken place on his land—the very land containing his dream home with the people he loved more than anyone in the world.

Mrs. Murphy told him to sit down at the picnic table under the pavilion. "Adrian, what I'm about to say will likely upset you, but I know you want to hear it. Just remember, it's all in the past, and what you are going through as a family is likely nothing more than a bunch of nonsense and coincidence."

Adrian sighed, "I appreciate all this, and you're right, it probably is just my overactive mind analyzing things that aren't real." Adrian's countenance radiated nothing but embarrassment. "Look, I feel ridiculous for even coming to you with all of this, and I know it's hard, but I need to know if I'm dealing with something that might be threatening my kids— something I can't fight against! I can't let anything happen to my—" His breathing was heavy, and his eyes glazed over with tears.

Mrs. Murphy cleared her throat. "Speaking of fights, did one of your boys—say Aeron—do that to your face?"

Adrian looked away and lifted his hand to his cheek. "How did you know it was Aeron?" he asked.

"Let's just say," she stated, "it's not the first time such a thing has happened in that house between a father and his son."

"Virginia, I have to know, so please tell me what is going on around here!" Adrian insisted. "I'm afraid my kids are in danger. Look, Seth keeps getting these mysterious nosebleeds; Aeron acts like he's possessed and going to kill us, and I feel he could do it; and my twins are *supposedly* playing with two kids who drowned in our lake almost a hundred years ago. Virginia, are my kids—" Tears clung to his eyelashes. "Are they going to be okay?" A tear raced down the contour of his cheek as his head drooped slightly toward the ground.

Lifting his chin, she said, "Seriously, you're not the first father from that house to come and talk with me about such things."

Adrian swallowed. "Please, I must know. I can't deal with this anymore. My wife and kids are everything to me, Virginia, and I'll never forgive myself if they get hurt, all because I moved them out here to some crazy *haunted house*!" Adrian stood. "It doesn't even make sense! I mean, come on! Haunted houses aren't even real! They can't be!"

"Adrian," Mrs. Murphy said, as she stood, and grabbed his hands, "I can't explain it all myself, but before I tell you anything further, I have to say that I have fallen in love with your family already, and I am so afraid you'll want to leave."

"I don't want to unless I feel I have to, Virginia."

Mrs. Murphy exhaled. "So, what would you like to know first?" she asked.

"I honestly don't even know where to begin," Adrian said. He sat once more. "I'm curious about the woman in black my boys claim to have seen. Is that Harriet, and did she drown her own kids?"

"Adrian, it wasn't Harriet who drowned her twins; it was Dolores." Adrian's mouth formed an oval, and his head turned slightly from the confusion he felt. "Yes, Dolores was seeking revenge for something that happened to her own child. She had given birth to a boy who lived to the age of 9-years old. His name was Henry. He was the offspring of one of her lovers, whom we believe was named Alastor, but no one was ever sure. That's why there was never a last name on his grave up there. It might have been this man from town named Mors, who also had a son to some other woman. That boy's name was Wyatt. Anyway, Harriet and Dolores were both raised in a strict, religious family, but when Dolores lost Henry, I think bitterness became a cancer to her body and mind."

Adrian's forehead crinkled. "How did Henry die?"

Virginia raised a handkerchief to wipe sweat from her brow. "He drowned in . . . a well." Adrian's eyes bulged in their sockets. "Yes, Adrian, it was the well that Seth fell into."

"Oh God! Virginia, please don't think I've lost my mind, but Seth said it felt as if he was being pulled under by something, but I assumed it was his shoes getting caught on some old debris in the water.

"My grandfather George was supposed to be watching Henry one afternoon, but he must have gotten busy, and the next thing they knew, Henry came up missing. They found a small toy boat bobbing in the well. About an hour later, they brought his poor, young body up from the bottom. It's as if he'd been trapped by something down there inside the well." She saw the shocked expression on Adrian's face. "There's more, honey, if you want to hear it."

Adrian's posture stiffened. "Yes, please tell me." He nodded and listened for her response.

"After Henry died, Harriet would often find Dolores out near the well, playing leisurely with the toy boat they found the day Henry drowned. She'd be humming her favorite lullaby she used to sing to Henry at night."

Adrian shook his head. "This is so bizarre," he said, "but I guess I could certainly understand her grief."

"Well," Mrs. Murphy continued, "not long after Henry died, Dolores asked Harriet if she could take the twins swimming. Harriet didn't suspect that her sister would do anything to the twins, so she agreed. Their bodies were found later, and they somehow got caught up in the weeds at the far end of the lake." I think I mentioned this to you before."

"Didn't Harriet suspect her sister?" Adrian questioned.

"I don't know that for sure, but Dolores claimed she saw some strange person earlier that day around the lake, and so she blamed the whole thing on him. I don't think my grandfather believed her. When he confronted her a few weeks later, after the details of her story changed several times, we think she hit him in the head with some heavy object and strung his body up in some old tree at the far end of the lake. He was hanging upside down, and his eyes had been gouged out." Adrian's eyes watered, as he grimaced. "It was as if Dolores was punishing him for not watching out for Henry the day he drowned. I think that's why his eyes were removed."

Mrs. Murphy swatted away a few gnats.

"What a horrible tragedy," Adrian said.

"Very much so," Mrs. Murphy confirmed. "It all started when those two came over here from Europe on that ship."

Adrian's curiosity erupted in his mind as he'd wondered what truly happened on that ship.

"As I'd mentioned several days ago, a ship was found adrift in the Atlantic, and on it, there were family members of many of the people already living in Inverness."

"What do you think happened?" Adrian asked.

"Harriet and Dolores claimed that another ship attacked them, but I think they murdered everyone on board and stole their possessions." Mrs. Murphy ran her fingertips across her necklace.

"Explain to me why Dolores and Henry lived out here," Adrian inquired.

"Dolores remained in Inverness, but she soon found herself with child."

"Well, I assume that caused a stir in a small town," Adrian surmised.

"Yes, a little, but the murders didn't stop. They started back up when Dolores moved out to the farm." Adrian shook his head. "You see, it was as if Dolores had a scarlet letter on her, like the woman in that Hawthorne novel. She lived in the town of Inverness above a saloon with Henry, but when the locals found out that she wasn't ever married, which she was able to hide for a while—claiming her 'husband' had died, they threw her out and she had to come and live with my grandfather and Harriet."

"So, it was the whole community she was against?" Adrian concluded.

"I guess you could say that, Adrian. Perhaps revenge was the only thing Dolores had left to live for, especially after Henry died. I believe she blamed it on the people of Inverness, because she was forced to move out here, and Henry ended up dying as a result."

"My God!" Adrian snapped. "So, let me get this straight: Dolores comes to live with Harriet and George, and she eventually ended up murdering George and their twins? That's so unbelievable!" Adrian shook his head again and rubbed his temples with his fingertips.

"You see, a profound mystery has always surrounded Harriet and Dolores, especially when they were the only survivors on that ship." Mrs. Murphy shifted on the bench of the picnic table.

"May I ask what they did with the bodies of the people on board?" Adrian's stomach tingled.

Mrs. Murphy cleared her throat and clutched her necklace again. She looked down toward the ground at first before lifting her head and arm at the same time. She pointed at the lake.

Adrian leaped to his feet. "No! You can't be serious!"

"Adrian" Mrs. Murphy said as she grasped his hand. "The original Inverness Cemetery wasn't located on the hill behind your house."

He pointed at the lake. "Are you telling me that our lake is built on a cemetery that was once filled with murdered people?"

Mrs. Murphy stood without releasing his hand. "Adrian, they did remove the bodies before putting in the lake, but those dear souls were never at peace to begin with. They died horrible deaths without getting to say goodbye to their loved ones. Some of the children came over with other relatives on different boats weeks or months ahead of them, so the murdered people never saw their children alive ever again. That would include the people from Inverness who were murdered here as well. There was no closure for *any* of them."

"So, am I dealing with a bunch of grieving souls?" Adrian asked. "If they are still lingering around my property, what would they want with *my* children?"

"Adrian," Mrs. Murphy surmised, "you have to remember, the

children of these immigrants grew up into adults, but they were children when their fathers, and some of their mothers, were murdered on that ship and after Dolores moved out here. To those dear souls, they are still hunting for their small children, not their adult children." Mrs. Murphy grasped Adrian's other hand. "Time stopped for them, but it didn't stop for their children who were already living in Inverness."

Adrian's knees buckled, and he fell back onto the bench of the picnic table. "So, are you telling me that there *might* be people from a hundred years ago who think *my kids* are somehow *their kids* that they never got to see ever again?"

Stepping over to Adrian, Mrs. Murphy sat beside him. "Yes, I think that is a possibility. I've heard of many cases where grieving souls were never at peace because they left so abruptly without getting to say goodbye to their loved ones."

"I guess some of that makes sense," Adrian agreed.

Mrs. Murphy gazed out across the lake, focusing on the far end where her grandfather had been hanging after he was murdered. "Thanks to Dolores and her lies, Harriet believed her husband was murdered by one of the locals, and that's probably why Harriet didn't mind being involved in the killings, or she was just trying to protect her beloved, younger sister. Dolores said that perhaps George was murdered because of an affair. Harriet obviously believed her. Over time, her lies must have convinced the locals that Grandfather George was an insane butcher who slaughtered the people who came up missing. My grandfather would have never hurt a soul."

"But by killing him," Adrian commented, "she made her stories about him practically impossible to prove or disprove. After all, your grandfather wasn't around to defend himself." Adrian said. "So, did Harriet ever suspect Dolores' involvement in George's death?"

"Harriet trusted her sister to completely take care of all the *sinners* in the world." Virginia crossed her arms for a moment. "I believe Dolores, at first, was obsessed with my grandfather's well-being because he had a lot of money. That's what makes me think they stole the money from those on that ship. Greed and jealousy can cause a lot of grief."

"That sounds logical," Adrian concurred. Adrian pressed his fingertips into each temple and shook his head. "So, Dolores kills George to get revenge for Henry, but she blames it on the locals?" He lowered his hands. "Then, she blames the death of your grandfather on the locals?" A burst of air shot from his lips. "Good God, what a twisted mess."

"You see, Adrian, I believe Dolores wanted my grandfather George's fortune, and she also wanted revenge on him for Henry's death. She also hated the locals for throwing her out of the town of Inverness, so she decided to kill some of them off as well by luring men out here to accomplish that very thing. She used Harriet's grief over Grandfather's death to set into motion one of the most tragic, evil plots I've ever known. She also influenced Harriet to turn against the world, in a sense, so that she could eventually blame Harriet for all the murders. I could be wrong, but that's how I imagined it to be."

"Man," Adrian surmised, "she was ingenious, I guess. She murdered people and got everyone to blame everyone else but her."

"Yes, she wanted revenge and got it," Mrs. Murphy said. "She even ended up getting the house and a lot of the inheritance when Harriet was hanged," Mrs. Murphy explained. "Thankfully, my father was the son of Matilda, Grandfather George's first wife. My daddy was already living in another town by the time Harriet came along."

Adrian shook his head and asked, "So how did some of Dolores' lovers end up living out here?"

"After my grandfather was murdered, I believe Dolores convinced Harriet that they needed a man around to protect them, so she had Alastor move in. However, he disappeared not long after that. No one, at the time, ever knew what happened to him. It was rumored that Alastor may have tried to blackmail the sisters for their fortune, and so they did away with him because of it. It must have been hard for them to trust each other. After all, they were all murderers."

"Yes, that makes sense," Adrian said.

"I believe Dolores had her other lover, Mors, chain Alastor in the basement," Mrs. Murphy said. "Don't ask me why she wanted him alive, but—" She stopped and grabbed Adrian's hand. "Do you know they left that poor creature down there in the basement for over a week before he died—likely from dehydration. When they found his body, the constable believed he might have survived for a little while on his own—" She stopped. "Well, you get the point."

Adrian's face grimaced. "Good God, Virginia. I can't believe all this craziness took place on my property!"

"Adrian, there's more, if you're willing to hear it."

Everything around Adrian ceased to exist. His mind closed off all reality, as his throat tightened, blocking any air from moving in or out. He squeezed his eyes shut as he strained to speak. When he opened his eyes, air suddenly rushed in, and he mumbled, "Yes, tell me."

CHAPTER 26

Teresa gathered some laundry and went to the basement while dinner simmered on the stove. The stench of mildew clung to her nostrils as she made her way over to the washing machine and dryer. Her face scowled from the odor of something dead. There was one window in the far end from where the washing machine was located. Two single light bulbs illuminated the entire area. For the moment, Teresa felt trapped in a dank prison seemingly designed for solitary confinement.

When she started filling the washing machine with water, her thoughts were still consumed by the events from that afternoon. Questions regarding Aeron held her mind hostage, and tears surfaced over the thoughts of what his outbursts and violence would mean to her family, as well as her son's future. Since Aeron was resting comfortably in his bed, she thought she would keep her mind occupied, so she gathered some laundry from their room and retreated to the basement.

As she sorted through the clothes, one of Aeron's favorite Ohio State shirts surfaced, causing her to pause. With her fingertips, she spread the shirt open and looked at the emblem. She wanted to smile over the way Seth taunted his brother with threats of buying him a Michigan State shirt, but sadness stole her joy and replaced it with fear of the unknown. Tears cascaded down her cheeks as she wadded up the shirt and held it against her chest. Tears dropped onto the shirt, darkening the scarlet fabric in various spots. Still holding the shirt, Teresa leaned forward and sniffled as her legs weakened. "Please, God. Please protect my Aeron from whatever is plaguing him," she whispered. "Please help us figure out what to do." She wiped her tears away with the shirt before tossing it into the machine.

The wooden panel under the stairs slowly opened with a slight hissing sound emanating from the cement floor. Emerging from the dark cavern was Alastor. He desired companionship, and Teresa was the object of his desire at that moment.

When Teresa closed the lid on the machine, the lights suddenly burned out. A cold chill raced through her tense muscles. Alastor stood motionless as Teresa stumbled around the room, feeling her way to the fuse box. The sunlight struggled to break through the single pane, dirty window on the opposite wall. Her eyes fought to adjust to the sudden darkness.

As she passed the window, a silhouette of her upper body and head appeared in the dimly lit basement. A few steps behind her, another silhouette was in pursuit.

"Thank God," she said, as she finally reached the box. She fumbled through several old packages of fuses that were placed on the bottom of the metal frame inside of the electrical box. As she sorted through them, she heard a squeaking sound coming from the stairs. She turned and dropped the fuses, which bounced across the cement floor like loose coins spilling from a pocket full of holes. Her breaths caused her whole chest to spasm, while her skin crawled from the darkness blanketing her. Teresa wondered if her legs would carry her to the steps, and into the salvation of the lighted kitchen.

Uncertain of the noise coming from the direction she wanted to go, she mustered the courage to move forward. Slowly, she traversed the path to freedom. "Okay, okay, okay . . . I can do this," she whispered. Instinct for survival had somehow taken over her stiffening muscles. She screamed when her foot accidentally kicked one of the fuses she'd dropped earlier. It danced wildly across the floor.

Only a few feet from the first step, the sound of chains dragging across the floor was a clanging cymbal to her ears. The noise caused her to bolt up the stairs toward the kitchen. A surge of adrenaline empowered her nervous, feeble legs to run even faster.

As Teresa reached the door and turned the handle, it wouldn't open, as if blocked by a heavy object on the other side. She started to pound on the door. "Somebody open this door right now!" she hollered. Unbeknownst to her, a thin, rotting hand reached for her ankle as she continued to bang on the door and plead for help. Several inches from her bear ankles, the hand took its final reach. Teresa felt something holding her leg. She kicked wildly and freed herself from whatever it was that held her captive. Her shoe bounced down the stairs. The door suddenly burst open, and Teresa fell into the arms of Aeron.

As Adrian and Mrs. Murphy continued to walk around the lake, Adrian shivered—not knowing whether the reason was due to the gentle breeze, or the story he'd been hearing. "To answer your questions, especially about Harriet," Mrs. Murphy responded, "it was the locals who'd caught on to a few things, such as a couple of the men claiming to be going to the Murphy farm, and then, not returning. Some of their wives went looking for them, of course. They didn't survive either. That left quite a few children without parents. Just as the people on the ship never got to see their children again, the same happened for these poor innocent children from the town." Mrs. Murphy pressed her hands together, as if saying a brief prayer.

"That is utterly horrible for those kids who were left behind," Adrian said. "So, you're right, the people who were killed from Inverness never got to say goodbye either. In their minds, their kids would always be kids to them forever."

"Yes," Mrs. Murphy added, "and maybe that's why your children are so important to these restless souls, whose final resting place is the lake."

"I honestly don't know what to think. There's a war going on in my rational mind, and I'm not sure what to do," Adrian commented. "One thing is certain: We will never set foot in that lake ever again!"

After grasping Adrian's hands, Mrs. Murphy continued. "So, Dolores held on to some of the personal belongings of the men and women they'd killed. However, unbeknownst to Harriet, Dolores—her own sister—hid those belongings in Harriet's room, and one day, when a vigilante group came looking for a murderer, Dolores opened the door and directed them to Harriet's room where they found the items. Can you believe she betrayed her own sister?"

"At this point, Virginia, anything is possible," Adrian scoffed.

"Well, some of the men were enraged at what they'd thought Harriet had done, so they dragged her out of the house and hanged her right out on the front lawn. They didn't even bother with a trial. In fact, they didn't even put her body in a casket. They just dug a hole next to Grandfather George and buried her up there on the hill. I was the one who had a gravestone put above her grave. I did it for my grandfather for some reason."

"So, did they ever catch on to Dolores?" Adrian inquired.

Mrs. Murphy patted Adrian's hand. "Yes, indeed they did. When Mors, the other lover of Dolores, found out how much money she had, he sought to find the fortune and claim it as his own. Dolores must have caught him stealing some of it, and they suspect that she attacked him with a hammer due to the injuries that were found on Mors' body. She must have waited until dusk before dragging his body up the embankment, weighing it down, and dumping him into the lake."

Adrian looked over at the lake and asked, "How did they know what had happened between her and Mors?"

"Well, the next day, the friends of Mors told the constable that he had been bragging about some money he was going to get from his companion, so, while investigating the farm, the sheriff asked to look around the property. Dolores agreed—obviously feeling confident he wouldn't find anything— but when he got to the lake, Mors' body was floating in the middle of it. He came loose from whatever it was she had him attached to before sinking his body."

"Is this the same sheriff, or constable, who did nothing about the vigilante mob that hanged Harriet without a trial?" Adrian asked.

"Yes, Adrian," Mrs. Murphy confirmed, "he didn't stop the mob. However, he ended up shooting Dolores when she pulled out a knife and tried to stab him while he attempted to arrest her for Mors' murder." Mrs. Murphy grabbed her cross necklace. "They did the same thing with her body as they did with Harriet's: They dug a hole and dumped her in it up there on the hill."

"So, that was the end of them?" Adrian asked.

"Yes," Mrs. Murphy responded.

"Virginia, how do you know all this? I mean, how would anyone know the details of things that happened way out here, and behind closed doors?"

"You know, Adrian, imperfect humans always leave some kind of evidence behind. Diaries, letters, and other means always surfaces when you least expect it."

"And I suspect that is the case here!"

"Yes, Adrian, you are correct."

"This is so . . . well, almost too much to take in." Adrian said. "My head is actually hurting."

Adrian looked at his watch. "Shoot, I better get home soon. Teresa is fixing dinner, and I promised I wouldn't be too long."

"Don't forget that I have to send that pie home with you, too."

"Oh, I haven't forgotten," Adrian said. They walked a little farther and Adrian started to laugh.

"What's so funny?"

"You've just scared the hell right out of me with the most terrifying story I've ever heard, and somehow, we abruptly ended our conversation with discussing dessert."

"I guess you're right," Mrs. Murphy chuckled.

As they continued walking to the house, Adrian asked, "Virginia, why did the other families move from our house?"

"The others left," she explained, "because they couldn't handle all the strange things going on around here. You've experienced some of those things, but I believe it's all a coincidence. I don't believe your house is haunted at all."

"What is that supposed to mean?" Adrian anxiously inquired.

Mrs. Murphy backed away and reassured him with a smile. "Adrian, I don't think you have anything to fear. Everything that's happened to your family can easily be explained by something natural. And ever since we first met, I bet your mind has played tricks on you, and that is the power of suggestion. Seth's head injury was strictly an accident, and his nosebleeds have to be from him falling into that dirty well. As for Aeron being so angry lately, the same thing happened to one boy when he moved out here, but it was probably just the stress of relocating to such an unfamiliar location." She patted his upper arm.

"I hope you're right, but I just don't know. I'm a little stuck now because of buying the house, but I really must evaluate whether to stay or sell it and move on," Adrian said.

Mrs. Murphy's head drooped, as she replied, "You're the first family I have really loved living there. I probably blew it by telling you all this nonsense." She looked up, and affectionately gazed into Adrian's eyes. "I don't want you to leave!"

Adrian's somber appearance caused Mrs. Murphy's eyes to shimmer with tears. "Virginia, I don't want to leave either, but I'm afraid for my family, especially my twins."

"To be truthful, Adrian, I was thinking about your twins earlier today. I believe the real estate agent heard that Darcy and Kieran were twins, so she probably mentioned those other twins named Lilly and Cain and how they once lived there, too. Your kids probably used those names for their imaginary friends just so they could deal with the stress of the move. After all, kids that age do have imaginary friends."

"Virginia, I think you're right; I'm only getting all paranoid, I guess." He leaned over and hugged her. "And besides, I didn't say I was going to move, but maybe things will calm down to the point where everything will seem normal again, especially when school starts for the kids. Maybe it's the move that has just gotten to me more than I'd realized." They looked toward the lake. "It is a beautiful place, regardless of the stories."

"Yes," Mrs. Murphy agreed, "it is a wonderful place, especially for raising a beautiful family." She smiled and winked her eye. "I barely know your family, but I can tell you that I really do love you all very much. Please don't leave!" They hugged again, walked back to the house, and she handed him their dessert for their evening meal.

On the way back home, Adrian's thoughts smothered his whole body with terror, but his rational mind refused to allow him to consider that the people from the past had anything to do with the events taking place in and around their new home.

Impossible, he rationalized.

When Adrian arrived at the house, he saw Teresa being comforted by Aeron. "What happened, Teresa?" He placed the pie on the stove and rushed to his wife.

Aeron stood and said, "Mom thinks some guy lives under our basement steps. Can you believe that, Dad?"

Adrian's heart convulsed—his eyes widened. "Aeron Douglas, that is definitely not funny," Adrian blurted out. "Where's the rest of the family?"

"Honey, I didn't call for them," Teresa mumbled. "I didn't want to frighten them. Aeron happened to be walking through the kitchen when I called for help."

After Teresa repeated the story about the basement, Adrian walked to the door, opened it, and flipped on the light. The basement was illuminated once more. "The lights are working now," he said.

"Honey, I'm telling you, those lights went out on me, and I never replaced the fuse!" Teresa insisted.

Adrian turned and said, "Yeah, but they're working now."

He and Aeron went down into the basement and looked under the steps. Teresa walked down part way and leaned over the railing. "Look,

Mom. There's nothing in here at all," he assured her, while closing the panel. Aeron bent over and picked up his mother's shoe.

Teresa grabbed it and returned to the kitchen. Adrian and Aeron followed. "Honey," Teresa said, "maybe I'm overwhelmed with everything happening, but I swear someone was down there with me, and someone grabbed my ankle. That's how I lost my shoe!"

Adrian walked over and embraced her. "Honey, I do believe you, because I really think you heard something down there in the dark. Maybe it was a mouse or something." A trace of guilt spread through his body like a static shock.

Could it be that man under the stairs? he thought.

"I don't know anymore. We haven't been here very long, and I'm already concerned for our safety," Teresa said.

"Look," Adrian said, "let's finish preparing the dinner and just relax together as a family. My head hurts too much to sort it all out right now." He grasped her hands. "Mrs. Murphy sent over another pie, and it sure smelled good while it was cooking."

Virginia finished cleaning the dishes from dinner before retiring to her room for the evening. Knowing she told more than she should have to Adrian, her heart pounded, and her hands trembled when she thought about the coming retribution that might occur. As she nervously meandered up the stairs toward her bedroom, shadows filled the living room walls behind her. Harriet and Dolores emerged at the bottom of the stairs, and their faces were adorned with malevolent grins.

As Virginia opened her bedroom door and stepped in, she shrieked from the shocking condition of her room. It was as if a hurricane had swept through. Her bed was overturned, and the dressers were wide open with clothes scattered about. Broken shards from a mirror were found close to the windows, which were covered with shredded curtains still hanging from the rods.

"Why are you doing this to me?" she cried out—her voice drowning in fear.

Her bedroom door slammed shut behind her, causing her to scream out in terror once more.

"Harriet, you need to stop this!"

As she turned and opened the door, standing in front of her were the decomposed corpses of Harriet and Dolores. Standing between them—waterlogged and swollen—was Henry. He looked up and opened his mouth. Henry's rotted teeth, and his pale, almost scaly tongue, caused Mrs. Murphy's stomach to churn. Just as she was about to scream, a small snake emerged from Henry's throat and slithered out of his mouth.

Mrs. Murphy collapsed.

CHAPTER 27

Reason and logic built a fortress around the Douglas house for several days, protecting them against suspicion and heightened paranoia. Fortunately, for the sake of routine, school was about to begin, and the household somehow felt normal again.

As Delaney was making her way down the hallway from her room that morning, she heard Darcy yell, "Kieran, it's his turn now!"

Curious about the fuss, she popped her head into the twins' bedroom and found Kieran facing one of the corners. He was counting upward to 10. "What are you two doing?" Delaney asked.

"We're all playing a game," Darcy said. "We take turns hiding things, and then we have to search for it. We got tired of that hide-and-seek game."

"Where did you learn this new game, Darcy?"

Innocently, Darcy smiled and replied, "Lilly taught us. She always plays it with Cain."

"So, Lilly and Cain are still playing with you?" Delaney asked.

Darcy pointed over to the opposite corner where Kieran was hiding his face. "Cain is over there with Kieran, and Lilly is over on my bed."

Delaney's forehead wrinkled. "I can't see them, Darcy," she said.

Darcy walked over to her bed and extended her hand. Lilly grabbed

Darcy's hand and walked over to Darcy's much taller, oldest sister. She was practically standing on Delaney's toes. Lilly's curls drooped in front of her eyes, which she brushed aside. "She's right here!" Darcy insisted, as she pointed at Lilly.

Delaney was relieved to see no one, especially after knowing all that she and Aeron had discovered about the *playmates* her brother and sister had been supposedly spending time with in their room. After all, she also had imaginary friends when she was Darcy's age. Delaney bent down and smiled. "It's nice to finally meet you, Lilly. I've heard so much about you lately."

Lilly smiled when she looked at Darcy. "Aren't you going to say something nice about Lilly's dress?" Darcy insisted.

"Oh," Delaney said, "you look beautiful in your outfit, Lilly."

Kieran dragged Cain over to meet his big sister as well. "Delaney, this is Cain. He's my friend—the best I've ever had. We're going to play together *forever*."

Once again, Delaney pretended to formally introduce herself to Cain before saying something nice about his outfit as well. Cain looked at Kieran and grinned. Delaney smiled, patted her brother and sister on their shoulders, and left the room.

Cain looked at Kieran.

Your sister is pretty. She's like Aunt Dolores.

Delaney saw Teresa and reassured her mother that when she was *introduced* to Lilly and Cain, she saw no one in the room. Teresa chuckled. "I can't believe I thought—" Teresa smiled and shook her head.

Later that night, unable to escape the trepidation she felt about attending a new school, Delaney left her bed and walked to the kitchen to make popcorn. She made her way to the living room where she snuggled up on the sofa and turned on the new television they'd purchased. The townhouse was a closet to her, and oftentimes, she felt destitute of any privacy. That night, however, she was the lone survivor on a deserted island in the middle of the ocean, and she didn't want rescued.

A self-proclaimed, hopeless romantic, Delaney finally found a love story she hadn't seen in a while. She nibbled on a few pieces of popcorn as the movie awakened her passions. The boy in the film reminded her of Jake Winters, the boy she'd dated throughout most of last year.

She picked up her phone and glared at it, knowing it could soon bring about her demise. Watching the consequences play out in her head, she paused before quickly returning it to the small table beside the sofa.

A few minutes later, the boy in the movie leaned over and kissed the girl. Delaney sighed before picking up her phone again and scrolling deep into the photo gallery until a picture of Jake surfaced. She studied his photo intently, hoping she wasn't tempted to flirt with the notion of a reconciliation. Her emotions were suddenly at war with her logic, but the curiosity of seeing his photo couldn't be constrained.

A quick glance won't hurt. Right? At least that's what she thought.

She lifted her phone and stared at the boy she hadn't seen in several months. Immediately, she remembered his chestnut-colored hair swooping down just far enough to partially cover his slightly darker eyebrows. His inviting, brown eyes would often hypnotized her when they gazed at each other on a date. Finally, his manly cleft chin and boyish dimples always caused her to grin with excitement when he smiled at her.

Her admiration tempted her to text him, and her hands trembled with both excitement and fear as her finger slid to the letter J.

Cain peaked around the corner into the living room before entering, and Lilly walked into the room behind him. The children held hands as they strolled quietly toward the back of the sofa and stood.

Unaware of the intruders, the anticipation of making contact with Jake was suddenly invaded by painful memories of a bitter betrayal. She truly fell in love with Jake, and as a couple, she stood by him throughout the devastating separation between his mother and father. The challenges to their relationship, however, seemed for a while, to draw them closer together, making them inseparable. After all, he was her first genuine boyfriend; the one she thought seriously about all the time, but Mariah Howard, Whitney's friend, abruptly ended that desire to know him more intimately. Whitney and Mariah—cohorts and best friends—had it all planned perfectly: attract, seduce, and keep Jake Winters and Aeron Douglas at all costs—one set of best friends for another.

Delaney's chest began to quiver as she thought about the occasion when she nearly gave into her most intimate desires on Jake's family room sofa sometime last spring. Delaney remembered gazing into his eyes, but she was unable to speak. The touch of her lips on his was all the conversation she needed to keep his attention at that moment.

Just as Delaney eased her body onto Jake's chest, the close sound of his youngest brother, Austin, startled them. Delaney sat up as Jake rapidly jumped to his feet, grabbing a pillow and holding it in front of him.

Once Austin entered the room, Jake yelled, "Didn't I say we wanted to be alone for a while?"

Dejected, Austin stood by the doorway and stared at his brother. "I was just coming to get another movie to watch in my room," he said.

"Just get it and leave us alone," Jake demanded. While Austin searched for a movie, Teresa, apparently having some kind of maternal premonition, texted a message to Delaney, telling her it was time to get home. With the moment interrupted—the mood diminished—Delaney knew it was best that she leave because she knew how close she had come to abandoning promises she had made to herself—promises she vowed not to compromise until she was with the one life partner she'd asked God to send into her life.

Lilly and Cain sauntered over to an overstuffed chair and sat.

Lounging quietly, gazing at the television, Delaney recalled again the unexpected pain that followed that intimate night with Jake. She soon remembered the rumors that spread like a virus around her previous school just days following that one night at Jake's home. Fortunately, it wasn't about their *close encounter*, but instead, she'd heard that Jake had escorted Mariah to her house after school the following Monday. He had been invited to stay, and after accepting Mariah's invitation to her bedroom, Jake had initiated the beginning of the end of his relationship with the only girl he truly loved.

Delaney was furious, and by the middle of May, their relationship was over. He did everything he could to apologize and make up, but it was a futile effort. Delaney's self-respect was a wall he couldn't scale. Aeron was pretty upset as well, and he and Jake almost ended up in a fist fight because of the betrayal to his sister. That was also about the time when Delaney first heard that Jake had been partying heavily on different occasions. Her heart had been ripped from her chest over the betrayals, and trust was destroyed, leaving Delaney to rebuild from the ruins Jake had left behind.

Adrian and Matt never allowed the drama with Jake and Delaney to come between them and the business; however, it put Adrian in a difficult situation after hearing about Jake's partying. The fact that Jake and Aeron were best friends caused Adrian to wonder if his own son might be involved in some of the partying as well. It later factored into his decision to remove his family from the *city life*.

Cain and Lilly rose from the chair and moved toward the doorway of the living room. Delaney sighed and placed her phone back on the table. As the twins stood together again, they turned and grabbed each other's hands.

When the movie finished its climactic ending, Delaney decided to turn in for the night. She stood and hit the power button on the remote. Once the screen turned dark, only the reflection of the hallway light was visible on the television screen. Unexpectedly, she noticed the silhouette of two small children standing under the archway at the entrance to the living room.

Thinking it was Darcy and Kieran, she turned and said, "What are you two doing up this—" Bewilderment covered her face.

She turned back toward the television and saw the two small children standing in the doorway. Looking back again, she saw nothing.

Adrian and Teresa scurried from their bed, along with Aeron and Seth when Delaney's scream echoed up the stairway and burst into their bedrooms. Delaney quickly turned to run, and as she did, the popcorn container fell to the floor. The pounding of footsteps from upstairs caused some rattling of various objects inside the curio cabinet, which sent even more chills across Delaney's skin.

Lilly and Cain quickly slipped into the shadows to avoid the family members barreling down the stairs. When they darted around the corner and raced into the living room, Lilly and Cain ran up the stairs and to the safety of their closet in Darcy and Kieran's room.

Delaney ran over to Adrian, and they embraced. "What happened?" he asked.

"Dad, I saw two small kids on the television!" she cried out.

Adrian pulled away. "What?" Anger burst from his chest. "What's so scary about two kids on television?"

"Dad, the television was off! I saw their reflection behind me! I swear to God they were standing right there!" She pointed toward the entrance to the room.

Confusion silenced Teresa and Seth. "Are you losing your mind, Delaney? The twins were asleep, so what kids are you talking about?" Aeron inquired. "They might be awake now."

After explaining again what she saw, Teresa said, "My God, Delaney. You fell asleep and dreamed it." Delaney was incensed by her mother's assertion.

"Come on, Delaney. I can't believe you woke us up over something so stupid," Aeron yelled.

"Screw you, Aeron!" she rebuked.

"Hey!" Adrian interrupted, "You two need to knock this off right now before you both wake up your little brother and sister."

Teresa walked over to Delaney and hugged her. "Adrian, she's trembling." Her mother let go and asked, "Okay, honey, are you sure you saw something?"

"Oh my God, Mom," she said in a bitter tone, "I was wide awake. I'm telling you guys that I saw two kids standing right there!" She pointed once again.

"Look," Adrian said, "I think we all just need to go back to bed. This whole move has us so uptight. We just need to settle down!"

Delaney rushed past everyone and stormed up the stairs. Aeron and Seth also returned to their room, annoyed by the interruption to their sleep. Adrian checked on the twins while Teresa sat in Delaney's room, calming her daughter down until she fell asleep. In her heart, though, Teresa was concerned, remembering her own experience in the basement. Her fears returned, and once again, she had another mystery to solve.

The next morning, Darcy looked up from the breakfast table and said, "Hey Delaney, I bet Lilly and Cain are sorry for scaring you last night." Teresa dropped her fork, as Darcy looked into the blank stares of her parents and older siblings.

Teresa reached over and stroked Darcy's hair. "How did you know they scared your sister, honey?"

"We heard Delaney scream, so we knew someone scared her. Lilly and Cain like to play tricks."

Teresa's breathing eased, relieved to hear their rationale for the incident from the night before. "Yes, you're right, it was all a trick by your *friends*, but everybody is okay."

Adrian, who was more than happy to change the subject, asked if Delaney would run Aeron and Seth to football practice that morning. "You have to get your official schedules and room assignments anyway, right?" Adrian asked.

"Yeah" Delaney said.

"My sister is not driving me to practice! I'll drive," Aeron insisted.

"My car . . . my keys . . . so tough," Delaney taunted.

"I'll walk," Aeron said.

Seth and Delaney laughed. "It's five miles, so you better get moving,"

Seth said.

"Come on, Mom!" Aeron pleaded. "Let me take your car, please!" Teresa rested her elbows on the table, folded her hands, looked over the rim of her glasses, and sighed. "I know that look," Aeron said. "We need to leave by 8:30, *Delaney*." He rolled his eyes and left the table.

Soon afterwards, the boys grabbed their football gear before heading out the door to the car. Seth sat in the backseat and as Aeron opened the passenger side door, nearly tearing the door from its hinges, Delaney dangled her keys in front of his face. He turned and stared at her.

"What are you doing?" Aeron asked.

"What does it look like I'm doing?" Delaney replied.

Aeron grabbed the keys and ran over to the driver's side door. He tossed his gear into the backseat and jumped into the car. Delaney laughed and got into the passenger side. Seth rested his head against the window and squeezed his eyes shut. He rubbed the bottom of his nose and looked down at his hand. Relief overwhelmed him.

As they traveled to the school, Aeron contemplated how he might start a conversation about the night before. He went over a few different ways he might approach asking whether his sister really did see what she had claimed. Before he could think of an appropriate way to ask, Delaney looked over at him and asked, "Aeron, do you believe me about what happened last night?" She stared at him, waiting for an answer. "I really did see those kids standing in the doorway."

He turned briefly toward her and replied, "I know you wouldn't lie about something like that," Aeron said, "but I just don't know what to believe." He looked back at the road. "And, I'm sorry for yelling at you about it, too." Aeron glanced over at her. "I just think our minds can play a lot of tricks on us, especially late at night." He refocused on the road. "We've all been anxious over so much weird stuff lately, and the stress of going to a new school might be causing us to imagine things that aren't there."

"Yeah, like the way you think you hear people in your head,"

Delaney said. "Seth's right you know."

Seth sat up and asked, "What am I right about?"

"What is Seth right about?" Aeron asked.

"About you being a jerk!" Delaney chuckled.

"Finally, someone agrees with me, Aeron," Seth said, as he tapped his brother on the shoulder.

"Shut up, Seth," Aeron rebuked. "It's not that I don't believe you, Delaney, but we've never had anything like this stuff ever happen to us before. Why is this happening now?"

"Aeron, I'm telling you that I saw two small kids holding hands in the doorway of our living room. I know it was a reflection in the television screen, but I know what I saw!"

Aeron placed his elbow on the door frame, and with his fingertips, he massaged his temple as he drove farther down the road. Silence filled the car for several minutes.

They were about a mile away from the school when Aeron looked over again and said, "If somebody can tell me what to think about all this, I'd believe it." Looking back at the road, he continued. "I mean, come on, we are talking about two dead kids playing with our little brother and sister, and now everyone thinks they're walking around the house scaring everyone."

Seth leaned forward and said, "I believe you, Delaney, but I understand Aeron, too. Dad pretty much convinced me that all of this is kinda in our heads right now. He says we're just obsessing over it, and maybe even seeing things that aren't real."

"I agree," Aeron said.

"Maybe Dad's right," Delaney said.

"Yeah," Seth echoed from the backseat.

Desiring to change the subject, Delaney asked, "So, what classes do you think you'll have, you guys?"

"Who knows," Aeron replied. "I hope they aren't too tough. I'm trying to get used to this move and all."

"Sorry, brother, but I don't think they have sleeping as a major course for you," Seth teased.

"Real funny. You couldn't pass a class on how to wipe your own—"

"Aeron!" Delaney warned, "he's just joking."

Aeron responded, "I know."

Delaney looked back at Seth and asked, "So, what classes did you fill out on that form the school gave to us a few weeks ago?"

"Just basic classes this semester. I'll take tougher ones next time."

"At least I won't have to put up with Whitney every day in the hallways," Aeron announced, which caused a smile to erupt across Delaney's face. He wanted to tell his sister everything he went through with Whitney, and he also wanted to get Delaney's opinion about a new girl he'd talked with after one of the practices, but he didn't want to deal with the teasing.

"Aeron, can I be honest with you about something?" Delaney said.

"Sure."

"I'm so glad you aren't with Whitney. She was only after you for one thing."

"What do you mean?"

"She only wanted some nice *eye candy* hanging on her arm around school. Sorry, but everyone knew it. She manipulated you right into her life."

Aeron laughed. "You're so full of it. She liked me because of my charming personality and intelligence." The snickering from Seth warranted a glare from Aeron in the rear-view mirror.

"You're the one full of it, Aeron Douglas," Delaney jested. "That girl had her claws into you so deep. And, I heard you weren't the only boy she was with at the same time. She always said you were *her world*, but you weren't the only one *rockin' hers*."

Seth laughed, as he leaned forward again. "Yeah, Delaney, we all know why he stayed with her this long."

"Oh really?" Aeron scoffed. "Well, at least I can get a girl to—"

"Stop! I don't want to hear this! You two drive me crazy," Delaney said.

Aeron reached over and pushed Delaney's arm. "Oh, come on, Delaney, we all know about you and Jake, so don't act so innocent."

Delaney blushed. "I told you not to bring up that name ever again! And besides, nothing *ever* happened between us."

"Sorry. I was just kidding," Aeron replied. "Jake would have told me anyway." Aeron looked over, and Delaney grinned. "I know Jake turned out to be a jerk, but he really did like you. He still does you know."

"Really?" Delaney's face was beaming red again. "I was actually thinking about him last night before I saw—well, you know who."

"He really wants to get back with you—big time," Aeron said. "We talked a couple nights ago, and he really regrets everything, but he's afraid you won't give him the time of day if he called you."

"Well, he should have thought about that before he cheated on me with that little troll he slept with behind my back. And besides, once he started partying, I was done." Aeron looked away—a hint of guilt struck his conscience. Bringing up the subject reminded him of the threats of retribution Whitney used against him in the barn days earlier.

Thankfully, Delaney changed the topic when she asked, "So, darling brother, who is this Brittany I hear is after you in a big way?"

Aeron flashed Seth a look. "You jerk, I told you to keep your mouth shut." Seth and Delaney started to laugh.

"Look, she's really nice, and I would *really* like to ask her out, if you must know," Aeron said—his face still as red as a sunburn.

Delaney smiled. "You know, *Aeron Tyler Douglas*, you are the new stud in town."

"Only in his dreams," Seth mocked.

Ignoring his brother's comments, Aeron asked, "What are you talking about? Besides, you only use my middle name when you are trying to get my attention." He grinned. "Well, you have my attention, so what have you heard?"

Delaney laughed and explained, "I was talking to some new people at our school already. I ran into them when I went up to check the class lists to see where my homeroom was going to be. I met these girls who happened to be talking about this *really hot guy* who just joined the football team. Of course, I introduced myself to them."

Aeron sat up. "Did you tell them you knew me?"

Delaney rolled her eyes. "What do you think, my love-starved brother? Of course, I did *no* such thing! I had to get the scoop you know." Delaney turned the radio down, as she proclaimed, "Yeah, and I asked who the new 'hot guy' was. They told me more about your body than I've ever wanted to know. And they mentioned your *gorgeous eyes* and even your *perfect teeth*. Oh, and of course, they described your *irresistible, charming smile*."

"Yeah, right," Seth choked out the words.

"Shut up!" Aeron yelled. "At least I have a body worth talking about! Now, go on, Delaney. Tell me more."

"Well, apparently, when you go walking around the field and gym shirtless, it is too much for them to handle." Delaney laughed and said, "I have to admit, it was a bit weird listening to them describing you, but I pretended not to know you. In fact, they saw your middle initial on the homeroom list, and they even argued over what your middle name was."

"They argued over my middle name?" Aeron chuckled.

"Yeah, it was really funny listening to them yelling at each other over different guy names that started with the letter T! Did you know your name could have been Aeron Toby Douglas?"

"Did you end up telling them you were my sister?" Aeron inquired.

"Certainly not! I really wanted to hear what else they had to say about you," Delaney teased. "Anyway, one of the girls named Shelley told the other girls to forget about you. Apparently, she plans on having you all to herself." All three of them laughed. "Yeah, baby brother," as Delaney pinched Aeron's cheek, "Shelley has major plans for you according to what she told me."

Aeron grinned again. "Now, are you *really* being serious?"

"Oh, have you already lost interest in that girl named . . . oh, now, what was her name? Have you forgotten her already?" Delaney mocked.

Aeron grinned and replied, "No, but this Shelley seems interesting. Of course, I'm not sure she can handle all this." He ran his hand down his chest and abdomen.

"God, what an ego!" Delaney said, while Seth groaned from the backseat.

"So, are you seriously thinking about asking that Brittany out?" Delaney asked.

"Well yeah, but I need your advice on how I should ask her, especially since I really don't know her that well."

Delaney slapped Aeron's arm. "What, the great *Aeron Douglas* is asking his sister for dating advice?" She laughed. "Now, I've already heard—mind you—that she is *very* interested in you, too," Delaney stated. "So, Aeron, you better not take too long or else she might lose interest. Oh, and please don't mention anything about Whitney. No decent girl will have anything to do with you if she finds out you have that drama queen still hot on your trail."

"Yeah, I suppose you're right," Aeron agreed.

As they pulled into a parking space, Delaney turned toward Seth and said, "And I also need to warn you, my handsome baby brother, that some of those girls have big plans for you, too."

"Really?" he inquires. "Like what?"

Delaney grinned and winked. She reached back and pinched his cheek. "You'll just have to wait and see."

Aeron got out of the car and grabbed his football gear. He laughed and replied, "Oh man, Delaney, he wouldn't know what to do with a *real* girl." The brothers pushed each other as they headed toward the field. "Hey, sis, don't forget to get our schedules, too," Aeron said. "I'd like to know where to find my classes before starting school."

"I won't forget. And I'll be back to get you around 12:00," Delaney said. "And, I believe you have something else you need to take care of today."

"Yeah, I'll ask her out, just so you'll get off my back." Aeron grinned.

CHAPTER 29

After their family prayer, a party atmosphere erupted at the dinner table the evening of the first day of school. The Douglas children amused their parents, and each other, by retelling their experiences from that day. To Aeron, contentment was finally beginning to take up residency in his soul; he was full of life once more.

Aeron looked at Delaney and chuckled. "Hey, Dad" Aeron asked, "what does PDA stand for?"

Delaney glared at her brother, wishing she had a roll of duct tape for her brother's mouth.

"What?" Teresa inquired. "Was a student caught in the hallway making out with someone on the first day of school?"

"No," Aeron replied, as he taunted his older sister with a smirk. "But if the girl had a *Chance*, I bet she would have!"

Unable to restrain her wrath, Delaney unleashed on her brother. "Aeron Tyler Douglas, you are such a jackass!" Delaney yelled.

"Exactly," Seth agreed. "That's what I've been saying!"

Kieran looked up from his plate and asked, "Daddy, what *is* a jackass? Delaney and Seth call Aeron that all the time."

Adrian patted his son's shoulders. "It means that Delaney thinks your brother is some kind of donkey, right Delaney?" Adrian raised his eyebrows at his daughter.

"Mom," Delaney pleaded, "I think Aeron needs to tell you about Brittany." She smirked at her brother and asked, "Don't you agree, Aeron?"

Aeron looked over at Seth, who had a napkin up to his mouth. Aeron snickered and said, "I guess someone has some *splainin'* to do, right Delaney?"

Teresa placed her elbows on the table and rested her chin on her hands. "Yes, young lady, it sure sounds like someone does have some *splainin'* to do." She then looked at Aeron and smiled. "And so does someone else at the table tonight."

Before Delaney could respond, Kieran tugged on Adrian's shirt and asked, "Daddy, what's PDA?"

Aeron laughed and explained, "It stands for 'public display of affection.' That means Delaney got caught hanging on a guy in the hallway." Kieran's nose crinkled with disgust.

Darcy thrust her hand to her mouth and giggled. "You mean you really touched a boy at school? That's gross!" Darcy said.

Delaney's expression was an explosion of fury; however, she smirked back at Aeron before saying, "Yes, the *captain of the football team* asked me out, Mom, and after he helped me with my locker, I thanked him with a hug before he walked me to my class." She scowled at Aeron and taunted, "At least it's nice to run into a gentleman once in a while."

Teresa winked and replied, "Oh, the *captain* of the football team. Gee, I married a guy who was the captain of his football team. Right, Adrian?" She batted her eyes at her husband and said, "Honey, I'm sure you looked *very sexy* in your football uniform as you ran up and down the field! I wish I would have known you then, babe." Darcy's laugh was like the squeal of a mouse caught in a trap, while Kieran's mouth was wide from the shock of his mother's words. Aeron and Seth broke into laughter as Delaney glared at her brothers, knowing her mother helped to somewhat settle the score. "I bet this new guy is *hot*," Teresa said.

"Oh, trust me, Mom, he *definitely* is," Delaney replied. "In fact, he's the best-looking guy I've ever seen. Girls were even panting as he walked by." She sneered at Aeron, who rolled his eyes.

"Yeah, right! Only you would hang all over the biggest nerd there!" He grinned. "Then again, that makes him the perfect match for you, sis! And there's no way he has guns like these!" Aeron flexed his biceps and kissed each arm before glaring back at Delaney, whose stomach tightened from her eruption of laughter, along with everyone else at the table.

"Dad!" Seth hollered.

Kieran dropped his fork as Seth looked down at his plate and then up at everyone who was staring at him. Blood was gushing from his nose and down the contour of his chin. It dripped into his mashed potatoes when he suddenly leaned forward.

Adrian, who was sitting at the end of the table next to Seth, jumped up and grabbed his napkin. "Oh my God, Seth!" he yelled. "What did you do?" Adrian pressed the napkin to Seth's face.

The napkin muffled Seth's voice as he insisted, "I was just sitting here laughing, and all of the sudden, it started!"

Teresa rushed to get another napkin from the buffet. She hurried over after ordering Aeron to get some ice from the freezer. Aeron's stomach churned from the sight of the blood, so rather than arguing, he gladly obeyed her order.

The rushing around of their parents startled the twins. Darcy started crying. "Mommy, why is Seth bleeding? Is he okay?"

Teresa looked over at Darcy, "Yes, honey, it's just a silly nosebleed. He'll be fine." She ordered Aeron to take the kids into the kitchen with their plates, once he'd returned with the ice.

Teresa's heart sank into her gut. "Adrian," she cried out. Worry was etched into her face.

As Adrian held his napkin up to his son's nose, Seth snapped, "This is crazy, Dad! Why do these keep happening?"

"You were laughing hard a second ago, so maybe that's what started it. It'll stop. We just need to give it time," Adrian reassured his son.

Teresa bent down and placed her cheek against the side of his head. "It's just a nosebleed, honey! Remember the doctor telling us that you might have caused some sinus issues when you got that old water from the well in your nasal passages? That's why he put you on the antibiotic." Teresa looked up at Adrian again, widening her eyes.

As Adrian and Teresa stood at the table, tending to Seth, a reflection of someone appeared in the glass of the cupboard door behind them. The mysterious image moved upward and hovered above Seth, who gagged from the taste of previously chewed food now mixed with the salty taste of blood. The apparition remained transfixed on Seth, as if admiring a famous painting in a gallery. When Seth stood, the image also rose higher and continued to levitate above him.

Delaney suddenly screamed. The intruder bolted from the room through the ceiling, disappearing like a mist being evaporated by the sun.

Both Adrian and Teresa jumped, which caused Seth to shout, "Ouch, Dad! That really hurt! Be careful with my nose!"

"Sorry, son!"

Teresa wailed, "What is wrong with you, Delaney?"

"I saw someone's reflection in the glass!" Delaney continued to gaze up at the ceiling. "It was like a shadow of someone, but it was cloudy and white. I could see it right behind you guys, but only higher above Seth!"

"Honey, it could have been a reflection from something outside, for God's sake! Maybe a passing car!" Adrian said.

"No, Dad! I really saw someone. It hurried away when I screamed. It just flew upward and disappeared."

Aeron, who'd rushed back into the dining room earlier when Delaney screamed, stood behind her, listening to what she'd described. When he spoke, she shrieked again.

"Ouch! Watch it, Dad! You jerked my nose again!" Seth pushed his dad's hand away.

"Delaney!" Teresa shouted. "Stop screaming! You're scaring all of us!"

"Fine, I'll stop, but I am telling you I saw someone in here with us!"

After helping Seth from the table, Adrian told Aeron to dump Seth's plate and wash it off. "Why me?" This time, he protested. "It's got blood on it."

"For God's sake, Aeron, just do as I told you!" he demanded.

Once they reached the upstairs bathroom, Adrian helped Seth remove his blood-stained shirt, as Teresa retrieved a wet washcloth to clean off his face.

When Adrian left to get another shirt, Seth looked up. "Mom, please tell me what's happening to me! I heard that the boy who lived here before us had the same thing happen to him all the time."

"Honey, I've already told you what the doctor said. You'll be fine. The infection will go away soon." Teresa got down on her knees and finished wiping off her son's face. The delicate feel of the cotton washcloth soothed his nerves, allowing his breathing to find a peaceful rhythm. Teresa eased her hand up to Seth's cheek. "I love you, sweetheart. Everything's going to be fine."

"Mom, I'm really scared. I don't understand how this happens so fast. What am I gonna do if I start having one at school, or even during football?"

Teresa brushed her hand through his hair. She whispered, "Honey, I'm upset, too, but the doctor isn't overly concerned, so I think we will just have to wait. Medication takes time to work. We'll check into it when we go get your stitches out tomorrow." Before she could stop it, a tear rolled down her cheek. Seth handed her a tissue. Teresa smiled and whispered, "Thank you, honey."

Later that night, Teresa looked up information about the reason for nosebleeds in teens. Her tears blurred the computer screen. As if in a race, two tears raced down her face at the sight of one word: *leukemia*. Eventually, she shut down her computer and slipped into her bed. Her mind was filled with images no mother should have to imagine.

Adrian put his arm around her and kissed her lips. He knew what was dominating her thoughts. "He'll be fine, babe. I promise," Adrian whispered. Teresa sniffled a few times, as Adrian held her, gently rubbing her arm.

Delaney slipped into her parent's room around 11:30 that night. "I can't sleep," she whispered.

"What's the matter, honey?" Teresa asked, patting the bed, inviting her to sit down.

"I'm worried about Seth, and I swear to God, you guys, I saw something cloudy hovering above him while he was bleeding at the table. It rushed away when I screamed."

"Can you describe it again?" Adrian asked.

"It looked like the shape of a person, and it was also right above him, watching what was going on."

As the conversation continued in one bedroom, Seth tossed in his bed several times, battling his sheet like he was struggling to escape a straitjacket. Seth wondered about his nosebleeds, and he shivered when he recounted the taste of the blood in his mouth. He sighed. When he closed his eyes, the sensation of falling into the cold, black water of the well haunted him once again.

What was grabbing his ankles? Why couldn't Aeron pull me out right away? He wondered.

The only comfort he had was the fact that the well had been finally covered with some boards. He rolled over once more, checking his nose for anything moist.

By 1:00 A.M., the entire house was engulfed in a serene stillness, especially after an evening of uncertainty and fear

CHAPTER 30

After arriving home from the doctor's office with Seth, Teresa started dinner as Delaney and Kieran set the table. Shortly after the clock in the hallway chimed six times, Adrian pulled into the driveway. When he walked into the kitchen, Kieran and Darcy ran to him for a hug. Their embrace always lifted his spirits, giving him a euphoric sense of comfort, and they grinned from the affection he willingly returned. He walked over to Teresa and kissed her.

"What's up with Aeron?" Adrian inquired. "I got a text from him, and he said not to pick him up after practice. I texted back, but he didn't respond."

Seth and Delaney smiled. "I bet his *new girlfriend* is bringing him home tonight," Delaney said. Adrian and Teresa smiled—a sense of peace embraced their hearts.

"So," Adrian inquired, "everything good with the doctor visit?"

Teresa smiled and nodded. "Yes, the stitches are out, and Wes still insisted that Seth's nosebleeds are nothing more than the result of an infection. He did some blood work, but he told me not to worry about—" Teresa stopped.

"Worry about what?" Delaney asked. Teresa shook her head and squeezed her eyes closed. A tear seeped from the corners of her eyes. She turned away quickly and grabbed a paper towel.

"We'll talk later," she whispered, as she continued cutting the lettuce.

As the family continued to prepare the meal, a car pulled into the driveway. Brittany turned down the radio and looked over at the boy she desperately wanted to kiss. "Thanks for running me home," Aeron said.

"Sure. I don't mind."

Aeron nervously stared at her. He swallowed. "Well, I guess I should get inside and get a shower." He reached for the door handle but turned back toward her. A wave of confidence struck him. "You know I'm kinda grimy right now, but I'd still like to kiss you goodbye."

A grin spread across her face. "Hey, just so you know, I love a guy who isn't afraid to get dirty during a good workout."

Aeron snickered and replied, "Oh, really? Well, trust me, I had a good workout, and I love a girl who doesn't mind getting dirty." Aeron's eyes swelled from the sudden jolt of his mind replaying what he'd just said. It was something he would have blurted out to Whitney—not the girl seated beside him.

What are you thinking, Aeron? Tone it down, dude!

"I'm really sorry. I didn't mean for it to come out like that. I meant that I was glad you aren't afraid of being next to a guy who's all messy . . . and . . . umm . . ." Aeron grinned, hoping she might say something to help bail him out.

Brittany grinned. "God, I just love that smile of yours! Your dimples get to me. That was the first thing I fell for when I saw you up close at your practice one morning."

Aeron looked out the window, trying to see if anyone was spying on them. He licked his lips. A familiar tingling sensation erupted deep inside of him. "I . . . ah . . . can't wait until after the game on Friday."

"Me too," she said. "I'm glad you finally asked me out." She tapped her fingers on the steering wheel, anticipating what Aeron might say next. Moments passed—the awkward silence was smothering them. "Do you like Inverness High?" she asked, even though she wasn't sure why.

"Yeah, it's okay." He started tapping his foot on the floor mat. "It's definitely smaller that my last school."

They suddenly spoke each other's names at the same time. "I'm sorry," Brittany said, "you go ahead."

"No, you go. I can wait," Aeron replied.

Brittany smiled and pulled a strand of her hair out of her face. "I was just going to say that I didn't know if you wanted me to drive this Friday."

Somewhat embarrassed that he didn't have his own car yet, he nodded and said, "Sure, if you want to, but are you sure you don't want to ride around in my mom's car? It's not a Mustang, but I guess a BMW isn't too bad either." They laughed.

"It's whatever you want, Aeron. It might be easier if we just take mine."

"Sure," Aeron agreed.

"On one condition, though," Brittany said.

"What's that?"

"You must open the door for me, and you have to do all the driving."

"Absolutely." Awkwardly, he put his hand on hers.

"Well, I like where this is going," she teased.

Dang, boy, you gotter goin'!

"Hey, you wouldn't be too afraid to kiss me goodnight, would you?" Aeron asked. "I know I'm all dirty and stuff, but—" Before he could finish his sentence, she leaned over and kissed him. Aeron smiled. "God, that didn't take much persuasion."

"Nope, not really." Brittany whispered. "When I see something I like, I don't hesitate to make go after it."

Seth stepped out the door from the sunroom and gestured for Aeron to come inside. "I guess I need to go." Aeron shook his head as he rolled his eyes. "Hey, Brittany," he said, "please don't say anything if Seth isn't at school tomorrow."

Brittany scrunched her eyebrows and tilted her head. "What do you mean?"

As Aeron reached for the door handle, he threatened, "I'm just gonna strangle him tonight for interrupting us. That's all."

Brittany laughed, as Aeron stepped out of the car. Brittany leaned over and said, "Hey, Aeron."

He leaned down and looked back into the car. "Yeah?"

"Don't kill your brother because I have a couple friends interested in him." She smiled once more.

Aeron snickered. "I didn't know you had dorks for friends."

"Now Aeron, you shouldn't say such things about a hottie like Seth."

"Oh please. He wouldn't be hot even if he was on fire." They chuckled. "Hey, thanks again for running me home."

"It was *definitely* my pleasure." Her grin made Aeron burn with desire. "Call me tonight."

"*Definitely*," he said. "Right after I kill my brother."

"You're so bad, Aeron Douglas." Brittany responded. "Hey, that reminds me of something I've been wanting to ask you."

"Sure."

"What *is* your middle name?"

"Tyler. It's my dad's middle name, too."

"Aeron Tyler Douglas. I love it!" Brittany said with a grin.

"You need to stop doing that," Aeron said.

"Doing what?" Brittany's eyes blazed with curiosity.

"Grinning at me like that," Aeron said with a seductive smile.

"Why? Does it make you happy?"

"Yeah, and something a little more than that." Aeron's gaze caused Brittany's heart to throb inside her chest. Their flirting was taking their minds in places they both wanted to explore, and they knew that Friday night could be that time.

"Well, I guess I'll have to keep doing it, then. Sorry for you."

Seth popped his head out the back door. "Hey, it's time for dinner." He waved to Brittany before leaning back into the house and closing the screen door.

"Don't you dare lay a hand on him. I need him alive." Brittany chuckled.

"I'll leave him alone tonight, but I can't guarantee his personal safety if he ever interrupts us again."

Brittany laughed. "I think you can control yourself." She started the car. "Now, go get a shower. I can't be seen in public with some guy who is all dirty. I have a reputation to uphold."

"Yes, ma'am. I'll take care of that right now."

"I'll see you tomorrow, Aeron."

"I can't wait," he replied. "Be careful going home. Text me when you get there."

"I love you, too," she said—her eyes glowing with excitement.

Aeron's head turned slightly, as confusion took control of his mind. "Huh?"

"You said 'be careful,' which is like saying "I love you." Brittany raised an eyebrow, expecting him to agree.

"Hummm . . ." Aeron mumbled. "I never knew that." He tapped the door. "Okay, then, I guess that's what I meant."

"I'll see you tomorrow, and you *be careful* as well," she replied, before backing out of the driveway.

After waving to her, Aeron stood in the driveway until she drove out of sight. "Whoa. That was definitely intense," he said under his breath. He grinned and walked toward the back door. Once inside the house, Aeron saw Seth in the kitchen. He grabbed his brother around the neck with his arm and held him in a headlock. "I could kill you!" Aeron said.

"What did I do?" Seth asked.

"I had her going, and you ruined it." Aeron released Seth.

"Yeah, right!" Seth mocked in a childish tone.

"Hey everyone," Aeron said, as he walked into the dining room where the rest of the family was setting the food on the table. Their faces were glowing with intrigue. "I . . . ah . . ." His eyes scanned the room, which was filled with curious onlookers with smiles stretching across their faces. Seeking the quickest retreat, Aeron said, "I'm going to grab a quick shower before dinner."

"Yeah, you do that," Adrian teased. "Oh, I can turn off the hot water if you'd like."

"Real funny, Dad," Aeron responded.

Kieran tugged on Adrian's shirt and asked, "Why would you turn off the hot water for him, Daddy?" Adrian chuckled and rubbed Kieran's head. He explained he was only joking. Kieran squinted his eyes and cocked his head.

"You'll understand it someday, buddy," Adrian said.

After throwing his football gear on the floor in his bedroom, Aeron grabbed underwear and strolled to the bathroom for a shower. After several minutes, Seth banged on the door and yelled for him to hurry up. "Can I get a shower without people bothering me?" Aeron yelled.

"Mom sent me up 'cause dinner's been ready for five minutes now."

"I'll be done in a minute!" Aeron hollered.

"Is that all the time it takes you these days?" Seth laughed as he closed the door.

When the door closed, it revealed that the man in black had been standing behind it. Steam pouring over the top of the shower curtain as the man stood and observed what Aeron was doing.

Aeron rolled his eyes, but soon chuckled at his brother's inuendo.

When he opened the shower curtain and reached for his towel, he was alone, once more, in the bathroom. After drying off, he slipped on his underwear and walked back to his room. Delaney was coming up the stairs as he walked down the hallway.

"For God's sake!" she said.

"What?" Aeron murmured.

"I know you think you're the stud of the house, but would you mind not walking around in your underwear all the time." Aeron ignored the comment. Delaney followed him to his room but stood outside in the hallway. "So, Brittany brought you home?" she asked.

"Yeah."

"So, are you still going out with her after the game this Friday?"

"Yeah."

After slipping on his shorts, he walked by her and said, "I'll see you downstairs."

"Gee," Delaney said, "I'm glad you know more words than '*yeah.*'"

Aeron took a seat at the table, while Adrian asked him if he owned a shirt.

"Why?" Aeron asked.

"Well, it might be nice if you decided to wear one at the dinner table once in a while." Adrian reached over and slapped Aeron on the shoulder and grinned. "How about you say grace tonight, if and when your sister gets down here," Adrian suggested.

Adrian yelled up at Delaney and told her to hurry back to the table. Even though Teresa and Adrian frowned heavily on any technology at the table, Delaney was afraid she'd missed a call or message from Chance Hilliard.

As she searched for her phone, a stranger darted past the door and appeared to glide down the hallway. Delaney didn't notice. Seconds later, another figure floated past her door. She stopped searching and stood up straight.

"Aeron? Is that you?" No one responded.

She walked over to the doorway and looked toward Aeron's room. In the opposite direction, and farther down the hallway, two children quickly ran from her parent's room and into the twins' bedroom. Delaney turned toward her parents' room but saw nothing. She walked back into her room and saw her phone on the dresser. She retrieved it and raced for the stairs.

Adrian and Seth were teasing Aeron about his new love interest as Delaney entered the dining room. Aeron flexed his chest muscles several times and said, "What girl could ever resist this?"

Delaney rolled her eyes and said, "Would you like me to start a list?" Teresa chuckled at their taunting of each other.

"Shhhhh. Aeron's going to say the prayer tonight, so let's all listen,"

Teresa announced.

They all bowed their heads as Aeron recited a familiar prayer.

As they passed the food around the table, Adrian looked at Seth and inquired about the doctor's visit. Seth tilted his head downward and showed his father the scar. "I can't really see it," Adrian responded. "Your hair has grown over it so much."

Kieran got up from the table. "Let me see, Seth." He walked over to his older brother and looked. "Yeah, Dad's right, you can't see it no more."

"*Anymore*, honey," Teresa said. "Now come and sit so we can eat."

Relief dominated the atmosphere, and most of all, their time together felt ordinary, something they all desired.

Later that evening, Adrian slipped into bed and moved close to Teresa. He pulled the covers up and kissed her. "I love you, babe."

"I love you, too." She rested her head on his arm. Moments later, a tear rolled from Teresa's eye and ran down Adrian's arm as it meandered through a maze of hairs. "Honey, I'm so afraid Seth might have—"

"I know what you're thinking, Teresa. I've looked up leukemia as well, and I really don't think it's that. Seth will be fine. We wouldn't even be dealing with this if it weren't for the well incident."

"Try being a mother, Adrian. It's not easy."

"Yes, and our kids are the luckiest kids in the world. You're an amazing mother. We'll get through this." Her flesh pressed even harder against his side.

Teresa lifted herself up and leaned on her elbow. "Honey, you never did tell me everything you and Mrs. Murphy discussed recently. I've been asking, but you seem to be avoiding me."

"All I can tell you is that she told me about some people who lived here years ago, and about the town of Inverness. Nothing worth repeating."

"Did she say anything about the people who lived here before us?"

"Yeah, but they simply left. They must have found a better place near a city."

Adrian rolled onto his side away from Teresa. She reached out and rubbed his back. She leaned up and kissed his shoulder. Adrian turned over toward her and kissed her on the lips as she eased onto her back. "I've missed you," she said. Adrian moved closer toward her, and they locked one of their hands together.

Nearly two hours later, as Adrian and Teresa slept, the rocker in their bedroom moved back and forth as Harriet rose and wandered toward the door. Displeased, Harriet was concerned Teresa might have enough influence over her husband to cause him to uproot the family and move away.

The children—she can't lose the children!

When she reached the door, she turned back and glared at Adrian and Teresa.

You both must die!

In the boys' room, Seth sat up and turned in his bed. After placing his feet on the floor, he stood and walked to Aeron's bed and sat.

Aeron awakened. "What's wrong," Aeron whispered.

"I can't sleep. I think Mom suspects something really bad might happen to me."

"What do you mean?"

Seth sighed. "I overheard her talking with the doctor, and he said he wanted to double check my white blood cell count. He mentioned *leuko* something. Why do you think he needed to do that extra bloodwork?"

"Probably looking for some kinda infection," Aeron inferred. "I wouldn't worry about it."

"I see a lot of worry in their faces when I get a nosebleed."

Aeron sat up. "To be honest, I've been praying about it a lot lately."

"You have?"

"Yeah, and I think everything will be fine," Aeron reassured his brother.

Seth stood and walked toward his bed. He crawled onto his bed and rested on his back. "Hey, Aeron."

"Yeah?"

"Thanks."

"No problem. I love you," Aeron said.

"I love you, too. Thanks for always looking out for me."

"I always will. I promise."

Seth smiled and rolled onto his side. He closed his eyes and prayed silently, thanking God first for giving him the best family he could have ever hoped for in this world.

CHAPTER 31

The Tigers celebrated their victory over one of their local rivals that Friday night. A feeling of normalcy swept over the Douglas family as they sat together and cheered for Aeron and Seth, along with their teammates. Teresa's mind replayed the numerous times that Seth's unexplained nosebleeds had plagued her thoughts, sending waves of panic over her.

Thankfully, nothing happened that night during the game, and Seth appeared to be at peace.

Several guys from school found their way to Delaney, who, uncharacteristically, didn't seem to mind the attention for some reason. Her focus, however, was on Chance Hilliard, and their plans to meet up after the game.

Delaney's heart fluttered like the wings of a moth dancing round a flame, and her stomach twisted into knots when she saw Chance coming out of the locker room with his gear over his shoulder. Several girls were there to greet him, but he knew who he was really looking for. Delaney waved at him, and he returned the gesture.

After making his way over to the bleachers, he'd finally reached Delaney. "Mom and Dad, this is Chance Hilliard," Delaney said. Adrian and Teresa shook his hand. "Chance, these are my parents, Adrian and Teresa."

"Yes, Mr. Douglas, we met the first day you brought Aeron and Seth to practice."

"Yes, I remember," Adrian said. "It's nice to see you again."

"You, too, sir," Chance replied.

Delaney turned around as Darcy and Kieran peeked out from the sides of their parents. "And these two are Darcy and Kieran." Both kids giggled.

"Wow," Chance said to Darcy, "you look a lot like your sister." She put her hand up to her mouth. "And you," he said, as he leaned down to Kieran, "look just like Seth."

"See Dad, I always tell you everybody says I look like my brother!" he bragged.

Adrian smiled and congratulated Chance on the win, and he invited him to dinner with them that night. Delaney grinned and replied, "Well, Chance already asked me out tonight, so I think we'll just find another place to go if you don't mind."

"Sure, honey, no problem," Adrian said. "And thank you, Chance, for being such a good friend to Aeron and Seth. They've really needed one. It's hard getting used to a new school.'

"No problem, Mr. Douglas. I guess I can keep hanging out with Aeron, without too much damage to my reputation." Chance smirked, as Adrian and Teresa laughed. Delaney blushed when Teresa winked at her and raised her eyebrows with a resounding approval.

Adrian and Teresa were invited to dinner with Chance's and Brittany's families, but not before Adrian told Aeron to be home by 11:30, and Delaney by midnight. Adrian was disappointed that Delaney and Aeron weren't joining them, but Teresa was relieved to find some adult companionship in an otherwise isolated new world.

Once Aeron and Brittany pulled into the driveway at the Douglas home after the game, Aeron turned off the car and sat quietly for a moment.

When Aeron placed his hand on hers, her stomach erupted into spasms, and her heartbeats pounded like the thundering hooves of a horse running a race. She was hoping that he'd make the first move. "That was so funny the other day when I dropped you off here at your house. You were so sweet," she said.

"Yeah, at least I was able to shower before I left the locker room tonight." Brittany glanced down at her outfit, hoping it was attractive enough for Aeron.

After noticing her gazing at her own outfit, Aeron said, "You look amazing, Brittany."

Aeron's breathing intensified when she turned in her seat and replied, "So do you. I've waited all week for us to be alone again."

"So have I," Aeron anxiously said. He turned sideways as well. "Can I say something without you taking it the wrong way?" he asked. Thankfully, the outside light on the house illuminated just enough of the interior of the car so they were able to gauge each other's facial expressions.

"Sure," she said.

"When I first moved out here, I hated it, but I had no idea I would meet someone like you. Spending time with you has been the best thing that's happened to me in a while."

Brittany tilted her head. "Why would you think I might take something like that the wrong way? That was really nice, Aeron."

He beamed. "Well, I thought you might be thinking that I was just using you as a way to keep my mind off of the move, but honestly, you're the most amazing girl I've ever met."

Brittany snickered. "Oh, come on, Aeron *Tyler* Douglas. I bet you say that to every girl you're interested in."

Almost embarrassed at sounding more cliché than he intended, Aeron said, "No, I honestly meant that. You're the most beautiful girl I've ever met!"

Her heart danced wildly, and she couldn't resist his advances. Aeron leaned over and kissed her. Her hand reached around to the back of his head, just as his hand did to hers. They soon withdrew from each other. Her grin caused his stomach to tingle, like freefalling from a cliff.

Aeron reached over and placed his hand on hers again, which was resting on the console. Their eyes were fixed on each other. Moments later, their intimate relationship was forged with another passionate kiss, and the joining of their hands. His breaths were short, and he began to sweat as the desire raged within him like a caged animal.

Appearing in Delaney's upstairs bedroom window was Dolores and Harriet. Their silhouettes were highlighted slightly from the light beaming in from the hallway. Obviously displeased with the activity they were witnessing in the car below, a dull grumble vibrated from their chests and reverberated throughout the bedroom. They gazed at each other and stepped back into the shadows.

Moments later, the sound of blunt objects being hurled against the walls emanated from the boys' room. The upstairs doors slammed shut. An angry, demonic scream pierced the air and echoed down the hallway.

Once Aeron and Brittany stepped into the kitchen, he pulled her close and kissed her once again. Aeron's will had been broken, as Brittany wrapped her arms around him. Aeron was gasping for air when he suddenly pulled away from her. Their eyes were filled with an intense craving for more intimacy, but they were unable to move for several seconds.

Brittany could hardly breathe as she reached forth one of her hands and locked fingers with Aeron's hand. Surprising herself with the boldness that leapt from her own lips, she whispered, "Where's your room?"

"Upstairs," he replied. His nerves were firing like cannons.

Aeron pulled her along through the kitchen and dining room. When they made it to the stairs, they raced to the top and soon arrived at his bedroom door. "Are you sure no one is coming home anytime soon?" she asked.

"They shouldn't be."

Aeron struggled to push the door open. After he turned on the light, they suddenly stopped. "What the—" Aeron bellowed. Scattered throughout the room were personal objects, along with overturned furniture. The sheets on his bed had been shredded, and his clothes were tossed about as if swept up by a violent windstorm and left to settle after the gale suddenly dispersed.

"God, Aeron, you might want to learn some organizational skills before inviting a girl into your bedroom." She chuckled, but suddenly ceased when she noticed Aeron's face drenched in rage.

"Someone's been in my room, Brittany!" He bent over and picked up a shattered piece of glass from the light that had been next to his bed. His lips clenched shut before exploding with a threat. "I'm gonna kill my brother. He did this as a joke!" He dropped the broken glass.

"Why would Seth do this?" she asked, as she stooped over and picked up a pair of underwear and chuckled again. "Wow, boxer briefs!"

Aeron turned to her and shook his head. "That jerk probably knew we might end up in here, so he was just trying to ruin *everything*."

Brittany shifted her weight to one hip as she flung the underwear in his face. "Oh, so you knew we would somehow *end up here* in your room. That's a display of confidence I've not seen in a guy before."

Aeron reached out and snatched her hands. "No, that's not what I meant. He knew we had a date, and he asked if we were coming out here alone tonight. I told him I wasn't sure what we were going to do, so he probably did this to our room anyway. I'm still gonna kill him!"

"I was just teasing, Aeron."

He gazed around the room. "My parents will kill me if they see my room like this. Brittany, I'm sorry, but I gotta pick up this stuff before they get home."

"I'll help," she said, "but if you think my evening with you is over, think again!" She leaned over and kissed him. His smile returned. "Oh boy!" she said, "That cheesy grin just tears me to pieces inside. Let's hurry this up."

He thrust his arm around her waist and pulled her into his chest. Their kissing continued. As their intimacy raged, they backed up toward his bed. Harriet glided past the door, and the twins ran down the hallway toward the attic in Delaney's room. Dolores was infuriated over the encounter taking place in Aeron's room. As the apparitions scurried up the attic's staircase, the door slammed shut behind them. All the bedroom doors flew open and slammed shut, except for Aeron's.

Aeron yelled, as he jerked away from Brittany. She screamed. "What was that?" he hollered.

"I'm thinking the same thing!" Brittany exclaimed. She was pressing her hand against her chest.

"I have to check it out," he insisted. Aeron dashed into the hallway.

As Aeron stepped out, Brittany glanced around the room and yelled, "Wait for me!" She grabbed his arm almost as if it was a lifesaver being tossed to her in stormy seas.

"The first door sounded like it slammed shut in Delaney's room," he whispered, as Brittany continued to grasp his arm. "It could have been the wind or something," he suggested. Brittany trembled much like she did earlier in Aeron's arms.

"Aeron," she whispered, "I know the rumors about this house. Everybody does!"

Aeron turned and said, "Me, too, but they're just rumors."

Brittany tugged on his arm. "Aeron, I wanna go. Please, just get me outta here!"

Feeling her trembling hands, Aeron pulled her close to him. "Man, you're really scared, aren't you?"

"Yes, and I wanna go now! *Please!*"

"Okay," Aeron responded. Brittany stayed by his side until they reached the car. Once they got inside, he asked, "Where do you want to go?"

"Let's go to my place instead. I hope that's okay."

"Yeah, whatever you want. I understand."

"Thank you, Aeron. I'm so sorry I ruined our evening, but that scared me a lot."

"Yeah, me too." He retrieved his cell phone. "I better call my dad about my room."

As they pulled out of the driveway, Dolores and Harriet reappeared in Delaney's bedroom window. Dolores clenched her rotting teeth tightly, and her hands squeezed into fists.

I will never let her have him!

CHAPTER 32

"Call your brother's cell phone, Seth!" Adrian ordered. "It's almost midnight!"

Seth called, and Aeron finally answered. "Dad wants you to get your butt home right now," Seth warned.

Adrian walked over and grabbed the phone. "Did I not expressly tell you I wanted you home by 11:30? Where are you, young man?"

"Yes sir. I'm on my way right now, but something happened, and Brittany wanted me to stay with her until her parents got home. Her dad's driving us back there now." Aeron replied.

"Her dad?" Adrian's head fell backward, as he placed his hand on his forehead in disgust. "What did you do, Aeron?"

"Nothing, Dad! Didn't you get my text message?"

"No, I did not! Now, get home right—" The signal was abruptly cut off, just like it did earlier that evening when Aeron tried to call his father about the bedroom.

"Aeron!" Adrian looked at the phone. He handed the phone back to Seth. "I hate these stupid things."

"Now, if I was late, you'd ground my rear end, Dad," Seth said, as he slipped his phone into his pocket.

"You wouldn't be late." Adrian exclaimed. "Even your sister made it home before him."

"That's right, Dad! That's because I'm the *good* son you've always wanted," Seth chuckled. Adrian didn't respond.

Teresa told everyone to get to bed, and as they left for their rooms, she whispered to Adrian, "Honey, it's okay that he's a little late. You only gave him a short time to take that girl out anyway. Besides, we didn't realize we'd be out so late either."

"I told him, Teresa, that he had to be home at a certain time! It wasn't negotiable!"

"He's not even a half hour late! And it sounded like he was already on his way back here?"

"Yeah, and her father is driving! He better not have been caught doing something with her."

"What? Why would her father be driving him? We just had dinner with them!"

"He better not turn this house upside down like he did with the last girl he dated! I'll not have it. I mean it, Teresa!"

"Dad, get up here *right now*!" Seth hollered. Adrian and Teresa bolted for the stairs. After arriving outside of the boys' room, Seth stepped out into the hallway. "What happened to my bedroom?" The rest of his siblings joined them in the hallway.

Adrian brushed past Seth. His rage erupted like a nuclear explosion when he saw the room. He grabbed Seth by the arm and screamed, "What have you two been doing in here?"

Seth jerked away, as he replied innocently, "Dad, I didn't do this! I mean it!"

Teresa thrust her hand to her forehead. "Seriously, Seth, this isn't funny. Now answer your father with the truth!" Teresa walked over and tried to push one of the beds back against the wall.

"You're grounded indefinitely, boy! It's not like there hasn't been enough weird things going on around here as it is!" Adrian yelled. He walked over and started helping Teresa.

Seth's mouth flew open in protest. "Dad," he pleaded, "I swear I didn't do this!" Delaney and the twins stared at the mess as the arguing intensified.

Adrian abruptly turned and rushed at Seth. He grabbed his shirt and pointed his finger in his face. "You're going to clean up this mess right now, young man!"

Teresa yelled at Adrian, telling him to calm down.

Delaney even pleaded with her father. "Come on, Dad. Maybe Seth didn't do it. After all, he's been with you guys all night."

Seth, thrust his arms out and sneered. "I'm not cleaning this up without Aeron being here. He's the one who probably did this!" he insisted.

Adrian grabbed Seth's arm. "Don't you dare talk back to me, Seth Matthew!" His hand raised into the air.

"Adrian Douglas! Don't you dare lay a hand on him!" Teresa demanded. Tears raced down Darcy's and Kieran's flushed cheeks.

Adrian quickly lowered his hand. Seth's hands were still protecting his face. "Dad! Please don't hit me!" Seth pleaded.

Tears flooded Adrian's eyes. "Oh God, Seth, I'm so sorry." He quickly hugged his dazed son. Seth hesitantly embraced him as well. They held each other as Delaney grabbed Darcy and Kieran's hands and left the room. "I can't believe I got so angry. I suddenly felt just like Aeron has been describing."

"Is Daddy alright?" Kieran asked, as his wet face glistened in the light from the hallway.

Delaney squeezed his hand. "He's fine, Kieran. Dad was just mad at Seth for not cleaning his room."

She hastily walked Darcy and Kieran down to their room and helped them get dressed for bed. After tucking them in, she kissed them and reassured that everything was fine. As Delaney closed the door to their room, Lilly and Cain emerged from behind the closet door and stood between the twins' beds.

My mommy and aunt are mad at Aeron.

"Why, Lilly?" Darcy asked.

They want Aeron to come and live with them, but he likes that bad girl. He was kissing her, too.

Darcy was puzzled. "He was kissing a girl?"

Yes! They were touching each other, and my mommy and Aunt Dolores are very mad! They want Aeron to live with them and Mors.

Kieran asked, "Where do they want Aeron to live?"

Cain tilted his head and looked out the window while Lilly pointed outside toward the lake.

My mommy and aunt and Mors love Aeron and Seth, and they really want them to live in eternity with all of us at the lake.

Her contorted face eased once Darcy was willing to accept the fact that Lilly and Cain's family also loved her brothers. "Is your mommy and aunt mad at Aeron?" Darcy asked.

I told you that he was with a bad girl tonight. My mommy and aunt hate her. Aunt Dolores said they were going to do something bad.

"Who is Mors?" Kieran asked Cain.

Mors lives with us. He says Aeron's real name is Wyatt.

"No, his name is Aeron, but why does your family want Aeron and

Seth?" Darcy questioned.

Because they miss Henry and Wyatt.

Cain slipped into bed with Kieran, and Lilly did the same with Darcy. About ten minutes later, Lilly and Cain heard the kitchen door open downstairs, so they stood, joined hands, and returned to the closet.

Aeron's heart pounded like a drum inside his chest as he heard voices upstairs. When he arrived at his bedroom, he saw everything still awry. "Dad, I was trying to tell you about our room, but I got cut off. My phone wouldn't even send out text messages."

"Aeron, you better have a good explanation about this mess," Adrian demanded.

Delaney heard her brother's name, so she went to his room.

"Dad, I didn't do this! Seth probably did it as a joke."

"Everybody better stop blaming me over this! I didn't do it!" Seth argued.

"You knew me and Brittany might come out here tonight, so you did it to scare us! Well, it worked. That's how we ended up back at her house."

Delaney snickered as Adrian's eyebrows shot upward.

Seth burst into laughter. "Oh really!" he teased. "Did you and Brittany redecorate before or after you had—"

"Knock it off, Seth!" Adrian demanded.

Aeron's face and eyes burned with fury. "Real funny! At least I know how to get a girl to—"

"Both of you, stop it!" Teresa ordered. "No one is doing anything but cleaning up this room!"

"Aeron," Adrian spoke, "if you messed up the room as a prank, please just admit it. I can't take another mystery in this house!"

"I didn't!" he protested. "Look, I was giving Brittany a tour of the house when all the doors slammed shut. Then, Brittany got scared, so we left."

"A simple phone call would have worked, you know!" Adrian barked.

"I did, but the phone wouldn't ring through, so I texted, but you said you didn't get it."

Seth lifted up Aeron's shredded sheets and spread them out. "Wow, Brittany must have long fingernails."

"Seth Matthew Douglas! I told you to knock it off!" Teresa yelled, before grabbing his upper arm. "Adrian, while I'm taking care of this one, would you please talk to your *oldest* son about some of the basic house rules, especially the one where I don't appreciate him being alone in *our* house with a girl, *especially in his bedroom*!"

She stormed out of the room with Seth.

Adrian thrust his arms into the air. "Well, I think your mother clearly stated what I was going to say. So, why didn't her dad come in with you?"

"I knew you were ticked off, so I told them to just leave once they dropped me off." Aeron picked up some of his clothes and threw them on his bed. "Dad, I honestly didn't screw up our room!"

"No, but apparently you were *screwing* in your room! You need to get your hormones under control! Isn't this your first date with her?"

"Dad, I didn't do anything with her in here! I'm serious! And I didn't do this to our room! You can even ask Brittany!"

"Yeah, right," Adrian scoffed. "I can see me calling her up and asking, 'Hey Brittany, after you and my son *fornicated* in his room, did you guys happen to redecorate it afterwards?'" Aeron blushed, but then he started to chuckle. "This isn't funny, young man. How do you explain all this?"

"First of all, Dad, I told you nothing happened between us tonight, even though I wanted it to." Adrian raised his eyebrows. "Look, I know I've ticked off quite a few of the guys this week at school 'cause I'm seeing Brittany, so maybe they broke in and did this. Remember, they know about all the ghost stories around this place, so maybe they're just trying to scare us."

Adrian's shoulders drooped. He sighed. "Yeah . . . maybe you're right. I thought you were going to lay low this first week of school," he said.

"Look, I'm sorry for being late, but I really like this girl, and she was really terrified up here earlier. We waited until her parents got home because she didn't want to drive me out here and then back to her home alone." Adrian shook his head in disgust. "Her dad said on the way back here that you all had a great time together at the restaurant."

"Yes, they are nice folks, but please be careful with everything concerning Brittany. This family can't go through another Whitney situation."

"I will, Dad." Aeron nodded. "It did get very interesting, though. She wants me bad!"

"Good God, Aeron, just make sure you're careful! I really wish you would try and wait on such things. We didn't bring you up this way. You certainly don't want to live through what Jake had to deal with."

Aeron nodded and said, "Okay, I get it, Reverend Douglas." Adrian rolled his eyes. "Look, Dad, she's *really* a great girl, and besides, she's a million times better than Whitney." Adrian sighed.

Adrian looked around the room. "You know, you're probably right about some kids from school getting even with you over Brittany. She is quite a girl, from what I can tell." After scanning the room once more, Adrian demanded, "Now, you two need to get this cleaned up. I'll help, too." He yelled for Seth, who was still getting a lecture in the hallway from Teresa.

Within the hour, Aeron and Seth were finally in their beds. "Aeron," Seth whispered, "what do you think happened to our room?"

Aeron rolled over onto his side and replied, "I don't know. At first I thought you did it as a joke, but I really do think someone from school did it. Maybe some of them are trying to mess with our heads. A few guys are really upset over me dating Brittany."

After a moment of silence, Seth asked, "So, what *really* happened between you and Brittany tonight?"

"What do you think?" Aeron whispered.

Seth sat up. "What was it like?"

Aeron tensed as he thought about his brief time with Brittney—before it was interrupted. "Are you sure you can handle me telling you all the details?" he taunted.

Seth wanted to say something sarcastic back to Aeron, but he was truly interested in what happened between his brother and his new girlfriend. "Yeah, so just tell me!"

Aeron grinned, as he responded, "Well, she started to take off her—" He suddenly stopped and whispered, "Well, it's time to go to sleep. I'm too tired to talk."

Seth groaned. "Come on, Aeron!"

"No, it's way too sinful to tell you."

"Come on, man. Tell me!" Seth pleaded again.

"Shut up!" Aeron demanded. "I told you I'm too tired and want to go to sleep."

Seth grunted and fell back onto his mattress. "Well, I suppose she wasn't too impressed, so she wanted to go home. Oh well," Seth teased. "Goodnight."

In the darkness, all Seth heard was "Whatever."

Silence filled the air, and not long after their conversation, both boys were sleeping soundly.

CHAPTER 33

Dolores stood over Seth, preparing to take possession of her desired companion for eternity. Her yearning for his body and soul was unquenchable. She leaned down and exhaled what appeared to be a kind of mist after opening her mouth. It penetrated Seth's nostrils; his chest raised slightly.

Seth stirred, and the demonic woman floated to the bottom of his bed and drifted toward the window. She vanished from their room and reappeared at the top of the embankment next to the lake.

Come to me, Seth. You must come to me now.

Seth's eyes squinted. He struggled to open them.

Seth, I'm here. Please come to me. Come to the lake.

Seth finally opened his eyes and rubbed them vigorously. They slowly adjusted to the darkness, and he shook his head, trying desperately to comprehend if he was awake, while wondering who was calling to him.

After swinging his feet around and placing them on the cool floor, he stood and stumbled his way to the window and gazed in the direction of the shimmering water that almost appeared to be glass. Drawn by some unexplained force, seemingly possessing his will, he couldn't resist the desire to follow what he'd heard in his head.

After pulling the drapes to each side of the window, he squinted again and finally saw a single glowing figure standing on the embankment across the road.

An angel? he'd wondered.

Seth, I need you. Come with haste.

Compelled by a force he couldn't understand, Seth slowly turned and walked from his room, down the stairs, and out the front door. He was quickly clothed in goosebumps from the cool, evening air. He walked steadily across the road and up the embankment to its summit. He stretched forth his hand, which was clenched by the cold, bony hand of Dolores.

We have been waiting for you, Seth.

Seth was silent—the trance released any inhibitions, and he was unable to resist her demands. Without hesitation, he followed her over to the edge of the lake. The glow of the moon illuminated the surface of the lake just enough for him to see the mist hovering inches above the water.

Dolores leaned close to his ear.

You must come with me now.

She stepped leisurely into the cool water; ripples spread out in all directions. Dolores's arm extended as Seth lagged slightly behind. When chilly water reached his groin, he shivered from the sensation of dozens of needles piercing every nerve in his body. Still unable to resist his lone companion, Seth was driven deeper into the unknown abyss.

Once the water reached his chest, Dolores turned and grasped his other hand from beneath the surface. She drew closer to his body and embraced him. His chilled skin brushed across the course material of her dress. Dolores, appearing young and beautiful, finally kissed his lips delicately, savoring the moment. When she pulled away, her soft voice uttered disturbing words . . .

They have come for you!

Tears filled Seth's eyes when a vision of his family appeared in the fog that was drifting across the lake. "Mom . . . Dad?" His heart sank when he desired to reach out to them, but the image dissipated as quickly as it had appeared.

Seth blinked several times, hoping for a clear view of the objects around him. Oddly, the fog glowed in a single, small spot on the opposite side of the lake. Emerging from the light was a stranger standing near the water's edge. There was a trace of fog floating around the strange being's feet, making it appear as if it had been standing on a cloud.

The stranger's arms rose outward from its sides and paused at shoulder height.

Again, Seth blinked several times.

The unknown creature slowly closed its arms in front of its chest before opening them swiftly, like Moses parting the Red Sea. The fog opened like a scroll, revealing a clearer image of the mysterious stranger.

Seth's eyes widened, and he shook his head, as if trying to clear fog from his mind. Unexpectedly, Seth wanted to back away; he wanted to rush to the shore and into the safety of his bed.

"No," he whispered. "No, I . . . I don't wanna go with you," he pleaded. "Please, leave me alone."

They are already here, Seth.

The water gyrated around Seth, and as he struggled to catch his breath, the tops of a dozen heads emerged from the darkness. A light from the moon above revealed the pale, grotesque features of every tormented soul that was rising from their watery grave. Their stringy, soaked hair clung to their faces and necks, and there was only blackness where hopeful eyes once looked upon the world with anticipation. Slimy entrails flowed outward from their abdomens.

Water droplets trickled from their arms—now outstretched toward Seth. Shriveled fingertips pressed into his flesh as he tried to back away. The feel of their bony hands was brushing against his bare back. He turned and the creatures grasped his arms. Seth's legs became entangled in a web of fingers now gripping his ankles and knees from below the surface of the murky water. As he attempted to scream for help, a rotting hand covered his gaping mouth, and he was quickly plunged beneath the surface.

As water flowed over his chin and into his nostrils, he tried to hold his breath before the liquid could flood his airway. As his head submerged beneath the blackness, his strength suddenly returned to his body. Desperate to free his limbs from the clutches of the creatures, who were resolute in taking his soul into eternity with them, he thrashed in the water, attempting to get away. When he resurfaced, he saw the faint outline of the pavilion, so he pulled away even more, trying to run in the slippery mud blanketing the bottom of the lake.

As he reached the shoreline, he collapsed onto the dirt, but his legs were still partially submerged in the water. He felt the grimy soil stuck to his face and chest. He tilted his head upward and wiped away what he could. Still choking from the muddy water, he spit what was left in his throat and mouth before collapsing once more onto the soaked earth.

Thinking he had freed himself, he chose not to move until he could regain enough strength to stand. His chest was aching from several stones wedged beneath his bare skin. As he struggled to roll onto his side, his legs were seized, and his body was pulled back into the lake. He hollered and was somehow able to yank his feet away from the hands of the corpses. He felt the sensation of a hand pulling him to safety, but nothing was touching him.

As they surrounded him again, he caught a glimpse of the stranger still standing on the opposite shoreline of the lake. An abundance of strength somehow surged throughout Seth's muscles, and he escaped the clutches of the souls still trying desperately to take him away forever.

He stumbled and fell down the embankment several times. He was desperate to get back to Aeron and the safety of his bedroom. Falling only once more, he managed to finally regain his footing and raced toward the house. He tripped up the stairs, managing somehow to make it into his room before collapsing onto the floor with a loud thud.

CHAPTER 34

"What in the world was that?" Aeron sprang from his bed and staggered to the light switch by the doorway. He rubbed his eyes and examined the room. At the bottom of his own bed, Seth was lying unconscious on the floor.

"Seth!"

Aeron ran to him and fell onto the floor next to his brother. As Aeron lifted Seth and rolled him over onto his back, the sight of blood gushing from Seth's nose and mouth caused Aeron to shiver and gag. He yelled for his parents.

Adrian and Teresa ran in from the hallway. "What's wrong, Aeron?" Adrian questioned.

"Seth must have fallen out of bed. This was where I found him," Aeron said. "His nose is bleeding again, Dad!" Teresa and Adrian joined their two oldest sons on the bedroom floor.

Teresa yelled for Delaney, who was just arriving. She ran back to the bathroom and soaked a washcloth in water and returned.

"I can't believe it's another nosebleed!" Teresa cried out.

After Teresa held the washcloth to Seth's face, he awakened and started to choke. "What happened?" Seth said in a cracked voice. He sat up quickly—his eyes frantically scanned the room. "Where are they?" he yelled, while grabbing Aeron's arm and squeezing.

"Where's who?" Adrian asked.

"The people who attacked me!" he hastily yelled. "They grabbed me and pulled me into the water."

"What people, honey?" Teresa asked.

"The people from the lake!" His family's empty expressions were plastered on their faces like mannequins. "Dad, they wanted me to go with them under the water!" Seth cried out.

"Seth, there's no one here but us. You had a nightmare," Adrian reassured his son.

"Dad, it wasn't a nightmare!" he argued. "They came out of the lake and tried to pull me under the water!" Seth insisted. "They tried to take me away from you guys forever! You can't let them take me, Aeron! You're supposed to always protect me! You promised!"

"Seth, you were just dreaming; I'm sure of it," Adrian insisted.

Seth looked at Aeron and pleaded, "It was real, Aeron. They tried to take me with them!"

Adrian looked at Aeron and shook his head.

"Yeah, Seth, you probably dreamed about falling into the well or lake," Aeron said.

"Mom, I swear I was fighting them, and I tried to get out of the lake, but I think someone else was there watching the whole thing. I think he might have helped me escape," Seth claimed. "I didn't want to leave you guys!" he cried out again.

"Adrian," Teresa said, as she tapped her husband's shoulder, "he's soaked! And how did he get mud all over himself?"

"I don't know, Teresa, but let's get him to the bathroom and get him cleaned up," Adrian insisted. "And we need to get his nosebleed stopped." Adrian and Aeron helped Seth to his feet. "You're going to be fine, Seth," Adrian said. "You probably bumped your face on something when you fell out of your bed." Adrian was baffled by the smearing of mud on his son's body; he knew there had to be a rational explanation.

Sleepwalking perhaps? Maybe he fell in the yard?

Once they got Seth to the bathroom, Aeron looked into the mirror and noticed his brother's blood on his own face and upper chest. Trace amounts were on his underwear as well. He told his father he was going to get changed, and Adrian asked him to grab some clothes for Seth as well.

Seth stood and glanced into the mirror. "Oh, God!" he said. "I can't believe this is happening again." As Adrian continued to clean off his son's face, Seth turned to Adrian. "Dad, I'm being serious about the people trying to drown me in our lake. You have to believe me!"

"Seth, I'm trying, but are you sure it wasn't just a bad nightmare, or maybe even sleepwalking?" Seth's body quivered uncontrollably.

"Dad, it *wasn't* a nightmare! *It really happened!*" Seth sat on the side of the bathtub while Adrian tried to stop the bleeding.

Teresa wet another washcloth and handed it to Adrian. "Honey, he needs a shower."

"Yes, I know." Adrian wiped more blood away. Seth grimaced. "Am I hurting you?"

"No," Seth replied. "I have to go to the bathroom. Can you give me a minute?"

"Sure, but you're always unsteady on your feet when you get these nosebleeds. So, be careful."

"I'll be fine, but will you stay outside the door?"

While Seth relieved himself, several drops of blood fell into the toilet water and mixed with the urine swirling around the bowl. "What is happening?" he whispered to himself.

After finishing, he walked over to the mirror. He bent over again and splashed water onto his face. When he looked up at his reflection, standing directly behind him, was Dolores. Her beauty had disappeared, and he saw her mangled, rotting face, which made him gag. Seth spun around, and his eyes quickly become fixated on the worms sliding down her decaying cheeks as she reached out to him. He felt the slow trickle of blood flowing from his nostrils and dripping onto his bare chest. Seth's lungs screamed for air, and his temples and neck throbbed with the throbbing of his untamed heartbeats. Seconds later, the room spun.

"Dad, I nee—"

Adrian heard a loud thump. He burst into the bathroom and saw Seth on the floor. "Teresa!" he yelled, "call an ambulance!"

CHAPTER 35

Dr. Gates walked into the waiting area, masked in bewilderment. His head shook back and forth. Adrian, Teresa, and Aeron quickly rose to their feet. "I don't truly understand what is going on with you guys. I see absolutely nothing showing up on any tests or scans on Seth. There's simply no reason why he's in and out of consciousness. He stirs a little at times, but he passes out almost immediately. It doesn't make any sense!"

"Wes, are you saying our son is in some kind of coma?" Adrian questioned.

"Not really," replied Dr. Gates. Adrian shook his head in disbelief. "It's as if he is under a spell."

"Isn't that a coma then?" Teresa asked, as she squeezed Adrian's hand.

"Teresa, it's like something shocked him, and he's paralyzed with fear," the doctor declared. "This is so crazy. I've taken care of Seth since his birth. I delivered him for God's sake, and he has had more things happen to him in just the last couple weeks than in the last fifteen years."

"Dr. Gates," Aeron said, "Seth insisted that there were these *people from the lake* who came after him, and he struggled to get away."

"Aeron!" Adrian yelled.

"I'm sorry, Dad, but none of us can explain why Seth was soaking wet and covered in mud." Aeron gazed back at the doctor. "Seth said these people were pulling him under the water in our lake, just like he said that same thing happened to him in the well. Seth swears that it wasn't a nightmare. He said the people are real!" Aeron glanced at his dad, whose expression was dripping with anger.

Dr. Gates motioned for all of them to sit down. He joined them. "Adrian, tell me what's been going on, and don't be angry with Aeron for saying something. We've been friends for way too long for you to only tell me half the story."

After explaining the details of the events in their new home, Adrian leaned forward and thrust his forehead into the palms of his hands. "I shouldn't have left him alone in the bathroom." Adrian lifted his hand and looked at Dr. Gates. "What if he hit his head on something, Wes? I mean, Seth seemed to hit the floor hard. That's when I rushed in and saw him lying there with even more blood, gushing from him." Adrian's head leaned backward, and he rubbed his hands through his hair. When he looked at the doctor, he said, "And one other thing I noticed. There was a lot of water on the floor right by him. It was a little discolored as well. I don't know if he peed himself when he hit the floor."

"I told you, Adrian, nothing came up as a serious injury," Dr. Gates said.

"Adrian and I were shocked at what we saw earlier in the boys' room," Teresa said. "The dressers and beds were scattered all over their room, and Aeron's sheets were shredded. It's as if someone was seeking revenge."

"Wes, please don't think we're crazy," Adrian interrupted, "but I really am struggling to explain all of this rationally. I'm beginning to think something supernatural is going on."

"Adrian, you're the last person I would think was crazy."

"Wes, it could also be something simple to explain. You see, I guess Aeron has upset some boys at the high school over a girl he's now dating," Adrian explained, "and they could have been the ones responsible for the mess while we were out either at the game or dinner afterwards."

Dr. Gates leaned back in the chair. He looked down the hallway, making sure no one was listening to their conversation.

"That's really true about some guys being ticked off at me," Aeron claimed, "and Seth said some boys were teasing him about the house being haunted, so I figured someone got in—or has a key to some door or something from the people who lived there before us—and they were trying to scare us by messing things up."

Dr. Gates smirked and said, "Yeah, and I think it's working. You definitely have me a little scared at this point."

Finally, the doctor stood and said for the three of them to follow him back to the unit where Seth was being monitored. "Don't let the machines scare you," he warned. "We have a lot of monitors running and there's some IVs in him right now, but it isn't life support like you think."

As the three of them entered, Teresa and Adrian held each other's hands. Even with the warning by the doctor about the equipment, Seth resembled a person about to succumb to death.

"Oh God, Adrian!" Teresa wept. Even Aeron was tearing up. Adrian could feel his courage draining from his body, leaving him vulnerable to overwhelming fear. A tear soon escaped and raced down Adrian's cheek.

Dr. Gates put his arm around Adrian's shoulder. "Adrian, I'm being very straightforward with you guys about his condition. The good news is that we are not seeing any type of physical trauma. And I know you guys were concerned about his bloodwork revealing some other illness. It's all clear, so you can relax over the thoughts you had concerning leukemia." Adrian hugged Teresa. "Look, I'm sure he'll come out of this any time now. We're going to try another medication shortly. We wanted to wait until you guys were in the room. It would be less traumatic for Seth if he sees family with him when he wakes up." He patted Adrian on the back and said, "Hey, I need to check on something. I'll be right back."

Moments later, a nurse named Amy walked in and greeted the family. "Seth is really giving us a huge mystery to solve," she said. "I've been a nurse for nearly twenty-five years, and your son is certainly a unique case tonight."

"He's going to be okay, isn't he?" Teresa asked.

"The great news is that nothing is showing up anywhere that he physically has anything wrong," the nurse insisted. "It's like he saw something that scared him into a horrible shock."

"Wes said he's not really in a coma," Adrian affirmed. "Are you sure you haven't had patients like this before?"

The nurse pondered for a moment. "You know, come to think of it, I had one other case about a year ago when a family brought their teen son into the emergency room after a bad nosebleed. He was also out of it like your son."

"Do you know where that family lived?" Adrian inquired.

"I think they lived in the town of Inverness just southwest of here."

Teresa's eyes lit up from the mention of their town.

"The address," Adrian demanded, "I need to know the address where that boy lived!"

The nurse was baffled by Adrian's insistence. "I'm really sorry, but I can't say exactly where they lived down there, but I guess you can find out if you ask the doctor." Adrian insisted that she call for Dr. Gates.

A few minutes later, the doctor returned. "Okay, Wes, I know you'll think I'm weird," Adrian said, "but the nurse was telling us about a similar incident about a year ago concerning a teenager brought in with a nosebleed, and the boy also seemed like he was in some kind of shock. It sounds just like Seth! We even heard the boy who lived in our house before us had the same condition with nosebleeds."

The doctor's eyes grew larger as he said, "Good God, Adrian! I'd almost forgotten about that case. A colleague of mine treated that boy, and even he was baffled by the boy's condition." The doctor whispered, "Let me check on something. There might even be some information I can check out to help us here with Seth." He sighed. "I can't believe I didn't think of the similarities between Seth and that other boy."

As Adrian, Teresa, and Aeron waited, they stood by Seth and held his hand. "Do you suppose there is something else going on around our house besides coincidence? After all, Seth was perfectly fine before we moved there," Teresa insisted. "Could it be something environmental?"

"Dad," Aeron whispered, "what are we gonna do? I can't take seeing my brother go through all this." He leaned over onto Teresa's shoulder. "Mom, I'm afraid something bad is gonna happen to Seth. I can't take this! I just feel weird inside sometimes, like something really bad is gonna happen. And what is this talk about leukemia?"

"Aeron," Adrian said, as he gently placed his hand on Aeron's back and rubbed. "Your brother is tough like you, and I'm sure he'll be fine. As for the bloodwork we had done, everything is fine now."

"Honey, I know you and your brother tease each other a lot, but I know there isn't anything you wouldn't do for him," Teresa said.

"Mom, did you *really* think Seth had leukemia?"

"Yes, because of the bleeding, but thank God he's okay," Teresa replied, as a lone tear rolled down her face.

Aeron pulled up a chair beside Seth and sat. He reached out and grabbed his brother's hand. "Come on, Seth. Please wake up!" Adrian and Teresa squatted down and hugged Aeron.

"Adrian, I can't believe it!" the doctor said, as he rushed back into the room. "The boy we treated . . ." He put his hand on Adrian's shoulder, almost as if bracing himself.

"What is it, Wes?" Adrian questioned. "Do you know where that boy came from?"

"I can't legally tell you the address, but why don't you tell me yours again!" After Adrian said his address, the doctor whispered, "That sounds *very* familiar, Adrian. And I mean *very* familiar!"

"It was Josh Wallace!" Adrian announced.

The doctor's head jerked backward. "I would say that sounds *very familiar* as well."

"I've heard that name from a couple people," Adrian replied.

"What's going on, Dad?" Aeron asked.

"Adrian," Teresa reminded him, "Delaney and the twins are home alone!"

Unexpectedly, Seth stirred in his bed. "Dad?"

"Seth, we're right here!" Aeron uttered as he stood.

Dr. Gates grabbed his stethoscope and held it to Seth's chest and listened. "Come on, buddy. It's Dr. Gates."

Teresa grabbed Seth's hand. "Honey, we're right here."

Dr. Gates stood and said, "Come on, Seth, you need to wake up for us." He looked at Adrian and Teresa and said, "His heart rate is slightly elevated, but he's probably anxious from a little disorientation." He looked down and asked, "Seth, are you feeling okay?" Seth tried to sit up in the bed, but the doctor held him back. "No, just rest a minute."

"What happened to me?" Seth questioned.

Adrian sat partially on the bed and placed his hand on his son's knee. "Seth, do you remember being in the bathroom before you passed out?"

Seth glanced quickly around the room as if he was terrified of something. "The lady in the mirror!"

"*What?* What lady? And what mirror?" Adrian asked.

"In the bathroom, Dad!" He gripped the bed sheet. "She was staring at me just a minute ago."

"What lady, Seth?" Adrian pleaded for an answer. "And besides, you've been passed out for nearly an hour."

A tear escaped from Seth's one eye and quickly veered off course and down the side of his face. He looked up at his father, annoyed that no one understood who he was speaking about. "The lady in the white dress from the lake—the one who tried to take me away from you guys forever. She was dead, and her face was rotting." Seth started to cry as the family glared at one another.

"Don't worry, sweetheart, I'm going to stay here with you tonight," Teresa said. "Everything's going to be okay."

"No, it's not, Mom!" Seth insisted.

Teresa leaned over and hugged him. "I promise that we will all be okay!"

CHAPTER 36

Aeron jerked awake and suddenly sat up. He was drenched in sweat. Delaney arrived in the living room as Aeron got up from the sofa. "I see my baby brother finally woke up."

"Where's Dad?" Aeron asked.

"He stayed here with us until early this morning. He said he had to run an errand before heading back to the hospital. I guess they're going to release Seth later this morning. He's doing fine," Delaney said. "Mom says he slept comfortably the rest of the night after you guys left."

"Why didn't Dad wake me up to go with him?" Aeron asked.

"He didn't want to leave us all alone here without you being with us. I guess he thinks you're a superhero or something," she chuckled. "Why don't you go and get a shower. I'll get you something to eat. Everyone should be home soon. Mom said they were waiting on some report from a test they did last night."

While waiting at a traffic light, Adrian stared at the piece of paper where he'd written the address and names of the former owners of their house. Joe, Gloria, and Josh Wallace had suddenly abandoned the house one year prior to Adrian's family moving in. Adrian wanted to make sure he knew the family members by name when he confronted them with the haunting tale hovering over his life, filling him with guilt and horror. Perhaps they might be able to make sense of something Adrian's rational mind couldn't grasp. At least that was his hope.

After finding the road, he slowed as he checked the addresses on the mailboxes. A few minutes later, 19576 appeared on the one he had been searching for on Williard Road. He pulled slowly into the driveway, put the car into park, and turned off the ignition. While gazing straight ahead at a garage door, he whispered to himself, "What are you doing, Adrian? They'll think you're crazy!"

His concern for his family's health forced him to step out of the car and nervously walk up a manicured stone walkway, somewhat reminding him of Mrs. Murphy's landscaping at her house. He tapped on the screen door.

Moments later, a teen boy appeared. Adrian was startled at first by his familiar appearance to Aeron: the same height, brown hair, well-built, but his countenance was rather depressing, unlike Aeron's, who always seemed to be easy going—until recently.

Adrian cleared his throat. "Hello, my name is Adrian Douglas, and I was wondering if Mr. or Mrs. Wallace was home."

The teen looked back toward the kitchen and yelled, "Hey, Mom!" He turned back to Adrian. "There's some guy here who wants to talk with you and Dad."

Around the corner came a slender woman with blonde hair pulled back into a ponytail. She was dressed in jeans and a T-shirt, and her attractive appearance was not diminished by her forlorn expression. She managed to smile as she asked politely, "Yes, may I help you?"

"Hello, Mrs. Wallace. My name is Adrian Douglas, and I've come to ask you and your husband a couple important questions. Is Mr. Wallace home as well?"

"Is there something wrong, Mr. Douglas?" She glared at her son. "Did Josh do something we should know about?"

"No, ma'am I don't know your son at all." Josh appeared nervous, as if he was afraid of Adrian for some reason.

"Mrs. Wallace, this does involve your son, but it has nothing to do with him doing anything wrong. Sorry if I made it appear that way." Josh's shoulders drooped in relief. "I understand that you lived in Inverness, and your son developed a lot of issues with his health while you were there. I have a son who is having some similar issues, and I thought maybe you could help, especially since my son is in the hospital right now." Tears began to fill Adrian's eyes.

"Joe," she hollered, "I need you to come here right away."

Moments later, a burly gentleman, with graying hair, sauntered down from the upstairs. After Mrs. Wallace introduced Adrian and informed Joe about the reason for the visit, he looked at Adrian and said, "Look, buddy, we don't really want to discuss the time we lived in that crazy place, so I think you need to go."

As he started to close the door, Adrian thrust forth his hand and stopped it. He looked at Mr. Wallace, and with tears rolling down his face, he begged, "Please, Mr. Wallace, I need to know if—well—if my son is going to be okay. Please don't turn me away! *Please!"*

Mr. Wallace looked at Adrian and understood the same concern he'd once had for his own son. His fear transformed into compassion, and he pushed the screen door wide open. "Come on in, Mr. Douglas."

After thanking Mr. Wallace, Adrian was invited to sit in the living room. Mrs. Wallace asked if Adrian would like a drink. He declined. "I've come here because I need answers, Mr. Wallace, and I need them fast. We purchased the house in Inverness after you moved out. That's when my son, Seth, started developing these strange nosebleeds. We accidentally found out that your son also had them after your family moved into the house."

"How did you find us, Mr. Douglas?"

"Adrian, please call me Adrian. And please forgive me, sir, but I searched for you in public records."

"Adrian," he sighed, "I'm sure we were told a lot of the same stories Mrs. Murphy has likely shared with you by now, but my family only experienced strange noises, and well, a few other weird occurrences. As for my son, he hasn't had a nosebleed since we left that place."

"My son just had another one last night," Adrian shared.

"Please call me Joe, by the way." Adrian smiled from the friendly gesture. "Look, Josh started having nightmares when we lived there. He would wake up in the middle of the night screaming about drowning in the lake. In fact, he would even pee himself in his bed sometimes because the dreams were so vivid."

"Joe!" Gloria protested.

"Honey," Joe said, "this gentleman needs to hear this." He looked at Adrian. "As I was saying, Josh would soak the whole bed because he was so frightened by what he'd experienced in those dreams of his." Adrian's stomach churned from nausea. He wiped sweat from his brow with his shirtsleeve.

"Mr. Douglas," Josh said, "in my dreams, I always found myself in the middle of the lake screaming for help. I did sometimes dream about people pulling me under the water."

Adrian shivered. "Well, Seth, my son, just had the same dream. At least I think it was the same as yours. That's kind of why I'm here." Adrian swallowed hard. "Last night, Seth was found on his bedroom floor. He was soaking wet and covered in mud."

Joe and Gloria looked at each other. Their expressions bore the scars of the battle they seemed to have endured as well.

When asked if they'd seen people in the reflections of mirrors or knew about any strange children playing in the house, the Wallace family looked at one another and denied any such occurrences. "This is so strange," Adrian concluded. "My youngest kids swear they are playing with these kids named Lilly and Cain who drowned in our lake about a hundred years ago. And my older boy insists there are strangers hanging around the house and barn. In fact, we recently came home to find our boys' room in shambles. It was like a revenge thing, I think. We're thinking it was probably some kids trying to get even with my oldest son over his new girlfriend."

"Mr. Douglas," Josh interrupted, "I would sometimes wake up and my sheets would be on the floor, and there would also be some green slimy stuff on them, like someone had it all over their hands when the sheet was pulled off me." Josh shivered. "Mr. Douglas. . ." he hesitated, ". . . my parents don't know this, but . . . well, I know I have to share it now." Josh glanced over at his father before saying, "My room was also a mess one time after my girlfriend and I were alone one night at the house. The doors slammed shut all over the house, but we never did find out why."

Joe looked at his son, who was too apprehensive to look back at his father. After a brief sigh, Joe said, "I sure wish you would have at least told me that, Josh. Is there anything else you might like to tell me now?"

"No, sir," Josh mumbled, while gazing down at the floor. "Mr. Douglas, I didn't tell my parents because I . . . I wasn't allowed to have her there alone, but my sheets were torn to pieces, and my clothes were scattered everywhere the next time I came back to my room later that night." Adrian began to sweat. "I almost couldn't get into my room because the dresser and bed were pushed up against the door. The glass in some of my pictures was even shattered."

Adrian's hand rushed to his mouth. As Josh lifted his hand and wiped away a tear, Adrian asked, "Is this bringing back some bad memories, Josh?"

Josh looked over at his father. "Dad," Josh pleaded. "I have to . . ."

His father's cheeks puffed out as he exhaled a burst of moist, warm air from his lips. "Adrian, I think my son would like to tell you something important. He shared it with me this morning. I haven't even told Gloria." His wife sat up suddenly. Joe looked at Josh and gestured. "Go ahead, Josh. Tell him."

"Mr. Douglas, I haven't had any nosebleeds lately, but the nightmares started coming back a few weeks ago. I had a really bad dream last night, so that's why I told my dad about it this morning." Josh's head slumped toward the floor again.

"You said the dreams started a few weeks ago?" Adrian inquired. "Well, that's about the time we started moving things out to the new house on Murray Road."

"Well, there's this kid in my dreams. I see him a lot. He's a little younger than me, but I see him screaming in a lake with people all around him. They're trying to drown him or something. I can't really tell for sure."

"Young man, can you tell me—" Adrian stopped. After several deep breaths, he asked, "Can you tell me what the boy looks like?" Tears were gushing from his eyes.

Josh squinted his eyes. He wasn't quite sure how he should respond. "Well," Josh swallowed, "it's always kinda dark in the dream, but there is a lot of thunder and lightning. I'm pretty sure he has dark hair, though."

Adrian's eyes opened wider. He immediately fumbled for his wallet. After turning to a family photo, he handed it to Josh. "Do any of these people look familiar?"

Hoping Josh wouldn't identify anyone, his heart shot into his throat when Josh quickly stood and blurted out, "That one!" He pointed to Seth. "It's him! He's the one in the water."

Adrian launched off the sofa. "Oh my God! Are you sure?"

Josh's eyes glazed over with tears, as he replied, "That's not all, Mr. Douglas."

Adrian reached out and grabbed Josh by the shoulders. Joe moved forward in his chair. "What do you have to tell me, Josh?" Adrian pleaded for answers.

"Tell him, Josh," Joe ordered.

"Well, I kinda saw your oldest son, too. He was surrounded by a bunch of dead bodies, and he was crawling on a wooden floor. It's covered with something like straw."

"Oh God," Adrian uttered. His heart nearly exploded from the terror fighting to get out of his body.

"I also saw the older girl in this picture in my dreams. She's always curled up next to her bed, and there are some smaller people—like kids— standing near her. There's a man with chains on his body and hands, and he's also standing over her. She's always screaming."

Adrian's hands shook uncontrollably, as he bellowed, "My twins! Did you see my twins in your dreams?"

Josh swallowed hard as he cleared his throat. His eyes pleaded for help from his father.

"Adrian, I think my son has reached his limit on what he can handle with all this."

"Joe, please, I must know so I can save my kids! Please!"

"Dad, I have to help him!"

"No, Josh. You need to stop!"

Unexpectedly, a stream of blood flowed from Josh's nostrils and cascaded to the floor. "Joshua!" Gloria yelled.

Joe jumped up and held his hand under his son's nose. "Gloria, grab a towel!"

Adrian stepped back, as Josh eased himself down onto the sofa. Gloria quickly returned with a dishcloth and held it to Josh's nose. Joe looked once more at Adrian. "Mr. Douglas, I'm afraid you'll have to leave now. My family can't go through this again."

Adrian nodded. "I . . . I understand. I'm so sorry. I didn't mean any harm." He stooped over and retrieved his wallet from the floor and slipped it into his back pocket. "I . . ." Adrian looked away, fighting his tears. "I'll show myself out."

As he turned and headed to the front door, Josh yelled out. "Mr. Douglas!"

"No, Josh!" Gloria pleaded.

"Joshua, just let him leave!" Joe insisted.

"No, Dad! I can't let this happen to them!" As he stood, Josh warned, "Mr. Douglas, I saw two young kids in the lake. They were floating by a bunch of weeds."

"No! Not our babies!" Adrian fell against the archway leading into the living room. "Oh my God!" Adrian looked at Josh and begged, "What about my wife? Did you see her in your dreams?"

"I don't think so, sir. I don't remember seeing her face. I think there was a couple in the barn in one of the dreams, though. I couldn't see any faces."

Mr. Wallace put his arm on Adrian's shoulders. "Look, I'm sorry, Adrian, it's not that I don't want to help, but that crazy place nearly took our son away from us forever. I'm no expert on these kinds of things, but you need to get your family out of that house right away."

"I plan to do just that," Adrian affirmed. He wiped his face with his sleeve. The sweat was running down the sides of his temples and cheeks, and his whole body shook violently as if he was going into battle—a battle he didn't know how to fight. "I can't thank you enough for this!" He turned to Josh and said, "Young man, I will never be able to repay you for your courage."

Mr. and Mrs. Wallace escorted Adrian to the front door, and exchanged a quick, but friendly handshake. After closing the door, Joe turned to his wife and whispered, "I don't think it's over for them. I think those creatures want his kids." Gloria hugged her husband. She looked up at him and nodded in agreement.

Josh walked over, still holding the towel, and embraced his parents. Gloria wiped more blood from his nose. "I think you're right, Dad. Isn't there anything we can do to help them?"

"I wish we could, son. I sure wish we could."

"Dad."

"Yes, Josh."

"Mr. Douglas didn't ask about himself being in my dreams."

Gloria wiped away a tear from Josh's eye with her thumb. "You're right, honey. Why are you telling us this?" she asked.

Josh broke down and cried. "Son, what's wrong?" Joe asked.

After looking up at his dazed parents, Josh cried, "In my dreams, I always see a man hanging upside down in the barn." He swallowed and said, "His chest was ripped open, and he has no eyes. His face is so distorted in my dreams, and I haven't been able to figure out who he is . . . until today." Josh's eyes glistened before he squeezed them shut. Tears raced down his cheeks. "Dad, I believe it might be Mr. Douglas!"

Joe hugged his son. "Josh, are you okay?"

"Dad," he insisted, "I have to do something!"

Joe pushed his son away from his chest, while still holding onto his shoulders. "Josh, I don't want you going anywhere near that wicked place. You got that!"

CHAPTER 37

On his way to the hospital, Adrian called his business partner, Matt Winters, and asked if he still had any rental properties available. Matt offered him a house with two bedrooms, which was all he had vacant.

"Seriously, Matt," Adrian said, "I appreciate even that right now. I'll explain later why I need it."

"Sure thing, Adrian, and I can drop the key off at your house if you'd like."

"No!" Adrian insisted. "I'll have Aeron drop by and get the key at your house."

"Just let me know if there's anything else I can do for you," Matt offered. "I'll have Jake go over and turn on the central air if you need it."

"Thank you, Matt, but I can manage that."

"How is Seth?" Matt asked.

"The doctor hasn't found any physical reason for him passing out, but everything is way too strange to explain over the phone. I'll tell you at work," Adrian promised. "I'm heading back to the hospital right now. I need the doctor to release him. We're not spending another night without all my kids right by our side."

"But, he hasn't even been in the hospital the whole day, right?" Matt stated.

"No, but either Wes releases him, or I'm signing him out," Adrian insisted.

"Wow, you really do seem concerned, Adrian."

"Listen, I would like to be in your rental house tonight. I have to talk with Teresa about some things, so I'll let you know when. Honestly, you don't know how much I appreciate this, Matt."

"No problem, Adrian."

Adrian walked into Seth's room at the hospital. He rushed over and embraced his son, squeezing tightly, like a frightened child refusing to leave the security of his parent on the first day of kindergarten. Teresa rubbed her husband's back while caressing Seth's hair. Adrian's tears dropped onto Seth's gown. "Dad, I'm okay now."

"I love you so much, Seth." Adrian curled his lips as they quivered from the intense thoughts flooding his mind. Everything Josh Wallace had told him caused Adrian to hold Seth even more firmly in his arms. He turned his head slightly toward Seth's ear and whispered, "I promise that I'm taking care of things, son." After patting his son's back, Adrian stood and said to Teresa, "Honey, can you walk down the hallway with me so I can get a coffee?"

On the way to the vending machines, Adrian grasped Teresa's hand. "I went to visit the previous owners. That's why I was gone longer than expected."

Teresa stopped abruptly. "You what?" Releasing her hand from Adrian's, she asked, "What did they say?"

"They just confirmed that their son had some similar issues like nosebleeds and nightmares."

"Adrian," Teresa said, grasping his hand once more, "what are we going to do?"

"I called Matt, and he has a house we can stay in until we figure out what to do with our new one. We can get into it tonight."

"That's good, honey, because I'm pretty certain that I don't want our family living there one more night," she said. "And, I'm not happy the rest of our kids are there alone right now without us being there."

"They were fine when I called on the way here," Adrian said.

On their way back to Seth's room, they stopped by the nurse's station and asked if they could talk to Dr. Gates. After getting him on the phone, Adrian stepped to the side and asked when Seth could leave. Adrian explained to Dr. Gates—after asking Teresa to check on Seth—what the Wallace family told him, especially about the dreams Josh was having. A release order was immediately given. He knew Adrian quite well, and he knew he wouldn't leave the hospital without Seth.

Within the hour, they were on their way back to the house on Murray Road.

After returning home, Adrian spoke with the older siblings in the kitchen. "Dad, there's stuff you're not telling us," Aeron said. "I can see it in your face. You're actually afraid, aren't you?"

"Aeron, I think we need to take a break from here to sort things out. We aren't sure if there's something environmental going on here, and maybe Seth's nosebleeds are an indication that we need to get someone in here to check things out."

He said nothing about his visit with the Wallace family.

Darcy and Kieran came down from their room with Teresa. "Hey, Daddy," Darcy said, "Mommy says that we're going to stay some other place for a while."

"Yes, honey. The doctor thinks maybe we should get the house checked out to see why Seth keeps getting nosebleeds. It's probably just for a little while."

"When you guys pack up some things, take enough clothes for school this week," Teresa said. "I'll be up to help shortly."

Seth rubbed his head. "What's wrong, Seth?" Aeron inquired.

"My head hurts. Do you mind if I take a little nap before we do all this packing again, Mom?"

"Honey, you really need to get ready to leave," Teresa insisted.

"I'll help him, Mom," Aeron said.

Once the boys walked into their room, Seth sat on his bed and rubbed his temples again. Aeron walked over and sat beside his brother. "Hey, I really am worried about you these days."

"Yeah, Mom and Dad said you were pretty torn up about me being in the hospital again."

Seth leaned his head onto Aeron's shoulder. "Man, my head really hurts." He sighed. "I have to admit that I'm a little worried, too. Last night, it felt like someone was telling me to go to the lake in a hurry. Could it be one of those sisters Chance told us about?"

Aeron cocked his head. "That's crazy, man. Those psychos have been dead for years, so I doubt it's one of them. Seriously!"

"Maybe," Seth replied. "You know, it's kinda like you said about the way you seem to hear things in your head when you get into a rage." He looked at his brother. "Aeron, I just don't know anymore. I'm afraid to stay in this place."

"Seth, are you really sure you weren't dreaming the whole thing about the lake?"

Seth nodded his head. "Yeah, I'm sure. How do you explain the mud and me being all soaked?"

After thinking, Aeron agreed, "I can't. Besides, Dad seemed really concerned about this house, too. I've never seen him like this before. He's not telling us everything. I know it." Aeron put his arm around Seth. "Hey, as for the rages I have, I promise I would never hurt you guys. I'm sorry for scaring you, man. Look, we're brothers, and we will always look out for each other." Aeron stood and helped Seth to his feet. "Let's get packing."

Before Aeron walked to the closet, Seth pulled his brother into his chest and hugged him. "I really do love you, Aeron. Please, whatever happens in our lives, please don't let anything happen to me."

"I told you I would always watch out for you. I mean that!" Aeron promised. "I love you, too."

As the family members tossed items into any suitcase and box they could find, Delaney remained in the twins' room to help them. Down the hallway in Delaney's room, the attic door opened and revealed Dolores and Mors standing beside each other.

The storm is approaching; they will come to us tonight!

CHAPTER 38

"Mommy, why do we have to pack again?" Darcy complained.

Teresa forced a smile and replied, "Honey, don't you remember me saying that we are having the inside of the house checked out for something that is causing Seth's nose to bleed, and we don't want to stay here until it's completely safe. Matt Winters is letting us stay in one of his houses for a while."

Kieran asked, "Can Lilly and Cain come with us, too? I don't want them to get sick."

"Oh, Lilly and Cain will be fine here, because you said they stay in the closet, and none of closets are the problem." Her guilt was attacking her conscience.

"Why don't we think about the new house as a little vacation?" Delaney suggested.

Darcy grabbed Kieran's arm and said excitedly, "We need some toys." Teresa hugged Delaney and thanked her quietly. Teresa said she needed to check on the boys, so she told the twins to finish sorting their remaining items. Delaney started to leave, but Teresa asked her to stay with the twins until she'd returned.

Several minutes later, however, Delaney said, "Hey guys, I have an extra bag in my closet I can get for your toys. I'll be right back. Stay right here."

Once the twins started putting toys they wanted onto their beds, the closet door squeaked open. Lilly and Cain stepped into the room.

My mommy and aunt said they are going to take you guys with us tonight when the storm comes. Now, we will all be together forever and ever.

Kieran shook his head. "No, Lilly, we can't go with you tonight, because my mommy and daddy are taking us to a new house."

Cain grabbed Kieran's arm with a forceful grip.

My mommy says you are going to live with us instead. Seth and Aeron are coming, too. Delaney will go with Alastor, who lives under the stairs.

Darcy was becoming annoyed by their persistence. "Oh no, you guys, we are going to a different house. Mommy says we can't stay here for a while. They're going to fix our house."

Lilly's patience began to fade, and her voice vibrated with a low, growling tone.

No! You will go with us instead. Your mother is lying to you.

"No, she's not lying. Mommy would never do that. We are having the house checked for some bad things that are making Seth sick, so we can't go with you."

Cain stomped his foot.

No! You and your brothers and sister are coming with us tonight.

"But what about our mommy and daddy? Can they go, too?" Darcy asked.

Lilly's eyes darkened, and her pupils flared into large black dots, filled in the center with a reddish tint.

They cannot go with us! Only kids can come where we are going.

"Where's that," Kieran inquired.

We will live in the lake forever.

Sensing something wasn't right, Kieran's eyes started to fill with tears. "But my daddy says we can't go to the lake without him being with us." He looked over at Darcy and said, "I don't want to go with them to the lake. Do you Darcy?"

Lilly glared at Darcy. Her gruff tone was full of rage.

You will go with us tonight or else!

"No! Not without my mommy and daddy," Darcy cried out. "We're not allowed!"

Lilly and Cain turned slowly toward each other and stared for several moments. Their pleasant appearances gave way to one of decay and death. Gaping sores covered their faces, and murky lake water oozed from the open lesions on their exposed skin. A hazy white film suddenly filled their eye sockets. Lilly's voice resonated in a deep, demonic timbre as the deceased twins whipped their heads around toward Darcy and Kieran and said together:

You will come with us tonight!

Terror seized Darcy and Kieran, and they grabbed onto each other as screams echoed around their room. An unrelenting swell of horror washed over the twins as the rest of the family ran toward their bedroom. Lilly and Cain turned and vanished into the closet before anyone else could see them. The door slammed shut, causing Darcy to holler once more.

"What happened?" Adrian yelled, as he darted into the room.

Darcy ran to her mother, while Kieran stood in the center of the room, his legs trembling as if standing in the frigid, harsh winds of winter.

"Oh my God, Adrian, they're scared to death!" Teresa said. She hit her husband's arm and whispered, "Adrian, Kieran's shorts are soaked." Teresa looked over at Delaney. "I thought I told you to stay in the room with them!"

"I'm sorry, Mom, but I was getting a bag for their toys. I was only gone a short time."

"Aeron, please take Kieran into the bathroom and clean him up." He walked over and grabbed his little brother's hand. Kieran was frozen in place, staring intently at the closet door.

"Kieran, please come with me."

He didn't move, but his head trembled as drool ran from the corners of his mouth.

"Aeron, get your brother out of here!" Adrian ordered. "Get him out of here right now!" Aeron scooped up Kieran and bolted from the room. Delaney grabbed some underwear and shorts and followed her brother.

Darcy looked up at Teresa and said, "Mommy, Lilly and Cain said they were going to take us with them tonight."

Stooping to her daughter's level, Teresa grabbed Darcy's arms and pleaded, "Where, baby? Where did they say they wanted you to go?"

Tears flowed unhindered down Darcy' rosy cheeks. "They said we were going to live in the lake with them forever and ever," she cried. "They said Aeron and Seth and Delaney are going with us, too!" Teresa's mouth opened wide. "Mommy, they said you and Daddy can't be with us ever again!" Darcy looked up at Adrian and cried out, "They talked really scary, and their faces got really ugly."

"Where did they go, baby?" Adrian asked.

Darcy glanced at the closet door and pointed. "They went away in there."

Both Teresa and Adrian embraced her. "Mommy and Daddy won't let them take you anywhere, honey," Teresa promised.

Adrian released Darcy and shoved several toys into the bag Delaney dropped onto the floor. He snatched the bags and suitcases from their beds and told Seth to go to his room and retrieve his and Aeron's belongings. "We are getting out of here *right now!*" Adrian demanded.

CHAPTER 39

After Adrian and the boys packed up Teresa's car, Aeron and Delaney were sent to get the keys from Matt Winters. "Matt will tell you what we need to know about the new place. He already gave me the directions, and he said you'd know where to go, Aeron," Adrian said. "We'll meet you there shortly. And I don't want you two going anywhere else!"

"We won't, Dad," Delaney replied.

On their way to the Winters' house, their conversation was dominated by the twins and their scary occurrence in their room before they'd left the house. "What do you think the twins saw?" Delaney asked.

"I'm not sure, but whatever it was, it made Kieran pee himself. I felt so bad for him." Aeron sighed. "Delaney, I'm really worried about Seth. Did you know that Mom thought he had leukemia?"

"Yes, she told me, but she didn't want everyone to worry, so she kept it quiet for a while." Delaney tapped Aeron's arm as he drove. "Aeron, you are never one to cry about anything, but ever since we moved into the house, you've been really emotional."

"I know, but it's been tough, and I'm honestly stressed about Seth," Aeron confided. "I know we argue and fight sometimes, but I don't know what I'd do if something happened to him. I promised to protect him, but I honestly don't know if I can. There's too much craziness in our lives right now."

"You'd give up your life for him, Aeron! You'd never leave him if he needed you," Delaney replied.

Aeron glanced at his sister. "Yeah, you're right." He looked back at the road.

"I think you'd even do that for me." Delaney raised her brows, waiting for a response.

With a grin spread across his face, he replied, "Yeah, I guess." Delaney hit his arm in protest. "I'm kidding with you. I'd protect you, too!"

Once Aeron and Delaney arrived at the Winters' house, Aeron—trying his best to appear calm—walked to the door and was greeted by Matt and Jake. "Boy, it sure is great seeing you, Aeron. It's been a couple weeks," Matt said.

"Not long enough, if you ask me," Jake teased. Aeron laughed nervously.

"Good to see you too, sir," Aeron replied. "And I guess it's good to see you, too, Jake," he said jokingly.

"Well, here are the keys you'll need for the house. Your dad didn't call me to send Jake over to turn on the central air, so it's going to be a little stuffy in there for a while," Matt said.

"That's okay," Aeron replied.

"Have your dad call me soon. I can fill him in on how to turn on a few things," Matt said. "I can still go over to the house with you if you'd like. Your dad seemed adamant that I not bother, but he said he'd explain later."

"No, sir, that's okay. We'll manage just fine."

Jake smiled, but he said nothing.

"Aeron, you seem nervous. Is everything okay?" Matt inquired.

Aeron smiled, trying to appear calm. "Yes. I'm just feeling rushed over the quick packing and all."

"Oh," Matt replied, "I understand." He leaned to one side, trying to see who was in the car with Aeron. "Hey, how's Seth?"

"He's had a bad headache today, but other than that, he seems fine."

"And how's your new school?" Matt asked, while Jake made awkward faces at Aeron, almost causing him to laugh. "Congratulations on the football game, too."

Aeron grinned and said, "Thank you. And the school, well, it's okay, I guess. It's just like any other school except I don't have to put up with this wimp every day," Aeron smirked when he pointed at Jake.

"Oh really? Well, it's a lot quieter now that we don't have to hear you bragging about yourself all the time," Jake teased.

Aeron looked toward the car. "I hate to run, but my mom and dad are going to meet us there, so I want to make sure I'm there with the key."

"Yeah, your dad did seem rather upset when I talked with him earlier," Matt said. "Remember, it's the house that you and Jake helped me renovate last October. The people moved out after about one year."

"Yeah, my dad said it's the one on Lisbon Road, right?" Aeron asked, while remembering the night Jake gave him the keys just so he could spend some time with Whitney all alone, without his parents knowing. The memory distracted him briefly.

"Yep, that's the one. Let me know if you need anything," Matt reminded him.

"Oh . . . yeah, I will, sir. Thanks again. My family really appreciates this."

"Hey," Jake said, "I'll walk Aeron out to his car, so he doesn't get lost." Aeron shook Matt's hand.

"Seriously, how is the new school? Is it okay?" Jake inquired as they walked to the car.

"Yeah," Aeron solemnly replied. "It's okay. The best part so far is Brittany. She's the one I told you about a few nights ago on the phone."

"And?" Jake inquired with a grin.

"Is that all you ever think about?" Aeron asked.

"And you don't?" Jake remarked.

"Well, just so you know, she can't resist me," Aeron bragged.

"You'll definitely have to tell me all about it," Jake said. "So, how's Delaney?"

"She's in the car," Aeron replied, "and don't tell me you were just being nice by walking me to the car. I saw you looking earlier." Jake punched Aeron on the arm.

Once they got to the car, Aeron slid into the front seat and closed the door. Jake leaned in the window and sheepishly said, "Hey, Delaney."

Delaney smiled, but her initial curt response was as warm as ice. "Hey." She blushed. Feelings she had once thought were subsiding, because of Chance, were suddenly rekindled. "How's Lauren doing?" Delaney asked.

"Being a pain in my butt . . . as usual," Jake said. "Aren't all sisters like that with their brothers?"

His boyish grin caused Delaney to sense more trepidation, prompting her foot to tap. "Well, tell her I said 'hello.'"

"I will. She's out with our new stepmom right now, or I'd go get her. So far, Ginny's been a great mom to us—unlike Joan."

Delaney shifted in her seat slightly and replied, "Well, tell Lauren to call me in a few days so we can get caught up on things."

"I will," Jake said. "Hey, if you guys need anything, just let us know." He and Aeron did this strange handshake that only they knew. As Jake stepped away from the car, he bent down and said, "It's good seeing you again, DD."

"Yeah," Delaney responded, looking straight ahead.

"You still get hot and bothered by him, don't you?" Aeron asked her, once they pulled onto the road.

"No, he doesn't get to me. I have a nicer guy now," Delaney said, trying to reassure herself. In her heart, there was something about Jake Winters that she couldn't seem to get out of her system.

"I think it's funny he still calls you DD." Aeron turned up the radio before asking, "Where did he come up with that nickname he always called you?"

"Duh! How about *Delaney Douglas*—my initials!"

Aeron laughed. "Yeah, that's right. I remember now. And he still calls his real mom by her first name. I can't blame him. Joan still doesn't make any effort to see them anymore. At least they really seem to like their new stepmom. She really is a nice lady."

Aeron turned the radio down. "You know, Delaney, I hated it when you broke up with my best friend, but I'm proud of you for sticking up for yourself and went after someone better for you. Chance is a great guy, and I really think he likes you a lot."

"Thanks," she said. "And, Aeron, I'm glad you've finally moved on from Whitney. She was such a manipulator. Brittany is a great girl, and she definitely likes you. After all, you got her into your bedroom on the first date."

They both laughed, temporarily forgetting about the lingering dilemma involving their chaotic lives.

CHAPTER 40

Aeron and Delaney arrived at the new house and started to unload the car. Aeron was almost finished when his dad pulled into the driveway with the rest of their personal belongings they'd gathered for the quick move.

"Matt's directions were easy to follow," Adrian said.

After unpacking both vehicles, and taking a few boxes into one of the bedrooms, Aeron reached for his cell phone because he wanted to call Brittany. It was gone. Panic surged through every fiber of his body. "Oh great!"

"What's wrong?" Seth asked.

"I can't find my phone." As they looked around the room, and in their belongings, Aeron stopped and whispered, "Oh man! I think I left it next to my bed at the other house. I can't believe I forgot it."

Seth shook his head. "Don't even think about it, man. Dad will kill you if you go back there, especially now that it's getting late."

"I *need* my phone," Aeron insisted. "I have to go back."

"Don't even think about it, or I'm telling Dad," Seth threatened.

"You're such a jerk sometimes, you know that!"

Moments later, though, Aeron left the room and walked into the bedroom his parents were going to share with the twins and Delaney. "Hey Dad, do we need anything from the store?" Aeron asked.

Adrian stopped and thought for a moment. "Yeah, your mom mentioned something about going to get a few things for breakfast and lunches. Go check and see if she's already left for the store."

Aeron rushed from the bedroom and found Teresa in the kitchen. "Hey Mom! Dad mentioned something about you going to the store. I can go if you want."

"Oh, thank God. I would really appreciate that, honey. I already made a list of a few things we needed. Go get some money from your dad so I don't have to dig through my purse. I really don't want to leave the twins right now. They are still shaken up over the incident at the house."

"Yeah, I understand." As he turned to leave, he looked back and asked, "What *did* happen in their room?"

"I don't know for sure. They had to have seen something horrible that frightened them nearly to death. I felt so horrible for Kieran. He's still not behaving like he often does."

"Well, at least we are safer here, I hope," Aeron stated.

"I hope so as well," Teresa agreed.

After obtaining his father's debit card, he walked toward the kitchen door after retrieving the keys to his mother's car. "I love you, honey," Teresa said.

"Love you, too, Mom."

"Please hurry back, and don't go anywhere else. Just GPS some stores near us."

"Okay," Aeron said.

A purple haze stretched across the horizon, so Aeron knew he had to hurry to the store—and the old house—before darkness blanketed the area. He passed the store and sped towards Murray Road first. He *had* to call Brittany—he wanted to be close to her, even if it was by phone.

As he turned on to their road, the brilliant colors of the sunset had finally subsided, sinking deep into the grip of nighttime. He accelerated towards the house, hoping to retrieve his phone before the ominous feelings of danger overwhelmed his mind.

As Aeron rounded the last bend before his house, two children darted out in front of his car and disappeared into the high weeds on the side of the road. "What was that?" he shouted, as he came to an abrupt stop. He lowered the window a few inches and yelled, "Hey!" No one responded. He put the car into park and opened the door, stepping out onto one foot. "Are you guys okay? Where'd you go?"

He heard rustling in the weeds across the road. The noise suddenly stopped when he hit the high beams on the car's headlights.

As he was about to get back into his car, the weeds and shrubs on both sides of the road thrashed violently back and forth. For a moment, he couldn't move. His muscles stiffened, and fear nearly paralyzed him. His throat pulsated wildly from his thumping heart. Frightening thoughts haunted his mind.

In the midst of the frenzied distraction of the weeds, he hadn't noticed, until then, that the car's engine had become silent. The pleasant song of the tree frogs, and the symphony of crickets, silenced their nightly serenade when the rustling of the weeds and shrubs immediately ceased their sadistic dance. His chest heaved with each breath, and his legs began to collapse.

"Who's there?" he timidly mumbled. The hush seemed to unleash a torrent of dread, causing spasms to erupt across his back. His footing started to falter. Thankfully, his knees gave way, and he was able to collapse into the front seat of his car.

After he slammed the door shut, he hit the locks. He turned the key, but the car refused to roar to life. His breathing resonated loudly inside the car. The lights were still on, so he had a clear view of the road in front of him. He could see the lights from their house in the distance. *"Come on! What in the world's going on?"* He frantically tried starting the car, but it was useless. "Please, God, just let me get to the house!" He even thought about running, but the darkness held unknown terrors he simply couldn't face alone.

He noticed the weeds moving again, but this time, the two small children emerged. They stood, holding hands, in the middle of the road about twenty feet ahead of him. Their white, hazy eyes glowed, reflecting the brilliance of the headlights. Aeron gripped the steering wheel as a dozen corpses also walked out from the tall brush. Some of their entrails dragged on the road as they wandered toward the car. Their garments were marinated in blood. The creatures maintained their course toward their intended desire: Aeron.

Aeron's eyes were fixated on the creatures who were only several feet away from the front and sides of the car. His constricting throat only permitted trace amounts of life-sustaining air to reach his lungs.

Bloodstained hands pounded on the windows. His driver's side window was down several inches, allowing a few hands inside the car. Out of instinct, Aeron turned the key and hurriedly closed the window. Crushed fingertips ejected from the rotting hands of several creatures and dropped onto his lap. He jostled about, causing the fingers to dance haphazardly on the front of his pants before tumbling to the floor.

He rolled onto his side and curled his petrified body into a fetal position. His screams ricocheted around the car as some of the creatures climbed onto the hood and trunk. Raw horror dominated Aeron's hopeless thoughts, as the car rocked violently, tossing Aeron back and forth. He screamed even louder, *"Leave me alone! Somebody help me!"*

The car was suddenly still. Aeron opened his eyes and turned his neck upward to see if the rotting, determined carcasses were waiting for him. He saw nothing—not even the fingertips of the corpses that had fallen into the car. He grabbed the steering wheel and pulled himself up—cautiously.

Standing in the center of the road, a lone corpse—with a radiant glow emanating from his body—gazed back at him. Aeron tried to swallow any saliva his mouth could generate; however, there was nothing left. The man stared intently at the tormented teen, now gripping the steering wheel as tight as a tourniquet. Aeron's breaths condensed on the windshield in front of him. Continuously clearing the glass, Aeron struggled to focus his sight on the stranger, who was still standing in the middle of the road. Aeron tried to conjure up the reason for the sudden disappearance of the nightly invaders.

Who is he? he wondered. *What does he want?*

The creature raised his hand and pointed a finger at the car. The engine roared to life. There was no sign of the beings that descended on him moments earlier. He looked down at the floor mat to confirm that the fingers had vanished, before looking to see if the smeared blood on the windows had disappeared as well. The windows were clear. His head turned rapidly from side to side as he looked for the grotesque nightly stalkers.

Finding nothing, except the man in front of him, Aeron reached forth his hand again and wiped some of the moisture from the windshield. He thrust the car into drive and sped around the outlander in the middle of the road. The strange man didn't move as Aeron traversed the short distance to his house.

After pulling into the driveway, he raced from the vehicle and darted into the house and up the stairs to his room. After finding his phone, he grabbed it and turned to leave.

The door slammed shut, trapping him inside. He pounded several times. "Oh, come on! *What else can happen?*"

As he tugged on the door handle in a frenzied fit of despair, the lights in the house flashed three times and went out. Aeron heard the closet door opening behind him with a familiar, eerie squeaking noise. Feeling molested by fear, Aeron heard thumping sounds emerging from the blackness of the room. He felt the vibrations of each step radiating across the floor. The creature was closing in on him, which caused Aeron to press his back hard against the bedroom door. The moonlight beamed through the glass, illuminating the creature's form once it moved in front of the window. "Who's there? What do you want?" Aeron screamed.

Come to me now, Wyatt. It is time for us to go.

"Who's Wyatt?" Aeron cried out, as his muscles froze. The creature continued its pursuit. *"No! Stay away from me!"*

When Aeron turned and tugged on the door, the apparition seized him around the neck and pushed him across the room. Aeron slammed against a wall and slid to the floor. He sat up and held his head, which felt warm and moist from what he assumed was his own blood. The darkness was pierced by flashes of light swirling in his mind. He was dazed, but he still managed to hoist himself up and onto his feet. "Why are you doing this?" Aeron hollered.

A burst of adrenalin surged through Aeron's body when he saw Mors reaching out for him again. He resurrected enough strength to push Mors out of the way before thrusting his shoulder into the solid wooden door. Aeron grabbed his shoulder and held it as he grimaces in pain.

Don't resist me, Wyatt. Come to me! We can start all over again as father and son!

Aeron pushed passed Mors and ran to the window. He tried to open it, but it, too, was jammed. Mors turned and walked toward Aeron, who was now pressed firmly against the glass.

"Don't touch me!"

Aeron fumbled in the faint light and found his nightstand. He turned and busted the glass before climbing through the frame. Mors snatched Aeron's shirt and tried to pull him back into the room. Aeron's shirt started to rip, as his hands pounded on Mors' wrists.

Aeron tumbled to the ground below as Mors stood in the window, holding Aeron's torn shirt. Aeron struck the ground with a thud, momentarily knocking him out. Mors turned and walked to the bedroom door and passed through it.

While Mors walked down the steps, intending to retrieve *his son,* Aeron awakened out on the lawn and staggered to his feet. He looked up at the window, but Mors was gone. As Aeron limped to the driveway around the other side of the house, Mors was walking toward the front of the car.

Aeron's hands and chest were coated with his own blood. As he fumbled with the keys, trying to get one of them into the ignition, Mors was only a few steps away from the car. Just as Mors grabbed the handle of the driver's side door, the car thundered to life, and Aeron raced out of the driveway. Once on the road, Aeron sped away—back to the safety of his parent's arms.

CHAPTER 41

Aeron burst through the door at their rental home and fell into the arms of his father.

"Oh my God, Aeron! What happened? You're bleeding!"

"Dad, some guy tried to kill me!"

"*What? Who?*" Adrian cried out.

"Some guy at the house. He kept calling me Wyatt!"

"What house?" Adrian inquired. Aeron was silent. "You mean the old house?"

Teresa ran in from the hallway. "Oh my God! What happened to you, Aeron?"

"I'm sorry you guys. I went back to the house to get my cellphone," Aeron apologized.

"You what! *What were you thinking?* You kids and your stupid phones!" Adrian rushed Aeron back to the bathroom. "We need to get you into the shower."

"How did you get cut up?" Teresa asked, as they rushed down the hallway.

"I fell out my bedroom window."

Teresa yelled for Delaney to find some towels.

Once they arrived in the bathroom, Adrian turned on the water and helped Aeron step into the shower. Adrian grabbed the hand towel on the sink and began wiping off his son's chest and back. Aeron was shaking uncontrollably, as if trapped outside in a snowstorm.

"I'm so sorry I went back there. I didn't mean for this to happen," Aeron sobbed as he described the horrifying events from the road and house. Seth and the twins arrived at the doorway, but Delaney rushed past them with a few towels.

"Seth, please take the twins to our bedroom," Teresa ordered.

"Dad, these zombies-like people came out of the weeds beside the road and climbed all over the car. Then, they all disappeared, but there was this one guy just standing in the middle of the road staring at me. He was glowing!" Aeron grimaced as his father touched his wounds. "Dad, I know I've seen that guy before, but I don't know where?" The bottom of the shower was flowing with blood and water. "Then," Aeron cried out, "when I got to the house, this other guy tried to kill me. He kept calling me Wyatt."

Adrian remembered what Mrs. Murphy told him about Mors and Wyatt. "Look, I'm just glad you're okay, but please don't *ever* do something stupid like that again, Aeron! You could have been killed!"

Teresa wet down another towel while Aeron grimaced from the touch of the fabric. "Mom, it was the scariest thing that's ever happened to me!"

Teresa turned off the water and Adrian began to pat his chest and back with a dry towel. "Honey, I know it was scary, but you're safe here with us." Adrian continued to dry off Aeron's upper body. "Honey, the most important thing is you made it out of there." Adrian told him to turn around as he dabbed the towel on various cuts on his back.

"My God, Aeron!" Adrian scolded. He shook his head, amazed by the crisscrossed designs of the cuts on his torso and back. "I hope we don't have to go to the hospital. I don't even know what I'd say to them."

"You guys," Aeron insisted, "I'm never going back to that house ever again!"

"I understand, Aeron. We're working on what to do."

After Aeron attempted to bend over to get undressed, he cringed and yelled out in pain.

"Delaney," Teresa asked, "could you please get your brother a pair of underwear and shorts." Adrian and Teresa helped Aeron sit on the toilet as they assessed how deep the cuts were on his body. "Adrian, we need to send someone to the store to get some bandages."

"Do I have to go to the hospital? Aeron asked.

"We're not sure yet," Adrian replied. "Give us a minute to see if any of the cuts need stitches."

Teresa and Adrian continued to press on various wounds, which were still oozing small amounts of blood. "Mom, I'm so sorry about not going to the store. It's all my fault," Aeron pleaded.

Teresa kissed the side of his head. "Honey, we need to focus on these cuts for now. Here," she said, "keep some pressure on this towel. We'll see if these cuts stop bleeding."

After Teresa returned from the store, she walked into the bedroom and found Aeron sleeping soundly with a few towels under his back. Adrian and Seth were sitting on the floor beside him. Adrian pressed a finger to his lips and pointed out toward the hallway. "Stay here," he whispered to Seth.

When he and Teresa stepped into the hallway, Teresa asked, "How long has he been out?"

"He dozed off about 10 minutes ago. He was petrified, and he refused to let me leave his side." A tear glided down Adrian's face. "Teresa, my boy can plow through football players like nothing, but now, he's afraid for me to leave his side."

"What do you think about some man trying to kill him, and what about those people he said were all over the car?" Teresa took her thumb and wiped the tear away on her husband's face. They embraced.

When Adrian pulled away, he whispered, "I haven't a clue, but I think we are okay with the cuts. That one we were worried about was still bleeding some, but if we bandage it, it might be okay."

"While I was at the store, I kept thinking about what might happen if we took him to the ER. We could say he fell through a glass screen door here, but I was afraid he would start panicking and mention those zombies he talked about earlier." Teresa sighed. "What then?"

"Look," Adrian said, "if it isn't better tomorrow, we will have to do something. Maybe by then, he'll be calmer."

"Maybe you're right," Teresa said. "Let's just let him sleep."

Before Teresa went to bed that night, she stepped into the boys' bedroom to check on them. Teresa's eyes filled with tears as she knelt beside Aeron and Seth on the floor. Aeron had rolled onto his side. She gently checked the larger cut, which had stopped bleeding.

As lightly as possible, she secured a large bandage onto his back. Aeron didn't move. She stood and walked to the bedroom door. When she started to close it, she paused. She decided to leave the door open before stepping into the hallway. "Please God, watch over my boys," she whispered. "Please watch over all my babies!"

When she stepped quietly into the room she and Adrian were sharing with the twins and Delaney, she knelt onto the floor before crawling into the sleeping bag beside Adrian. She thought to herself: *Lord, thank you for saving us, and please keep us all safe no matter what happens.*"

CHAPTER 42

Come to us, Seth. You must come to the lake. Come now!

In the distance, lightning flashed in the darkness. At 12:14 A.M. Aeron flipped his head and crumpled his pillow under his neck, trying to relieve some of the pressure on his upper back. Seth's eyes fluttered from the disturbance in his head.

Seth's eyes opened, and he sat up. His disorientation caused a brief panic before he stood and walked toward the bedroom door. Dressed only in shorts and a T-shirt, the central air caused him to shiver as he strolled down the hallway toward the kitchen.

Come to us, Seth! We need you!

The keys to Teresa's car glistened on the counter. The spotlight above the garage was streaming through the window. Seth felt a sense of haste when he picked them up and rushed to the door.

Twenty-five miles down the road, Josh Wallace was restless in his bed—haunted by the ferocious visions of his nightmares about the Douglas family. Just as creatures were about to seize a dark-haired boy in the lake, Josh's eyes opened, and he sprang up from his bed. The sweat covering his body 'caused a chill, as the cool air from the ceiling fan descended upon him. His labored breathing was drying out his throat, so he walked to the kitchen for a glass of water. Upon returning to the upstairs hallway, he stepped into the bathroom to wash his face.

I must do something, he thought, gazing at the fatigued image in the mirror. *I can't let them take that boy!*

As he rubbed his chin, and glanced into the mirror, he saw a stream of blood flowing from one of his nostrils. It dripped onto the sink counter. "Oh no!" As he wiped blood from his nose and upper lip, Josh realized where he needed to go. "Dad's gonna kill me," he whispered. In his mind, he somehow knew the boy in his nightmares was going to the lake that night. "You have to go," he whispered again to himself. Josh walked to his room, put on more clothes, and went to the car.

The house—I have to get to the old house!

While driving to Inverness, Seth heard the cries of lost souls beckoning him to come to the lake. Their shouts reverberated in his head like echoes recoiling off canyon walls. By the time he turned on to Murray Road, screams of terror boomed in his head. His mind saw people in agony as they were being lifted into the air by their ankles from a rope that had been thrown over rafters in a barn.

Only yards from the house, the screams had grown into torturous pandemonium, and Seth shook his head vigorously to silence their cries.

Seth was drawn deeper into a trance as he pulled into the driveway of their abandoned home. He gazed straight ahead, refusing to leave the vehicle at first.

Come, Seth. Join us forever.

Seth couldn't move; he sat still as the hum of the engine soothed his weary mind.

A violent crash of thunder awakened Aeron. He sat up as an explosion of thunder rattled their house. "Man! That was close!" Aeron said, as he fought to gain full consciousness. "Seth, did you hear that?" There was no response. "Seth?" Aeron stood and turned on the light. Observing an empty sleeping bag, Aeron rushed out from room and ran to the bathroom. Seth wasn't there, so he dashed to the living room.

When Aeron stepped into the kitchen, he darted for the kitchen door and opened it. "What is going on around here?" Aeron said to himself.

A flash of lightning caused him to look toward the garage. He'd noticed that his mother's car was gone.

No! He couldn't have! Aeron thought.

Aeron rushed into his parents' room and tapped his father's shoulder. Adrian's eyes opened. "What's wrong?"

Aeron motioned for his father to come with him. Once they walked into the hallway, Aeron blurted out, "Mom's car is gone!"

"What?" Adrian raced to the kitchen door and opened it. "Someone stole her car!"

"No, Dad! Seth is missing, too!"

"What? He's missing?"

Teresa walked into the kitchen. "What's going on?"

"Your car's gone," Adrian said.

"Is it stolen?" Teresa asked, still trying to be as quiet as possible.

"I don't think so. Seth is missing, too" Adrian said.

"Oh my God! Where'd he go?" Teresa cried out.

"I'm not sure," Adrian replied. "Aeron, go get your sister. You both need to get dressed. Now hurry!"

"We have to call the police," Teresa insisted, as she picked up her cell phone.

"No! We can't do that, Teresa. Are you going to tell them our son, who doesn't even have a license, is out for a joyride in the middle of a thunderstorm?"

Teresa paused and stared at Adrian. "Good God, you're right." She frantically tried calling Seth's cellphone, but she heard it ringing in the other room.

Aeron ran into the kitchen holding his brother's phone. "He didn't take it with him!" Aeron stated.

"Adrian, we have to find him!" Her hand rushed to her forehead. "I'm going with you!"

"No, Teresa, you need to stay with the twins. They'll need you if they wake up."

"No, I'm going with you!" she insisted.

"Teresa," Adrian reasoned, "what if the twins wake up and neither one of us is here with them?"

Teresa paced the floor. "Okay, you're right. They'll panic." Teresa froze in place as her hand rushed to her forehead. "Please find him, Adrian! I don't know what he was thinking!"

Moments later, Delaney hurried into the kitchen. "What's this about Seth stealing your car, Mom?"

Adrian embraced Teresa. "We'll find him, I promise!"

"Adrian, hurry!" Teresa pleaded.

As Adrian rushed past Delaney, she inquired again, "Mom, what is going on?"

"My car is missing, and so is Seth. We are sure he took it."

"You've got to be kidding me! Why would he do such a stupid thing? He isn't even old enough to drive on his own!" Delaney stated.

Adrian rushed into the room with his keys. "Come on, kids, we have to go right now!" A crash of thunder rumbled outside.

"Please be careful!" Teresa begged.

"We will, honey, and we'll find him. Don't worry," Adrian promised.

As Adrian and the oldest siblings sped toward Inverness, Aeron asks why they were going there instead of looking near the rental house. "I think he might have gone back to the house. That's the first place I think we should look."

"Dad, why would he go there by himself?" Delaney questioned.

"You've got to be kidding me!" Aeron said. "You really think he went there?" He grimaced from the seat pressing against his injured back.

Adrian put his hand on Aeron's knee. "Aeron, you guys just have to trust me." Delaney leaned forward. "Look, I visited the Wallace family today—the previous owners—and we just need to get to the old house. That's all I can say!"

"Dad, who is this Wallace family?" Delaney asked. Adrian offered a brief explanation, leaving out the details of the deaths described by Josh.

When they turned at Murray Road, a deluge of rain slammed onto the car. Lightning illuminated everything around them. "Dad, it's getting really bad all of the sudden," Aeron insisted.

When they approached the area where the corpses surrounded Aeron in the car, he abruptly yelled out, "I remember him!"

"Remember who?" Adrian inquired.

"The guy who was standing in the middle of the road after the bodies went away."

"Aeron, what are you talking about?" Adrian asked.

"I saw him at my school!" Aeron replied. "Dad, maybe he helped me, because the people disappeared before I looked out and saw him standing on the road."

"At this point Aeron, I'm ready to believe anything," Adrian said.

Seth finally stepped out of the car. Lightning flashed, allowing him to momentarily see one of his eternal companions standing on the embankment by the lake. The rain drenched Seth's body, as the wind whirled around him.

Still in a somewhat catatonic state, he finally arrived on the top of the embankment, and Harriet stretched forth her hand and grasped his. They walked to the lake's edge. As the cool water touched Seth's feet, he started to resist.

I want my family! he thought. Tears, along with rain, streamed down his face when he thought about his parents and siblings.

Harriet pulled him closer and exhaled a mist into his face. He inhaled some of it, which caused his eyes to become heavy, and his pupils to dilate. Unable to resist now, he stepped into the water with his ghostly companion. Lightning illuminated the sky, and he saw Dolores standing waist deep in the lake with her arms outstretched in anticipation of her cherished possession for eternity. Seth's eyes began to roll around in their sockets as if he was slipping deeper into a spell. Harriet led him farther into the chilly lake. Once the water reached his knees, his awareness began to return.

"*No!* I don't want to go!" he cried.

We will take care of you forever!

He was soon waist deep in the murky waters—his eventual, eternal grave. Dolores stretched her arms out farther and pulled Seth closer to her bosom.

The crowns of a dozen heads rose from the blackness. Their brazen attempt from before may have failed; however, they were determined more than ever to claim Seth as their own companion in death.

Seth saw headlights in the distance. "*Wait! No! I don't wanna go with you!*" He was seized by the people from the lake. They pulled him farther out toward the middle where his footing started to founder. Smothering his body with cold, bony hands, the creatures pulled him under several times, but Seth managed to fight back. "Leave me alone!" he cried.

Seth struck many of the corpses with his fists, which enabled him to break free of their grip. He maneuvered his way toward the shoreline before collapsing and hitting his head on the course surface on the shore. He succumbed to the trauma—leaving him unconscious.

CHAPTER 43

After pulling into the driveway, Adrian, Delaney, and Aeron saw Teresa's car. The driver's side door was wide open. "Oh God!" Adrian exclaimed. His stomach twisted—his heart plummeted into his gut. They rushed from Adrian's SUV and yelled for Seth. The rain pounded their skin, and the rumble of thunder muffled their frantic calls. "We need to go to the lake!" Adrian yelled.

Delaney hollered. "Dad, a light just turned on upstairs. Seth's in my bedroom!"

Adrian looked toward the lake, desiring to go there instead, but he stayed with his son and daughter. All three of them rushed into the house, but Delaney stayed by the kitchen door. "I can't go up there! I just can't!" she insisted.

Adrian told her to remain by the door. "Honey, no matter what happens to us, you get out of here and head back to your mother!" Adrian ordered.

"Gee, Dad, that's reassuring," she cried.

"Come on, Dad!" Aeron said. "Seth, we're coming!" He tugged on Adrian's arm.

Adrian handed Delaney the keys and quickly kissed her forehead. "We'll be right back!" He ran with Aeron to Delaney's bedroom.

Aeron was first to arrive, and when he opened the door, there was no one in the room. They checked the two closets and then opened the attic door. Just as Adrian turned on the light to go up to investigate, two doors slammed shut down the hallway. "Dad, he must have gone into another room," Aeron suggested.

Once they dashed into the hallway, they looked in both directions. "You go check your room, and I'll go to mine." Adrian said.

Forgetting his previous attack, Aeron bolted into his room and turned the light on. His chest pounded from terror when he suddenly remembered the fight he had for his life just hours earlier in his room. Regardless of his fear, he knew he had to save his brother. "Seth! Where are you?" The wind whipped his curtains wildly as they clung to the rods above the broken window. Rain was pouring into the room.

Adrian thrust his bedroom door open and ran in. "Seth! Please answer us!" He flipped on the light. Rain cascaded down the windows as he scanned the room.

As the two searched each of their rooms, both bedroom doors slammed shut with a thud. The entire house went dark.

Delaney's screams roared up the stairs.

Aeron rushed to the door and pounded on it as he yelled for his father to come and rescue him. Adrian tried several times to thrust open his own bedroom door with his shoulder. "Aeron, are you okay? I'm stuck in here!"

"I can't get out, Dad. Hurry!" Behind him, Aeron heard the familiar sound of a malevolent voice, somewhat muffled by the rain and wind rushing in through the gaping window.

Come to me now, Wyatt!

Aeron frantically plunged his shoulder into the door in a futile attempt to escape the impending clutches of the creature whose putrid hands were several feet away from seizing his throat. "Dad! Hurry! That guy's in my—”

The squeeze of Mors' hands closed off Aeron's throat. Mors hoisted him up by his neck against the door before hurling him across the room. Aeron crashed into a dresser and fell to the floor. He was unconscious and vulnerable to Mors' will.

Delaney heard the booming thud upstairs, causing her to scream even louder for her father. Adrian tackled the door as if he was barreling through a bunch of linemen on a football field, only to bounce backward and fall onto the bed. He quickly stood and raced toward the door once again, failing miserably to break through it.

A deafening, sadistic shriek resounded around the room, causing Adrian to force his hands to his ears. Furniture seemed to dance across the floor as other objects were hurled around the room like the chaotic excitement of dozens of birds escaping a predator. Adrian was suddenly knocked to the floor when a vase struck his head and smashed into pieces. Blood squirted from his forehead before he was left motionless on the floor.

"Dad, Aeron, you guys need to answer me!" Delaney pleaded.

Delaney, I need your help! Come up here! They're hurt!

"Seth? Is that you?" she cried out.

Yes, please come up here and help me!

"I'm coming, Seth! Wait there for me.

Delaney moved blindly through the darkness. The sudden scooting of a kitchen chair startled her, but she went with haste to find Seth.

Just as she was moving through the dining room, she heard the cellar door opening with an eerie creaking sound.

She stopped. "Seth? Is that you?" No one answered. The clanging sound of chains dragging across the floor caused her skin to crawl.

"Seth? Please answer me!" she cried.

A flash of lightning illuminated the dining room and revealed the corpse of Alastor moving toward her. Her shriek caused Aeron to stir, and he suddenly saw Mors only inches away from grasping his neck and likely snapping it.

"Get away from me!" Aeron begged. He kicked violently. Mors was unable to latch onto Aeron, who ran over to the door and tried to thrust it open with his broad shoulder. He slid down the door and yelled for help again. He thought about exiting through the broken window again, but Mors blocked his path.

Delaney shouted for help when another bolt of lightning revealed Alastor moving closer. She sprinted up the stairs, but she lost her footing in the dark and fell. As she regained her balance, the lightning revealed Alastor now ascending the stairs behind her. His hands were bloody from the tight chains wrapped around them. The banging of the metal on the wooden steps was louder with each moment.

"Delaney!" Aeron yelled.

"Aeron! Please help me. Someone's coming after me!" she pleaded. After regaining her footing, she dashed for the top of the stairs.

She ran to her room because it was the only door that was wide open. After slamming it shut, she slid onto the floor and forced her back against the door. Thunder rattled the glass in the windows.

When Alastor pounded his fists on the door, Delaney crawled over to the side of her bed and curled up next to her nightstand, but she froze when she heard the attic door opening with a shrill, squeaking sound.

The deceased twins emerged from the attic and walked toward Delaney. "Who's there?" she called out into the blackness.

Lightning illuminated the room and revealed Lilly and Cain moving nearer to her. Their ghoulish faces, still seeping with lake water, were still glowing with decay. Delaney shrieked as her back slid along the mattress. Another flash revealed the twins approaching closer with their arms outstretched. Delaney slumped over, hoping not to pass out.

Aeron, not willing to surrender, stood and lunged once more into the door with the force of a charging bull. The frame buckled under the pressure, and Aeron fell aimlessly into the hallway. Delaney sat up and hollered for her brother. The creaking of the floor around her caused her to press her body even harder into the side of her mattress.

Aeron launched himself from the floor to his feet and saw Alastor pounding on Delaney's door. With the determination of a soldier charging into battle, Aeron rushed at the creature. He plunged his hands into the rotting, maggot-infested torso of Alastor. The force caused the decomposing carcass to tumble backward and fall over the banister. He crashed onto the floor below.

Aeron felt the putrid slime on his hands, and he flung them several times in the darkness before wiping them on his clothes. He banged on the door and pleaded for Delaney to let him in. She crawled to the door and stood, propelling her frightened body into her brother's arms, which were still covered with the remnants of Alastor's chest.

"Aeron! Thank God it's you. I heard Seth yelling for me, but I couldn't find him." As Aeron attempted to run into her room, Delaney grabbed his arm and yelled, "Don't go in there! Those twins are in my room!"

Aeron still rushed into the room. Lightning flashed, revealing no one. "They're gone, Delaney!" She rushed in and latched onto his arm. "I can't find Seth either," he said, "and that same guy tried to kill me in my room again!" Aeron turned around to see whether the male apparition was following him. They saw no one in the darkness. "Is Dad still in his room?" Aeron asked.

"I don't know. I've called for him, but he won't answer me," Delaney replied.

"Aeron, what is that smell?"

Gagging, Aeron found his way into the bathroom and wet a towel. He wiped off the remains of Alastor's rotting flesh. "Let's find Dad!"

They stumbled to their father's bedroom. The door opened without any force. Searching frantically around the room, Delaney tripped over something solid near the center of the floor. After she bent down, she felt her father's warm, unconscious body.

"Aeron, it's Dad! I think he's been knocked out!" She felt his face, which was soaked with something wet. "I think he's bleeding!"

Aeron heard a noise in the hallway. Knowing Mors was likely in pursuit, he slammed the bedroom door shut and locked it. He cautiously walked through the room and bumped into the side of a dresser. He dragged it to the door to block it before crouching onto the floor to be with his wounded father. "Help me get Dad onto his bed," he ordered. The lightning bathed the room with light and allowed them to identify the source of the bleeding. Delaney found a pillow and slipped off one of the pillowcases and pressed it against her father's head.

Aeron! Help me!

"Did you hear that, Delaney?"

"Hear what?"

"I think I heard Seth yelling for me. I think it came from outside." Aeron rose from the bed and told Delaney to stay there with their father. "I have to go and help him. I know I heard him!" Aeron felt under the bed and retrieved the baseball bat he knew his father kept there for protection. He handed it to Delaney. "Listen to me!" he demanded. "Hit anything that looks dead! I mean it!" Aeron's breathing was rapid and shallow. "Where's your cell phone?"

"I left it at the other house," Delaney answered. "Where's yours?"

"I can't believe I did it again!" Aeron's frustration with himself became an anchor around his neck. "I had Seth's at the other house, but I can't remember what I did with it. I don't have it on me."

"I'll check Dad's pockets," Delaney said. There was nothing.

Aeron rushed cautiously back to the door and pulled the dresser away. He pressed his ear to the wood and listened. He unlocked the door and opened it. Nothing was there but blackness. "Lock it behind me and push the dresser back in front of it."

"Are you sure you heard Seth?" Delaney whispered.

"Yes, now lock the door and push the dresser in front of it. Try to get Dad awake."

Just as Aeron was about to descend the steps, lightning revealed the figure of someone standing on the landing of the stairs in front of the ornate stained-glass window.

It was Mors.

Aeron, I need you! Hurry!

"I'm coming, Seth!" His heart seemed to be running a marathon inside his chest. He saw the silhouette of the creature moving toward him. Adrenaline catapulted him into action, and he ran forcefully down the steps and struck Mors with his fist. The creature stumbled backward, causing its head to smash out the stained-glass window. Rain and wind poured in like waves overtaking a sinking ship. Mors staggered forward and plunged over the railing and crashed through a small antique table below.

Alastor was no longer there.

Aeron descended into the darkness, and he soon burst through the kitchen door and out into the side yard. "Seth, I'm coming!"

CHAPTER 44

Aeron—the well—I'm drowning!

Aeron retrieved a flashlight from his father's car. It finally lit up after he banged on it several times. He darted past the garage and made his way to the well, slipping occasionally in the sea of mud. "Seth, I'm coming!"

Aeron plummeted to the ground at the edge of the well. The boards had been tossed to the side. He hollered for Seth as he frantically plunged his hand down into the murky water and thrashed back and forth.

"Seth, where are you?"

As he removed his arm from the water, Henry's hand shot out of the abyss and seized Aeron around his wrist. Aeron struggled to grasp the soggy ground around the edges of the well, but his fingers helplessly slid in the slimy muck, and he fell into the chilly water.

Aeron submerged when Henry tugged on his legs. Aeron kicked forcefully, allowing him to resurface, but Henry also emerged and grabbed Aeron around his neck. Aeron slipped beneath the surface with barely enough air to survive. He was forced to ingest the rancid water. His throat strained, and grunting sounds echoed in the water as Aeron exerted as much force as he could to reach the surface for the life-sustaining air his body craved. Aeron thrashed about, finally freeing himself from the assassin desperately trying to take his life.

Aeron grabbed onto enough soil to pull himself out of the well. He rolled several feet away from the edge and rested in the sludge. His chest was heaving from the struggle that almost claimed his life. He coughed until he regurgitated the contents of his stomach.

Aeron, get them away from me!

Seth's cries somehow carried over the howling winds. Aeron wondered if the frantic cries were all in his head. He pushed with his arms against the ground and sat up. He rose to his feet. "Seth, is that really you?"

Aeron! The barn! Please hurry! They're trying to kill me!

Aeron grabbed the flashlight from the grass and ran across Murray Road and up the embankment. He collapsed onto the ground near the lake, but his determination to rescue his brother sent a surge of adrenaline into his muscles, and he was able to get up and run to the barn. Shrill screams of agony echoed in the roaring winds. Aeron stood listening to the agony that echoed around him. He was certain the slaughtering had begun.

"Seth, I'm coming!"

Aeron sprinted into the barn. Thunder shook the structure with a foreboding sense of doom, as shadows surrounded him from another quick flash of electrical charges filling the night sky. The blustery wind whistled through the loose boards on the sides of the barn, and along with the pounding rain on the roof, it caused Aeron to shiver, making him feel as though he'd been thrown into a damp dungeon.

"Seth, are you in here?"

With the flashlight held firmly in his hand, he walked forward cautiously, shining the light across the floor. "Seth?" His tightening chest made breathing nearly impossible, and the rank taste of the well water caused him to gag and cough. He pleaded, "Come on, Seth, if you're in here, answer me!"

A drop of water splashed upon the top of his head. Aeron shuddered from its coolness. "Come on, Seth, you need to stop this and answer me right now!" Another drop struck him on the shoulder, but he ignored it. An odd odor caused him to grimace while one more drip of liquid from high above landed on the side of Aeron's head and rolled down his temple and cheek. He brushed it away. Oddly, the substance felt oily. Curious about the fluid, he shined the flashlight onto his hand and discovered a smear of blood. "What is this?" He wiped it on his shirt, while gagging from the sight of it.

Lightning pierced the darkness and illuminated some of the interior of the barn. Creaking sounds rang down from above but were quickly muffled by the vibration of thunder racing through the warm, moist air.

Aeron raised his flashlight upward into the loft and ceiling high above him. His mouth opened wide at the sight of a dozen bodies hanging upside down from the rafters above. They were bound around their ankles by ropes. Blood dripped from their intestines, which were hanging outside their abdomens, and their arms were limp, as if pulled from their sockets.

Nausea seized Aeron's stomach, and his heart sank at the grotesque assembly of corpses swinging above him like the pendulum of a clock. As he stepped backward, he fell onto his back. The flashlight was still clenched tightly in his fingers.

Stunned from the fall, he stayed on his back for a moment, begging for the return of the air that had been knocked out of him. After his breath was finally restored, he shined the light upwards into the ceiling. As the flashlight's beam moved rapidly back and forth, Aeron stopped when he saw a dark creature standing in the loft looking down at him. The apparition was still clothed in the bloodstained leather apron. The creature grinned as if preparing for another victim to slaughter.

Aeron couldn't speak. His eyes burned from the dust he'd kicked up from the floor when he fell. The killer in the loft meandered steadily toward the ladder with his machete at his side. Aeron flashed the light once more into the ceiling. The bodies still dangled above him like chandeliers.

Unexpectedly, their eyelids opened, revealing hollow cavities filled with blackness.

Still unable to scream out, Aeron shined the light back into the loft. The butcher was no longer there. He frantically moved the light back and forth along the edge of the loft, but the apparition was simply gone from his sight.

There was a thump, and a slight vibration across the floor. He pointed the light in the direction of the noise. Standing at the bottom of the ladder, facing Aeron, was the butcher. He moved toward Aeron, steadily raising the machete into the air.

"*Noooo!*" Aeron finally screamed out in terror. Strength returned to his limbs, and he bolted for the doorway. He slipped on the loose hay and fell forward into one of the stall doors, which banged shut from the force. He hoisted himself up and turned the beam of the flashlight back in the direction of the approaching creature. "*Go away!*" Aeron begged.

Hellish, high-pitched shrieks recoiled throughout the barn, causing Aeron to shine the light into the rafters. Still hanging high above him, the mangled creatures screamed out in agony as their decaying bodies convulsed and thrashed about, causing them to slam into one another.

As Aeron attempted to run, he slipped on the hay-filled floor and fell again. The flashlight was hurled across the floor and landed about ten feet away. It rolled around once in a semi-circular path and stopped. The blood-stained shoes of the butcher could be seen in the beam of light. It was still moving closer toward him as the innards of several of the cadavers detached from their cavities and splattered onto the floor.

The sound of what seemed like boulders crashing onto the floor of the barn caused Aeron to jerk with fright. He pulled his legs into his chest and covered his head. The dead bodies had ripped loose from their ropes and fell to the hard, wooden floor below.

Gut-wrenching moans surrounded Aeron, who was again trying to hoist himself up from the floor. He ran toward the flashlight, hoping nothing was in his way. The murdered victims thrashed about, causing Aeron to rush even faster to the only light source he had available.

Once he reached the flashlight, he twisted around and saw the monstrous beings rising from the floor. Several were blocking the only exit Aeron saw ahead of him. Their shrill cries of anguish forced Aeron to cover his ears—almost causing him to drop the flashlight again.

Aeron pulled his hands away and shined the light into the congregation of death seeking to take him as another soul into their torturous, eternal existence. Standing in the center of their outstretched arms was the butcher. The flashlight beam reflected off the long, sharp blade he held high into the air. As if tackling players on the field, Aeron yelled as he charged through the wall of decay and exited the barn.

A crash of thunder triggered him to look upward into the blackened sky. He slipped and fell, burying his face in the mud when he hit the ground. Moments later, he regained his footing and ran toward the top of the embankment—his muscles burned with fatigue.

Aeron, I'm here! The lake! Come to the lake!

"Don't do this to me, Seth!" Aeron sobbed, fearful that he was being led into another trap.

Lightning stretched across the sky and emerging from the barn was the butcher and several of his slaughtered companions. Seeing the throng of ghouls heading toward him, Aeron backed up and slid into the lake.

When he stood up out of the water, a dozen disembodied beings were standing around him. Several creatures seized his legs and pulled him away from the shore. They were fully intent on drowning him. His screams went unheard in the tempest, which was churning around his weakened body.

Aeron surfaced and gasped for air. Rotting hands captured his arms and legs and pulled him under the water once more. Aeron flailed violently, trying to free himself. A sudden, razor-sharp pain raced through one of his legs. The water penetrated his nostrils and flowed into his mouth. After he surfaced, he frantically tried to see who was surrounding him. He was pulled back under the surface of the turbulent water and held there. Jagged, bony fingers pressed harder around his throat, robbing him of the precious air his muscles needed to fight off the onslaught of terror. He resurfaced, but quickly submerged again. For nearly ten seconds, the water buried him in the throes of darkness and hell.

Finally punching his way free, he burst through the surface of the water. He swam to the edge of the lake and collapsed onto the shore. The stinging sensation of the rain battered his bare back. He hollered out in agony when he attempted to stand. He saw the flashlight still illuminated and laying in the soaked grass. When he attempted to run, he collapsed onto the edge of the lake. He crawled to the flashlight and scooped it up into his muddy hand.

Aeron hollered out in anguish when he tried to stand. The flashlight revealed a huge gash in his right leg. "No! This can't be happening!" He wept as he massaged his wounded, throbbing leg.

When he heard sloshing in the mud, he shined the flashlight into the lake. He saw his shirt floating in the water. The corpses were still in pursuit. He shined the light toward the barn, which revealed the butcher and the slaughtered ghouls closing in on him.

He blinked several times and wiped the rain from his brow. *"Daaad! I need you!"*

Aeron turned, as lightning revealed a body lying near the pavilion on the other side of the lake. "Seth!" Aeron yelled. "I'm coming!"

Delaney heard moaning in the darkness. "Dad! Are you okay?" She squeezed his hand.

"Yes, honey, I think so. Something hit me. What happened?"

"You were knocked unconscious, and right now, Aeron's out looking for Seth."

In the blackness, Delaney was still able to help him stand. "Can you walk?" she asked.

"Yes, I think so." Adrian held her hand as he stood. "Where's Aeron now?"

"I don't know, but I heard him shouting a few minutes ago in the yard," Delaney replied. "Should we go after him?"

"Yes," Adrian said. As they approached the door, nearly falling over objects scattered about the floor, Adrian bumped into the dresser. "Why's this here?"

"Aeron thought someone was after him, so he told me to block to door. Can you help me move it?"

After Adrian and Delaney moved the dresser, she opened the door. Lightning illuminated the hallway, revealing Alastor standing at the top of the stairs. He reached over and yanked Delaney from her father's side. She fell to the floor.

Her shrieks echoed throughout the upstairs as Alastor dragged her down the hallway by her arms. "Dad! Help me!"

Just as Adrian darted in the direction of his daughter's screams, Mors latched onto Adrian's throat and forced him to the floor. "Del—" His words ceased.

Delaney was able to wedge her foot around the leg of a heavy dresser in the hallway. Alastor pulled harder, but she refused to let go.

Adrian rallied the strength to swing his fist into the darkness. He struck Mors, causing the creature to release his grip on his throat. Adrian pushed himself backward and into the bedroom. He felt into the darkness for the nightstand beside his bed. He was able to retrieve his gun from the drawer.

"Dad!" Delaney hollered. "Help me!"

The lightning continued to rage outside, allowing Adrian to see Mors standing in the doorway. The flashes of light coming from the barrel of his gun, and the ear-piercing shots ringing out into the darkness, caused Delaney to scream. Mors stumbled backwards and tumbled down the stairs. His body came to rest on the landing.

Like a wrecking ball tearing through a wall, Adrian charged down the hallway and smashed into Alastor, causing the creature to let Delaney loose from his grip. Adrian felt in the darkness and helped Delaney to her feet. They found the banister and held onto it as they rushed down the stairs, past Mors, and out the front door.

The howling wind offered up the faint sounds of Aeron shouting out into the tempest. "The lake, Delaney! I know the cries came from the lake!"

Adrian and Delaney raced toward the cries for help.

CHAPTER 45

As Aeron limped to the other side of the lake, fear ravaged his body, forcing him to accept the possibility that his brother was dead.

Seth was motionless, lying face down in the mud at the water's edge.

"Seth!" Aeron fell beside his brother. He turned Seth over and hoisted him onto his weakened, trembling legs. "Oh God, come on, Seth! Wake up! *They're coming!"* Aeron peered out into the fierce squall—desperate for any living soul who might rescue them. "Seth, we gotta go—*I mean it!"*

The storm raged as Aeron violently shook Seth, trying to stir life back into his unconscious brother. As the roaring winds muffled Aeron's frenzied cries, wind-driven torrents of rain pelted Seth's limp body. Blood poured from his mouth and nose, leaving a crimson flow running down Aeron's forearm like the splintered veins of lightning raging overhead.

"Oh God, this can't be happening *again!"* Aeron tightened his embrace around his brother and cried out, "Come on, Seth . . . *please!"* Aeron attempted several times to lift his brother out of the lake, but his wounded leg, and the slippery mud, caused him to fall hard onto the saturated ground.

"Dad, I found him!" Aeron's cries were devoured by the violent, howling winds. *"Daaaad!"* His heart was thrashing about in his chest, as his lungs begged for precious air. *"I need you!"*

As Aeron gazed into the blackness, lightning blazed across the sky, revealing nearly a dozen decaying corpses standing waist deep in the turbulent lake. The menacing creatures were determined to abduct the brothers from the realm of the living.

"God . . . help us!" Aeron wailed. He forcefully shook Seth again. "Come on, Seth! *Pleeease!"*

As another flash of lightning dashed across the sky, Aeron saw the rotting, outstretched arms of the deadly creatures even closer than before.

Spasms seized control of Aeron's muscles as he struggled again to stand and lift his brother from the edge of the water. He collapsed once more. *"Noooo! Leave us alone!"* he pleaded.

Drowning in weakness and despair, Aeron finally lowered his chin and rested it on the top of Seth's soaked, wet hair. Seeing no escape, but to punch into the darkness, Aeron frantically rocked back and forth with Seth held firmly in one of his arms. *"Please wake up, Seth!"* Aeron cried out. *"They're gonna kill us!"*

In desperation, Aeron attempted one last spine-tingling shriek. *"Someone help us!"*

Streaks of lightning shot across the sky, affirming Aeron's worst fears: the hands of the creatures . . . only inches away.

A banket of dread smothered him in hopelessness. His throat pulsated from the sadistic hammering of his heart, which was accompanied by the sensation of a dozen knives piercing his back. Forcing his cheek hard against his brother's head, Aeron cried, "Seth . . . I'm sorry!"

The pale, decaying hands of the corpses were seconds away when Aeron was startled by someone grabbing his shoulder, causing him to shriek from fear. "Hey," a strange voice yelled, "We need to get outta here!"

Aeron opened his eyes and looked up, but he was unable to see clearly from the rain and tears flooding his eyes. "Who are you?" Aeron hollered.

"Come on!" Josh Wallace yelled, as he pushed several apparitions backwards into the lake. "Give me your brother!"

Josh grabbed Seth under his arms and dragged him about ten yards away from the edge of the lake. Aeron pushed himself back toward the pavilion and was able to use the picnic table as leverage so he could stand. He hobbled over to his brother and fell to the ground beside him.

"Who are you? Aeron asked.

"My name's Josh. I used to live here." He glanced up and thought he saw the creatures walking steadily toward them. "Come on, man, we need to get outta here!"

Together, the boys struggled to lift Seth, but they still managed to hoist him over Josh's shoulder. A streak of lightning penetrated the atmosphere, allowing Adrian to see his sons. "Aeron! Seth!"

"Dad?" Aeron yelled. "Is that you?"

"Yes!"

"Where's Delaney?" Aeron inquired.

"I'm here!" she yelled.

As they rounded a tree in the yard, they were able to see lights shining in Mrs. Murphy's house. "Look!" Josh hollered. "Mrs. Murphy's lights are on. We need to go there!"

Surprised, Adrian shouted, "Josh? What are you doing here?"

"I saw this happening in my nightmare. I couldn't stay away!"

"Thank God you came!" Adrian praised.

They looked back and thought they'd heard moaning coming from the direction of the lake. "Hey, we have to get moving!" Adrian yelled. "Something's after us!" He helped hold Seth on Josh, as Aeron tossed his arm around Delaney's shoulders.

Once they arrived at the door, Adrian pounded desperately, while yelling for help. Mrs. Murphy came to the door and told them to get out of the storm. "Joshua, is that you?" she asked. "Why are you here so late, and in weather like this?" She grabbed his shoulder. "And what happened to Seth?"

"I had to come and help these guys. I can't explain it, but I just had to save them!" Josh said.

"I don't know what happened to Seth, Mrs. Murphy, but I think we have dead people coming after us!" Adrian roared. "We have to lock the windows and doors!"

As she rushed them into the living room, Josh collapsed onto the sofa with Seth. Josh rolled over and slid to the floor—weakened from the strain. Aeron sat on the sofa with this brother, still trying desperately to awaken him.

"Why are you all here?" Mrs. Murphy asked. "It's way after midnight!"

"Seth took our car and drove out here for some reason," Adrian replied.

In a frenzy of movement, Adrian and Delaney closed and locked the doors. They scurried to the windows and locked them before pulling the blinds closed.

Seth started to cough, and Aeron shook him several times. "Thank God! Come on, Seth. You have to wake up! We're in trouble!"

"Where am I? What happ—" Seth gagged from the phlegm in his throat.

"I found you at the lake. Those people tried to take you again!" Aeron exclaimed. "Josh and Dad rescued us!"

Seth draped his arms tightly around Aeron's neck. "You can't let them take me, Aeron. I don't wanna leave you!" Delaney sat beside him and draped her arm around his shoulders.

Aeron grabbed a blanket from the back of the sofa and wrapped it around his half-naked brother. "There's no way anybody's gonna take you away from me!" Aeron yelled.

"Adrian . . . Josh!" Mrs. Murphy hollered. "Come here!" They ran to the window where she was standing. Aeron ran and joined them. "Wait until the next flash of lightning," she said. "My porch light doesn't shine out that far."

"Oh God, are they here?" Aeron gasped.

"Just wait!" Mrs. Murphy insisted. Regardless of their efforts, death was still stalking them, like a determined predator. The reflection in the glass revealed their terror-stricken faces, as they anxiously waited for the next bolt of lightning.

A brilliant streak of light soon revealed the hellish assembly of phantoms in the yard. Aeron's eyes bulged. "Oh, God!" he cried out.

"That's definitely not God, honey," Mrs. Murphy replied.

Mrs. Murphy ran over to the sofa and held onto Seth. Aeron hobbled back to his brother and embraced him. Josh and Adrian backed slowly away from the window. "No! You can't have any of us! We won't go with you!" Josh screamed.

Shaking uncontrollably, Seth pleaded, "Dad, I don't wanna go with them! Stop'em! *Please!*"

The doors and windows began to rattle from the pounding fists, barely covered with flesh. "Make them stop, Aeron! Make them go away!" Seth cried.

Mrs. Murphy stood and yelled, "Harriet, knock this off right now! *You can't have them! Damn you all to Hell!*"

Without anything to impede their determination for the young companions they desired, several of the apparitions broke through the glass. As the tenacious creatures climbed over one another through the gaping holes, the living occupants of the house bolted up the stairs and stood on the landing. Aeron's leg gave out several times, but Adrian and Josh helped him up to safety.

Shadows soon assembled near the bottom of the stairs, led by Dolores.

"Go away!" Seth hollered, as he grabbed onto Aeron and begged, "Aeron, please don't let them take me!" Aeron hugged his brother tightly, as Delaney clung to her father.

"Wait!" Mrs. Murphy yelled. "Stay here, and don't let them up here!"

"Not a chance, Virginia," Adrian yelled.

"Who are you?" Seth asked Josh.

"I'm Josh Wallace. I used to live in your house."

Mrs. Murphy dashed to the small table in the hallway and retrieved two kerosine lamps. "Here," she said, as she rushed back and pushed one lamp into Josh's hands and the other into Adrian's. "Unscrew the caps!"

"I know what you're thinking, Virginia!" Adrian said. "Let's finish this!"

After they unscrewed the caps, she ignited the wick in each container and yelled, "Throw them hard at the floor below!"

"What?" Josh bellowed.

"Just do it . . . now!" Adrian demanded.

"But they're all soaked," Delaney said.

"It's kerosine. Trust me, they're burn!" Mrs. Murphy said.

Adrian and Josh hurled the glass lamps onto the hardwood floor below. Once the containers shattered, the kerosine splashed onto their clothes, causing the creatures to burst into flames. The fire quickly spread across the floor, forcing the living occupants to retreat to the end of the hallway of the second floor. The ghouls shrieked with agony and terror.

"We're trapped!" Delaney hollered.

Delaney screamed, as she pointed toward the staircase. Dolores was consumed by flames, but she was still determined to seize her desired possession: Seth. Her outstretched arms were torches lighting the way.

Aeron stood in front of Seth and yelled, "No! You can't have my brother!"

Adrian spotted an antique chair next to the long table with photos. He grabbed the chair before rushing back to Seth.

Dolores finally reached the top of the stairs and turned toward the frightened inhabitants huddled together in a corner.

Adrian raised the chair high above his head. "You're not taking my children away from us!"

The courage of a dozen soldiers surged through his body. He rushed at her and forcefully swung the chair, striking Dolores on the shoulder. Her flaming carcass hurled backward over the banister and fell into the blazing corpses below. Adrian dropped the remaining pieces of the chair and ran back to his sons and daughter. They embraced.

"Adrian, they're still coming!" Mrs. Murphy grasped his arm. "Here, we have to go here!" Mrs. Murphy insisted. She opened a door leading out onto a small porch. Everyone followed. "You boys jump to safety first," she ordered.

"We're not leaving you! You're jumping with us!" Aeron demanded.

"I can't!" Mrs. Murphy cried out. "I can't jump that far!"

Josh tugged on her arm and begged her to go with them.

"We're not gonna let you die!" Adrian insisted.

Aeron climbed over the iron railing and lowered himself onto the railing of the porch below. He slipped and fell backward into the yard after his leg gave out on him, but he managed to stand and ordered Seth to climb down. Seth lowered himself and fell into Aeron's arms.

"Delaney, you're next," Adrian demanded. "Your brothers will help you."

Adrian and Josh latched onto her wrists. "Now, make sure your feet are on the railing below, and hold onto the bottom of the railing up here," Josh said. A few seconds later, Delaney was safe in her brother's arms.

"Come on, Mrs. Murphy," Adrian ordered. "You're next."

Mrs. Murphy closed her eyes for a moment and recited a brief prayer. She opened her eyes and looked down. "Please, don't drop me!" she begged.

"We won't! We promise!" Josh said.

Adrian and Josh slowly lowered her, and when her feet were almost into Aeron's hands, a bolt of lightning struck the tree next to the house. The ear-splitting, thunderous discharge caused Josh to release Mrs. Murphy. She slipped from Adrian's grasp as well and plummeted into Aeron and Seth's arms. All three of them tumbled to the ground.

Adrian turned to Josh. "Hey, this smoke is getting thick, so we need to hurry this up!"

Josh lowered himself over the railing and jumped the remaining distance to the saturated earth below. He ran to Mrs. Murphy and helped her up from the ground.

"Dad! Hurry!" Aeron yelled.

As Adrian climbed over the railing, one of the creatures seized him from behind and pulled him back into the house. "Dad!" Aeron yelled, as he attempted to climb back up on the railing.

Delaney screamed out in terror. "They got Dad! We have to help him!"

"Get everyone over to our house, Delaney!" Aeron ordered. "I'm going in after him!"

Just as Aeron got up onto the first railing, his leg gave out again, and he fell backwards into the yard.

Shrieks could be heard from inside the house—like the revelry of a pack of coyotes capturing prey. "*Aeron!*" Adrian's call echoed over the howling winds.

"I'm coming, Dad!" Aeron pushed Seth and demanded they retreat to their house. "Go! I'll get Dad."

"I'm coming with you!" Seth vowed.

"No," Aeron demanded, "you have to get everyone to safety."

"Seth," Josh interrupted, "get your sister and Mrs. Murphy to the house. I'll help your brother."

"You don't have to, man. I can't risk anyone else's life," Aeron pleaded. "I need you to make sure my sister and brother get to safety. I mean it!"

Josh's hands tightened into fists. "I can't let you do this alone."

"Yes, you can. I need someone to protect them over at the house in case there's creatures over there."

"Alright," Josh agreed. "Just go get your dad!" He turned toward Delaney, Seth, and Mrs. Murphy. "Come on, guys, let's go!"

"Come on, let's get to my house," Seth insisted. "Delaney, come on!" He grabbed his sister's hand, and they darted through the yard toward the house.

The rain subsided as they tried their best to assist Mrs. Murphy toward the other house. A symphony of anguished cries emanated from inside her home, which was almost fully consumed by flames.

CHAPTER 46

Aeron hobbled onto the front porch and attempted to open the door, which was locked. He ran to the open window that had been broken out by the ghostly intruders. "Dad! Where are you?"

"Aeron! Help me!" Aeron heard the cries coming from upstairs.

"I'm coming, Dad!" Aeron rushed to the bottom of the stairs, but he couldn't get up the stairs because of the throngs of ghouls blocking his way. "Dad, I can't get to you! What do I do?"

Harriet heard Aeron's voice and turned. She steadily made her way back down the stairs toward him. Several corpses continued to beat on the upstairs bedroom door, while other creatures retreated with Harriet.

Some of the corpses that had been consumed by the flames, had fallen onto the floor upstairs, while some had fallen down the stairs in an attempt to return to their watery grave. Harriet stepped over them in her pursuit of Aeron.

"I've locked myself in one of the bedrooms," he hollered. "I don't know—" Adrian was choking on the smoke spreading throughout the upstairs. "I can't hold them back forever," he finally yelled. "I'm going out one of the windows. Come around and catch me!"

"Okay, I'll be there to catch you," Aeron yelled. He also coughed from the vortex of smoke billowing out the living room window that had been smashed out.

Just as he unlocked the door and attempted to open it, Harriet grabbed him from behind. Aeron spun around and fell against the door. Rage consumed him, and he drew back his fist. "I've about had it with you, lady!" He struck her in the face, causing Harriet to fall backwards into a few of her ghostly companions. "You're not taking my brothers and sisters anywhere!"

Aeron rushed out the front door and around to the other side of the house. As he limped as fast as he could, he heard the smashing of glass from the side of the house.

"Aeron, where are you?" Adrian hollered.

"Here I am, Dad! Hurry! The house is really burning."

Adrian threw out the window the end of a couple sheets that had been tied together. As he was climbing out the window, the bedroom door burst open. A flood of creatures meandered to the window, but Adrian had already climbed out and was half-way down the makeshift rope.

When a couple of the corpses began to haul the rope up toward them, Adrian jumped the remaining distance and fell into the grass.

"Dad, are you okay?"

"Yes, but let's get away from the house. It might explode," Adrian ordered. They began to sprint toward the other house, but Aeron grimaced and fell to the ground. "Let me help you," Adrian said.

"I think my leg might be broken!" Aeron hollered. As he was helped from the ground by his father, Aeron asked, "Why would the house explode?"

"Mrs. Murphy uses—" Adrian paused. "Wait a minute!" Adrian turned back toward the burning house. "Listen, get over to our house right away. Get as far away as possible."

"Dad, what are you gonna do?"

"Just go! I'm going to end this once and for all!"

Adrian pushed his son toward their house and ran back to the side of Mrs. Murphy's home. Adrian kicked in the kitchen door and rushed in. He yanked the stove away from the wall, making sure the gas line had ruptured. As fast as he could, he rushed out the kitchen door and dashed toward his own home.

Just as he reached Murray Road, a shockwave of heat and fire lit up the night. Mrs. Murphy's house exploded, knocking Adrian forward across the road before he collapsed onto his own front lawn.

"Dad!" Aeron hollered, as he ran to his father. "Are you okay?"

Adrian rolled over and sat up. He examined his body for a moment before looking up at his son. "Yeah, I think so."

Delaney, Seth, Josh, and Mrs. Murphy emerged from the side of the Douglas home. "Dad," Seth yelled. "What happened?"

"My home!" Mrs. Murphy lamented. "My home is gone!"

Adrian and Aeron rushed toward the others. "I'm sorry, Virginia, but it was the only way," Adrian said. Her stomach erupted into spasms.

As they all stood in the diminishing rain, Adrian and Aeron held on to Mrs. Murphy.

"Adrian, listen!" Mrs. Murphy demanded.

"I don't hear anything," Adrian commented.

"Exactly," she replied. "It's so quiet. No more screams." She smiled at Adrian.

The lights came on inside the Douglas house. "Look at that, Virginia. Our lights came back on. Do you suppose that means something? Do you think it's all over?"

"Maybe," Mrs. Murphy stated, "but Harriet's been pursuing me all these years. She doesn't give up until she gets what she wants."

Josh joined them. "Mr. Douglas, my mom used to say that the ghosts from our past always come back to haunt us in some ways." He wiped the rain from around his eyes. "Like Mrs. Murphy said, they are never satisfied until they get what they want."

"Let's hope you're wrong about that," Adrian said. "I've had enough ghosts to deal with out here."

"Mr. Douglas," Josh stated, "I hate to leave, but I better get back home before my parents find out I'm missing."

Adrian embraced Josh. "You helped save us, Josh."

"I couldn't stay away," he explained. "My nose started bleeding again, and in my nightmare, I saw everything that happened to Aeron and Seth. But listen, my dad honestly doesn't know I'm here." Josh stepped back from Adrian.

"Josh," Aeron asked, "how can I ever thank you?" He shook Josh's hand. "You saved our lives, man!" They embraced.

"I just wanted it to end, and I didn't want you guys to get hurt," Josh replied.

Seth walked over and hugged Josh as well. "Thank you." Seth whispered into Josh's ear. "I'd be in a different place right now if you hadn't shown up and helped us."

"Hey, Josh," Aeron inquired, "have you ever seen some stranger at our school that also shows up around here sometimes?"

"Yes," Josh replied. "His name was Stewart Ward. He's the guy who always seemed to watch over me when I lived here. I didn't know who he was until I found out that he once owned this land."

"How long ago was that?" Aeron asked.

"Over a hundred years ago. His headstone is in the cemetery on the hill. It's like he's a guardian angel or something."

"I saw him earlier tonight," Aeron explained. "Yeah, I think he is a guardian angel, too."

"Yeah," Josh said, "I think his name means 'protector' or something like that."

Adrian pulled Seth close to his chest, embracing him as if it was his last time to ever hold him. "Are you okay, buddy?"

"Yeah, I think so."

Mrs. Murphy grasped Adrian's hand. "Adrian, do you *really* have to move away?"

"I hope not," Adrian answered. "But I can honestly tell you that I feel differently than before. I'm not afraid like I was." The two of them looked over into Mrs. Murphy's yard. "Virginia, I'm really sorry about the house, but I think it might be you who will have to move away now." They embraced each other. Tears flooded their eyes.

"Dad," Seth commented, "Aeron also saved my life again tonight."

Tears continued to roll down Adrian's cheeks. "What did he save you from?"

Seth gazed into his father's eyes. He pointed toward the lake. "Them!" he said. "I remember them pulling me into the water, but when I woke up at Mrs. Murphy's house, Aeron was right there with me. He promised he'd never let anything bad happen to me."

As they embraced in the yard, Harriet, Mors, and the twins appeared at the window in Delaney's room. At the well, water moved in a circular pattern from the center. Across the road, miniscule bubbles rose to the surface of the lake in a dozen spots, scattered throughout the watery grave.

Aeron walked closer to Seth. "Are you okay?" he asked.

Seth threw his arms around Aeron. He nearly squeezed the air out of his brother. "Thank you for saving me, Aeron."

"I'm not sure exactly how I saved you this time," Aeron said. "The whole thing seems like a blur to me now."

"You definitely saved me from them," Seth stated, while pointing toward the lake.

"Them?" Aeron questioned.

"Yeah, *the people from the lake!*"

CHAPTER 47

ONE YEAR LATER ON MURRAY ROAD

Noah Taggart walked into his newly purchased barn. He was searching for a specific toolbox containing several items he needed for fixing a latch on a closet door in his kids' bedroom. The door had been found open every morning since his family had moved into their new house. As he sorted through an old wooden toolbox his grandfather had made years ago, he finally found one of the screwdrivers he needed for the task.

When he closed the lid, a drop of blood fell onto it from above. Noah's eyebrows turned inward as bewilderment seized control of his mind. Another drop fell from above. He ran his finger through the crimson spot and rubbed the substance between his fingers.

When he looked up, Adrian and Teresa Douglas were hanging high above him by their ankles. Their carcasses had been sliced open, and the look of terror emanated from their bulging eyes.

Joanie Taggart finally took some time, while her husband went to the barn for a few tools, to run a load of laundry to the basement. As she opened the lid and started the cycle of filling the washer, the wooden panel under the basement stairs moved slowly across the cement floor.

Joanie was sorting the clothes into two different baskets when a hand emerged from behind the panel. Oblivious to the threat stepping out from under the stairs behind her, Joanie continued sorting without hesitation.

Just as she began loading the clothes into the washing machine, Delaney Douglas stood several feet behind the unsuspecting woman.

Joanie added the last remaining shirt, and she closed the lid and turned to leave. Delaney's chained hands stretched outward.

The basement lights went out.

Twins, Nathan and Madison Taggart, were alone in their bedroom while their mother went to the basement to do laundry. As they opened a container filled with toy cars and dumped them onto the floor, their closet door opened behind them.

As each twin chose the cars they wanted to play with on the floor, Darcy and Kieran Douglas stepped out of the closet and gazed at the unsuspecting twins. Darcy and Kieran joined hands and turned their heads toward each other.

They smiled and looked back at Nathan and Madison. They realized that eternal companionship with new playmates was only moments away.

Matthew and Michael Taggart stepped into the refreshing water of their new lake while their twin brother and sister played alone in their room. As the teen brothers joyfully splashed each other with water, they didn't notice bubbles rising to the surface all around the lake.

When Michael expressed how excited he was to finally have a lake to swim in on hot summer days, Matthew ridiculed him for being too obsessed about the lake.

When they lowered their upper bodies deeper into the water to cool off, they continued to talk about their move to the new house on Murray Road. They also discussed the thrill of taking a walk to the cemetery on the hill behind their house.

The brothers were unaware that standing in the water behind them was Aeron and Seth Douglas. After Aeron and Seth glanced at each other and smiled, they gazed again at the backs of the unsuspecting teen brothers who had ventured into their watery grave. Once Aeron's and Seth's hands emerged from below the surface of the lake, they seized the Taggart brothers from behind and dragged them under the water.

ACKNOWLEDGMENTS

I can't really pinpoint the exact time some folks inspired me to write
something in the horror genre, but the idea for a story hit me right after I'd
taken my daughter to a volleyball clinic not far from a property my family
used to visit frequently when I was younger. I called up Sandy, a friend of
mine, and asked if I could stop by for a visit while Madison was at a local
school. We were eager to get caught up on fond memories about the many
times our families enjoyed gatherings at her and her in-law's properties.
There were countless times we had reunions at the pavilion next to their
beautiful lake, and the old farmhouses and barns on the land had their own
unique characteristics. Before leaving that day, I snapped a few pictures of
the area, and that night, a story was born.

     Photos of the pristine lake, the old farmhouse across the road, and
the wooded hillside, all wove a tapestry of plots and subplots in my mind
as I downloaded the pictures. Also, about one hundred yards from the
farmhouse is a cemetery. So, the combination of the lake, the legendary
farmhouse, and the cemetery, stirred an irresistible tale that beckoned me
to begin *People from the Lake* that night. Two months later, the manuscript
was completed.

     This story did eventually take a backseat to my other novel,
Song of the Tree Frogs, which was in the process of being considered

as a motion picture (which did occur a couple years later). However, with a little coaxing from my agent, I decided to "resurrect" this story, work on some editing, seek cover models, and eventually find possible representation. You now hold the final product.

Even though I am known more for my Christian literature, I was somewhat skeptical that a paranormal thriller would come to fruition. Believe it or not, my first story (at the age of 10) was a thriller about a creature terrorizing a local farmer, along with the livestock. Who would have ever guessed that years later I'd be the co-producer for a film (*Beast of Our Fathers*) about a creature terrorizing a local family living in a large farmhouse!

That said, I knew *People from the Lake* had to be a different kind of "ghost story." I wanted to focus on a special family struggling to cope with supernatural forces far beyond their rational understanding of their world. I wanted the three teen siblings to have a special bond for my targeted YA audience, and I sought to use the youngest children (the twins) as the voice of innocence in the chaotic world of the Douglas family. I wanted a strong female character who was a professional, and a father who was vulnerable to the emotional aspects of being a parent. I also wanted most of the character names to symbolize something significant to the themes presented in the novel. For example, the name Murphy is an old Gaelic word for "sea warrior," and the name Douglas also has a Gaelic root, meaning "black stream." Hence, the names tend to have something to do with water. The last name Ward (named after my neighbor who was like a father to me) means "guardian." Indeed, he was the embodiment of that to me!

Now that you have some background, which inspired the story, I must take this time to thank some very special individuals who made this tale possible. I want to thank the Mathias family for the many years of memories they helped me build over so many decades. Thanks especially to Sandy for allowing me the use of the lake as part of the back cover of this novel. I absolutely had to have an actual picture of that lake as a part of the book. I also want to thank Jimmy Joe Savage (an amazing photographer) and Matthew Ketchum and Michael Loy (representing Aeron and Seth on the cover) for being great models. They did an excellent job at capturing that first chapter of the book. Michael has an endorsement in *Song of the Tree Frogs*, and Matthew has become a very special young man to us. In every sense of the meaning, he is family to us, just like Nathan. Matthew also had an important role in the movie, *Song of the Tree Frogs*. We are proud of them all!

Josh and Danielle, from the award-winning Menning Films, are some of the best people my family will ever know. Their talents in photography and moviemaking far exceed most, and Josh's cover designs were exceptional at capturing a snapshot of the setting and two characters from this story. Together, their creativity is stellar! Josh also designed this cover for this 2nd Edition.

I would also like to thank Josh, Don, Zach, and Jenna for helping with the book trailer, and to the four families who allowed us to use their properties. I can't thank the following people enough for their great efforts in filming the book trailer: Rob, Kelly, Matthew, Michael, Jessica, Benson, and Mia (who represented the Douglas family). Also, I would like to thank Joanie, Missy, Noah, Helen, Heidi, Dakota, Nick, Rocco Sr., Rocco Jr., and Sammi for being great ghouls for the filming. Thanks to my wife and Linda for providing some of the meals as well. I apologize if I inadvertently left anyone out.

Lara Helmling is not only my editor, motivational guru, and my agent, but she is also a genius when it comes to helping authors develop their entrepreneurial mindset. Another friend who has also encouraged me is Brooke Harman. Thank you, Annie Inge, for also being a great support. Brooke is always my go-to person for ideas and the initial editing of my manuscripts. I want to thank my wife (Connie) and daughter (Madison) for putting up with me when I write. Living with an author isn't easy. I love them so much!

People from the Lake is intended to "immerse" readers into an unusual world far beyond our reality. It is not an endorsement of paranormal events, nor is it to be taken too seriously. It is just a story I invented out of pure fun from my many years of enjoying those scary movies that tended to keep me up at night. Writing different genres pushes me, which I need. Over the years, I've also enjoyed scaring family and friends, and their revenge on me has given us a lot of laughs, especially involving Tabbie (Tabs) out on Williard Road. I sure miss her. She would have loved this story because we loved scaring everyone. Most people don't mind a good jolt to their nerves from time to time, and I happen to be one of them.

I certainly hope you enjoyed getting to know the Douglas family, and perhaps now, you might be inclined to sleep with one eye open at night.

I love connecting with my readers, so check out my website at www.jwkitson.com. Take care, do your very best to have happy dreams!

HOW TO CONTACT
J.W. KITSON

I'd really love to hear from you! For more information regarding this novel or special gatherings for speaking engagements and book clubs, please contact John at Kitson Books, LLC:

Email: info@jwkitson.com
Online: www.jwkitson.com

Kitson Books, LLC
P.O. Box 2886
East Liverpool, OH 43920

Get updates on this and other projects at:
Facebook: www.facebook.com/kitsonbooksllc
Twitter: www.twitter.com/jwkitson
Website: www.jwkitson.com

To purchase bulk copies of this book at a discounted rate for schools, organizations, and clubs, please contact Kitson Books, LLC at www.jwkitson.com.